Canadian **Dani Collins** knew in high school that she wanted to write romance for a living. Twenty-five years later, after marrying her high school sweetheart, having two kids with him, working at several generic office jobs and submitting countless manuscripts, she got The Call. Her first Mills & Boon novel won the Reviewers' Choice Award for Best First Book in Series from *RT Book Reviews*. She now works in her own office, writing romance.

When **Emmy Grayson** came across her mother's copy of *A Rose in Winter* by Kathleen E. Woodiwiss, she sneaked it into her room and promptly fell in love with romance. Over twenty years later, Mills & Boon Modern made her dream come true by offering her a contract for her first book. When she isn't writing she's chasing her kids, attempting to garden, or carving out a little time on her front porch with her own romance hero.

Also by Dani Collins

His Highness's Hidden Heir
Maid to Marry
Hidden Heir, Italian Wife
The Greek's Wife Returns
Boss's Christmas Baby Acquisition

Also by Emmy Grayson

Brides for Greek Brothers miniseries

Deception at the Altar
Still the Greek's Wife
Pregnant Behind the Veil

Red-Hot Icelandic Nights miniseries

Enemy in His Boardroom

Discover more at millsandboon.co.uk.

WANTED: BILLIONAIRE'S WIFE

DANI COLLINS

EMMY GRAYSON

MILLS & BOON

All rights reserved including the right of reproduction in whole or in part in any form. This edition is published by arrangement with Harlequin Enterprises ULC.

This is a work of fiction. Names, characters, places, locations and incidents are purely fictional and bear no relationship to any real life individuals, living or dead, or to any actual places, business establishments, locations, events or incidents. Any resemblance is entirely coincidental.

Without limiting the exclusive rights of any author, contributor or the publisher of this publication, any unauthorised use of this publication to train generative artificial intelligence (AI) technologies is expressly prohibited. HarperCollins also exercise their rights under Article 4(3) of the Digital Single Market Directive 2019/790 and expressly reserve this publication from the text and data mining exception.

® and TM are trademarks owned and used by the trademark owner and/or its licensee. Trademarks marked with ® are registered with the United Kingdom Patent Office and/or the Office for Harmonisation in the Internal Market and in other countries.

First published in Great Britain 2026
by Mills & Boon, an imprint of HarperCollins*Publishers* Ltd,
1 London Bridge Street, London, SE1 9GF

www.harpercollins.co.uk

HarperCollins*Publishers*, Macken House, 39/40 Mayor Street Upper, Dublin 1, D01 C9W8, Ireland

Wanted: Billionaire's Wife © 2026 Harlequin Enterprises ULC

Business-Deal Bride © 2026 Dani Collins

Wed for the Headlines © 2026 Emmy Grayson

ISBN: 978-0-263-41819-4

Printed and Bound in the UK using 100% Renewable Electricity
at CPI Group (UK) Ltd, Croydon, CR0 4YY

BUSINESS-DEAL BRIDE

DANI COLLINS

MILLS & BOON

To my amazing fellow authors writing for Presents, past and present. Writing can be a lonely occupation, but this supportive bunch is always ready to celebrate milestones and commiserate over manuscripts that won't write themselves. I wouldn't have this career if these fabulous authors hadn't written all these fabulous books that have entertained and inspired me for decades. I love and admire every one of you.

CHAPTER ONE

AXEL SEVERIN READ through the marriage contract again. He had only one question for the man who had been his employer and mentor: Why was the name of his prospective bride not spelled out on these pages?

He didn't ask, though. He already knew the answer.

Otto Braun had no love for his daughter. She was "the biological issue of Otto Braun." Otto took every opportunity to dismiss Mira. It was among the many reasons Axel had agreed to this arrangement—to compensate Mira for the glaring injustice of her father's disregard.

Axel wasn't a particularly compassionate man, but he did know right from wrong, and the way Otto treated Mira was wrong.

"Problem?" Otto asked gruffly from behind his marble-topped desk. He was a barrel-chested man well into his sixties. He wore his customary charcoal suit with a dark blue tie. His hair and beard were white and neatly trimmed. His eyes held the gleam that warned he was at his most cagey.

"Simply doing my due diligence," Axel replied, even as he braced like a spider perceiving vibrations in the web.

The contract stated clearly that, on the date of their marriage, Otto would allow Axel to assume full control of the global engineering firm. That meant he would no longer be plagued with Otto's last-minute interference. Then, after a full year of marriage, Otto would sign over his shares in Vorstoben to Axel and his wife.

It was exactly what Otto had promised Axel two years ago, when Axel had told him he was leaving to start his own firm.

Stay, Otto had urged. *I'll promote you to CEO. Marry my daughter, and I'll gift the company to the two of you.*

Axel had already been chafing under a decade of Otto's dictates. He had caught Otto's notice when he'd been a hardworking junior engineer of twenty-two and had been climbing the corporate ladder ever since. In the beginning, earning money had been Axel's sole aspiration. Once he had his mother squared away, however, and built enough of an investment portfolio to ensure he would never fall back into the nothing he'd come from, he'd been ready to do bigger things. To be his own boss.

What if Mira doesn't want to marry me? Axel had asked Otto.

I'll never leave the company to her, was Otto's dismissive reply. *I wish I had a son. Marry my daughter, and I'll have one.*

The offer was too good to pass up. Sitting behind the CEO desk for the last two years, Axel's ability to curb Otto's worst impulses had resulted in steady expansion and record profits. He felt very proprietary toward Vorstoben these days. He ran it well and wanted it.

He glanced at Mira. She was a polished brunette in a dark skirt suit, hair in a stylish chignon, face drawn with strain. Axel had known her as long as he'd known Otto. He considered Mira a friend to the extent that either of them was capable of a close relationship. In reality, his predominant feeling toward her was pity. She had joined the firm after finishing her business degree three years ago. Since then, she had worked tirelessly to earn her father's good opinion—while Otto took every opportunity to erode her confidence. He was cold and critical and dismissive for no reason that Axel could discern.

She was Otto's only child. She ought to inherit the company and everything Otto possessed, especially when she had done her best to contribute to its success. Otto had deliberately held her back, though, refusing to promote her beyond a midlevel accounting position. She yearned to be taken seriously. To be *noticed*.

So, in an attempt to appease Otto and have a real chance at rising in the ranks here, Mira had agreed to Axel's proposal.

Every time they had tried to set a date for the wedding, however, Otto had pushed them off. It had become enough of a frustration that Axel had issued an ultimatum last month. Otto had to make good on his promise or he was leaving.

Finally, the contract was in his hand. No more delays. Once they signed it, they could marry. Otto would retire and, in a year, Axel and Mira would jointly take possession of Otto's shares, giving Axel the de facto ownership he'd been promised.

Mira's jaw was set with hurt that her father hadn't had the decency to put her name on the document beyond her signature line at the bottom, under a statement about her being of sound mind and agreeing to the conditions set forth herein, but she scrawled her name upon it.

Axel took the pen and rasped his name with a few hard strokes of black ink. He handed the pen to Otto.

Otto signed. Otto's assistant witnessed and left the room.

Otto handed the contract to his lawyer, Umberto, a

sixty-ish man who had a weariness in his expression that Axel knew had been stamped there by decades of working with the intractable Otto. Axel often thought he would look like that himself if he didn't step onto his own path soon.

Which he was doing today. *Finally.* His inner tension eased.

"Give him the other," Otto said.

Axel's shoulders snapped back to rigidity.

Umberto didn't meet Axel's gaze as he placed the signed contract into his briefcase and offered a fresh envelope.

An acidic pang of premonition entered Axel's gut. It was a sensation from his childhood, the one he had experienced every time the class bully noticed the new kid in school. Or his mother's drug dealer had shaken him down for money she owed. Or the landlord had turned them out because he didn't like finding his mother unconscious in the stairwell.

That sensation of being powerless—helpless—was suffocating. Axel had grown out of being a victim, though. He was too self-sufficient. Too *smart.* Wasn't he?

His hand turned cold as he took the envelope and broke the seal. He glanced at Mira. She bit her lip, watchful, expression mirroring his sense of dread.

Axel held the pages so she could read with him.

The first was a paternity report from twenty years ago. It stated Mira was *not* Otto's daughter.

Mira's shocked gasp cut through the thick silence. She grasped at her throat as though the noise had caused a physical tear there. She shot a glare of stunned hurt at Otto. "This is why you've always been such a bastard to me?" she asked on a gust of disbelief. Then she turned on Axel to accuse, "You knew?"

"No." He felt concussed by this. He was dazed, unable

to work out what it meant beyond a realization that Otto had tricked him. If Mira wasn't Otto's daughter, the contract they'd signed meant nothing. This entire engagement had been a ploy to keep him here so he wouldn't strike out on his own.

A ball of fury began to condense in his gut.

"Read the rest," Otto commanded.

Axel turned to the next page. It was a notarized letter to Otto from a woman named Lorena Fontaine, dated three years ago.

As I face the end of my life, I find myself regretting that I never told you I gave birth to your child…

"Oh my God." Mira recoiled.

Mira's mother had been expecting Mira at the time, the letter continued. Lorena knew Otto wouldn't leave his wife. She provided the name of the agency in America where Otto's daughter had been relinquished for adoption.

"How could you *do* this?" Mira's fingertips lined up against her quivering bottom lip.

Marry my daughter…

Axel was far more practiced at stuffing his reactions deep into a cavern within himself. While Mira was exchanging heated words with Otto, asking about who might have fathered her, Axel was slipping into survival mode. His agile mind quickly filtered through his choices.

He could walk out. This bait-and-switch of Otto's was unforgivable. He'd kept Axel here under false pretenses, setting Axel back on his goal to form his own company. It would be thriving by now if not for this subterfuge. It would serve Otto right if Axel left Vorstoben in the lurch. The conglomerate would falter under the older man's erratic command. Axel could pick over its bones soon enough.

Or he could remain here as CEO under Otto. It was not an attractive option, but Otto would die eventually and the board would likely keep Axel on. At some future date, Axel would gain full control of the company, if not the ownership of it. *If* he wanted to be patient a little longer.

He didn't.

"Umberto believes he's found her." Otto's deep voice cut into Axel's churning thoughts. "I have instructed him to reach out and request she take a paternity test. Once we have a positive result, he'll ask her to come meet me. If she's willing to marry you, then I will make her my heir and honor that contract." Otto nodded at the briefcase, looking smug.

Or I could do that, Axel mentally acknowledged, even as he saw how Otto was trying to keep him on a string while bringing a third puppet into this farce. Otto wanted to hold his biological daughter like a carrot before Axel and keep him dancing.

"You bastard." Mira was trembling with fury. "Why did you even keep me around? Why did you stay married to Mama after you learned that?" She flung a hand at the pages Axel still held. "Why have you let us believe for *two years* that you wanted him to marry *me*?"

"To keep me here," Axel said through his teeth, so filled with disgust he could hardly contain it.

"I didn't care for the scandal. Until I learned I had a *real* daughter—" Otto's lip curled disdainfully "—I had to carry on with the charade that you were mine."

"Liar," Mira choked. "You wanted access to Mama's money. You knew she would have taken all her assets and more besides if you divorced her. I *will* take them," she warned, sending a vindictive look between Otto and Axel. "That will sting, won't it?"

It would. Vorstoben had leveraged against properties that belonged to Mira through her mother. She had allowed those arrangements because she had been desperate for Otto's good favor.

It was yet another nefarious motive for this false engagement Otto had engineered.

Axel had believed himself inoculated against being taken advantage of. He wasn't naive, but he hadn't seen that Otto was deceiving him this entire time. It made him livid, but he didn't allow any of that volatile emotion to bleed into his tone or expression.

"Is that contract worth the paper it's printed on?" he asked Umberto. "After such blatant misrepresentation?"

Umberto's wince claimed he was only following orders.

"I am the majority shareholder. I can dispense those shares as I see fit," Otto asserted, telling Mira, "There's a settlement offer in there if you keep this out of the press. But I can bequeath Vorstoben to my *biological* daughter if I want to. *If* you marry her," he added, turning the cunning gleam in his eye onto Axel.

He really thought he had Axel over a barrel.

"You've finally given me something I wanted. *Freedom*," Mira bit out, no longer the meek, biddable daughter Otto had conditioned her into. "Prepare to be made sorry, old man."

"Mira," Axel said as she headed to the door.

"No, Axel." She flung around to face him. "Do whatever you have to. Marry his *real* daughter if you want to. I don't blame you for trying to get what he promised, but take a lesson from this backstabbing. He'll find another way to undercut you. He always does." Her eyes were glistening as she shot Otto a final look, but they weren't tears of hurt or sadness. It was the glow of vengeance.

A similar flame had been lit inside Axel, an incendiary refusal to lose again. He *would* get what had been promised to him.

He folded the envelope Umberto had given him and tucked it inside his suit jacket. If Umberto could find this secret baby of Otto's, so could he.

CHAPTER TWO

Joy Youngston was midway through a stag spin on the pole when she glimpsed *him* entering the club.

Her grip almost slipped. She wasn't sure why. It wasn't as though she recognized him. She only clocked him as not someone she'd seen before. Someone she *would* remember because he brought such an aura of wealth and sophistication in with him. Power. Not only was he not a regular to this club, he didn't belong on this side of the city. Not in that suit. It must have been made for him because it moved as though it was part of him, accentuating the line of his wide shoulders and the length of his legs.

She mindlessly continued her routine, swinging around and kicking out her legs in a provocative eye-opener, then hooking the pole behind her knee so she could catch the spiked heel of her shoe and lean back in a rainbow.

As she held the position, she watched his upside-down image walk unhesitatingly toward her. His movements were as fluid as an athlete's, his bearing tall and commanding. There was a watchfulness to him. Not fearful. Aware. He recognized the dangers in a club like this, especially to a man who looked like he carried abundant cash and a nice watch, but he was blade-sharp and ready to respond to any sort of trouble.

She contorted into a back arch, then grasped the pole

and brought her legs down, one–two, before sinking into splits against the stage.

Other men watched the titillating movement of her breasts or tried to catch a wardrobe malfunction in her string bikini. This one kept his attention on her face.

She couldn't help staring back. He had a square, clean-shaven jaw and straight, dark eyebrows to match his straight, closely shorn dark hair. He was more compelling than conventionally attractive. Roughly hewn and uncompromising. Beautiful in the way of wrathful storms.

Disapproving?

A savage pain hit her breastbone. *Go to hell*, she thought darkly, trying to retreat into her bubble of self-containment, but he had pierced her shell from the second he walked in. She couldn't look through him the way she usually could. Couldn't look away, either. He was too magnetic, pulling her gaze against her will.

Anxious electricity zipped in opposing currents under her skin, setting all of her buzzing. She tried to hide his effect on her as she swung her front leg around to meet the back and pushed against the stage, first a cobra, then she hinged her knees and lifted her butt high while her chest pressed low to the floor in a speedbump.

His piercing gaze didn't slide to the undulation of her body. He didn't look at her thighs with the garters she wore around the tops of them, or the tulle skirt that was more of a ruffle since it started at her tailbone and ended above her mostly bare cheeks. He didn't acknowledge the girls on the other two poles at all.

Joy did these moves for hours every night. It was pure muscle memory and didn't usually cause her pulse to pick up or her breath to labor.

Tonight, her bones felt like melted crayons. Her limbs

twitched with conflicting signals. She grew breathless and hot. Wired.

Because the way he stared into her soul thrust alarm into her belly.

And spiraled erotic shivers into her blood.

His lips moved. He didn't try to compete with the music, but she read her name as he shaped it. Not her stage name. Her legal name, Joy Youngston. He jerked his head in a signal to leave the pole and talk to him.

Her heart dipped in shock. She had the sudden fear she was about to be arrested. Exotic dancing was strictly regulated in Illinois, but she had her paperwork in order. She abided by all the rules—no touching chief among them.

Still on her hands and knees, she held his gaze as she slid her toe back along the floor, extending one leg. She reached up and back to find the pole, readying to mount it again, letting him know she didn't take orders from strangers.

He drew a money clip from his jacket pocket and pulled a hundred-dollar bill from it.

She stayed exactly as she was. The position opened the front of her body for his perusal. Still his gaze stayed locked with hers in a battle of wills that felt dangerous and exciting and terrifying.

He jerked his head again, but she wasn't giving up her spot on the stage for anything less than what she normally took home from a six-hour shift.

She lifted her chin, urging more from the clip.

He thumbed a second and a third bill, then held them out to her.

She took the money and tucked the notes under the strings at her hip, then rolled to take a low grasp on the pole with both hands. In a blatantly sexual move, she planted her feet and slowly lifted her hips, straightening her legs so she was bent forward, facing him. She held the pose with her shoes spaced wide while she exaggerated the dip in her lower back, affording him a good view of her breasts as they swayed inside the tiny cups of her black bra.

It was a little treat for his generosity and a show of insolence on her part. She would cooperate, but in her own time.

Slowly, she climbed her hands up the pole until she was standing straight. She pointed to the batwing doors that wore an Employees Only sign.

"Wait there," she mouthed before she walked backstage into the dressing room. Her knees were weak, and her pulse knocked around her rib cage like a pinball.

"What's wrong?" The girl on break was touching up her toenail polish.

"I have to meet someone." Joy pulled on a cheap blue bathrobe with yellow ducks, having learned that anything nicer than this grew legs and walked away. "You can take my spot."

"Yeah? Thanks. I need the money." The young woman hopped to her feet.

Don't we all, Joy thought as she filled a clean glass from the water cooler and gulped it down.

Was that guy from the government? The military? Her brother was serving overseas. Her sister-in-law was pregnant in California. She would be informed if anything had happened to David. What about their father? Paul Youngston was on medication for Parkinson's, and Joy had made sure he had taken it before she left home this afternoon. Their neighbor, a retired nurse, came by in the evenings to check on him and help him into bed. If there was a problem, she knew to reach Joy here at the club or when to call an ambulance.

"Joy Youngston?" The voice was like black coffee, dark and bitter.

She spun around to face him. "You're not supposed to be back here."

The lights were brighter in the changing room, glaring an unflattering yellow. She could see his suit was navy, not charcoal, and held a fine pinstripe. His tie was silver blue, like his eyes. He would be able to see her makeup was applied heavily with thick eyeliner and lips that were artfully painted to appear plumper than they really were.

"Who are you?" She lifted her brows in the haughty way she'd learned to face down all forms of male attention, whether shy or friendly or aggressive.

His stare was…impossible to read. Not lecherous, but sexual energy crackled on the air. She normally felt she had the upper hand when she knew she was desired, but she realized she had never been attracted to the men who came onto her.

This stranger had reversed that on her. She found him compelling but also intimidating. He was delving into her gaze as though looking for something. As though deciding something. It set her back on her spiked heels.

Want me. She hated that deep yearning, but she had come to accept it was written into her DNA. Or had been stamped there with the seal on her adoption certificate.

"Axel Severin." He had a slight accent, one that rounded the *A* to *ah* and threw the *X* into the back of his throat. "You've been ignoring my messages."

Her heart swerved. She belted her robe more tightly.

"This is about my birth father?" Her ears rang with alarm. She had started receiving weird messages from Germany a week ago. "It's a nice variation on the foreign prince scam, but…" She managed to sound pithy as she cocked a negligent hip and shrugged, even though she was unsettled that this had escalated into a confrontation at her workplace. "Dancing on a pole does not make me stupid. Kindly take me off your list of potential marks and never contact me again. Willis!"

She hoped the bouncer had noticed him come back here and stationed himself nearby in case there was trouble.

Willis poked his head in.

"Can you show him the exit, please?"

Willis gave Axel an up-down glance and set his jaw, expecting resistance. Axel was close to Willis's six-five, but Willis was built like a bulldozer and removed angry drunks on the regular.

Axel was neither angry nor drunk. He was also formidable enough to halt Willis with a casually raised hand. "You can spare me ten minutes for a conversation," he said to Joy.

The messages had been unsettling her for days. She might have taken them more seriously if she'd actually been looking for her birth father—or if these messages hadn't withheld her birth father's name because "a great deal of money" was involved.

"If it seems too good to be true, it is." She'd learned that when her college boyfriend had talked her into using her own college fund to pay his tuition, claiming he would support her once he completed his degree and was established as an orthodontist.

"I didn't say there weren't strings," Axel said with a derisive twist of his lips. "Let me tell you what they are."

She blamed herself for this. She was fairly open about the fact that she was adopted. She had even let a friend interview her about it for a lifestyle blog when she'd still been living with Todd. She had specifically mentioned how frustrated she was that she didn't have any information on her birth father. It would be very easy for someone to read that post and decide she was a ripe target for a scam like this.

"Who are you?" she demanded. "A lawyer or something?"

"Or something."

Okay, Captain Cryptic.

"Look, my time isn't free." She inspected the miniature kiss prints on her black nail polish. "If you want to talk to me, we can go into the Champagne Room. It's a thousand dollars for twenty minutes." It was actually two hundred for thirty, but she was trying to scare him off.

He offered Willis a black credit card. "Give us an hour."

CHAPTER THREE

The bouncer started to lead Axel out of the changing room, but Joy hung back to flick through a rack of costumes.

"What are you doing?" he asked her.

"Changing." Her chin came up so she could look down her nose at him. "What would you like? Schoolgirl? Librarian? Bondage? Cheetah?"

"That." He nodded at her robe, trying not to think of the lush curves barely contained by her provocative black bra and butt-floss bottoms. The way she had stared at him while writhing had caused exactly the reaction intended, which was irritating in the extreme. He needed cold clarity, not dull-witted lust. Not a hot weight throbbing behind his fly, urging him to rearrange his priorities.

How was he supposed to erase from his mind that image of amber-honey limbs moving with superb grace, though? Or platinum-streaked hair falling around her shoulders and across her cheek, begging his fingers to brush it from her eyes and tuck it behind her ear? A mutinous, pouted mouth that—

Stop.

What the hell was she even doing here? His research had told him she was studying to be a nurse, not working as an exotic dancer.

The woman he was contractually obligated to marry was a stripper.

Axel strove to be a modern man who didn't judge other's choices. He'd been in the position of having few choices himself. He knew you had to make the best of what little you had. God knew, there'd been a time when he would have thought being able to afford a private room in an adult-entertainment establishment was the height of luxury—not that he had ever thrown his money away in places like this.

He curled his lip as he entered the round room with its cushioned bench and pole in the middle. A funk of sour beer and sweat permeated the air.

He had scratched tooth and nail to get out of traps like this and resented the hell out of Otto—and this woman—for dragging him back into this world, even for a minute. If he wasn't so furious at Otto, so determined to win this hand and the pot, he would have walked out and never looked back.

Even as he thought that, however, his gaze snagged on a muscled calf and a narrow foot in a black stiletto. The turn of her ankle kicked fresh lust into his groin.

"I'll be back with the champagne," the bouncer said.

"Don't bother." Axel had had champagne. They didn't serve it here.

The bouncer left, enclosing them in silence.

"I don't have my phone for the music." Joy adjusted the knob on the wall near the door, filling the room with the relentless rhythm playing in the front of the club.

She was trying to seize the upper hand. He recognized the tactic because he did it himself with a shake of his head. She lowered the volume to silence again.

"Are they recording us?" He glanced at the dark bubble protecting a camera lens above the closed door.

"They watch to be sure there's no touching. Martini could lose his license."

Which probably didn't stop the behavior from being tolerated if the dancer was willing and the customer was known to be discreet.

How would she react if *he* touched her?

He yanked his mind from going down that path.

"Why do you work here?" he asked in a voice that sat like grit in his throat.

"A deep need to express myself through the art of exotic movement." She set the inside of one spiked heel against the base of the pole, picked up her inner leg, and grasped the pole as she leaned out, taking a slow spin around it.

Her long hair fell in a curtain that brushed his sleeve as she went by. She batted purple lashes at him and offered a buttery smile.

"You need the money," he surmised.

She touched her nose.

"For?"

She straightened to set her back against the pole. "Are you going to sit? Lap dance is extra."

"No." He could afford as many bespoke trousers as he needed, but he didn't throw them away by sitting in... He didn't care to identify what those stains were.

This was a ridiculous room. There was no space to move without bumping into her. Nowhere to escape the enticing image of cheap, shiny polyester lying against the swells of firm, high breasts. He couldn't avoid the glimpse of her black bra, or the firm length of her tanned thighs encircled by those tantalizing garters. He wanted to tangle his fingers in them. Close his teeth on them.

"I was under the impression you were in a nursing program."

"I am. Part-time. Why? Is my birth father offended by my career choice?"

"He doesn't know." Axel hadn't known about it until he had landed and went to a bungalow in the suburbs to find her.

A matronly woman had answered the door, clutching her cardigan against the March wind as she studied him through round-rimmed glasses. *She's at work. Is there a problem?*

Axel had said it was a legal matter. Concerned, the woman had helpfully told him where to find her.

Even at that, Axel had assumed Joy was serving drinks, not dancing in a place called Martini's Cabaret. Not until he'd walked in and had his eyes nearly pulled from his skull by the raw sexuality she exuded.

He loathed feeling anything but completely in control of himself and his surroundings, but he hadn't been able to look away from her. She'd been mesmerizing. Bold in the way she met his gaze. His mind was still imprinted with the image of lithe, muscled limbs, the shimmy of her generously endowed chest and the flex of her firm, rounded buttocks.

Every time he met her hazel gaze, his sexual awareness of her ratcheted up another notch. Looking into her eyes tempted him to look at her mouth with her lush upper lip, and her long throat that he wanted to trace down to—

No.

"If you need money, you should have replied to my messages."

"Why would I do that when I can make you pay me to speak to you?" she mocked. "I get twenty percent off the fee for this room. Are you sure you don't want me to…?" In a move of supple power, she brought her knee up, then caught her arm under her calf to finish drawing her leg up, up, up until she was holding herself in the splits against the pole, hugging her raised leg and artfully dropping her other hand to grasp the pole exactly where his gaze most wanted to zero in.

She rolled her shoulder, and the robe slipped off her shoulder. A seductive smile drew itself across her lips.

A fresh zing of lust struck below his belt, one that dulled his brain and dimmed his vision. Before he realized what he was doing, he grasped the cool brass of the pole next to the ankle she held aloft. He leaned near enough that his nose was a millimeter from hers, close enough to feel the electricity between them.

Her breath hitched, and her lashes quivered, but she didn't move.

"No touching," she reminded, lips parted enticingly. Her gaze traveled over his face, scraping like sensual nails against his control, until her stare landed on his mouth.

He was nearly pulled off his feet but held himself with steely discipline. "You want me to want you," he noted in a rasp. "You think that gives you power over me. I do want you."

Her startled gaze came back to his. Wariness entered her gaze, but a glow of wild excitement blossomed beneath it. That flare of reaction dug talons deeper into his libido, trying to drag it out to play.

"But I can wait until we've conducted our business," he continued, never breaking eye contact. "Can you?"

He let the beast in him steal one thorough look, all the way down to where the hem of her robe had ridden up to expose the tops of her thighs. To the narrow band of black that revealed she waxed to a Brazilian. Or less.

He was fully hard, if she cared to notice. The thud of his heart was a hammering pulse behind his fly.

In an abrupt move, she bent her upper leg around the pole, forcing him to take a step back or catch a spiked heel in the face. She seeming to defy gravity as she kicked her bottom leg out straight and spun in a slow circle, forcing him back another step, flashing him the frill that fluttered against the tops of her ass cheeks as she went by.

After three spins, she ended with both feet coming to rest on the floor.

"What I want," she said as she lifted her chin and set her shoulders back, "is for you to touch me so you'll get kicked out."

Lie. She was meeting his gaze, but her color was high. Her nipples were pebbled hard enough to show against the twin layers of bra cups and robe. It wasn't cold in here. Not at all. He was sweltering in his tie and jacket.

Damn it. This sexual pull between them was not something he'd factored into this arrangement, and he didn't have time to recalibrate. The stubborn street dog in him was fighting to take what was his. He was determined to beat Otto at his own game and quickly, especially now that Mira had partnered with a man who had his own ax to grind.

If Axel didn't take over Vorstoben soon, it might not be there at all.

He had wasted precious time trying to reach Joy through social media, then a couriered letter. She had ignored both. After asking Umberto if she'd responded to his messages, and hearing Umberto confirm she hadn't, Axel had invented an appointment in London and carried on here to Chicago to confront her in person.

"I don't have time for games," Axel stated. "I need you to take this seriously."

She stiffened at his commanding tone, but unsnaked her arm from around the pole, shifting so she grasped it behind her back.

"Would you take it seriously if you received messages like these?" she challenged. "My birth father wants to meet me, and I stand to inherit *hundreds* of millions of euros? Along with a company I have no idea how to run? And all I have to do is submit to a DNA test and show up in Germany? *Then* I will meet him and learn his name? Please," she dismissed the idea with scorn. "Would you like my bank details up front, so you can start pouring those millions into my account?"

She shifted her weight, causing her robe to slip a fraction of an inch, exposing more of her bra and a wider sliver of skin below it.

He dragged his gaze upward. "It's a delicate matter. He can't risk you selling the story before you've agreed to his narrative." Just as Axel couldn't risk her speaking to Otto first or tipping Otto off to his presence here. "I will need that DNA sample but..."

He told himself he was looking so closely at her features to compare her to the photo of Lorena as a young woman. Joy had her same arched brows and narrow, high-bridged nose. Her cheekbones were spaced with perfection in her oval face. Her lips were definitely her mother's, despite the makeup that made them seem fuller and plumper.

He didn't see much of Otto in her, thankfully, beyond her height and a feminine version of a mulish chin, which was good because he didn't want to kiss—

He bit back a curse. This was a business partnership he was courting. He had no intention of getting personal with her, let alone physical.

"But?" she prompted.

"Hmm?" DNA. Right. "Your birth name is Enja Fontaine, is it not?"

She tried not to react, but the way her expression blanked was its own tell.

"I'm confident you're the woman I'm looking for." A strange buzz arrived in his ears as he said that. He cleared his throat. "I don't have time to mollycoddle you. There's urgency around proving your identity and proceeding to the next steps."

Mira hadn't gone to the press yet, but she could. Revealing she was *not* Otto's biological daughter would embarrass him, which Otto deserved, but it could also harm her chances of getting at least a compulsory portion of his estate in the future.

Otto thought he had the upper hand with both of them, believing he could keep Axel on a leash while they waited for Joy to show up, but Axel wasn't waiting. Not anymore.

"Do you know what the top signs of fraud are?" Joy asked conversationally. "I looked them up. They include pretending to represent a family member…" she touched a fingertip, counting them off as she continued "…pressuring the victim to act quickly, asking for personal information—my DNA feels very personal—and asking the victim to spend their own money in order to get whatever is promised. Like paying for a DNA test?" She blinked her overly long, purple eyelashes before stating clearly, "No."

"I'll pay for the test. Maybe I'm wrong, and you're not her. There's only one way to find out, isn't there?"

"Are you hoping I'm not?" She smirked and looped her elbow around the pole, tilting her head against it. "What's wrong? Now that you've seen my profession, you're worried my father won't be so keen to meet me? How do I know who you're comparing my sample to, anyway? No." She shook her head. "It's too fishy."

"This won't affect his desire to meet you." Not when Axel introduced her as his wife and staked his claim on Vorstoben.

"But I haven't decided if I want to meet him." Her playfulness dropped away, leaving a solemn expression that held no subterfuge whatsoever.

That was a wrinkle Axel hadn't anticipated. "You're not curious about him?"

"I was curious about my birth mother," she admitted. "But when I contacted the agency, all they could tell me was that she had already died. Which was a huge bummer." Dark shadows entered her eyes. "I knew that she didn't put my father's name on my birth certificate because he was married. I've always assumed that meant she didn't want him in my life or the other way around."

"That might have been true when she had you, but she signed an affidavit that was delivered to him after she died. I have a copy in my hotel room."

"Why didn't she want him to know about me until after she was gone?"

Spite, Axel suspected. Otto didn't invite many other emotions from those close to him. "His wife was pregnant at the time."

"I have a half sibling?" Her face brightened with wonder.

"No." Damn. For one second, she'd glowed with such delight, she'd hurt his eyes. Now all of that dimmed, and she glared at him as though he'd kicked her.

"Dead? See, this is why I don't want to do this. It's a roller coaster that I don't need." She looked to the door.

"His wife had a baby who isn't his. We'll get into all of that once I confirm your identity."

She shook her head. "If he's so interested in meeting me, why isn't he here himself?"

"There's a lot of money involved. It's complicated."

"And delicate." She threw his word back at him with ample mockery. "My life is also delicate and complicated. I have an ailing father who would be gutted to hear I have a rich birth father who wants to take his place. The person who was helping me with his care is pregnant with her second baby, so she moved closer to her own parents. That means my brother will go to California the next time he gets leave, rather than coming here. My sister-in-law was living with us, so we've lost her income, too. That leaves me covering the mortgage that Dad took out to cover his medical bills. My dancing keeps us sheltered and fed, so I can't go chasing waterfalls. Windfalls? Either way…" She rolled a dismissing shoulder. "Thanks, but no thanks."

"Prove you're his daughter, and your financial problems will be gone." He emphasized that with a cutting swipe of his hand through the air, still amazed himself with how many obstacles could be removed with the application of cash. "What would you do if you had unlimited funds? Move your father closer to your brother? Hire him a rotation of private nurses to offer care twenty-four-seven? I can start arranging that tonight."

"All you need is a vial of my blood?" she guessed with an acidic smile.

"I will pay you for a vial of your blood. How much do you want for it?" He had her now, and he would reel her in.

The last vestiges of sex kitten disappeared. She stood

tall, arms folded, eyes narrowed with shrewdness, mouth firmed in deliberation. "I've been down this road, you know. I let a man snow me with false promises of a big payout, and now I'm dancing here instead of Broadway."

"Is that what you stand to lose if you leave with me tonight? This rewarding career of yours?" He sent a derisive look around the room. "I'm confident you can find similar employment if it turns out I'm wrong about you."

"You mean if *I'm* wrong about *you*." Her smile was a pained stretch of her lips.

"Take the test and find out."

"Twenty thousand dollars. Up front," she demanded.

He snorted. She'd already fleeced him for a room that couldn't be worth more than five hundred dollars for an hour, but he would have added a zero to her extortion figure if it meant he could claim Vorstoben. "Your money will be waiting with a nurse at my hotel. Let's go."

"Now?" she asked with alarm.

"Now."

CHAPTER FOUR

I CAN WAIT. Can you?

Joy hurried to the changing room, even more shaken than ever by her reaction to Axel Severin. Men wanted her all the time. She never wanted them. Not like this, but when he'd loomed over her in the Champagne Room, she'd been struck by an overwhelming urge to kiss him.

That would have been disturbing if he had been any stranger, but he was here on her birth father's behalf. She was beginning to believe that much, at least—that he was on a legitimate quest to find the offspring of Lorena Fontaine.

After losing Wendy, the mother who'd raised her, to a congenital heart problem, then learning the mother who'd birthed her was dead, Joy had shrunk inward. She'd tried to convince herself she didn't care where she came from. Her birth family didn't matter because her adoptive family loved her unconditionally. They had welcomed her home with open arms, hadn't they, after she'd made such a fool of herself over Todd?

Her disappointment over not being able to meet her birth mother had contributed to her falling for Todd's BS, though. She saw it clearly now that she had distance from it. She had been sad and adrift and had clung to the one close connection she'd had at the time. She had been so afraid to lose Todd, she'd put him above her own autonomy and aspirations, never seeing how one-sided and flimsy their relationship really was.

Now Axel was offering a new connection, one that he held just beyond her reach while saying, *I'm confident you're the woman I'm looking for.*

Her skin tightened as she remembered the specific timbre of his voice. She was still breathless and fluttery, still feeling accosted by his tightly contained energy and the sexual charisma that pierced her belly with yearning.

After removing her makeup, she quickly looked Axel up online, but only wound up with more questions than answers.

The first email about her birth father had come through the adoption agency. She'd been asked to reply to a lawyer called Umberto. She had still been deciding whether to respond and how to tell her father, Paul, about it when she'd received a private message from Axel through one of her social accounts.

She had blocked it, certain it was a bot. But receiving that message had made the one from the agency seem suspicious. When the couriered letter arrived two days later, she'd lied to her father and said it was about her student loans, but she'd been baffled and alarmed at the persistence of the scammers.

Axel wasn't a conman, though. Not according to the internet. Either he'd gone to great lengths to create this online persona or he was the CEO of a big infrastructure conglomerate in Germany.

If he was a CEO, what was he doing here, on her birth father's behalf?

She flicked through some photos of Axel. One showed him at a podium for a trade conference, another showed him arriving at a charity gala with his fiancée.

Fiancée!?

The sound of screeching brakes arrived in her ears, causing a sick lurch in her stomach.

Wow. Mira Braun was beautiful in an ultrasophisticated way. Even so, she didn't look particularly fulfilled wearing something that Joy presumed was a designer gown. Her sparkly earrings were probably real diamonds, and Axel wore a tuxedo, but they both wore similar, aloof expressions.

The photograph struck her as staged. Like the kind actors took with their costars when they secretly despised each other but had to do a press tour and act as though they were in love.

Maybe she was being uncharitable. Jealous, even. Of what, though? She didn't have any feelings toward Axel besides hostility. She sure as heck wasn't looking for love or romance. She was a complete cynic about those things, thanks to Todd. If anything, learning Axel was engaged filled her with contempt—and little surprise.

I do want you...

She shrugged her shoulders as a shiver chased down her spine.

Why were men such predictable jerks? And why was she attracted to him when he obviously was one?

She dropped her phone into her bag and finished dressing, pulling on jeans with short boots and a diamond-knit pullover with a puffy jacket. She plopped a black motorcycle cap on her head and turned up her collar because the March wind off Lake Michigan was still cold enough to cut her in half.

She had half a mind to walk out the back door, but Axel was waiting in the hall, just inside the batwings.

"Ready?"

She clenched her teeth and followed him outside to a

waiting SUV. He held the door for her, then directed the driver to the Ritz-Carlton.

The vehicle was tricked out like a limousine with a tiny refrigerator in the console between their armchairs. It held single-serve bottles of champagne and glass flutes along with a variety of snacks, including fresh fruit.

"Help yourself," he invited when he saw her taking inventory.

If this was a kidnapping—and she was only convinced it wasn't because she had nothing worth being ransomed for—she could see how easily Stockholm syndrome happened.

"I read that you're engaged," she said belligerently while fingering through playbills from the seat pocket, wistful that she wasn't in any of these musicals.

"It's been called off," he said dismissively.

"Convenient." She flicked him a glance of undisguised doubt.

He turned his head, face shadowed and unreadable. "It has."

The wall of derision she'd erected as a defense against him turned to sand. His masculine energy sparked and crackled in her direction again, licking like flames against her skin.

"You seem like a bigwig at a huge company." She changed tactics. "Why are you here, running errands for my father? Who is he to you?"

"We'll talk at the hotel."

So annoying.

They traveled in silence until they walked into the lobby of the hotel. A young man met them there. He wore a suit that rivaled Axel's and held a tablet inside a black leather cover.

"My assistant, Heskel. Ms. Youngston," Axel provided.

"It's nice to meet you, Ms. Youngston. Would you both come with me, please? Everything is ready upstairs." Heskel escorted them toward the elevators, speaking to Axel as they walked. "I made a reservation in the restaurant, but it's very busy. The chef has agreed to send something up if you prefer?"

"Three courses with a paired wine," Axel said with an absent nod.

As they stepped into the elevator, Heskel opened his tablet cover and extracted something. "For you, Ms. Youngston." He offered a slim red leather sleeve that held what looked like a single credit card.

She didn't take it, only moved her gaze from the card to Axel's impassive expression.

"You asked for twenty thousand dollars," Axel said. "That's preloaded with thirty, to assist with legal costs. You'll want someone you can trust."

Heskel continued holding out the card like a barker on the street, trying to entice passersby into his peep show.

Axel plucked the card, then picked up her hand and pressed the card against her palm, folding her fingers around it.

No touching, she thought, even as fireworks shot through her. His hands were warm. Strong and insistent. Magical in their ability to halt the elevator midair. To stop the earth from rotating and make her feet leave the floor.

We called it off.

A vibration between longing and apprehension arrived in her breastbone, sending skittering sensations into the depths of her abdomen. The vibration dropped low, like embers that stayed hot and heavy in the notch of her thighs.

She yanked her hand away and shoved the card into the

back pocket of her jeans. "Must be nice, being able to arrange something like this at the drop of a text," she said, using a snotty tone because she was so disconcerted.

"You'll soon find out, won't you?"

The elevator doors opened, and Axel waved her to exit first.

Joy had been working up her courage to have her blood drawn. She hated needles, but it turned out to be a cheek swab. She had barely removed her hat and jacket before the nurse was leaving with the sample, Heskel on her heels.

Blinking with astonishment, Joy suddenly found herself alone with Axel. This time there was no bouncer beyond the door or a CCTV to record what happened between them.

"Happy?" She rose and touched the credit card in her back pocket, wondering if it would really work. She reached for her jacket where it was draped over the arm of the sofa.

"Wait." He picked up the card the nurse had left on the coffee table, the one with Joy's file number written on it. "Email Umberto. Tell him you've sent your sample to this lab and give him this number. Tell him that when you receive confirmation that it's a match, you'll make arrangements to travel to Germany to meet your father. It's the middle of the night there, but he'll see it first thing. By the time you wake here, you'll know."

"Give you an inch, and you take a mile, don't you?" she muttered as she dug in her bag for her phone.

"What is that in metric?" he asked with false interest.

"A crap ton of arrogance," she provided with a sweet smile. "I can't just drop everything and fly to Germany, you know. I have responsibilities." Even so, she took the card and sank back onto the sofa while she began to scroll through her trashed emails.

"All of that will be taken care of. Don't mention me in the message."

"Why not?" She looked up.

"Because I asked you not to."

She snorted. Arrogance didn't begin to cover his brashness. "This all sounds very shady. Are you making me an accomplice in something illegal?"

"No."

"As if you would admit to it," she grumbled.

"I will explain after you send the message." He took on a tone of weary patience and walked over to the bar. "Would you like something before dinner arrives?"

"What is this, a date now? Because I don't care how much money is on the credit card. You paid for a test and a conversation."

"Then make the test happen, and we'll continue our conversation." He didn't even look at her, only focused on unboxing a bottle of scotch.

Dictator.

She found the email from the agency and typed her response to Umberto, reading it aloud before she sent it. "My sample number is yada yada at the lab yada yada. Once a match is confirmed, we can discuss a meeting with my birth father." She looked to Axel for confirmation.

"Perfect. Thank you."

She hit Send, and the whoosh filled the quiet room.

He poured a finger's worth of amber liquid into a glass. "None for you?" he asked again.

"No. Thank you." She stood as nerves arrived with a return of her crackling awareness that she was alone with him. It had been different in the private room at the club. She always felt confident in her costume. Yes, it left her mostly naked, but it was still a type of mask, one that gave her a certain power.

Wearing her worn, dated jeans and thrift-store sweater was a different type of revealing. Things had been financially dismal before she'd moved home and discovered her father's coffers were also empty.

She moved to the window. The luxurious corner suite was one of the hotel's finest with a full-size lounge, a dining table for six and views of Navy Pier. Out on the black lake, the pinprick lights of ships bobbed like untethered stars.

"Don't results take a few days?" she asked over her shoulder.

"Not when you pay for a lab tech to remain on standby."

Axel's level of wealth was hitting her like a wrecking ball. Or rather, the fact that he didn't seem to need to squeeze money out of an overdrawn exotic dancer from a very middling middle-class family. It made all of this more distressingly real.

"Tell me about your relationship to my birth father." She turned to see he'd taken a seat facing her.

His gaze came up from her jean pockets. Even though half the room separated them and neither of them moved, she had the sense of the walls shrinking inward and him coming up against her. It was a wild rush of heat that curled around her, pulling her close. Caging her.

Her heart lurched, and a sting exploded in her chest, rising into her throat and blossoming in her cheeks. She pretended it wasn't happening and lifted a brow in challenge.

He tilted his head in a self-deprecating, *You caught me*.

But there was no sheepishness in him. He was too direct, letting her see the power and ferocity within him. The desire.

She heard his graveled voice again. *I do want you. But I can wait*.

Her stomach swooped. It should have been with alarm,

but it was the vertigo of being on a swing with her eyes closed or the uneven, hysterical thrill of being swept along whitewater rapids.

"My information on you was incomplete." He sipped his drink. "I didn't know about your side hustle. That leads me to wonder what else I don't know. Are you involved with anyone?"

"What *do* you know about me?" She crossed her arms, not liking how easily he put her on her back foot. Did he know about Todd? "Have you been having me followed?"

"No. I glanced over your social profiles." He spoke dismissively, as though it should be obvious that was all anyone needed to do. "You began your degree in performing arts with a focus on modern dance but quit in your third year. You were living with someone at the time but moved home last year, possibly because of your father's declining health? Parkinson's, is it?"

"Yes." She had come home for his birthday and realized how badly Carrie was struggling to work around caring for a toddler and an adult who needed increasing levels of assistance.

Since she had already dropped out of school, and Todd was bleeding her dry, Joy had cut her losses. She had told Todd she wasn't coming back to Connecticut. He'd squeezed one final month of rent out of her and kept the good coffee maker, but eventually sent her a box of her things, COD. of course.

"You've since enrolled in a nursing program," Axel continued. "Presumably because it's a stable career that would allow you to help your father. Your brother is an air force pilot with a wife, a small child and another baby on the way. You like animal videos and avoid political content. You don't advertise your alter ego or where you perform."

"Gee, I wonder why, when strangers show up and admit to stalking me."

"I'm not a very good stalker if I don't know whether you have a boyfriend, am I? Do you?" he pressed.

"Why? Does my birth father expect him to ask permission to date me?"

"No. I do."

"Ha!"

He only sipped his drink, reeking of patience while her heart galloped in her chest. How did he look so damned sexy and, yes, dangerous, sitting there relaxed and watchful?

"Silly me, I thought whom I date would be my choice."

"You would think, but we've both been pushed into a corner." He looked into his glass, tilting the liquid this way and that. "I'd like to put my cards on the table, Joy. It's more expedient, rather than waiting until we have the test result. If I do that, I want your assurance that what I tell you will stay in this room." His gaze came up.

"Or?"

"Or you will be made very uncomfortable. That's not a threat. It's the truth. Your birth father has a high enough profile there would be significant publicity. Whatever you might make in selling this story, you would spend on hiring a PR agency and personal security to manage the fallout."

"Good grief, who is he?"

"Do I have your word?"

"Fine. Yes." She glanced toward the bedroom. "There's probably a Bible in here if you need me to swear on it. But please, for the love of all that's holy, tell me what's going on."

"We'll need that Bible," he said with a faint quirk of his lips. "I'm here to marry you."

CHAPTER FIVE

SHE BARKED OUT a laugh. Because he had to be joking. How could he not be?

"With a sturdy prenup," he said as though he hadn't blurted out something so absurd she had already dismissed it. "After a year, we'll quietly divorce and go back to our separate lives."

"This conversation has officially jumped the shark." She walked across to pick up her bag and jacket again.

"You promised to listen."

She removed the credit card from her jean pocket and left it on the coffee table.

He picked up a manila envelope from the end table and dropped it next to the credit card. It landed with a slap.

She froze. "What is that?" she asked suspiciously.

"The letter from your birth mother to your father." He sat back. "And a list of assets you're in line to inherit along with a copy of the contract that proves you *will* inherit the lion's share of your birth father's fortune if you marry me. You'll be very wealthy, Joy."

"I don't care for this judgy attitude of yours." She waggled her finger at him. "Acting like I'm driven solely by money."

"I don't judge you for that." His brow quirked as though he was affronted by the accusation. "Everyone is driven by money to some extent. I'm here because I want the piece of your fortune that was promised to me. Sit down." He nodded at the sofa. "Let me explain."

She told her feet to take her to the door, but the envelope and its secrets called to her. She inched back to stand on the far side of the coffee table from him, arms folded, staring down at the envelope as though it contained a viper that would slither out and sink its fangs into her. But she was too fascinated by its sway to look away.

"Your father is Otto Braun."

"The father of your fiancée." She lifted her surprised gaze to his.

"Ex," he corrected. "And he's not her father. But you've got the gist of it." He leaned forward to set down his glass and opened the envelope. He shook out its contents across the tabletop. Catching at the corner of a photo, he drew it away from the rest, pushing it toward her.

She picked up the photo and studied the man who was well-kempt with a longish face and a neatly trimmed white beard. He carried some middle-age weight and his features were lined by age. He was handsome, but there was a certain hardness to his expression.

Was this really where she had come from? She slowly sank onto the sofa, feeling porous and suddenly needing to absorb everything Axel could tell her.

He reached forward again and pushed a photograph of a woman toward her. "Lorena Fontaine. French. She moved to New York when she became pregnant and returned to Europe a few years later."

Joy picked up the dated photo of a woman taken when Lorena was close to Joy's twenty-four. She was elegant in a timeless way, wearing a dress with chiffon sleeves and holding a cigarette in two fingers. Her lips were tilted in a half smile around a whistling exhale of smoke, as though she was amused by whoever was taking her photo.

Joy recognized enough of herself in the woman's features to feel knocked off her equilibrium. Her body reacted as though she'd been pushed or struck or grabbed. Her blood was singing with adrenaline, urging her to run. Or fight.

"This is her letter to your father. They rekindled their affair about five years after your birth. His wife was still alive then." He found a photocopy of a handwritten letter and offered it to her. A notarized translation into English was stapled behind it. "Lorena says she knew he wouldn't forgive her for giving you up, but when she was diagnosed with lung cancer, she decided to tell him about you. I don't see any reason she would lie about him being your father. Not if she was waiting until after her death to inform him. What did she have to gain?"

He fell silent while Joy scanned the translation. There wasn't much more to it than what he had just said. Lorena mentioned the name of the adoption agency and hoped that Otto would *provide your daughter the lifestyle she ought to have had.*

Joy had always felt like she was her birth mother's dirty little secret. Learning that Lorena had waited until after her death to tell her father reinforced that impression, sending a deep pang into her heart.

"Does she have any family? Do they know about me?" she asked, trying to keep the husk from her voice.

"I couldn't say. Her parents are gone, but her brother is still alive. I have no idea if that's something she would have shared with him."

"Especially if she wasn't even telling her baby's father."

Joy frowned, trying to understand. Trying not to be stung by her complete erasure from her blood relatives' lives.

"Given the timing of their second affair, my suspicion is that Otto had recently learned his wife had also had an affair. The child he believed was his daughter was not."

"Mira." She lowered Lorena's photo into her lap.

"Yes. Until I learned that, I couldn't understand Otto's ambivalence toward her." Axel was doing a good job of seeming completely impassive, but a muscle ticked in his cheek. "I don't imagine Otto was in a mood to hear he had a biological daughter he couldn't claim. I'm guessing that's why Lorena didn't tell him and wound up breaking things off again."

"But now he knows and wants to meet me?" She was having trouble controlling her expression, feeling her mouth wobbling toward a smile even as her chin crinkled anxiously.

"I'll be frank with you, Joy." He leaned forward, and his hard voice gave her inner child a pinch on the arm, then twisted it. "Otto wants to use you to keep me at Vorstoben."

She frowned. "Isn't that what you want?"

"Not exactly." He picked up his drink and sat back. "I want to quit working for him and work for myself. I told him two years ago that I was leaving to open my own firm. I wasn't intending to compete directly with him. Vorstoben takes on complex, billion-dollar projects. Factories and resorts. I've always seen a need for highly skilled, bespoke services. Projects that are challenging in a different way. When I told him I was leaving, Otto promoted me to CEO. He said he would retire once I married his daughter and gift us the company after a year of marriage. He let me believe all this time that his daughter was Mira."

"Oh." Until Axel said that, his proposal had been a joke. Now the determination she read in him was rolling over her like a cool, frothy tide. It should have frozen her to the bone, but it rocked her while sand shifted beneath her feet. Nothing was solid. She was being tossed around and tugged out to sea.

Tugged by a god who would not take no for an answer. *That's been called off. You're the woman I'm looking for.*

Her heart began to thud as though he was pursuing her through the dark city streets.

"I agreed to his offer." He was still holding her gaze, filling her ears with the smooth timbre of his voice. "I poured myself into Vorstoben, believing it would be mine as soon as Mira and I married. He wouldn't let us set a date. Wouldn't finalize the terms." He took a gulp of scotch and bared his teeth at the burn. "A month ago, I said I wouldn't wait any longer. He offered me this." He took up a slim envelope from the pile and unfolded what looked like a contract of several pages. "It promises that if I marry his *biological* daughter, he'll honor the terms he set two years ago. That was when Mira and I both learned she isn't his daughter. And that you are."

"That's how he told her?" She didn't know Mira, but she felt the other woman's shock on a visceral level, and the unmooring sensation it must have caused her. "That's horrible. Why do you even work for someone who acts like that?"

"Call it a deep need to express myself through executive movement," he said with heavy sarcasm. "He gave me opportunities and valuable experience when I needed it. That inspired a certain loyalty in me, but you're right. He's not nice. On the other hand, he's made it clear he won't leave the company to Mira, so I'm not trying to steal it from her. I only want what he promised me."

"I don't understand how you think he could use me, though?"

"He'll offer you his fortune if you marry me," he said simply and pointed at the contract. "He knows damned well that you would feel this hesitancy you're showing. Who would marry a stranger? It's a ridiculous ask."

"Thank you." These were the first sensible words he'd said all night.

"He would use your reservation to string me along, but I've reached the end of my forbearance. According to this contract…" he gave the pages a ruffle "…upon marrying me, Otto's *biological* daughter stands to inherit all of this." He filtered through the papers again and showed her a list of properties. The value tallied up to a hefty nine figures. The largest asset was Vorstoben, making up more than half.

Joy almost swallowed her tongue.

"I imagine Lorena felt some guilt at denying you the fortune you were entitled to inherit, once she realized Otto was balking at leaving it to Mira."

"But that's adoption." Joy shot to her feet and paced away in agitation. "You can drive yourself crazy thinking about the life you might have had if you had been raised by your birth mother. I'm really happy with the upbringing I had, though." Wendy hadn't been able to get pregnant again after having David. She had longed for a daughter, and Joy had arrived days after David started school. Joy had had her full, doting attention. "Mom and I were super close. That's why I waited until she was gone to even contact the agency. I've never had fantasies that anyone would come along and *rescue* me."

"Good. That's not why I'm here."

"No, you want to marry me to get your hands on things that aren't even mine!" She waved at the table.

"Only Vorstoben." He swallowed the last of his drink and sucked his teeth. "I already own a number of shares in it. Once I gain the ones that contract awards me, I will be the majority shareholder, which grants me total control. So I won't let him renege. Not again."

"But that comes at *my* expense. I don't want to be used by either of you." She shook her head, honestly wondering if she'd taken some of that weird cough medicine that gave her squirrely dreams. "No. There's no reason for me to agree to any of this."

At that moment, the door lock hummed. Heskel stepped inside and held the door open for the room service trolley to be pushed in by a server. As the server began setting the table, Heskel gave Joy a diffident nod.

"I apologize for the interruption, Ms. Youngston, but I have a few questions regarding your father's care. Is there any interest in a full-service senior building? There's one located near your sister-in-law that seems very well recommended. The cost is comparable to purchasing and retrofitting a home for accessibility, then hiring appropriate staff, so I thought it makes sense to explore it?"

"Puh… Pardon? I haven't agreed to anything." She threw that at Axel, alarmed.

"This is for discussion purposes." Axel rose and set aside his empty glass. "Heskel is pulling together options to present to your father. You seemed concerned that your brother will visit your father less often, now that his wife lives across the country. I asked Heskel to include a plan that moves your father closer to his grandchildren. If he chooses to stay in his current home and have a nurse come daily, that's up to him, but with my resources you can offer more far-reaching solutions."

"But I don't have your resources. Not unless—"

"Exactly," Axel cut in. "Include it," he instructed Heskel. "With a timeline on when the move could be accomplished."

"Of course. I'll be across the hall. Please text if you need anything." Heskel accepted the bill from the server and signed it, then followed the server out the door.

Axel drew out a chair for Joy at the dining table.

She sat as though in a trance, mind incapable of grasping a solid thought. She was halfway through the soup course before its delicate taste traveled from her tongue to her brain. Even then, she couldn't have said if she liked it.

"I'm probably not even her." At this point, she didn't know if a negative result would be a relief or a devastating loss.

The server had lit a candle. The soft glow painted flickers of golden light against Axel's cheekbones and brow and mouth. His eyelids blinked once, slowly. Almost suggesting pity at how she was grasping at straws.

"You'll still have thirty thousand dollars and a story you can never tell," he said dryly.

She choked slightly and pulled her spoon from her mouth. "Lucky me."

Thirty thousand dollars was not chump change, but it would only give her breathing space. Deeper pockets could alter the course of her father's care altogether, vastly improving the quality of his golden years.

She rowed her spoon in her soup.

"Could I really afford to move Dad into a senior building?" she asked tentatively. "A *nice* one?" Because she'd seen the ones she could afford, and it was another reason she'd started dancing at Martini's.

Triumph flashed in Axel's fierce blue eyes, telling her she'd tipped her hand, but it was too late to backtrack now. "The level of care you can offer him will astound you," he assured her.

He was stepping right on her Achilles' heel. She knew he was manipulating her with her emotions because it had happened once before. This time was different, though. It wasn't about her fearing abandonment. It was actually a fierce desire to give back to the man who had raised her and given her a warm and loving upbringing. Paul might be dependent on her now, but for most of her life he had been her safety net. He had done his best to give her a solid foundation to launch from. It wasn't his fault she had flubbed it.

"All I have to do is marry you?" she asked tentatively. "And meet my birth father?"

"We have to stay married a year. You'll behave as my wife in public."

"Where do you live?" she asked curiously.

"Vorstoben's head office is in Berlin, but I have a number of residences that you can retreat to. We don't have to live in each other's pockets."

A number of residences...

It was mind-boggling. Nothing about this made sense.

"What about..." Her voice dried up.

His attention lifted from his plate and settled on her in a way that was almost as physical as feeling him press her into a mattress. He was attractive. She couldn't help but be aware of that. She could cut her finger on the edge of his jaw, and those masculine lips would kiss it better.

Her pulse fluttered at the mere idea of his lips against her fingertip.

She looked away, embarrassed. She'd never experienced anything so carnal. An inappropriate fantasy of walking around the table and straddling his lap came into her head. He looked strong enough to pick her up and carry her to the sofa from there.

The corners of his mouth dug in, making her think he could see her thoughts like he was watching a film. She couldn't tell if he was amused or satisfied or if that reaction was something more reciprocal.

"When I said I want you, I meant it." His gaze slid to her mouth, and her blood turned to fire.

She knew when men were ogling her, and this wasn't that. He wasn't looking at her like a source for his sexual pleasure. He was looking at her with a mixture of intent and appreciation. As though they already had secrets between them. Delectable, seductive secrets.

"I'd rather you came to me with your own wants." His features took on a more concrete implacability. "Managing public opinion around your recent occupation will be difficult enough without you partaking in extracurriculars."

"Excuse me," she blustered, erotic thoughts scorched away by an indignant blush. "You're making a lot of assumptions. I don't partake in extracurriculars. I dance for money, but that's all I do for it. I don't go home with men. Not for money or recreation. So don't presume you can take possession of *me* along with everything else you think I can get for you."

"I'm only making clear that if you do have an itch, you'll come to me to scratch it."

"Keep dreaming," she muttered but only got an unimpressed mouth twitch in response. "I haven't even agreed to marry you, in case you haven't noticed."

"I noticed." He switched out their soup for the entrees, lamb chops with asparagus and cherry tomatoes atop ravioli. The sauce smelled like mint. "What else do you need besides the arrangements for your father? I can pay off your student loans."

"That's what the credit card is for." Those loans had been hanging over her like an anvil on a fraying rope, but they were hers to pay. Actually, they were Todd's, but paying them off was a punishment to herself for being so stupid. She wouldn't make them anyone else's problem.

"I'll clear them along with your father's mortgage. Call it a wedding gift. Shall we discuss your allowance?"

"I'm not twelve."

"Stipend? What do you want to call it? It's only for budgeting purposes. You'll have leeway to overshoot it."

"You're moving too fast," she muttered.

"I told you there was urgency. Let's find the clincher." He set his elbows on the table and laced his fingers together, imposing his iron will upon her. "If you could have anything you wanted in the world, right now, what would it be?"

"I don't know." She couldn't imagine a life without all these stressors and obligations that had been accumulating for years.

But as she sighed and looked into the flickering flame on the candle, her heart wrenched with yearning toward the one thing she'd been pretending she was okay with losing. The thing she sought and found, in a watered-down form at least, whenever she walked onstage and grasped the pole. The one place where she had always felt she belonged.

The words came out of her like an incantation. "I want to dance."

His brows shot up.

"To finish my degree," she clarified crossly. "I want to perform with musicians and artists." For a real audience, not a bunch of men looking to scratch their own itch.

She'd lost so much time on that aspiration. It broke her heart to consider where she might be if she hadn't let Todd derail her. Dancing at Martini's had been as much about regaining the condition of her body and rejuvenating her skills as filling the coffers because, deep down, she secretly dreamed of returning to dance. Somehow. Even though it seemed impossible.

Axel picked up his phone. "I'll put Heskel onto researching academies."

"No. It's..." Against her best judgment, her heart lifted with anticipation. Hope.

She hadn't allowed herself to feel that emotion in so long, it brought a sting of tears into her eyes. If she had a chance to train again, she should take it. Shouldn't she? Before age and all the other vagaries of life made it even less likely that she could?

"What about the wedding itself?" he asked as though she'd agreed. "I'd prefer simple, but if you have your heart set on something bigger—"

"For a fake marriage? No," she scoffed.

But there was one girlish dream she had all but abandoned. One that she saw could still come true *if* she acted soon. Oh, he was cruel to offer this to her when it meant everything to her and their marriage would mean nothing.

Still.

"I want..." She had to swallow the thickness from her

throat. "I want my father walk me down the aisle. My real one. Paul."

"Of course. Let me relay that to Heskel." He tapped his phone.

She was still reeling from how easy he made all of this sound when his phone pinged.

He read the reply. "Heskel says we can marry twenty-four hours after we purchase the license. We'll do that first thing tomorrow morning, so we can marry Thursday. We'll fly overnight and meet Otto on Friday morning."

"Wait. What?" Her heart nearly came out her mouth. "I haven't even told my father that Otto reached out." She rose, truly needing to run away from all of this. It wasn't real. It couldn't be.

"Would you like me to speak to him with you?"

The way he was capable of railroading a person? Her poor father wouldn't know what had hit him.

"No." She hurried across to pick up her jacket and pushed her arms into it. "This will hurt his feelings. His condition has taken a downturn lately, and he's not rich like Otto. I don't want him to feel like he failed me or anything." She needed a couple of tries to close the zipper on her jacket. "I don't care about the money." She lifted her face and looked him in the eye as she said it, so he would know it was the absolute truth. "I want to meet my birth father to satisfy my curiosity about where I came from. I don't have to marry you to do that."

It was a reminder to him and herself that she still held agency in this situation.

"True," Axel agreed, picking up her hat and all the documents from the table, bringing everything to her, including the credit card. "Read the contract, though. Otto expects you to marry me if you want to inherit from him. If you go to him without me, I will refuse."

She felt struck by that bluntness. There was such a lethal finality in his voice, it emptied her chest while opening two paths before her. She had the same feeling she'd had when she had dropped out of school. She had known she would regret it. She had known she wouldn't be able to go back to that moment and take the path she *really* wanted.

Which path did she really want today?

"If Otto sees that you're no use to him, he'll discard you. You'll be back in the cabaret within the week," Axel warned in that dispassionate tone.

"I'm not afraid of that," she claimed, even though she wished every day that she didn't have to be there.

"Then don't be afraid to accept a bigger payout for an easier gig," he said tersely.

Her backbone lost some of its steel. She took her hat and set it on her head, then accepted the papers from him.

"Joy." He gave her hat a slight adjustment, centering it, then smoothed her hair back from her temples.

He was barely touching her, but it sent tickling frissons of sensation through her shoulder blades. The pleasure was at odds with the apprehension she felt when she studied the hard angles of his expression.

"I want your allegiance." His gaze locked with hers. "I will only know I have it if I've purchased it before you meet him. You don't know yet how badly you need my protection from him, but you do. So give me your promise now. If the test proves you're his daughter, you'll marry me before you speak to him."

"We met two hours ago," she protested. "You want to marry me in *two* days." Her voice cracked.

His expression didn't change.

She searched his eyes, wishing she knew whether she could trust him. She wouldn't know until she did, though.

Which was how she had learned that she couldn't trust Todd.

She *wanted* to believe in Axel, though. That was a very alarming realization when she had pretty much sworn off trusting any man after Todd.

What Axel was proposing could break apart what was left of her life. Or he might help her rebuild it so it was strong and unshakable. He was making her a very alluring offer when she didn't know how she would manage another few months, let alone years of carrying so much financial baggage and a parent who was growing more dependent on her.

Maybe she wanted her troubles to be washed away with money and maybe she wanted to dance again. But she knew, deep down, that she wanted something else, too.

She was fighting against acknowledging it but had to face it when he touched her chin, urging her to lift her gaze. A hot streak of sensuality ran down her throat.

He was attractive and intriguing and powerful and inscrutable.

She tried to swallow but couldn't. She wanted to close her eyes and hide. But couldn't. She wanted him to kiss her with those wickedly beautiful lips.

"Do I have your word?" he asked gravely.

Her heart was beating so hard and fast, she nodded as an escape tactic, so he would release her.

"I'm probably not her anyway," she repeated in a thin voice.

"We'll know soon."

He took her home. They didn't speak beyond, "Good night," and, "You have my number."

Her father was already asleep. She sneaked into her bed and read through everything Axel had given her, then tossed and turned until her phone pinged at three in the morning.

It was an email from Umberto with the test results.

Probability of paternity: 99.9999%

She stared at it for a long time before she sent it to Axel.

Even though it was the middle of the night, he texted back immediately.

I'll be there at nine to buy our license.

CHAPTER SIX

Axel refused to check his watch.

Aside from how it would affect his battle with Otto, being left at the altar was not something that would bother him too much. The only guest was his bride's father, who wasn't here yet because he was coming with Joy. The ceremony was being held in a quiet, hundred-year-old mansion on the lakeshore. An equally small brunch would be wasted, but most of what Axel had spent on bribing Joy to agree to this marriage could be stopped or recouped.

Axel had never aspired to marry anyway, not until Otto had made it a vehicle to getting something he wanted. Agreeing to marry Mira had been an easy choice. A safe one. Until the last time he'd seen her, Mira had always been even-keeled and cooperative. Axel had liked that about her. She had never riled more emotion out of him than sympathy or a snort of amusement at one of her facetious comments.

Marrying Joy would not be that inert.

Which bothered him. He had been shoved around by life enough that he no longer allowed it. Coming here to marry Otto's "real" daughter was him grabbing the wheel on his future, refusing to be driven by anyone's will but his own.

Yet here he was, tying himself to a woman who was

already igniting more reaction in him than he'd allowed himself to feel in years.

It was sexual, of course. He couldn't get the vision of her undulating, nearly naked body out of his head. He had had to take himself in hand more than once over the last day and a half just to be able to think.

But she was scrappy, too, not giving ground easily. It was annoying to come up against. He'd risen to a level where few people pushed back on him, but he couldn't help but respect her for it. She would need that feistiness, given what he was asking of her.

He was asking a lot, he had realized, once he met her father and saw how severely Paul was impacted by his condition.

"I told him we've been dating a while," Joy had confided yesterday when he had arrived to take her to the courthouse for their license. "I said I hadn't mentioned you because I wasn't sure how serious we were, but that you asked me to come live with you in Europe. I said I would only go with you if you married me first, so you proposed. I didn't mention Otto." She grimaced at the lies and omissions. "I didn't want to fully stop his heart."

They had detoured through a jewelry shop on their way back to the house. Joy had looked at modest solitaires, but Axel had picked out a three-stone engagement ring with channel-set baguettes down the shank. The band was a matching design.

Then he played the part of a doting bridegroom when she introduced him to Paul. That had given him the excuse to hold her hand and touch her waist, and he'd found it entirely too gratifying to see goose bumps rise on her arm when he did.

Her reaction made it easy to convince her father that

they were smitten and *had* to be together, but Axel didn't like how much he felt it within himself. Each minute he spent with her planted another seed of want in him. Another fantasy of having her in his bed every night.

After a childhood of wanting things he couldn't have, he'd hardened himself against needing much. He liked his creature comforts—who didn't?—and he was willing to work hard to afford them, but aside from food, water and shelter, he didn't *need* anything.

He didn't need this marriage, he insisted to himself. Especially to a woman who provoked such prickly discord in him. Such want. He'd be better off if she didn't show up.

In a failure of willpower, he dragged his brooding gaze off the black marble of the fireplace and looked over his shoulder.

Heskel hurried up to him from his position by the door. He lowered his voice as though there was an audience of guests when there was only the pianist and the officiant, both of whom had given up trying to make small talk with Axel and were speaking to each other in hushed tones on the other side of the room.

"I just had a text from the driver," Heskel said. "There was a delay leaving the house. Her brother called. Explanations had to be made. They'll be here shortly."

Axel nodded, and Heskel went back to his position.

Axel ignored the pound of his relieved pulse in his ears. He told himself he was only pleased he would get what he'd been striving for most of his life: true self-reliance.

Too much of his life had been lived in circumstances he couldn't control, answering to people with more power than he had.

Why do you work for someone like that?

Axel's sarcastic reply about working his own pole had

been all too true. He had grasped what was available in order to pull himself up.

His parents had been children themselves, ill-equipped to raise him. There'd been drugs and arguing and petty crimes even before his father had been killed in a bar fight. Axel had had no say when he was taken away and given back to his mother. The foster system might have ensured he had clean clothes and vouchers for food, but he'd been disparaged for being a drain on the system. For being poor.

At twelve, desperate for money that didn't involve following his parents into unsavory means, he'd lied about his age and got his first job pushing a broom at a building site. His coworkers, grown men, had laughed at him, calling him a weed and a bookworm because he never laughed and scribbled through his homework while eating a jelly sandwich in two bites like a feral dog.

But he'd been able to keep his landlord from evicting them from the squalid room they occupied and that had been something.

Learn a trade, a bricklayer had advised him when he was fourteen and showing competence at anything he was taught. He'd been strong in math and already understood drawings and building principles. He applied to a trade school at sixteen, thinking to become an electrician, but the career counselor at school had encouraged him to aim higher.

So he'd studied engineering. Between his university classes and his night watchman job, he interned at Vorstoben, specializing in industrial projects. They hired him full-time the day he graduated with honors.

Axel hadn't rested on his laurels. He continued his education, taking a master's degree in business management, drawing the attention of his superiors. Eventually, the big man himself had noticed him.

Otto's mentorship had meant something to him. No one else had backed him in the same way. He had been loyal to Otto. That was what made Otto's bait-and-switch betrayal so galling.

That was what made Axel so determined to get what he had been promised.

Voices murmured at the entryway. Heskel nodded at the pianist to take her seat and for the officiant to stand before Axel, then he opened the pair of doors wide.

Gentle notes began to fill the room.

Axel's bride entered, and all his ire and grim memories evaporated.

Nothing about her appearance was extravagant. Her makeup was far more understated than the night he'd met her. Her gown was a creamy satin that draped in a slim column down her graceful form. Her sleeves fell in folds off her shoulders, leaving her upper chest bare but for a silver locket that looked like an heirloom. Her hair fell in big curls held back from her face with a band of white flowers. Her bouquet was only three peach-colored roses with a sprig of greenery.

She was undeniably beautiful, but her true beauty was in the way she looked at her father. The expression on her face wrapped a fist around Axel's lungs and squeezed. *That's love*, he thought as she walked slowly, very slowly, alongside her father's struggling, lopsided gait. Axel had never seen such a blatant display of that particular emotion. He wouldn't have known how to recognize it, if he hadn't had the context of knowing how much that man meant to her.

Guilt pinched his conscience. He had extorted her cooperation by leaning heavily on her love for her father, thinking nothing of taking her away from the warm fold of her family and dropping her into a war zone.

Otto would never look at her the way Paul did, with pride and tender affection.

Joy glanced at Axel, sending another punch into his chest because her expression shone with poignant gratitude. *I want my father to walk me down the aisle.*

Of all the things he'd bribed her with, this was the one that meant the most to her? A strange lump formed in his throat, one he reflexively cleared, pushing away sentiment.

This marriage was a means to an end for both of them. That was all.

Joy and Paul arrived before him. She stooped so her father could kiss her cheek, then watched him shuffle to his seat before she faced Axel again.

Now there was somberness in her pouted mouth and trepidation in her eyes. The petals on her bouquet trembled.

All Axel could think was that he wanted to touch her. Seize her.

A prickle of alarm went through him. He never allowed himself to feel anything deeply, but this was intense and carnal and sharp. Chaotic. He wanted to claim her as badly—maybe more—than the things their marriage would gain him.

Which should have been a red flag.

It was.

But he ignored it.

"You look beautiful," he told her, then ordered the officiant, "Begin."

"Thank you for being here today," the officiant began.

Run, the adrenaline in Joy's veins kept urging.

Call it off, her brother had insisted, not buying for a second that she'd been having a secret affair with a foreign tycoon. *What the hell is really going on?*

She didn't know. It had all happened so fast. The twenty-four hours she might have used for second thoughts had been eaten up by lawyer visits and interviewing nursing staff and shopping for a dress.

"I have the chance to meet my birth father," she had admitted in a whisper to David behind the locked door of her bedroom.

"You don't have to marry a stranger to do that."

I want to. She hadn't said it, but there was a trapped bird inside her that kept batting its wings against her rib cage, panicked and urgent and, for some reason, trying to fly straight to Axel.

Which didn't make sense. She knew it didn't. Especially when she stood before him and the ceremony started and each word inched her further and further toward the end of the proverbial plank. Soon she would be over the edge, plummeting into a bottomless ocean that was miles over her head.

Axel's voice dropped deep into his chest as he made his vows to honor and respect her, to build a marriage that would grow stronger and more caring as time passed, blanketing her in a belief that he meant it.

Her chest filled with currents and eddies as she repeated the words to him, feeling dizzy. The vows felt real, the ring weighty as he slid it onto her finger. His gaze flashed with satisfaction as he did it, and her knees grew weak.

This was a business deal. He was doing this to get a company, she reminded herself, blinking against silly, emotive tears. If she felt an urge to cry, it was only because she hadn't slept.

"You may seal your bond with a kiss."

He drew her into his arms, and she stiffened, trying not to give in to whatever this force was that had taken possession of her deepest self. She lifted her mouth, expecting a brush of his lips in a chaste observance of tradition.

But as the strength in his arms and the warmth of his thighs penetrated her gown, this unnamed, shimmering grip he had on her coiled tighter around her. It changed her, molding her to a shape that fit against him like a matching puzzle piece. There was an audible click in her ears that assured her she was exactly where she was meant to be.

Then he fit his mouth to hers as though he'd been kissing her for weeks, months, centuries. His aftershave filled her nostrils, and the lights went out as she closed her eyes. His hand brushed her naked shoulder, and she parted her lips under the pressure of his.

His taste filled her senses.

It was nothing like any kiss she'd ever experienced. Time stopped. There was only heat and wildfire. Devastation as he tore down her defenses and slowly rebuilt her, altering her so she was utterly his. So she wanted to be his.

As surrender shuddered through her, the officiant said something. Her father chuckled.

Oh no.

Axel's breath hissed in. He reluctantly lifted his head.

Joy resisted losing the taste of him, clinging to his lips with her own, then didn't know where to look so she stared at his tie. She must be glowing red as a traffic light at having put on such a display. At having revealed how reluctant she was to stop.

Axel's gruff voice abraded her ears. "Let's finalize this. We have a plane to catch."

* * *

Joy had never been so aroused from lengthy lovemaking, never mind a single kiss. She was utterly destroyed, but despite Axel's relentless push for the marriage, he seemed content to take his time over brunch with her father, his assistant and the two strangers who had performed their nuptials. In fact, he put up with a number of probing questions from her father before they left for the airport.

Thanks to Paul's quavering inquisition, Joy now knew her husband was an only child. His father had passed when he was young, he enjoyed skiing in winter when he had time, he traveled for work, not pleasure and had no pets. He missed the challenge of being directly involved in the design process with complex projects but took great satisfaction in overseeing multiple international projects and making top-level decisions.

He had politely asked about her father's lifetime working in mortgage and loans, then reassured him that he would bring Joy back for the big move to California. The unit Paul had chosen would be ready by the time Carrie's baby was due. In the meantime, a private nurse had been hired along with a daily housekeeper. An assistant would also help Paul downsize and pack.

Joy's marriage erased her father's financial worries and ensured his day-to-day life would be much more comfortable. Leaving him was still hard. And even though her stress over providing for him was lifted, Joy was more anxious than ever.

Marry in haste, repent at leisure, her lawyer, LaShonda, had said with a glower of warning. Joy had picked LaShonda from the three she'd interviewed because LaShonda had been the only one to ask if she was out of her damn fool mind. Then she had proceeded to wield her red pen like a rapier on the prenuptial contract, building in enough protections to raise Axel's eyebrows.

"If she wasn't working for you, I'd hire her myself," he'd drawled, then signed off on all the changes.

Before they left for their flight, they changed into travel clothes. Axel now wore dark green trousers with a black sweater that hugged the musculature of his shoulders and chest. He pushed his sleeves up to expose his forearms.

Why that detail seemed so important, Joy wasn't sure, but she found herself staring at his strong, flat wrists and the light hairs decorating the fading tan on his skin. She kept thinking of their kiss. Kept thinking, *I'm his now.*

That knowledge sank deeper and deeper into her psyche, swirling in her belly as they climbed aboard a private jet. This was her very last chance to reverse this mad decision she'd made, but within minutes, her opportunity to escape had folded and disappeared with the landing gear.

They were in a luxurious cabin with deep swivel chairs facing a dining table while Heskel retreated to a smaller cabin in the back.

"Do the pods back there recline into beds?" Joy asked curiously, stifling a yawn.

Axel glanced up from reading something on his tablet. "Are you tired?"

It was only the middle of the afternoon, but she admitted, "I was too nervous to sleep last night." Or the night before. "Do you think they'd mind if I used one?"

"You're not sleeping in the staff cabin," he said disdainfully. "We have a stateroom." He rose and moved to open a door she had thought led to a bathroom.

She followed out of curiosity.

Like the rest of the jet, the stateroom was furnished in

a style of minimalist luxury. The bed was huge, made up with a snowy white duvet and overstuffed pillows. Big windows revealed an indigo sky over a layer of pink clouds as they headed into dusk. At the foot of the bed was a flat-screen television recessed into a bulkhead of cupboards and drawers.

Axel acted as though a private jet was a perfectly normal way to travel, but all of this was completely surreal. Especially the part where she was married to him.

What if he's dangerous? David had asked in predictable big-brother protectiveness. Joy had tried to play it off that this was a normal thing to do, that this was merely a business deal.

Nothing about their kiss had felt normal or businesslike, though. Kisses were acts of affection. Sometimes they warmed her up for a more intimate encounter, but they never sent bolts of lightning crackling through her nerve endings, igniting a desire in the pit of her belly that lingered for hours afterward.

"Do you want something to sleep in? Or dare I hope you sleep naked?" Axel leaned his shoulder against the bulkhead. He let his gaze stray unabashedly and possessively down the formfitting yoga pants and loose pullover she wore.

"I—" her heart lurched "—don't think I'm ready for that."

His gaze rose to hers, full of lazy amusement. "Sleeping naked?"

"With you," she confirmed in a quavering voice. It felt like a lie. She definitely didn't feel tired anymore.

"The bed is big enough we won't bump into each other unless we want to." His tone altered, becoming more businesslike. He straightened off the wall. "I expect Otto to attack the validity of our marriage. He may even report us to immigration. If he doesn't recognize our union, he won't have to honor the contract. For that reason, we'll share a bedroom."

"And I should lie back and think of Vorstoben?" she asked with acerbic irony.

"I do enjoy that bite of yours." He ambled toward her. "You're going to need it."

Her stomach flip-flopped with nerves as he neared, but she stood her ground and bared her teeth, clacking them in a threatening snap.

"Not with me," he chided. "You're tired. I respect that. I won't touch you until you say you want me to. But do you? Want me to touch you?"

He was so close, she had to tip her head back. Her neck felt weak as a broken flower stem, helpless to the crushing weight of his sex appeal. She felt the trace of his gaze against her lips as though it was his fingertip. His tongue.

She licked away the tickling sensation and saw the flash in his gaze.

"You have to say yes, Meine Schönste." His maddening voice seduced her. "Say you want me to kiss you again. Küss mich bitte," he prompted in a voice that was wickedly compelling. Mesmerizing.

"Küss mich bitte," she repeated, trying the words, but also because she did want him to kiss her again.

It's only a kiss, she thought before he cupped the side of her face and sealed his mouth over hers.

Immediately, they were back to that wedding kiss, but this time there was no one to stop them. This time, he rocked his mouth to part her lips and his tongue invaded her mouth. It should have been too blatant too soon, but she hadn't stopped thinking about this. Wanting it. She brushed her tongue against his and delicately sucked.

A feral noise resounded in his throat, one that pleased her into almost smiling. Then his hand bracketed her waist, ran to caress her hip, then back to her rib cage and across her lower back.

Swirls of pleasure unraveled like yarn in her abdomen. His touch felt so good.

She moaned into his mouth and slid her arms up to his shoulders, angling her head in offering, twisting her body to invite the delicious stroke of his hands. *Touch me*, she telegraphed as he set her ablaze.

His mouth ravaged hers while his hands claimed the rest of her—spine and shoulders and the cheeks of her ass. His palms slid to draw drugging circles on her backside, then clenched her buttocks, making her lift onto her toes in erotic delight.

"Say mehr bitte," he commanded in a rasp against her ear before his busy mouth moved to her neck. "More," he translated. "Ask me for more."

She couldn't think, could only tremble while his lips sent shivers into her throat and delightful tingles into her breasts. Her nipples stung, and her arms clung, and she was arching to feel the thickness behind his fly against her mound.

"What do you want, Joy?" His head came up. His tongue flicked at the corner of her mouth. Then his wide palm pushed into the notch of her thighs, claiming her swollen mound with such deliberate, possessive pressure, lightning shot through her.

A ragged groan left her.

"You want this?"

No one had ever made her feel so good with so little

effort. She had always had to self-serve if she wanted an orgasm, but she was already so aroused, so delirious with lust, she said, "Yes. More. Bitte."

His kiss drew her back into the velvet darkness, and his hand pressed more firmly. Rocked. Deliberate and unhurried.

She was dimly aware of fisting her hands into his pullover and arching to ensure his touch was exactly in the perfect spot. Exactly the right amount of pressure.

Breaking from his smothering kiss, she gasped urgently, "Don't stop. Please don't stop." She was taut as a bow, supported by the strength of his arm across her back. *This is paradise*, she thought. This was how it was supposed to feel. This was the kind of sex she'd been promised by books and movies and whispers and giggles over wine.

"What do you need?" He kept up the delicious rubbing, but added a tiny bit more pressure. A fraction more friction. Some low, filthy words about how he wanted his tongue *right here*...

His touch pressed the center of her pleasure, and she broke, crying out as contractions struck her middle, collapsing her knees.

He kept his hand there, practically holding her up while she clung and shook and panted. Her pulse had its home in his palm, ringing through her body while she turned her face against his shoulder and saw the door was still open to the lounge.

"Anyone could have seen us," she said in horror, lurching away from him on shaking legs.

"We're newlyweds. No will come looking for us," he said dryly. "But I'll leave you. Sleep well."

She stared with bewilderment at the door he closed behind him.

* * *

A hand on her shoulder woke her.

Joy snapped her eyes open, completely disoriented to find herself in bed, the room lights dim, the white noise of the jet's engines filling her ears.

"I didn't mean to startle you." Axel sat on the edge of the mattress and soothingly stroked his hand down her bare arm. It sent titillating tingles through her bloodstream that were deeply unwelcome when her defenses were still below zero. "We'll be landing soon."

She sat up, then regretted it. It put her too close him. She inched away. "I didn't think I would sleep so hard."

"No?" Was he laughing at her? Jerk. It had actually taken her a long time to fall asleep while she stressed out over marrying a stranger, one who could take her apart without any effort whatsoever, then walk away.

Eventually, she had stripped down to the T-back bra and boy short underwear she'd been wearing beneath her yoga clothes. It was more than she wore onstage, but she felt very naked wearing so little right now. Sensitive. And deeply aware of him on a sexual level.

An image of him flattening her to the mattress sprang into her head. It should have been accompanied by alarm, but the fantasy sent a golden heat spiraling through her, making her breasts feel heavy and their tips tight. An ache hummed to life between her thighs, carnal and wet. Receptive. Her skin called out to him, begging for his touch.

Embarrassed and confused by this potent, relentless attraction, she moved farther toward the middle of the bed. She glanced over to see an indent in the other pillow and a discarded blanket atop the wrinkled covers.

"You slept here?" That made her feel even more vulnerable.

And resistible. Unwanted, even. It was a lesson in how uneven this relationship truly was. She would have to guard herself more carefully against him.

"For a few hours," he replied. His eyelids were heavy, his mouth relaxed. He was watching her in a way that said, *I know what you're feeling*.

Mortification became a hot coal in the pit of her stomach while a guiltier heat throbbed in the notch of her thighs.

"Would you like to join me in the shower?" His voice was so low, she felt it more than heard it. It resounded inside her, making her heart thud.

"No." It should have come out firm and strong, but it was thin and high. Strained but also defiant as she took back a little of the control she'd surrendered earlier.

His fingers twitched into a loose fist where his hand rested on his thigh, then relaxed. He rose abruptly, making her stomach swoop. "Wise. We'd be on the tarmac for hours."

"You really take a lot for granted, don't you?"

He only looked down at her with those flame-blue eyes. "Do I?"

He walked into what she'd already seen was a spacious lavatory, especially by airplane standards. It didn't have a bathtub, but the shower could easily accommodate two.

Don't think of it.

As the door closed behind him, her exhale burst out of her. She dropped her forehead onto her knees, wanting to run, but where? She was on an airplane a mile over the ocean. Or Britain, maybe, since they were getting close to landing.

Close to meeting her father.

She had so many mixed feelings about all of this, but now she had to confront her worries over meeting Otto.

Was he really as callous as Axel had implied? She'd read the contract he'd had Axel sign and practically memorized the letter from her birth mother. It did seem dodgy that Otto had known about her for three years but had only reached out to her a week ago, but maybe Axel was misrepresenting things. She'd only heard his side of it, and he'd blinded her with his generosity toward her and her adoptive father.

She knew Axel's support wasn't coming from the goodness of his heart. He was using her to one-up Otto.

Leading up to the wedding, she had told herself she didn't mind because she was using him, too. She wanted better care for Paul. She wanted her family together in California. She wanted to dance.

And she wanted to meet her birth father.

What if Otto was angry with her, though?

Over the years, she'd talked to other adoptees and had had several in-depth conversations with her sister-in-law, Carrie, who was a family therapist. Joy would have sworn she had long ago made her peace with being relinquished by her birth mother. Wendy and Paul had given her a very stable, privileged, loving upbringing. Yes, there were times Joy had felt like an outsider in their family, but that wasn't because of anything they had done. It was all in her own head.

Then Wendy had died, and Joy had felt so adrift she'd reached out to the agency, seeking a connection with her first mother only to learn that she was gone, too. They had refused to provide more than her name. That loss had hurt in a way Joy hadn't expected.

That was when she had realized that she harbored a deep, hidden sense of rejection along with a heavy weight of obligation toward her adoptive family. They would never want her to feel that way, but it was there all the same.

As for her birth father, he'd remained a mystery. She had considered doing one of those ancestry tests, but learning Lorena was dead had been such a kick in the stomach, she hadn't had the courage to look for her father. She'd also had all that drama with Todd messing with her head, then moved home. She had been struggling to survive ever since.

Now here was Axel claiming he would protect her from Otto.

Maybe, deep down, she had latched onto that promise because she was so fearful of another rejection. Maybe she was still looking for a connection beyond her adoptive family, one that didn't come with tangled emotions of gratitude and indebtedness.

And maybe she had married Axel because she knew she wouldn't see him again otherwise. She had been enthralled with him from her first glimpse of him. She didn't want to be, but she was.

She had also thought this intense attraction was mutual, but he really seemed to be able to turn it on and off at will, which was painfully lowering.

The bathroom door opened. Axel emerged in a towel, bringing a spicy fragrance of aftershave with him, sending a punch of sensuality into her middle.

She was still sitting in the bed and pushed her legs toward the edge of the mattress. "You're quick."

"I can be," he said laconically. "When the occasion demands." He pressed a section of wall to open a closet, revealing a handful of suits.

She stared at his naked back. Had that been a *sex* joke?

She threw off the covers, starting to rise, but he turned

to show her a small gift bag. He ambled toward her with his towel sitting low and loose and precarious across his hips.

"What—" She had to clear her dry throat as she was confronted by his stacked abs and the sprinkle of hair that arrowed down from his navel. She fixed her gaze on the black bag with its gold embossing and satin ribbons for handles. It matched the shop where they'd bought the wedding rings. "What is it?"

"A thank-you," he said. "A sweetener, maybe."

She hesitantly took it and peered into the bag, drawing out the black octagonal velvet box. Not another ring? She pried it open.

"Oh my God." It was a ring. Two pear-shaped stones, an emerald and a yellow sapphire, sat at angles to each other on a coiled platinum band caked with small round diamonds. "Why...?" She looked up, up, up at him.

"I saw it when we were picking the wedding rings." He rolled his smooth shoulder. "It reminded me of the way you wrap yourself around the pole."

A sweetener. Do you want to join me in the shower?

"And how do you expect me to thank you?" she asked with a thrum of disenchantment, offering it back. "Wrap myself around your pole?"

"You already said no to that," he reminded pithily. "So I took care of myself."

The ball of heat that exploded within her was impossible to hide, especially because *he* knew she was picturing him erupting into his own soapy hand.

"I can also be quiet when the occasion demands," he said with a mocking smirk. "But don't feel you need to be. Shower's all yours."

"Oh shut up." As if she would do *that*, knowing he was

out here listening! She dropped the ring and the box onto the rumpled blankets and stood.

He caught her arm before she'd taken a step.

She flung a glare of temper at him, as if she wasn't looking for an excuse to wrestle with him across those tangled covers. As if his burnished skin didn't make her mouth water and she wasn't dying to know how the point of his nipple would feel against her tongue.

"Wear it to our meeting with Otto." He turned into the jaded executive before her eyes, naked chest and slipping towel notwithstanding. "He'll interpret that you've thanked me appropriately and know you're firmly on my side. That you're mine."

His crude, possessive words crashed through her, inciting a flutter of intrigue but toppling her belief that they were anywhere near equal in this sea of sexual attraction that was drowning her.

"I really am just a pawn to you, aren't I?" She shook off his grip and locked herself in the bathroom.

CHAPTER SEVEN

NOT A PAWN. A queen. One with enormous power to run the board. That was why he'd captured her.

Axel hadn't amassed this much wealth and power so he could be treated as a pawn, though. And that was what Otto wanted to do. Axel's solitary focus right now was performing this checkmate on Otto.

Or should be. He was having a hard time thinking beyond the way his wife had shattered under his touch a few hours ago. And how sensual and flustered she'd looked when he'd had to wake her.

He hadn't meant to let their kiss flare out of control, but she had smelled so damned feminine and sweet. Her body was both strong and softly curved. He had felt her shiver and heard her breath catch, and the most primal part of him had taken over.

He had nearly lost himself behind his zipped fly. Everything in him had wanted to pick her up and set her wilted body on the bed. To continue what they had started.

She could unravel him as easily as he had her, he had realized while she'd been trembling and panting in reaction. That was sobering enough to make him walk away if only to prove he could. The last thing he wanted was to be under her sexual spell if Otto managed to turn her against him.

He was reminded he had higher priorities than consummating his marriage when he picked up a panicked message from Vorstoben's CFO a few minutes later. Mira was making good on her threats to pull the properties she'd allowed to be used as collateral. Refinancing was necessary. And urgent.

A second message from Otto demanded Axel come see him the moment he landed, to discuss their plan of action.

Axel's plan was to oust Otto and negotiate with Mira. He would have to hit the ground running if he wanted to keep the financial impact of her anger from cratering the whole organization, but he was confident he could do it.

The stateroom door opened, and Joy came into the main cabin.

Wrestling his libido back into its crate was next to impossible, however, when she looked so delectable. She wore a fitted, cream-colored dress that closed with two gold buttons beneath her left breast. It hugged her curves to her knees and dipped modestly in the front to reveal the beaded lace that decorated the top of her slip. Her muscled calves made his mouth water.

"Do I look okay?" she asked with a self-conscious brush of her hand against her hip. "I bought it when I got my wedding gown." She smoothed her hands down her backside as she sat in the chair across from him.

He'd blamed their prickly banter in the stateroom on sexual frustration and lack of sleep, but it struck him that she was nervous about meeting Otto.

"You look perfect." She wore enough makeup to hide her jet lag and her hair was gathered into one of those braided patterns that mysteriously consumed its own tail. She looked chic and feminine. Aloof, sophisticated.

Yet there was an underlying vulnerability that pierced through his thick armor.

"Don't let his opinion matter to you," he asserted. "I've seen that movie. It ends poorly."

"I can't help how I feel." She defensively crossed her legs and looked to the blur of gray morning clouds they ducked beneath to land.

A protest rose in him, but he couldn't allow softer feelings like pity and protectiveness impact him too deeply. He needed to be completely impervious as he faced down the man who had double-crossed him.

They deplaned for his car and, a short while later, arrived at the Vorstoben building amid the usual morning bustle.

Axel was greeted with respectful nods. Security guards hurried to open gates and press buttons for elevators, glancing curiously at her, but Heskel had already registered their approved guest. No one asked her to identify herself.

The way Joy twisted her new ring while they rode the elevator had Axel capturing her cold fingers in his, refusing to allow any show of weakness. Her nails cut against his skin as they moved through the top floor of white and chrome decor, spiking the aggression simmering within him.

Outside Otto's office, they were greeted by a pair of assistants who scrambled to open the doors for him and Joy to walk through.

Otto was at his wide desk, the city showcased through the floor-to-ceiling windows behind him. It was a deliberate arrangement. Otto liked to be backlit and make people squint.

His features were sagging with age, but his golden-brown gaze sharpened as he sat back. He didn't smile, only stared at Joy in a way that picked her apart.

"Joy, Otto Braun." Axel heard her swallow. "Joy Youngston," he provided to Otto. "Your daughter."

"Enja." Otto rose to come around to the front of his desk. "Umberto said you'd done the test." He gave her a calculated study. "You look like your mother."

"Axel showed me a photo of her." Joy's expression flickered with a hesitant, unsteady smile. "I have so many questions about her. And you. It's nice to meet you." She tried to take her hand from Axel's so she could move forward and offer it to Otto.

Axel didn't allow it. He kept her by his side in the middle of the room.

Otto's attention swept down to their locked hands, then snapped up to meet Axel's gaze. Questioning. Narrowing with suspicion.

Axel smiled with raw satisfaction. Grim triumph.

"You insisted I marry her." He lifted her hand and turned it, flashing the ring he'd given her on the plane before twisting the other way to reveal the plain band on his own finger.

"You were supposed to come to me first," Otto snarled at Joy.

Axel felt the jolt of shock travel through her. Her features contorted with injury.

"Don't take this out on her." Axel stepped forward, reflexively angling to shield her while drawing their linked hands behind his back so his bulk was between them. "This is the deal you struck." Axel had no compromise in him. "I've held up my side. Now honor yours."

"Like hell." Otto shifted so he had a line of sight on Joy. "He's taking advantage of you. He married you because he thinks he can get my money. My company. I was saving it for you."

This was why Axel had wanted her vow to him before she met Otto. The old man was already trying to manipulate the situation to favor himself. That infuriated Axel, but it didn't surprise him.

"She's seen the contract," he told Otto. "She knows exactly what you expected from your biological daughter."

"I wouldn't have forced you to marry him. Is that what he told you? That you had to marry him? If he bullied you, this can be annulled," Otto said.

Over my dead body, was Axel's very primitive and disturbing thought.

"Come. Let's talk." Otto waved at the sofa, cannily trying to read Joy, trying to find the inroad to turn her against Axel.

She looked to the sofa, confused. Tempted. "Why did you want to meet me?" Whatever optimism had been in her face had faded into a frown of anxious wariness.

"You're my daughter. Why wouldn't I want to meet you?"

"But why did you set up that contract before you had?" she asked. Her nails were cutting into Axel's hand again.

"That was business," Otto dismissed with a patronizing wave that said, *Don't trouble your pretty little head.*

"He's known about you for three years," Axel reminded her with brutal honesty. "He didn't reach out until I threatened to leave. He wants to use you to keep me in line. She's no longer available for that." Axel turned spitefully toward Otto. "She's already my wife."

Otto muttered a word in German that was very foul.

Joy didn't need a translator to know what he had called her. Her breath cut in as though he'd struck her.

"Watch your mouth," Axel warned in a lethal tone.

She looked to Axel with eyes full of disillusionment. Blame. *How could you bring me here for this?* Tears gathered in her eyes, and she flexed her fingers, trying to extricate them.

He held on, unable to regret bringing her here even though she might never forgive him for it. "You're already bleeding cash reserves," he reminded Otto. "Step away from the company, and Mira will have no reason to continue her attacks on it."

"It's my company," Otto insisted with a rabid shake of his jowls. "I decide what happens here."

"You signed a contract. Honor it."

"You questioned the validity of that contract yourself," Otto threw at him. "We'll see what the courts say."

"Lawyers it is, then," Axel said darkly. "But make no mistake. I will get this company if I have to join forces with Mira and take it, brick by brick."

Joy didn't pay attention to where Axel took her.

She was aware of feeling cold until the weight of his suit jacket was draped over her shoulders. She heard him say something in biting words she couldn't understand. Her vision was blurred, and there was a scorch in her throat that stretched into her chest, making even her shoulders ache with the effort to hold back her tears.

In those first seconds of meeting Otto, her hopes had been sky-high. Surely Axel was wrong about him. Surely her birth father—who had asked her to come meet him—would be glad to see her. Surely, he was eager to know everything about her, the way she wanted to know everything about him.

Seeing him had given her a disconcerting sense of recognition, one that disarmed her because she thought she ought to feel a sense of belonging from that vague familiarity.

But as she had looked for an answering interest in his expression, her soft, jumbled emotions had collided with instinctual dislike.

It wasn't Axel's warnings poisoning her opinion. Otto had radiated coldness. He had kept a distance between them and made her bristle with the way he looked at her. His gaze hadn't had the lecherous quality of the men at the club, but it had been a cousin to it. He had called her by her birth name and mentally calculated her intrinsic worth based on her off-the-rack dress and how likely he was to get what he wanted from her. He'd regarded her as an object, not a person. She'd felt it.

Despite all the things she'd told herself for years, all the *just curious* justifications she'd made in the last forty-eight hours, she had come here yearning for a sense of homecoming. She had wanted him to open his arms to her. She had wanted to feel wanted. She had wanted to be missed.

Instead, she'd been disdained. Scorned. She was suffering a depth of disappointment that threatened to drown her. She was in such pain, she didn't want Axel to touch her, but she needed his help drawing her out of the car. The strength of his arm across her back was necessary as he guided her stiff, frozen body into a new building.

He brought her into a silent apartment. She had the sense of being on the top floor because the ceilings were high above exposed rafters. Angled windows poured light onto the combined kitchen, dining and living area. There was a terrace, but she only stood at the closed double doors that gave access to it, staring blindly at concrete tiles and empty flower boxes.

"You're upset," he said grimly. "You have a right to be. His behavior was appalling."

"His?" she choked and swung around to confront him.

"He was always going to be exactly as you met him today," he asserted as he yanked off his satin tie. It was such a dark blue, it was almost black. "You would have come here whether we married or not. Wouldn't you? You wanted to meet him."

She clenched her teeth, refusing to admit that because it sat too close to the hidden longings inside herself. No, she had never expected anyone to show up and save her, but she had wanted them to want to. She had wanted someone to say, *I would have kept you if I could.*

She had wanted Otto to say, *If I had known about you, I would have found you sooner.* She had wanted him to say there was a good reason—a really good one—that he had waited to reach out to her.

Otto had let her down so crushingly, she felt sick with it. She wanted that not to matter, but it did.

"He would have tried to use you, one way or another," Axel continued brutally. "Against me, against Mira. Whatever served him." He opened his collar button with an impatient twist, then his cuffs so he could roll them back. "He would have tried to use your family troubles to keep you in line. By marrying me, you took control and made that impossible. He can't hurt you now."

"He already has," she blurted, voice catching raggedly. "I want to go home." She wrenched at the rings he'd give her, struggling because her fingers had swollen overnight. "I'll find a way to pay you back f-for everything—"

"Joy, stop it." His hands tried to capture hers, and she knocked him away. "You're angry with him so you're trying to run away from me," he said sternly. "Stay and fight."

"I don't want to fight," she cried. "I was happy as I was."

"Like hell you were," he snapped back. "You were already in a fight, and you were losing."

"So what?" She stepped in close to confront him. "I didn't ask you to fix it for me! I sure as hell didn't ask you to bring me to *this*." She was starting to break apart, emotions rising to burn hot against the backs of her eyes, elevating the pitch in her voice. "I just wanted my father to be okay. And you took advantage of that." She poked him in the chest. "You knew how desperate I was, and you used it."

"Yes," he agreed flatly. "But I'm on your side."

"You're on *your* side." She clenched her eyes tight. Tears solved nothing, and it felt so weak to weep, especially when she had done this to herself. She had agreed to come here. She had married him, deluding herself into thinking this would work in her favor.

"We're on the same side," Axel insisted.

"How? I can't trust you. How could I?" She snapped her eyes open.

"I told you exactly what was going to happen." His unflinching stare hammered that home to her. "I didn't lie about any of it."

That was why this was worse than what had happened with Todd. Axel might not have lied the way Todd had, but she had still fooled herself into believing things would be different. She was devastated by her own gullibility. She was hurting and exhausted, far from home and very alone. That was what she was facing as she stared at him. She was starkly alone. She always would be. It was terrifying.

"Can I trust you?" The bite in his voice sent a chill across her skin, raising the hairs on the back of her neck. "Because you promised me a year."

She'd seen how he reacted to people who broke their promises. And backing out now would mean more than dissolving this marriage. She would have to find a way to cover her father's bills again. Beg the neighbor to help with his care. It was so daunting, hot tears rose afresh behind her eyes.

Axel had her cornered, and he knew it.

A phone rang, startling her so badly she jumped.

"It's the doorman telling me my lawyer is here." He moved to a cordless phone on an end table and spoke briefly before clicking it off and setting it aside. "What's it going to be, Joy? I need to know whether you're staying so I know how to direct him."

He sounded completely removed from the outcome. He didn't care whether she stayed, not beyond how it affected his plans, only that she be clear in which way she would jump.

"I don't have a choice, do I?" she said in a garbled voice. Then, because she needed to collect herself and wash off her makeup before she cried it down her cheeks, she asked, "Where are my things? I want to change."

"Upstairs," he said remotely.

The elevator dinged a warning that it was about to open, so she hurried to trot up them.

CHAPTER EIGHT

JOY HAD NEVER felt more powerless in her life. Axel had taken more than her body into his hands in the last twenty-four hours. Her finances and her family's welfare were also in his control. Most painful of all, she'd let him make one of her most deeply hidden dreams come true, and it had turned into a nightmare.

Not that it was his fault that Otto was utterly disinterested in her. She hadn't seen anything more than calculation in the older man's gaze even before he'd known she and Axel were married. No curiosity or sentimentality. Her initial thought had been, *This is why she didn't put his name on my birth certificate.*

In fact, Joy had to wonder if her birth mother had been protecting herself by not telling Otto about her pregnancy. Lorena would have been tied to Otto forever if she had kept Joy and told him about her.

Axel was also correct in saying that if he hadn't interfered, she would have come here to meet Otto. And, yes, she would have wound up exactly this disappointed.

By marrying me, you took control...

It didn't feel that way at all! She felt overwhelmed and raw and homesick, but it was too early to even call her father to let him know she'd arrived safely. There was nothing he could do to help her, anyway. She texted that she had landed safely and sent another to her brother. David was in Guam, but he typically only replied when he was off duty. It wasn't unusual for days to pass before she heard back from him.

At this rate, David was only going to say *I told you so*, and she deserved it.

This was the deal she had struck, however. Had she really thought there would be no cost to her?

She snorted at herself, realizing she had to shake off whatever expectations she'd had and deal with what was. She had to accept that she had landed herself into this situation and figure out how to take charge from here.

She started by pulling herself together physically. She changed into her favorite jeans and a snug striped top, then brushed out her hair and washed her face, reapplying just enough makeup to hide the distress around her eyes.

Then, because she hadn't had more than a cup of coffee since leaving Chicago, she made her way downstairs, planning to raid the refrigerator.

Heskel was here, setting the table for two. "Frau Severin," he greeted with a polite smile. "Are you hungry?"

"Starving," she admitted, then glanced around warily, bracing herself for the aggressive energy that her husband gave off with a single look.

Can I trust you? You promised me a year.

She had, and it was really landing on her what a daunting promise that was.

"Where's Axel?" she asked.

"In with Gerard." He nodded at a closed door. "He said you should eat while it's hot. He'll join you as soon as he can."

He removed a covered dish from an insulated bag and

set out a plate for her. The crepes were still steaming and had a bluish-purple compote drizzled across them.

Her stomach panged, and her mouth began to water.

"Please," Heskel invited, holding her chair. "Would you like coffee? Juice? A mimosa?" He set out a basket of pastries and a pretty parfait of yogurt, berries and muesli.

"I'd love a coffee, thank you."

While she was trying to eat with more grace than a lion pouncing on a kill, Heskel set a cappuccino above her plate. A swimming swan was drawn into its foam.

"That's beautiful." She was charmed. "Were you a barista in a past life?"

"I was." He glanced over the table with a critical eye. "What else can I do for you? Unpack?" He glanced to the loft.

"You could call me Joy," she suggested. "And keep me company." She was feeling very friendless at the moment, trying to imagine how she could make this work.

"When we're not in public, of course. Joy," he conceded with an amiable nod. "I have the same arrangement with Axel."

"Have you worked for him long?"

He hesitated, then said, "Four years."

"Was that too personal? I didn't mean to be."

"No," he said on a slight laugh. "It was a trick question. Until an hour ago, I was employed by Vorstoben, but also as his assistant, so my answer stands."

"Did they fire you because of this?" She used the tip of her knife to motion between herself and the closed door, appalled to have any part in his losing his job. "I'm so sorry."

"Don't be." He waved off her concern. "They offered me a raise to stay and assist Herr Braun in Axel's absence. I'm privy to the status of all the ongoing projects and have a good rapport with contacts inside and outside the company. I prefer to work for Axel, so I declined."

"Oh." She considered that level of loyalty as she chewed a bite of cheese-stuffed crepe. "I'm not asking what they offered you, but I'm curious how much a good salary for an EA at a company like Vorstoben is?"

"In US dollars?" He looked upward as he performed mental math. "They offered me around one hundred fifty?"

"Thousand?" She dropped her fork so it clattered against her plate, nearly choking on her bite of food. She forced herself to swallow, then gasped, "And you turned that down?"

He brought her a glass of water, biting back a grin of amusement.

"Axel and I have a standing agreement that he will better any offer I receive, including and especially from Vorstoben. It was in my best interest to hear them out, so I did. When they'd gone as high as they were likely to go, I texted him the amount. He asked me to pick up breakfast on my way over."

"Oh my God. I mean, good for you, but oh my God." She cleared her throat with another sip of water, boggled. All of the money Axel had thrown at her and her family now seemed like pocket change. Apparently, it was. For him.

She was starting to think she'd sold her own loyalty at far too low a rate.

"The truth is, I'd work for him for a tenth of that," Heskel confided. "He helped my husband and me out of a very tight spot a few years ago."

"You're married? You seem young for that."

"So do you," he said with an ironic tilt of his mouth. "Klaus and I weren't married yet, but we were living together when he was in a terrible car crash."

"How awful. He survived, though?"

"Yes. And he's mostly recovered, but he still has some pain if he sits or stands too long. That's prevented him from taking full-time work again. He's an industrial engineer. Axel had just recruited him to Vorstoben when it happened. It was a good job, so we thought it was the right time to buy a home together. Nothing extravagant, but when he couldn't work, things became difficult."

"Don't you have social programs here?"

"We do. And they gave him a package that covered lost wages, but it was a reduced rate. Even so, I was only working part-time around finishing my degree. I had to quit both to care for Klaus. We were looking at having to sell our new home and move to something smaller. It was a lot to deal with, but Axel heard what had happened and checked in with me. He wound up covering the shortfall on our mortgage." Heskel shook his head and looked away, dampness in his eyes. "I asked him how I could repay him. He said to work for him when I was ready. I'm resourceful and have good communication skills, but my background is marketing in the food industry." He shrugged, seeming perplexed. "He said he wanted someone he could trust. He can. With your marriage, I extend my loyalty to you." He turned a magnanimous palm toward her.

"Unless my needs conflict with his," she surmised with a tense smile.

"How do you foresee that happening?" He canted his head in curiosity.

"Well, you haven't given me back my passport. I take that to mean you won't help me leave if I decide I want to go home."

"I always hold the travel documents when I fly with him." He moved to a leather messenger bag and brought her passport to her. "I'm sorry if you felt I was restricting you. That's not the case at all." He set the passport on the table.

She checked that it was hers, feeling churlish when she saw that it was.

"If you ask me to book your flight or make arrangements for you," Heskel continued, "I will feel compelled to tell him what I'm doing. But you have your phone and credit cards. You can do that yourself if you want to. He expects confidentiality from me, not blind obedience or illegal confinement."

"I sound paranoid, don't I? My ex gaslit me constantly. And everything you just told me seems so..." She couldn't call it out of character for Axel since she didn't really know him. All he'd shown her was a ruthless will to get Otto's company, no matter what it cost in dollars to him or heartache to her. "My impression is that he's very practical and single-minded and only helps people if it serves his own agenda."

He couldn't have known whether he was buying Heskel's loyalty, though. That suggested a decency she hadn't credited him with.

"He's an engineer," Heskel said with amused affection. "I say that because I'm married to one. Their priorities are efficiency and finding a way to get the result they want in a consistent way. But I don't want to gossip about him. I want to carry out the tasks he has assigned to me. He asked me to support you in looking for a dance academy. A friend of a friend owns a studio here. He studied at the Royal Ballet in London. May I set up a meeting for you? I'm sure he could give you some guidance on how best to pursue your goals."

Her jaw almost unhinged and fell onto the floor. "When did Axel ask you to do that?"

"During one of our meetings in Chicago. It took me some time to get to it, what with the wedding and everything else."

"I'm not complaining." They'd only landed a few hours ago. Her suspicious mind had leaped to thinking Axel was trying to make up with her after their argument, but this wasn't a bribe or an apology. He was only holding up his end of the deal they'd struck. That was a little deflating, but also reminded her that if she was going to stay in this marriage, she might as well get what *she* had been promised. "I would love to meet your friend. Thank you."

The idea of speaking with a professional dancer lightened her mood considerably.

"I'll call now to set that up." Heskel stepped away.

The door to the office opened a moment later. Axel came out with a man who could have been thirty or fifty. He had more salt than pepper in his closely shorn hair, but he didn't have a wrinkle on his dark brown complexion.

"Joy. My lawyer, Gerard."

"Hello." She found a smile and rose to move to Axel's side. "It's nice to meet you."

"My wife, Joy." There was a note of something in his voice—pride, maybe? Whatever it was, it felt at odds with the anxiety she felt in being his wife, leaving her flustered and blushing.

The way he casually set his hand on her lower back sent unexpected warmth shooting into her limbs, but she did her best to play her part, shaking hands with Gerard.

He warmly invited them to dine with him and his wife as soon as possible.

"I'd love to meet her, thank you," Joy said sincerely.

"I'll have my assistant set it up, but please excuse me."

Gerard nodded wryly at Axel. "I have a mountain of work ahead of me."

They walked him to the door. The second it closed behind him, Joy stepped away from Axel's touch.

His brows went up in question.

She only hurried back to the table, thinking that if she was staying and playing the part of his wife, she needed a better grasp of what he expected of her. She might react to him, but he seemed very take-it-or-leave-it about her.

Heskel was setting out Axel's plate while wearing his earpiece, speaking German to someone. His tone held a distinct, *I have to go* flavor as he hurried to end his call with, "Bis später."

"Klaus?" Axel guessed as he held Joy's chair. "Take a few days at home with him since I won't be working. We'll be in Paris." He nodded at Joy as he took his seat.

"Paris? We just got here." This man refused to let her get her feet under her, didn't he?

"You need clothes. Our wedding announcement has gone out?" He glanced at Heskel, who looked up from texting to nod a confirmation. "Invitations will start coming in. I instructed Gerard to sue Otto for breach of contract. He agreed that Otto is likely to attack our marriage, so we need to show people it's real."

But it's not. She didn't say it aloud, but Axel's gaze was waiting to snag her own when she flashed a look at him. He held the eye contact in an implacable way that had her throat flexing in reaction.

By marrying me, you took control...

She absolutely needed to do that, but how?

"My work phone was confiscated before I left the building," Heskel said. "I'm sure people are trying to reach you. Would you like me to do anything about that?"

"No. Let Otto answer for my absence. If he doesn't see the light and retire before we return from Paris, I will open my own firm. Vorstoben's clients will turn to me out of frustration. If anyone reaches you in the next few days," he added as he dug into his breakfast, "let them know I'll be in touch after I return from my honeymoon."

Joy choked on her bite of parfait. *Honeymoon?*

As a courtesy to Mira, Axel hadn't taken a lover in two years. Celibacy hadn't always been comfortable, but sex wasn't something he had ever felt he needed.

Not like he did today.

And when it came to sex, he was all for edging. To a point. Now that he knew how responsive Joy was, how she melted and sounded when she shattered, he wanted more. Needed more.

"He will attack your marriage any way he can," Gerard had warned him during their meeting. "How strong is it?"

"We've known each other three days. What do you think?" Axel had asked dryly.

Otto's potential attack wasn't why Axel wanted to bind Joy to him physically, though. Nor was it his lengthy dry spell, though that was definitely a factor. They were married. Why shouldn't they have sex if they both wanted it?

This particular shade of want, however, was biting and primitive and disturbing.

For that reason, he kept trying to put a lid on it. He didn't want to want her this hard. It felt too much like those times he'd wanted other things he couldn't have, like parents who took care of him or a hot meal.

Maybe if she wasn't so frosted by how things had gone with Otto, things would be different, but he couldn't change what had happened and wouldn't if he could. At least she had stayed and would continue this pantomime they were calling a marriage.

He didn't want it to be pantomime, though. He wanted the reality of touching her. Covering her. Claiming her.

Don't, he ordered himself, but his ears were ringing with the sound of her footsteps as she explored their suite in the Paris hotel.

His eyes refused to look away from her, only noting very absently the backdrop of tasteful creams and dull bronze, white sculptures and pink floral arrangements.

She wore boots with her jeans, giving her strolling steps a swagger that entranced him. She paused in the rounded nook of windows that offered a view of the Eiffel Tower shining golden against the purple clouds of fading dusk.

They had both fallen asleep on the plane from Berlin. It was too early to go for dinner. What else were they going to do right now?

"Heskel told me how you helped him and his husband. Do you mind if I ask why?"

He lifted his brows. Heskel wasn't usually so forthcoming.

"I knew Klaus from school. We'd kept in touch, which is how I knew to recruit him. I was working in Hong Kong when his crash happened. It took a few weeks for me to get back here to visit them. When I saw Heskel, I saw myself." He winced at how uncomfortable it made him to refer to his darkest days even in passing. "I recognized how much stress he was under, trying to keep them afloat. It looked a lot like the way you were drowning when we met," he said sardonically.

Her brows came together crossly. "I was fine."

He ignored that blatant lie, saying, "I threw him a life ring because I wished someone had done that for me. You asked me why I continued working for Otto even after I knew what sort of man he was. Because, in many ways, Vorstoben was my life ring. Seeing the way Otto dismissed Klaus without telling me was the beginning of me making plans to leave, though."

"Hmph." She moved past the doors to the balcony, skirting the end of the sofa to the bookshelf. Hardback copies of French classics stood next to framed black-and-white photos of Paris streets. She peered into the bedroom.

"Only one." She sent him a cool look. "I'm sure you think I'm very casual about sex, given my line of work."

"I didn't say that."

"You didn't have to."

"I don't care how you made ends meet, Joy. I was poor for the first half of my life. If I'd had a skill like yours, I would have used it, so I don't judge how you leaned into yours."

"What did you have?" she asked with a curious tilt of her head. "To rise to a life like this? Besides a job at Vorstoben?"

"Hunger." Literally. He tucked his hands in his trouser pockets and leaned on one of the square mirrored columns. "A ferocious desire for security and control over my future. Single-mindedness." Desperation, at times. "I was fifteen when I worked on a hotel like this." He glanced around. "An iconic building getting an upgrade. The furniture they threw out was nicer than anything I'd ever seen. I stole a chair from the dumpster and took it home to my mother. She still has it. She loves it. I remember promising myself every morning, when I arrived on the jobsite, that one day I would stay in places like this and not think twice about the cost."

"Is this the first time you've thought about the cost today?" she asked with a twist of humor on her lips.

"I haven't at all. Heskel booked it." He shrugged.

"I've been pinching pennies for so long, I can't imagine that sort of confidence." She touched the bouquet on the bookcase, realized the flowers were real and cupped a bloom, bending to inhale its fragrance.

He let his gaze trace the line of her back, the roundness of her ass, the beautiful length of her legs.

She glanced up and caught him, not that he was hiding his interest.

A light blush stole into her cheeks. She dropped her gaze to the flowers, toying with the petals. "I keep wondering if you're still in love with her."

"Who? Mira? No," he dismissed firmly.

She angled her head, studying him from the corner of her eye. "That sounds like you don't even like her. But you were going to marry her?"

"She's fine." He heard how lukewarm that sounded and curled his lip at himself. "We're friends. Soldiers in the same infantry, maybe. I've never wanted love in my relationships, and she knew that." It was probably a good idea to make that clear to Joy as well.

"Why not?" She blinked in a way that asked, *Who doesn't want love?*

"It weighs too much. Fills you with obligation and gives others leverage over you."

"Like the way you exploited my love for my father to pressure me into marrying you?"

"Yes."

Her brow flinched, but that wasn't new information. She seemed to mentally brush it aside. "You were marrying Mira for the company? Same as me?"

"Yes. We've known each other for years. I've dined with her and Otto enough to say we're more than acquaintances.

Once we were engaged, we went to a lot of functions together, but..." Could it even be called dating? "Honestly, *that* was more of a paid escort situation. Without the sex," he added with self-deprecation.

"You didn't have sex with her?" She tucked her chin, skeptical.

"Now who's making snap judgments about promiscuity?"

"It's not promiscuous to have sex within a committed relationship. You were engaged for a long time." She was still wearing a look of incredulity. "It's a reasonable assumption that you would have slept with her."

"I barely kissed her." It seemed important to him that she know that, but he didn't dwell on why. "I wasn't attracted to her, and I was under the impression her interest was directed elsewhere."

"But you were going to marry her anyway?"

"It was a business arrangement."

"Isn't that what this is?" She pointed between them. "Would you have had sex with her if you actually married her?"

"Probably not," he said truthfully. "We had planned to divorce after a year, same as this. I didn't expect our engagement to last so long, but it turns out you don't actually die if you don't have sex. It just feels like you will."

"But you want to have sex with me?" That was not an invitation. It was barely a question. Her arms were folded, her shoulders stiff. Unreceptive.

"I do," he said, keeping a tight rein on his libido.

"Why? Because you're horny after going without for so long? And I'm convenient?" Her jaw lifted to a belligerent angle, but her eyes were full of watchful, vulnerable shadows.

His desire for her was far more personal than that, not that he was comfortable admitting it. "I want to have sex with you because we react to each other. Whether this level of desire is convenient is very much up for debate." His guts were tangled in knots of want and his own resistance, not wanting to be pulled this hard. "What exactly is the reason for this line of questioning? Are you angry that I called this a honeymoon? We don't have to have sex if you don't want to." It hurt at a cell-deep level to say that. His libido howled and fought being shoved into its crate.

"I don't think I'd sell that lie very convincingly after what happened on the plane, would I?" She looked past him to the windows, cheeks bright pink, brow gathered in disgruntlement. "That's why I thought you must think I'm someone who falls into bed with anyone who flips a bill at me."

"I don't." The sharp claws that were clenched around his vitals shifted, taking a piercing grip into his groin. "This is a conversation we should have, though, so tell me what you're thinking."

"That I wish I was the sort of person who did sleep around," she admitted with a tight press of her lips. "I've only slept with one man, and I attached way too much emotion to it. That didn't serve me at all."

One?

"The man you lived with?" How could he instantly feel so much resentment toward a stranger? A single, solitary man with whom she regretted becoming too attached. "What happened?"

"Short answer? I let him use me." She sent him a faint, ironic smile as she let that penetrate. "Not in the way you're doing it. At least you're open about how you want to use me." She looked to the floor, brow heavy with self-recrimination. "I didn't see what he was doing for a long time."

"Why not?"

"I don't know. It was gradual. Like, he forgot his wallet so I would buy lunch. Then it was bigger items. A jacket he wanted. He would promise to pay me back, but when I asked him about it, he'd point out that his parents hadn't set up a college fund for him the way mine had. Somehow, he made me feel petty for having more and wanting to be paid back. It was a rough time. I had just lost Mom and learned that Lorena was dead. I wanted someone in my life I could count on."

"And he took advantage of that." He really did hate this other man.

"He said that living together would be cheaper, and it was. For him," she said on a snort. "I paid the rent. He swore that it would all wash out as soon as he got through dental school and started working. I don't know if it was a line or if he really believed it, but I believed it. So, when he couldn't finish an assignment, I did it for him. When his tuition was due, I paid it. And when it came down to choosing between my dance aspirations or working full-time to pay the bills, I picked the wrong horse. I thought he was my person, though. That we were in love. You support the people you love, right?"

This was the problem with love. It became a liability. It might be nice to have, but it did not pay the bills.

"He told you he loved you? To keep you there?" It was exactly the guilt trip that tightened his skin and made him prickly with ire.

She nodded, expression flexing in shame.

"I will never lie to you like that, Joy. If you need love in order to have sex, then I understand. I'll leave you alone."

And he would throw himself off the balcony because the next year was going to *hurt*.

She searched his gaze until he began to feel it like too much sun on his face. "I don't think I could sell that lie very well, either," she said with a break in her voice and looked away.

The tug in his groin was visceral. Dear God, she was going to kill him, dancing around the pole between yes and no.

"That's one of the reasons I thought I could go through with this marriage." She trailed her fingertips along the edge of the desk. "I confused sex and love before, but I don't love you. How could I?"

Ouch. He didn't know why that stung, but it did.

"We've only known each other a few days," she clarified, brow pulled in consternation. "I thought that meant I was safe from you yanking me around by my emotions. I didn't expect we'd jump straight into a physical relationship. I didn't know you would make me want one."

He bit back a groan. His ears stung, he was straining so hard to catch every word spilling from her lips.

"You already hold all the financial cards. Now you want this from me, too?"

"Most of my relationships are transactional. I admit that," he said grittily. "But you already gave me leverage with Otto that I wouldn't otherwise have. As long as you stay married to me and play your part, you don't owe me a damned thing. I'm not trying to extract *more* from you."

"No?" Her brows went up.

"No. If we have sex, it's because we want each other."

"Do you want me, though?"

"You doubt it?" No one had ever said anything so astounding to him.

"You're very hot and cold." Her mouth softened into a pout. "'I can wait,'" she quoted mockingly. "You had no trouble walking away from me on the plane."

"Do you think that was easy?" he asked with a rasp in his throat. "I only meant to kiss you, and you damn near turned me inside out. One of us has to keep a few brain cells working. Otherwise, we're liable to burn this place to the ground."

"Really?" Her mouth tilted with shy amusement, and her lashes flared. He suspected if he stood closer, he would have seen her pupils explode.

The air became fully charged with the electricity they'd both been trying to ignore. Sparks of heat began to catch in him like hungry flames on dry grass, threatening to surge forward in an uncontrolled sweep of licking fire.

"Really," he said in a voice that had dropped into the pit of his chest. "If you want more orgasms like that one on the plane, get the hell into that bedroom and take off your clothes." He pointed.

Oh, she hated being told what to do. It was very exciting, the way she stood taller and lifted her chin to that haughty angle.

Wordlessly, in the way of an old aristocrat dropping a glove, she pushed her jacket off her shoulders and let it fall to the floor. She set her boot on the edge of the chair and lowered the zip. The boot hit the floor, then the other. She held his gaze as she peeled her shirt up and off, revealing a pale purple bra with translucent arcs across the tops of the cups. Her jeans relaxed across her hips as she released the button and fly. With a wiggle, she dropped them, leaving her yellow thong in place.

When she reached to open the front closure on her bra, he let his beast off its leash.

CHAPTER NINE

"I'm not in the bedroom!" Joy gasped as Axel pounced on her.

She pushed her hand against his shoulder, not sure what had possessed her to provoke him like this. A desire to see if she could get a reaction out of him? Gain the upper hand in some way? No chance of that!

"You chose the bed, Honigbiene. Lie on it." He tipped her, pressing her to the lacquered top of the Louis Quinze replica, shoving the small lamp out of the way so it fell with a dull thud to the floor.

This was what she had wanted, she realized, as he filled his hands with her. The way he claimed her made her feel wanted.

Even so, the hard desktop had her arching in protest. "It's cold!"

"You'll warm it." He used his weight and leverage and the cup of his hand on her breast to keep her in place while he buried his lips in her throat.

Her skin felt so sensitive, the desktop was almost painful, as was the friction of his trousers between her thighs.

"Axel," she gasped, cradling his head in her hands.

"Too fast?" He lifted his head and kissed her, but his wicked hands were on her breasts, teasing her nipples until she twisted beneath him, unable to bear the tendrils of heat sparking from her breasts to her loins. "This is all I've thought about since the moment I laid eyes on you."

She sobbed out a noise of acquiescence, pleased with that confession, but she was bombarded by so many sensations she didn't know how to cope with it all. The brush of his tongue swept against hers. The faint stubble on his chin rasped her skin. The knit of his pullover slid against her chest and stomach and beneath her hands as she clutched at the flexing muscles of his back, sending her plunging straight back into the eroticism of their encounter on the plane.

She jerked her face to the side, trying to catch her breath.

He moved his seductive lips to her ear, wafting a wicked chuckle against her cheek. "Open your eyes, Honigbiene." He licked beneath her ear, over to her throat.

She dragged her heavy eyelids open and turned her head to look up at him.

"No. There." He turned her face to the side again. "That woman has been driving me insane."

They were reflected in the mirror mounted on the pillar. She was essentially naked with one breast exposed, nipple standing high, beaded with arousal. The other was hidden, possessed by his hand, the tip soon captured by the hot suction of his mouth.

She cried out as dangerous, thrilling sensations shot into her pelvis.

As though he knew exactly how fiercely she yearned for his touch there, his hand swept down her waist and hip and thigh, caressing behind her leg until she lifted it to his waist, allowing his clever fingers to follow the crevice to where her thong was damp with arousal.

She groaned and wriggled again, but he was too strong

to evade. Too enticing to resist. He mercilessly sucked her nipple while tantalizing her needy core.

A gruff curse left him. "I want to eat you up." He straightened and easily lifted her hips, pulling her underwear free so she was naked to his gaze.

Before she could close her thighs, he was hooking her legs over his shoulders while dropping to his knees at the edge of the desk.

"I don't—" Her voice was lost in a groan as he used his thumb to caress and part her folds.

"Let me have this," he said with a catch of intense craving in his voice. "You don't know how badly I need this."

She had never responded to oral, but she'd never responded to being felt up before, either, and he'd nearly killed her with an over-the-pants fondling.

Her flesh remembered exactly how adept he was. She was already achy and needy and soft. Shaking in nervous tension and painful anticipation.

It was beyond blatant, the way he was looking at her. Talking to her in a soothing way as if he had some kind of pity in him when he clearly had none. Not the way he was toying and avoiding, then spooling out the expectation in her with a soft "hah" of his hot breath against her most sensitive flesh.

"Axel, please," she groaned, somehow remembering, "Bitte."

He rewarded her with a slow, benevolent lick.

She could have screamed, it was such a tortuous relief. She turned her head, but her vision was blurred with lust. Her hand was trying to form a fist in his hair, but the strands were too short. She could only catch the silky tufts between the fingers of one hand while she gripped the edge of the desk above her head with the other. She braced one foot on the shelf in the wall and the other dangled off the edge of the desk.

It was the height of debauchery. She had completely abandoned any sense of propriety. Of self. In the mirror, she watched the rock of his head as he lewdly pleasured her and it turned her on. All of this turned her on so much, she could only groan in ragged ecstasy.

He teased her with the addition of a finger, then a second, and found a rhythm that paired his penetration with the sweep of his tongue. She knew she was making the most lascivious noises, filling the room with them as she dug her foot onto the shelf and lifted her hips into his pleasuring.

Maybe she was even saying "please" again. Over and over because the coil of sexual tension in her was so tight she thought she would explode from it.

Then she detonated, and it was as powerful as before. More. It went on and on because he did not let up. Her powerful climax rolled into a fresh, intense arousal that made her sob in frustration. How could it be so good and not enough?

Gently he withdrew his touch and left a wet bite against the inside of her thigh. She instinctively tried to pull away, but she was utterly wrecked. She had the vague thought that she ought to close her legs or tell him she wanted a real bed. Something. But she was too weak to move, and she'd fallen too deeply into the well of lust to do anything but watch as he peeled off his sweater.

He withdrew a condom from his trouser pocket before he opened his fly and dropped his pants enough to bare his ass and his erection.

Since when did she think *that* organ was beautiful? But that most brutally masculine part of him, turgid and aggressive, made her ache with yearning. She watched him apply the condom and had to swallow an agony of need.

"Say yes, Schatz. I will die if I can't have you right now."

"Yes," she gasped and started to crook her knee, but he drew her legs up so her ankles were on his shoulders.

His cheeks were flushed, his expression intense as he guided his thick length to the sultry flesh that was still tingling with sensitivity. Still pulsing with greed.

As his hardness began to fill her, he hugged her legs, keeping her still for the careful pulse of his hips. The shallow, testing strokes sent delicious spikes of heat through her whole body, making her shake and groan.

"Good?"

"So good." She bit her lip and clutched the edge of the desk again, holding herself still for a deeper thrust that told them both she was more than ready.

"Now, my pretty wife." He caressed all around where he was penetrating her, awakening her into a fresh flood of heat and yearning. "I want every last person in Paris to hear you scream my name when you come."

They did.

I confused sex and love before.

Had it been sex like that? Because Axel could see how it rewired the brain.

That was a disturbing thought, mostly because he didn't care to think of her with her ex, giving that other man even a fraction of her extraordinary passion.

His animosity wasn't jealousy, precisely. It was a deeper, more justified contempt toward someone who had taken advantage of her when she'd been struggling with grief, tricking her into financially supporting him.

Was he any better, though? Axel wasn't bankrupting her,

he reminded himself. Quite the opposite. And he wasn't lying to her about how he felt, either.

He still found himself brooding on whether he was treating her fairly. What more could she want, though?

I don't love you. How could I?

And why in hell would he feel a compulsion to give her more than he already had?

Because that sex had been outstanding.

After defiling the desk, he'd carried her in here to tear up the bed. She was magnificent. Strong and flexible, and she had a stamina and sexual appetite to match his own. Her sensuality ran deep enough to bury him. She wasn't afraid to push back. Or demand.

Ringing cries of ecstasy from her had been as satisfying as his own incredible orgasms. It had been spectacular. Euphoric. He wanted to envelop her and hide her from the world. *Mine.* But he also wanted to worship her. Celebrate her.

He reminded himself that he was breaking a long fast. The physical relief and sexual triumph from that alone was profound. But he instinctually knew sex wouldn't have been this intense with any other woman. What was it about Joy? Purely chemistry? Or was he drunk on the way their marriage had given him the upper hand with Otto?

That was a prickly thought, but there was some truth to it. Certain exultant emotions were riveted into this act that he didn't care to examine right now, because his battle with Otto wasn't finished. Axel was merely enjoying a moment of respite while he gathered his forces for his next move.

Joy was a key member of his assault. That was why Axel was so eager to spoil her, he reasoned. He wanted this marriage to appear watertight.

Was *that* transactional? Manipulative? Perhaps. But

throughout his life he'd been taught that he could get what he wanted if he provided what others needed, whether that was food, labor, technical skill or other resources. That was how he'd climbed the ladder at Vorstoben. He'd met Otto's need for a leader with business acumen and management skills. In return, he'd gained the secure, comfortable lifestyle he wanted. When his desire had shifted to wanting autonomy, Otto had appeared to offer that as well, while needing Axel to marry his daughter.

Axel was a transactional person, but woe betide the person who tried to cheat him once they'd agreed on a price. He would get Vorstoben or an equivalent repayment of the time he'd put into it. That was nonnegotiable.

Not that marrying Joy felt like a high price right now.

He sent a look of consternation across to her angelic face, relaxed in sleep.

No, he knew what was really bothering him. She had accused him of being hot and cold, and he was. He preferred his walls and autonomy, but he wasn't a heartless bastard. He couldn't completely shut down on her after she'd given herself so generously to him.

This was why he'd been okay with marrying Mira—he didn't like bumpy emotions or the ability to bruise someone's feelings. He didn't like that hurting Joy was now a conduit to harming himself. She had become as much a liability as asset.

He needed distance from those barbed thoughts and her.

He left the bed. As he snapped his briefs into place, she drew in a sharp breath and blinked, brushing her hair off her face.

"What time is it?" she asked with soft urgency, picking up her head.

"Six thirty."

"I need to call Dad." She dropped her head back onto the pillow, eyes fluttering shut again while her brow flexed. "I texted when we landed in Berlin and told him I'd call once he was up. He must be worried."

"Do you want me to find your phone?"

"No. I'll, um—" She sat up, pulling the sheet up under her arms as she did. "Is there a robe in the closet?"

"Really? I've seen everything you have under there." And had run his hands or lips over every square centimeter, in case she'd forgotten.

"*I* decide how much skin I reveal and to whom," she said with a clash of her gaze into his.

She was putting her own defenses into place.

His logical, civilized brain said, *Fair*, but the possessive animal in him bristled and said, *Actually, that's mine. No one else will ever see that much of you again.*

What a hypocritical reaction.

Dismayed with himself, he moved to the closet, then held plush robe ready for her, rolling his eyes to the ceiling with great sarcasm. "Should I order room service? Or would you rather go out?"

She *tsked* at the way he held the robe and stood to shrug into it, yanking it from his grip as she closed it across her front and tied the belt. "Whatever you prefer."

"What I prefer…" He caught his fingers under the cinch of her belt. "Is to eat in, drink wine in the tub, then climb back into that bed for another round or three. Lights off, if you prefer not to show me what you have."

"I'm allowed to have boundaries." Her chin came up in shaky dignity. "Don't make fun of me for it."

"I wasn't joking about any of that."

She sniffed, but some of her tension dissipated when she said, "Fine." Her brows gave a haughty little jump.

"To all of it. But the lights can stay on. Wear a blindfold." She started to brush past him.

He snagged his arm around her waist, amused and, yes, titillated. "Really?"

"I don't know!" she said with exasperation. "Maybe it will give me the upper hand for once."

As if she needed it.

Tightening his arm, he brought her hip into the twitching flesh at his groin and clasped a fistful of her hair with his other hand, slowly dragging her head back so her hands clutched at his arm and her lips parted on a startled inhale.

He kissed those soft lips, taking his time with it, savoring the way she softened and leaned into him.

When she danced the tip of her tongue against his, when she was breathless and her lashes seemed too heavy for her eyelids to lift and her lowered gaze was hazy with desire, he drew back and released her.

"Say hello to your dad for me." Before outrage could take hold in her eyes, he added, "I need to order dinner. And a scarf."

"Springtime in Paris!" her sister-in-law had exclaimed, very taken with their honeymoon location.

Joy promised to send photos but suspected the city was overhyped. That is, until she and Axel were actually walking through the streets where trees and flowers were coming into bloom.

"I feel like I'm in a movie," she said, stopping on one of the pedestrian bridges over the Seine to snap photos of the river, swollen and glugging slowly beneath them. It was flanked by buildings freshly washed by last night's rain. Everything smelled fresh and gleamed in the morning sun, inciting a sense of possibility in her while breaking her eyes at how pretty it all was.

"Including the Hollywood makeover," she added when she turned the camera for a selfie and was freshly startled by her polished appearance.

Axel had booked her into the hotel salon first thing, then bought her a new outfit from its posh boutique before they left. She wore a pair of wide-legged designer jeans with a snug crop top and a black satin jacket.

"Do you want a trophy wife or something?" she asked him now.

"I have one," he said laconically as he leaned his forearms on the rail.

She captured his possessive look in the frame as she clicked.

"I knew we'd be photographed once the news got out." He straightened to draw her into his arms, pulling her hips into a light collision with his own, one that sent delicious sensations sloshing through her belly.

The press release had been very brief, stating only that Axel Severin had married American Joy Youngston on the heels of his broken engagement to Mira Braun.

"Won't people assume I'm the reason you two broke up?" she asked, trying and failing to be as casually unaffected by their closeness as he seemed.

"Probably." He brushed at the bangs she'd had trimmed into her hair after the color was adjusted to a more natural honey and molasses tone. "That's why we must appear smitten."

This was all an act for him, but it was nearly impossible for her to think when he touched her.

"What if, um, they find out that Otto is my father?"

She dropped her voice to a near whisper. "Isn't it PR 101 to stay ahead of something like that?"

"The only way they'd learn it is a leak from Otto or Mira. Otto isn't likely to acknowledge you until he has to. He would have to admit to having an affair while his wife was pregnant. It then opens the question of whether you have any rights to his fortune. I don't think Mira will say anything, either. She hasn't made public yet that she's not Otto's daughter, probably because she's exploring her own legal options. We're at an impasse. Which suits me. It allows you and I to establish ourselves as a couple before Otto takes any shots at us."

"Is that why you're kissing me right now? Are you paying to have us photographed?" She tipped her head back and narrowed her eyes in suspicion.

"No. But I might have if I'd thought to do it. My mind has been on other things." He was obscenely handsome when one corner of his mouth kicked up that way.

He'd relaxed significantly from the first time she'd seen him. She didn't have to wonder why. After getting a little drunk over dinner last night, they'd bathed together, spending a lot of time tenderly washing their dirtiest parts. Afterward, they made love again, slept hard, then barely got through breakfast before they were at it again.

If he had suggested going back to the hotel right now, she would have gone. She was smitten. Or infatuated, at least. Sexually.

And disconcerted because, as much as he seemed beguiled by their sexual connection, she didn't think he was anywhere close to as enthralled with her as she was with him.

"Didn't you say I had an appointment?" she reminded

him, trying to gather some of those brain cells he said they ought to keep hold of.

"You do." He finished walking her over the bridge to a designer's showroom.

The next few days were spent browsing exclusive boutiques, picking up everything from dance shoes to sunglasses. Everything. The lingerie purchase alone would have bought her a new car. A nice one.

Between shopping excursions, Axel wined and dined her at street cafés and high-end restaurants. They went out in the evening to art galleries and visited a nightclub and watched a musical production.

He seduced her constantly. He set his hand on her leg while they watched models parade their fashions. He kissed her nape when he seated her in a restaurant. There'd been a particularly erotic and clandestine grope in a darkened alcove when they were walking back to their hotel one evening, one that he ended while she was still tense and whimpering with need.

"If you can't be quiet, I have to stop," he scolded in a way that suggested he was denying her on purpose. "Otherwise, we'll be arrested."

She had thought Todd's manipulation of her emotions had been bad. She was completely at the mercy of Axel's whims. Even when she was anointing him with her mouth, trying to make him break, he was fully in charge of their play.

He cradled her jaw and the back of her head, thrusting with slow, hypnotic precision, saying, "Touch yourself while you do this. I want to come together. I'll tell you when."

She did. And it was so hot, she nearly crumpled to the floor afterward.

This was exactly what a honeymoon should be, she supposed, but on their last night, she pointed out, "I thought this was supposed to be a time when spouses got to know each other, but I don't know much more about you than when I met you."

They were in one of the small dining rooms of a converted four-hundred-year-old residence. The high ceilings wore decorative gilded plaster. Intricate tapestries covered the walls, and intimate light glowed from wall sconces and dripped from crystal chandeliers.

The staff had greeted Axel by name and welcomed her warmly, not giving them menus and bringing champagne without being asked.

"What do you want to know?" he asked, seeming to withdraw several degrees.

That was something she'd become very familiar with.

"I don't know," she mused.

She had learned a few incidental things. He didn't care for seafood and rarely had more than one or two glasses of alcohol. He didn't need much sleep. Twice, she woke to find him out of bed in the night, working. He had a villa on a Greek island, a vineyard in Portugal, a pied-à-terre in London and a unit in a Singapore building that he had helped design, getting in on the ground floor so to speak.

"I guess I'm curious about your childhood. What was it like?"

"Impoverished," he said with a twist of his lips. "Is that not obvious?"

"No, I mean, you told me that's why you were ambitious and why you wanted to live like this." She waved at the amuse-bouche. It was a single bite of puff pastry that turned out to be cheese. It melted in her mouth and made her next sip of champagne explode with flavor on her tongue. "But what were your parents like?"

"Young. Too young," he added with a dismayed curl of his lip. "They were both born in East Germany. When the wall fell, my mother's family moved to Berlin for work. She was thirteen at the time. My father was sixteen and left his family in Leipzig, also looking for work. After a few years, my mother's parents went back to Dresden. By then, she had a job in a café and was finished with school, so she stayed. She and my father went on a few dates and…" He motioned at himself.

"She was eighteen? Nineteen?"

"She turned eighteen two days before she went into labor."

"Oh. That is young. Especially when you don't have family nearby. Your grandparents weren't supportive?"

"They weren't in a position to help. Reunification was a difficult time. There was a lot of unemployment, prices went up. Everything my parents had known growing up had changed. They married because it seemed like the right thing to do, but they didn't have much between them beyond hormones and a baby they weren't ready to parent."

Everything in her went still, concerned about what that meant. Afraid to ask.

"They weren't abusive. Not intentionally." He spoke conversationally but seemed to have retreated a million miles into himself. "They tried. And argued because they failed. My father did whatever he had to, to keep us fed. Stole. Sold drugs. My mother took them, trying to cope. She's sober now, but after my father was killed, that was a dark time."

"Axel, I'm so sorry." She put out a hand on the table, but he ignored it, face looking carved from granite.

After a moment, feeling spurned, she slowly pulled her hand back into her lap. "Were you ever put into care?"

"A few times. I didn't like it." He grimaced in distaste. "It was too regimented. I'd been raising myself since I could walk. I didn't trust their charity and didn't want to answer to anyone. I didn't want their pity. I hated their judgment." He picked up his wineglass.

Joy had experienced something similar. Not often, but she knew the quizzical look that searched for the flaw that explained why her birth parents had failed to look after her.

"But you still see your mother?" she asked gently. "How is your relationship with her now?"

"She lives in a house I bought for her in Dresden. We talk every week or so. I told her about you and said we'll visit as soon as we can. She tries." His shoulder jerked. "She made amends with me a few years ago, acknowledged her shortcomings and asked me to forgive her. I do. I can see that she was set up to fail, being so young, but…" His brows lowered in dismay. "She wants me to feel the kind of love a child is supposed to have for their parent, and I don't. It's not a grudge. I just learned that it didn't matter if I loved her. Loving someone doesn't mean your needs will be met. All it does is make you feel like you owe them something."

Joy's heart took that like a punch. She wanted to argue that maybe, if his parents had loved each other, things might have been different for all of them.

But maybe they wouldn't have. How could it be proved either way?

"I can't say Otto was a father figure to me. It was never like that, but once he began recognizing my efforts, I was able to leave struggle and instability behind. So I felt some loyalty and obligation. I'm furious with him for tricking me, but much of my anger is with myself. I let myself believe in him when I already knew I'm the only one I can count on."

She had thought she was cynical. The hardness in his expression sent frost creeping through her chest.

"That's why I can't let him get away with cheating me," Axel continued grimly. "There were too many times in the past when I had to accept the insults, the theft, the beating. What I'm after isn't vengeance, Joy. It's justice."

She nodded, understanding, but stunned with hurt over what he didn't spell out—that he would never give up his heart. Not to her or anyone else. And didn't want hers, either.

It's only one year, she thought for the millionth time.

And, paradoxically, also thought, *That's not enough.*

CHAPTER TEN

AXEL HADN'T EXPECTED to like being married. In fact, he'd braced for the worst since his parents' marriage had been a strong advertisement for cutting line before things got worse than they needed to be. Plus, after living on his own for so many years, he had developed an appreciation for order and quiet and minimalism.

Joy's things were everywhere, especially when they got back from Paris. They had to convert the spare bedroom into a dressing room to accommodate it all.

Oddly, he liked seeing her clothes next to his in the closet. He liked hearing her talk to her family over the tablet before they went to bed. He liked coming home to someone and eating meals with her, and he liked being out with her.

They'd gone out every night in Paris, but she was visibly nervous the first night he took her to a cocktail party in Berlin. She was worried there would be a language barrier and judgment over their quick marriage.

She charmed everyone they met, of course. She was naturally curious and wry and so attractive in a beaded black cocktail dress, everyone was dazzled to be in her sphere.

The next day she had her first meeting with Heskel's friend, the dance instructor. She was nervous about that, too.

"I'm rusty," she said as she anxiously tried to choose

between two leotards that looked identical to him. She was packing a duffel so full, it looked as though she was leaving for a week. "The school I was at was good, but it wasn't the Royal Ballet in London. I want him to be honest, but I don't want him to be too honest, you know? A wrong word from him could kill my dreams."

His hackles went up. "Do you want me to cancel my meeting and go with you?"

"No. I don't want you to see me humiliate myself." Her tone asked him how he dared make such a stupid suggestion.

Heskel arrived then to take her to the studio.

Axel quietly relayed in German that his assistant should ensure zero wrong words were spoken to his wife and was told, "I'm confident he'll be completely professional."

Axel was distracted through his meeting, though, troubled by thoughts that this instructor would deride Joy in some way. He wasn't used to being concerned about someone, not beyond the level of basic decency. His mother had been a source of constant distress when he'd been a child, but this was different. Joy wasn't engaging in risky behavior like drug use. She was worried her feelings would be hurt.

So was he.

Unable to stand it, he cut his meeting short and had Heskel text him the address so he could catch up with them before she finished.

When he arrived, she was kneeling on the floor in the middle of an otherwise empty dance studio. Her eyes were closed. She wore a black sports bra and pair of matching yoga shorts, but nothing else.

Heskel motioned him to quiet while a recording of a haunting female vocalist began to play.

With slow grace, Joy took hold of her own head, drawing it down so her body followed. She flowed into a snake-like move and kicked one leg up straight. That turned into a cartwheel that put her on her feet. After quickly tiptoeing across the room, she crumpled into a handful of bends and swooning movements that synced with the music. The emotion in the song poured from her limbs and her face and the butterfly lightness of her leaps. The yearning of the vocals chased her around the room, making him catch his breath and clench his fist in an agony of longing as she stood on one foot and reached toward him, the distance seeming to be a thousand miles.

Axel was spellbound until the final moment when she returned to the center of the room and did a slow spin that pulled her down, down, down until she was only a ball on the floor.

What else could he do but throw his hands together in claps that reverberated around the big, empty room?

"My employer," Heskel said ruefully when the instructor, a man in his sixties with white hair and a lean, tall posture, shot them a frown.

"My husband," Joy said as she popped up from the floor, scolding, "You distracted me." She hurried toward the instructor and listened attentively as he critiqued her performance.

"Look after yourself when you get home," the instructor reminded her as he brought her to where Axel and Heskel were waiting.

"I will. Thank you so much." She was damp with sweat, but her smile was pure radiance.

I gave her this, Axel thought, and found himself despising her ex yet again for taking dance away from her.

"It went well?" he asked when they were walking to the car. "No humiliation?"

"Oh, he didn't pull a single punch," she said with a

sheepish laugh. "But in terms of a master class, that single opportunity to have his one-on-one attention for an hour was beyond anything I could ever hope for. Thank you." She hugged his arm.

He slipped his arm around her, pleased to see her showing so much exuberance. "Will he take you on as a student? What happens next?"

"Flatterer. I'm not that good! No." She tucked herself more fully under his arm as they walked. "His focus is ballet, anyway. He said my foundation skills are solid, that I have nice musicality, but that I need to work on my physical strength. He could tell I've been developing certain muscles and not others, which affects my alignment and some of my transitions. He liked that I learn fast and know how to correct myself, but I need more height in my leaps. He's going to put me in touch with a student choreographer who is putting something together for a festival in May. It's a shoestring budget, but they're holding auditions soon. He said if I can get in with them, the training and networking will help me find my track."

She was still in high spirits the next evening when they met Gerard and his wife at a restaurant. Axel could hardly take his eyes off how dazzlingly pretty Joy was as she relayed her excitement about the dance opportunity and traded misadventures with Gerard's wife around the other couple's children and Joy's toddler nephew.

"I miss him so much," she confessed wistfully.

I can give you that, too, Axel thought abstractedly, then frowned because children had never been on his radar. With his upbringing? No. He had always thought to spare a child whatever baggage he would bring to parenting.

Joy glanced at him and must have seen his consternation. Her smile faltered.

"I'll visit the powder room while we're waiting on dessert," she said with a strained smile.

Gerard's wife accompanied her, and Gerard took advantage of having Axel alone to catch him up on his legal position with Otto.

"As we expected, Otto is questioning the veracity of your marriage," Gerard said. "He's claiming to protect Joy's interest. What if he gifts you the company and your marriage dissolves?"

"It won't." The words came out more forcefully than Axel intended, grunted out by the inner Neanderthal who was having the best sex of his life with the woman he'd dragged into his cave.

"He's leaning into the 'married for a year' stipulation," Gerard added.

"He doesn't have a year," Axel derided. "He's scrambling for investment funding to replace what Mira has yanked. Now that she's working with Rocco DeStefano and tying up Rocco's resources, the timing has never been better for me to start my own firm. I can poach from both of them. Tell Otto that his refusal to honor the marriage contract nullifies my noncompete clause. I will act accordingly."

Not that he had been waiting on anyone's permission to start his own firm. He'd already put Heskel on finding office space and staffing it.

When they returned home, he was still turning over the longing in Joy's voice when she had spoken of her nephew.

"Do you want children?" he asked her.

"I—" Her voice turned strangled. She halted in removing her earrings, eyes wide as a deer confronting headlights. "Because of what I said about missing my nephew? I saw you frown when I said that. I wasn't trying to hint that I want a baby. I've actually been meaning to ask you to help me find a doctor so I can use something more reliable than condoms." She turned away to finish removing her jewelry and started on the pins from her hair.

"Meaning you don't want children," he clarified.

"Maybe. Someday. Not now."

"Not with me." That shouldn't be such a kick in the crotch, but it was.

"Not when I'm about to get back into dance. Why? Do you want children?" She turned to face him but contorted her arms, trying to lower the zip on her dress.

He moved across to do it for her, turning her so he could reach. "I wasn't planning to become a father, no. But it crossed my mind tonight that starting a family would go a long way to proving our marriage is more than a piece of paper."

"This is about Otto?" She spun around to face him, affronted. "What are you thinking? That if I continue the man's bloodline, he'll bestow his riches upon me? There is a limit to how far I'll let you use me, Axel. It does not extend to being a vessel that literally carries your 'justice.' I sure as hell won't let you or anyone use my child for anything. Ever." She started to brush past him.

He stopped her.

She knocked his hand off her arm and glared up at him.

"That wasn't what I was suggesting," he ground out. "I thought a family might be something you want. I thought we should talk about it."

"Why would I want to have a baby with you when our marriage has an expiration date?"

"It doesn't," he said in another knee-jerk response. "We can choose whether we end it and when."

"I can't." She took a step back, coming up against the dresser. She grasped the edge of it as though needing the support. Her mouth tightened. She looked trapped. Hurt. "You can decide tomorrow that you don't want Vorstoben and discard me immediately. I can't leave for a year, or there will be unpleasant consequences for my family."

His heart lurched. "Are you saying you want to leave?"

"No." Her brow pleated, and she swallowed. "But don't..." Her voice cracked, and she blinked fast.

"Are you crying? Joy." He hadn't meant to upset her. He reached for her.

"Don't *do* that." She shoved at his chest and stalked past him until she was across the room. "You know you can fry my brain with sex, and that's not fair! What happens when the sex fades? Huh? Do you really see us staying married all our lives? Having a family? That's a real question, Axel. Do you?"

"I don't know." How had this escalated so quickly? "It was just a question."

"Well, stop and think for a minute how loaded that question is for me! My birth mother gave me away. The man who made me, the one you dragged me here to meet, has no interest in a relationship with me. Now you're saying maybe you want to keep me around a little longer, but only maybe? Only if I have a baby that gets you what you want? A baby you don't even want except for what it gets you? Do you hear how cruel that is to say to *me*?"

He snapped his head to the side as though she'd struck him. He felt her sharp words like claws against his cheek. It was an attack he deserved because he hadn't really seen how tender this was for her. She was so good at hiding that particular scar, acting as though her adoptive family had given her all she needed, that he'd forgotten the very real pain of loss and rejection she carried.

"You didn't like it when Otto changed the rules on you," she pointed out shakily.

"I'm not changing the rules." He did want to change the rules, though. He didn't want a hard end date on this marriage. It bothered him to think of her counting down the days. It didn't matter that he understood why she was doing it. He didn't like it. Not at all.

This was the sort of inner turmoil that he had thought to avoid by marrying Mira. They would have easily ghosted through a year of a marriage that was more of a financial partnership, one that wouldn't have caused any ripples in his life. Or his equilibrium.

"I want to give you what you want," he said tightly. Because if he gave her what she wanted, he could have what he was increasingly feeling like he needed: her. "If you wanted children, I wanted you to know I'm open to discussing it. That's all."

She was still standing across the room, arms crossed to hold up the loosened dress that was hanging off her bare shoulders. Her expression was dejected. "I want to be loved, Axel. I want someone to say they want me in their life forever. I want to know that I belong with them for the rest of my life. Can you give me that?"

The sensation that jolted through him could have been the electric charge off a cattle prod. It seared so deeply and painfully within him, it damn near stopped his heart. Because how was he supposed to pay that steep a price? "No."

He heard her breath hiss in as though he'd stabbed her.

"I need to make some calls. I'll join you later." He walked downstairs.

It took Joy a long time to fall asleep.

She hadn't meant to react so strongly to what had actually been a fair question, given they were married and having sex, but it was a very touchy subject for her and not just because of how temporary their relationship was.

The question of children had always been a sharp jab against her skin with a two-pronged fork. She wanted children, and she also wanted a career in dance. It wasn't impossible to have both, but she knew that each was taxing and demanding and required a devoted level of commitment. Both also had a biological clock, one reproductive, the other related to joints and tendons and whatever muscles she might sprain or injure during hours of training and performing.

She still had time to pursue both, but this marriage was eating a year.

It was buying her a year of dance, she reminded herself, which gave her a second chance at the career she'd nearly given up hope on having.

That made Axel asking her to put that aspiration aside and start a family rankle, especially when his reasons had seemed so mercenary.

At the same time, the idea of having Axel's baby was incredibly appealing. One of the reasons she had finally left Todd was the stark realization that she didn't want to have his children.

Axel had all the qualities of strength and health and a well-built nest that would shake awake anyone's ovaries. The ache of yearning went deeper than biology, though, to the part that she had alluded to when she had said she wanted to be loved. She wanted her baby born into love. She wanted *his* love.

Because she was tipping toward that emotion herself.

They were still new, she hurried to remind herself, as though that would stop this flailing sensation inside her.

She couldn't expect declarations of love, especially when that emotion was so very sharp-edged for him.

For Axel, making love didn't *make* love the way it did for her.

That was what was happening to her, though. She grew more enamored and more vulnerable to him by the day.

Which made the fact that he held all the power in terms of ending their relationship all the more pointed. And made his casual suggestion that they could have a baby and stay married tear at the scab on her heart, the one she pretended wasn't there.

She didn't remember falling asleep but woke in the night to an awareness of him beside her.

The distance across the mattress was mere inches, but it felt like an intolerable chasm.

She slid closer, not wanting to wake him but seeking contact. Reassurance at a very basic level.

"Cold?" He was awake and rolled toward her, drawing her into the heat of his body.

He always slept naked while she usually pulled on a short nightie over a soft sleep bra, even if they'd made love. That was what she wore now. She laced her bare legs with his and her lips met the hollow of his shoulder without her even thinking about it.

At the brush of her lips against his skin, the shift of his hand against her back stilled. He was hardening against her stomach and started to draw back.

"I don't want to fight," she whispered into his throat, touching her lips under his jaw. She let her thigh stroke higher against the outside of leg, so her nightgown rode up to her hips.

His breath hissed in, and his hand roamed lower, catching under the lacy hem and pushing it to her waist as he rolled her beneath him. He kissed her. Not rough but hard. Greedy. As though they hadn't seen each other in months. Years. As though he had felt the distance and hated it as much as she did and was determined to close it.

His tongue swept between her lips, telling her what he wanted. *Now.*

There was an urgency in him that tensed all his muscles and made her feel pounced upon, but not in a bad way. There was something exciting in the way he pushed her legs apart with his hard thighs and dragged his mouth to her breast, raking aside lace and cotton as though he'd been waiting too long to feast on her.

He was lighting a fire in her that was more of an explosion, alarming but thrilling.

He wet his finger and pressed it into her, rasping something she didn't catch because her senses were under assault. What she had thought would be tender makeup sex was more of a claiming; one she encouraged by arching herself in offering.

He slid beneath the covers to lick fire into the very core of her, making her twist against the weight of the blanket and the strength in his arms as he hugged her thighs. She couldn't get away and didn't want to, but his caresses were almost too much to bear. Deliberate and demanding.

For the first time, he did not seem to be in control, though. Not to the extent that he usually was. Each of her responses made him growl or dig his fingers into her thigh muscle or hold her tighter.

As the tension in her belly coiled to exquisite levels, she dug her heel into his back, lifting her hips, seeking the climax he was driving her toward.

He rose and threw off the covers.

She released a loud sob of protest. Agonized denial.

They were both panting. He remembered to put on a condom, which was a nearly intolerable delay, then he dragged a pillow beneath her hips and hooked her legs over his arms.

His first thrust, imperative and wild, pushed a ragged groan from her lips.

He froze. "Too hard?" he asked through gritted teeth. His whole body quivered with strain.

"Too good," she breathed and set her hands against the headboard so his next thrust went even deeper.

"Stay with me," he growled as he quit trying to restrain his power, thrusting with all his strength, fast and ferociously intense as he drove them straight to the peak.

The second her breath hitched and the first flutter of orgasm arrived, he let go, locking his hips to hers while he bucked, joining her cries of pleasure with his own shouts of helpless triumph.

Waves of ecstasy rolled through her for long minutes, keeping both of them in exquisite stasis, pulses fading slowly, slowly, until he sagged all his weight onto her, both of them sweaty and shaking and trying to catch their breath.

She was utterly wrung out, barely able to breathe under the press of his body, but she twitched in protest when he started to gather himself. "Don't go," she whispered.

His hand clenched in her hair, and his damp lips scraped across her cheek to the corner of her mouth. "I'm not going anywhere, Meine Schönste. Don't you, either."

He had to roll away to remove the condom, but he returned immediately and gathered her close, allowing her to believe what he'd said with her whole, glowing heart.

Until the party on Saturday.

CHAPTER ELEVEN

Joy was gaining confidence with these parties and events, but this charity gala was the fanciest yet, increasing the pressure on her to look her best. To reflect well on Axel.

He was making important connections at these things. He'd been a little more open since their argument the other night, telling her how things were going with Otto—(poorly)—and that he was moving forward with his own firm, courting investors and preparing to take on his first few projects.

That worried her a little. What did he need her for if he had given up on taking over Vorstoben?

He hadn't, he assured her. He had merely accepted that his dealings with Otto would take time so he was pursuing what he'd really wanted all along.

His new venture had lit a fire in him that was exciting to be around. She was already on cloud nine, having made the first cut at the audition process for the festival. Axel's support in her dance aspirations meant the world to her, which increased her desire to do whatever she could to help him get what he wanted.

To that end, she had a professional style her hair and apply her makeup. She broke out the most expensive gown in her closet, one of pale blue satin that made her feel dipped in liquid moonlight. It flowed off one shoulder and down her body, clinging enough to accentuate her curves without being blatant about it.

"You look incredible." He seemed transfixed as he watched her come down the stairs.

"So do you."

He was in a tuxedo, jaw shiny and sharp, ice-blue eyes gleaming with such pride in her, her heart panged with pleasure.

He opened a box and held out a gorgeous bracelet with an aquamarine that closely matched her gown. It was set in ornate filigreed white gold that cuffed her wrist.

"I love it," she said, biting her lip. "But why?" They had made up from their fight.

"I wanted to." He kissed the heel of her palm, then her fingertip.

As he held her gaze, a potent silence fell between them, one that was becoming familiar. It was filled with a helpless sort of energy on her side. His was more difficult to interpret, but she had the suspicion he wanted to be closer to her, he just didn't know how.

"Thank you," she said softly, stepping closer to lightly touch her lips to his, taking care not to stain him with her lipstick. "You really don't have to spoil me, you know."

I'm here, she conveyed, basking in the warm admiration of his half-lidded gaze. She was starting to think she would be here forever. If he would let her.

If he wanted her forever.

Please let him want me forever...

"You're too beautiful," he chided. "We should go, or I'll take you back upstairs."

Perhaps he'd given her the bracelet so she would fit in better, Joy thought when they arrived. She'd never seen so many designer gowns and extravagant jewelry—real diamonds and emeralds and sapphires—outside of watching a red-carpet event on TV.

The wearers were celebrities and high-level politicians, filling her with awe as she recognized them.

Axel seemed comfortable around all of them. Unimpressed, which amused her into relaxing. He introduced her, and most people were polite if not effusively warm. A few were genuinely nice, like the Canadian woman Joy chatted with as they left the powder room.

"I love your bracelet," the woman said. "Can I ask where you found it? I'm looking for something for my sister-in-law's birthday."

"Let me ask Axel."

He was watching for her and approached the moment he saw her looking for him.

The woman introduced herself as Quinn Gould. She was a wholesome-looking redhead with freckles, which wasn't to say she lacked sophistication. Not at all. Her gown was a gold confection that suited her slender figure, and she did *not* look as though she needed advice on where to find good-quality jewelry. She wore emerald earrings and a choker with a square-cut emerald at its center.

"Your husband is Micah Gould?" Axel asked. "We're acquainted. I've been wanting to catch up with him, actually."

"He'll come find me," Quinn assured him. "I ditched him when he was dragged into a conversation about microelectronics. He knows my eyes glaze over when he talks shop," she confided.

Quinn was in the middle of offering tips on where Joy could take language lessons when an older couple approached the three of them.

Axel introduced them, mentioning the husband ran a

company that had been a longtime supplier of steel to Vorstoben. Joy could see him eyeing up the man, trying to discern whether the couple were being polite or if the man's loyalty to Otto was fading.

"I hear you're a dancer," the man said to Joy, cutting though the small talk with the delicacy of a sledgehammer. "Is it true you were stripping in a club when Axel met you?"

Joy heard Quinn's indrawn breath. Maybe it was her own. Adrenaline spiked through her while a heavy blanket of mortification encased her. She wasn't ashamed of dancing at Martini's, but she was sorry her previous line of work had chased her to the other side of the world and was being used to stain Axel's hard-won image.

Especially as he was trying to establish his new company.

"You did not just say that." Axel's voice was positively lethal.

"Am I mistaken?" The man feigned surprise, looking around. "I've heard it from several sources. These things have a way of getting around." He flicked a disdainful look toward Joy as though she was one of those things that got around.

"I think—" Quinn started to say.

Axel stepped right into the man's space and said something in German that had Quinn gasping again.

The other man's wife wore a stony expression, not looking at any of them, but her eyes flared with shock.

"Axel." Joy touched his arm, still feeling stabbed in the lung but not wanting to make this scene any worse than it already was.

"Do not tell me it's fine. It's not," he growled at her.

"No, but I've dealt with this before. Men like him come

into the club all time." She let that statement land before adding, "They think I'll put up with being put down, but I don't. You shouldn't, either," she said to the man's wife, startling the other woman into a look of wide-eyed entrapment.

The man's patronizing smirk faded into his own shock.

"I know how hard it is to leave." Joy continued speaking to the wife. "Even when you're being treated poorly. But it's worth it. Reach out to me if you need help. I promise I'll do everything I can to assist you."

"Who the *hell* do you think you are? You—" The man lurched toward her, but Axel fully blocked him, shoving his chest right up against the other man's, pushing him back a step.

"I will rip you in half," Axel assured him.

At that moment, a server came up to ask urgently, "Is there a problem?"

"No." The older man stepped back and grudgingly brushed at his jacket.

"Yes," Joy contradicted, thanking her months in the club for the ease with which the next words rolled off her tongue, firm and assertive. "That man is being insulting and aggressive toward me. He needs to be removed."

Then she walked away, head high. She didn't know where she was going or what happened behind her. She wanted to steal a glass of champagne off a passing tray, but was shaking so badly, she was sure she'd spill it down her front.

She was almost at their table when she realized Axel hadn't come with her. People were glancing at her curiously.

These things have a way of getting around.

More like that man had spread rumors through this room like a virus.

Oh God. Her throat started to ache. She wished the floor would open and swallow her.

"Well, that was some serious badassery." Quinn looped an arm around her. "You and I are going to be *very* good friends. I can tell. Let me introduce you to some of the most sarcastic people I know. You'll love them."

"I—" Joy couldn't help looking back the way she'd come. There was no sign of Axel, which made her heart swerve and dip anxiously.

"I put Micah on him," Quinn said. "He's big enough to hold your man back from the murder he was about to commit. You're welcome for keeping him out of jail."

"I didn't mean to make a scene," Joy said with agony.

"A scene? It was a master class in dealing with ass clowns. 'He's the kind of man who goes into strip clubs and scorns his wife? I'll help you leave him?' That was sniper-level assassination of character. Teach me."

"You're being nice," Joy said, but she found a weak smile as Quinn introduced her to someone from the British embassy. She was acutely aware that Axel still hadn't come after her.

I'll kill him.

Axel was in such a haze of rage, so ready to remove that scumbag himself, he didn't realize Joy had walked away until he heard Quinn say stridently, "Micah! I told Axel you'd find me. He wants to speak with you. I'll go after Joy."

That was when Axel had snapped out of his locked stare to see Joy wasn't here. His whole world screeched to a halt.

"I've got this, big guy." Quinn patted his arm. "You take

a beat. And *you*," she advised the piece of crap who'd insulted Joy, "should go save your marriage."

The other man's wife had already walked away as well.

Where was Joy? The ladies' room? Axel looked around. He couldn't spot her.

"What happened?" Micah asked. He was one of the richest men in Europe, running a family conglomerate that had weathered some ethics scandals in his father's time but was now recognized for its green initiatives and commitments to diversity and transparency.

"Gossip." Axel spat the word as though it was the most obscene curse ever uttered. Considering how it had been wielded against Joy, it was.

He pinched the bridge of his nose, sickened that Joy had been attacked. He was livid with himself that he'd put her in the position of becoming fodder for those ugly rumors, then ambushed by such gross behavior.

He glanced for the man who'd insulted Joy, still wanting to close his hand on the man's throat, but that vile filth had wisely dissolved into the crowd. If he had any sense of self-preservation, he had left the party and was on his way out of the country.

"The rumors around you opening your own firm?" Micah said with a frown. "I was hoping that was true. I wanted to talk to you about it."

Axel didn't have much interest in business at the moment, but he exchanged a few terse words with Micah, promising to set up a meeting.

"I need to catch up with my wife and take her home," Axel said.

"If Quinn has her under her wing, they're likely near our table." Micah led him to a small clutch of people who were all laughing except Joy.

She wore a strained smile and clung to a glass of wine, looking brittle enough to break.

"Let's go," Axel said.

She said a stilted good night, and they left.

Joy was both relieved and sick with apprehension. Her enjoyment in this evening was fully gone, but she wasn't ready to face the censure she was certain was coming.

The drive home was completed in ominous silence, making her stomach churn.

The second they walked into the penthouse, she blurted, "I'm so sorry."

"*You* are. Why?" Axel asked with muted outrage. "I knew where you worked when we married, Joy. There's no reason for you to be sorry. God." He poured drinks for both of them, asking sharply, "Have you told anyone?"

"*No.* Only Heskel's friend, Zander, the dance instructor he took me to that one time, but Heskel asked him to keep it confidential." Would Axel balk at her pursuing dance now, worried it would inflame the rumors?

"This stinks of Otto." Axel brought her a glass and took a deep gulp from his own. "The next time you speak to your father, ask if anyone has been snooping around."

"He knows not to talk to reporters." Axel had warned her their marriage would generate curiosity. "But the neighbor knew," she recalled.

"He must have had someone investigate you, looking for something to undermine our marriage. He's trying to damage my reputation when I'm on the verge of competing with him. He's trying to—" He bit that off and looked away, profile flexing with remorse.

"What?" she prompted, sensing something unpleasant was coming.

His mouth tightened, before he said reluctantly, "He's trying to build a case for not accepting you as his daughter."

For rejecting her.

Against her will, a low sob resounded in her throat, leaving an ache in her chest.

"I shouldn't have said that," he said.

"Why not? It's true." Her throat hurt. She had been fully prepared for *Axel* to reject her over this, but he seemed to be infuriated on her behalf. "What are you going to do?"

"Everything in my power to destroy him," he said with a curl of his lip and another sip of his drink.

"I mean about how this ruins your reputation."

"I didn't say it ruins it. I said he's trying to damage it. If he wants to play dirty, I'd like to issue a press release that he's your father and sought you out for a marriage contract he refuses to honor. But that affects you and your family." He emptied his glass and set it down hard. "So I'll find another way to gut him."

He took the glass she offered that she hadn't touched.

"Can I…" She cleared her throat. "Can I talk to Dad first? To explain all of this so he's not blindsided by it?"

Axel's brows crashed together. "You would consider making a statement? You don't have to acknowledge that Otto is your father, Joy. He's caused you enough pain. Tonight—" He closed his fist and stalked a few steps away, shoulders a hard line. "I'm sorry. That should never have happened. The fact that you knew how to deal with that bastard's remark because you've faced derision like that before? You wouldn't have had to work in the club if Otto had reached out to you when he learned about you."

"I don't care about that." Her voice broke a little at how ferociously he was defending her. "It's not about money that he did or didn't promise me. I don't care about getting one up on him, either. I just don't want him to have the power to ambush me like that. If all of my secrets are out, and Dad knows about him, Otto can't use any of it against me. He ceases to have any power over me."

Axel set aside the glass and came to her. He settled one hand on her hip, the other alongside her neck. His brow was pulled with concern, his gaze shadowed by remorse.

"I know I should apologize for drawing you into this, Joy, but Otto was always going to come after you. If not to keep me, to push out Mira. I'm sorry for what you're going through, but I'm not sorry for getting to you first and making this hard for him."

Her lips quivered. She had to press them together to steady them before she could speak.

"I thought you'd be angry at me. And think I was a liability." *I thought you'd send me home.* "I don't know what I bring to this marriage except—"

"You," he said, shifting his hand so he could set his thumb against her lips. "You bring you. That's enough."

Oh. Now she really was going to cry.

CHAPTER TWELVE

JOY'S FATHER TOOK the news really well.

"I thought there was more to this marriage than you were letting on," Paul said in his creaky voice. "Your mother and I always expected you to be curious about your birth parents, sweetheart. You didn't have to hide this from me. I completely understand."

That made her feel weepy enough to want to hug him through the screen, especially when she confessed her meeting with Otto had not gone as well as she'd hoped.

After some consoling words, Paul said, "What about your husband? Please tell me you're still happy with your marriage?"

"I am." She blinked with shock at how true that was. Her life here with Axel was more fulfilling than she could have anticipated.

She went on to describe the dance company and the performance she was hoping to be picked for, the language classes she had signed up for and her upcoming getaway to Sicily with Axel, for business and sunshine.

A friendly journalist came by the next afternoon, bringing a photographer who took candid photos of her and Axel lounging around the penthouse and standing at the rail of the terrace. Joy wore off-white trousers with a torso-hugging, long-sleeved lace top in the same color. Axel wore a black suit with a black shirt and a black tie.

"You make a striking couple," the journalist said. "How did you meet?"

Joy let Axel take the lead. He was using this opportunity to announce he'd fully broken away from Otto and had opened a competing firm, confirming what was already floating through the headlines.

When Axel casually mentioned he had met Joy after learning she was Otto's daughter, the woman's eyes popped in realization she was being given a scoop.

"I only learned my birth father's identity very recently." Joy didn't mention Lorena's name but filled in a few blanks about her adoption into her American family, adding that she had wanted to meet Otto, but that they didn't have a meaningful relationship.

"Is my research correct? Were you performing as an exotic dancer prior to your marriage?" The journalist was giving Joy a chance to deny it.

"I was."

"Plug the company you're with now," Axel prompted her.

"I'm still in the audition process," Joy demurred. "But Axel is right. The choreographer deserves a mention for the production she's putting together." Joy offered up the dates and venue for the expected performance.

"Does your marriage have anything to do with you leaving Vorstoben?" the woman asked Axel. "By that, I mean the timing of your broken engagement to Mira Braun? She left the company, too. There seems to be some conflict between her and her father?" she probed.

"I can't speak for Mira," Axel said firmly. "Otto was aware for years that my plan was to run my own firm. I would prefer we hadn't come to legal action, but I'm confident the courts will side with me in our dispute."

The article came out the next day while they were on the ground in Sicily.

A small media storm ensued, but Axel was busy closing a deal on a massive resort complex that had ground to a halt due to various issues. That evening, they attended a mixer of executives and their spouses, and even though people seemed aware of the article and Joy's former job, everyone was more excited that their project had been saved than interested in gossiping about her.

When they returned to Berlin, Joy felt lighter than she had in years. Her family was thriving and looking forward to being together in California. Her financial troubles were gone. She no longer felt she had to hide her work at Martini's, and she was making new friends among her fellow dancers while doing what she loved.

The only thing she loved more than dancing every day was coming home to her husband.

They had fallen into a routine of discussing their plans for the day in the hot tub, parting after breakfast, then coming together again in the evening. Often, they went out again because they had engagements, but Joy was no longer afraid of those. She was seeing familiar faces and had been invited onto a charity board for performing arts that interested her.

She was on top of the world and told her brother that when he called one evening.

"I'm still trying to get used to this," David said with concern. "It doesn't feel like *you*, Joy. I thought you wanted to be a nurse? What if you need something to fall back on?"

A wave of exasperated affection washed over her. David

was caring and protective, but he didn't have a clue who she was at heart. Not the way Axel understood her.

"I'm dancing. I'm happy," she insisted. "You'll see when we come to California."

That trip was another month away, but she was looking forward to it. She and Axel would touch down in Chicago long enough to collect Paul before flying him to California themselves so Joy could help him get settled in his new home while meeting Carrie and David's newest addition.

"How's your brother?" Axel asked idly when they were undressing for bed.

"Good, but he asked me why I gave up the nurse training. You knew the day you met me that I was only pursuing it for Dad. That it wasn't my real passion. David was genuinely baffled that I would walk away from what he views as a solid profession. It made me realize how different I am from him. From all of them. They love me. I know that. And I love them, but I always felt this sense of being a bit of an oddity. Even my mother was very practical, working at City Hall because they had a decent pension. She encouraged my dance as a hobby while I was growing up, but it wasn't something she thought I should pursue as a living. They were concerned that I chose performing arts at college. When I gave it up for Todd, I think they were a little relieved. No one asked how I really felt about it."

"That's probably why you did give it up. You were trying to fit into their expectations."

"I really was," she said with dawning understanding. "I always had this lingering fear they'd reject me if I didn't stay between the lines. On the surface, Todd was cookie-cutter husband material. That's why I tried so hard to make it work with him."

"And when you realized he wouldn't make you happy,

that their way didn't make *you* happy, you took up dancing for money, trying to show them that you could support them on your own terms."

"I wasn't that passive-aggressive about it. Not consciously, anyway." But he wasn't wrong. "I was trying to keep my dream alive in whatever way I could make it happen."

"Then I played on that to force this marriage on you, but I don't regret it. Not as much as I should." He took her hands and pulled them behind his back so she came up against him. "I see how much it means to you. It's where you feel you truly belong, isn't it?"

She nodded, growing emotional because he saw her so much more clearly than her family ever had.

I love him, she thought as she tightened her arms around him.

As his arms enfolded her, she knew she would remember this as the moment she fell. It wasn't even a fall. It was a sense of coming to rest. Because Axel might be demanding and remote and ferocious, but he always took such care with her.

His hands moved over her, and as so often happened with him, she felt pulled into him as though magnetized. This was where belonged, she thought, closing her eyes against the press of heat behind them.

She tilted back her head, and they kissed, long and slow and with such a deep tenderness, her heart ached in the best possible way.

His hands moved lazily over her. They were still capable of frantic lovemaking, but neither of them was in a hurry tonight. This was a coming together that went beyond their bodies. For whatever reason, he was making her feel cherished, and she was drinking it up, wanting to give him all of herself. Not just her body, but the heart that felt cradled by his palm when he cupped her breast. The soul that condensed on the air when she gasped in pleasure.

I love you, she thought, as she licked beneath his ear and breathed his name toward the ceiling.

When she reached between them to caress his erection, he swore and said with quiet urgency, "I need to be inside you."

His hands went under her butt, and she hopped, grasping her arms around his neck and her legs around his waist. As he carried her to the bed and came down on her, she felt his erection against the tender folds that were aching to envelop him.

"You're shaking," he said.

"I want you so much," she said helplessly, feeling hot and wet and so aroused, she thought she would combust. "I don't know how to…" Express it. Reveal it. Make him feel it.

"Me, too."

Then they were tumbling across the bed, stripping off clothes until finally he pressed inside her.

They both calmed. Now his kiss turned languorous. He shifted so his weight was on one elbow, and he could send tingling pleasure through her with the lazy stroke of his hand. His knee crooked, and he secured their hips tighter, so they were locked like one of those brain-teaser puzzles she had never figured out how to unravel.

Who would want to? This was how they were meant to be. It was where she wanted to be. *This is home.*

I love you, she thought as he shifted over her and began to move in slow, powerful thrusts. *I love you*, she thought as the glorious tension built and sunlight filled her veins. *I love you*, was the only thought in her mind as the pleasure coalesced into a pinpoint of utter perfection, then expanding in waves of ecstasy.

His hand clamped on her shoulder, and his sweating body shook. A broken shout left him, and she lifted her hips for his final, rocking thrusts.

It was seismic. Cataclysmic. For a long, timeless moment, they were melded into one, caught in pure, shared ecstasy.

Joy wanted to stay in this liminal space of blissful unity forever, but physical reality crept in. Their hearts were pounding, their skin tacky enough to sting as he made the monumental effort to roll off her. Her body was weak, her mouth dry from panting.

But she was still in the glorious and dazed state of harmony. The words left her before she'd thought them through.

"I love you."

CHAPTER THIRTEEN

AXEL WAS ON his back, scraped clean of thought while his body was still recovering from lovemaking that had been intense even by the standard he and Joy usually set. His heart was still hammering, his chest billowing as his lungs snatched for oxygen.

She was on the pill now so he didn't have an excuse to roll away to remove the condom. He was too weak to do something like that anyway. And he couldn't do that to her. He might not know how to return that emotion, but if Joy was offering it to him, he couldn't reject it. Not when he knew how sensitive she was to being scorned.

But, *I love you*?

It shouldn't hurt like an acid burn, but it did.

"I didn't mean to say that," she whispered in an agonized voice.

"Did you mean it?" He turned his head on the pillow. "It's only been six weeks."

"I know." Her brow flinched, and her lashes dropped to hide her eyes. "I know that you…don't."

He looked to the ceiling, experiencing a new version of an old emotion: helplessness. He hated to hurt her and didn't know how to avoid it. It made him feel powerless—another emotion he couldn't bear.

His whole reason for marrying her had been to prevent

Otto from taking advantage of him, but more frequently these days, he felt as though he'd taken advantage of Joy, building expectations in her that he couldn't fulfill.

"Joy—" He started to roll toward her, not sure what he would say, but she turned her back on him.

"I should get some sleep. Inga has already let a couple of dancers go. I want to be on my game tomorrow." She reached to turn out the light on her side.

He bit back a curse, aware he'd handled this badly but unsure how to fix it.

Things remained stilted between them. Axel was frustrated and mentally likened it to the way a storm or other natural event might thwart a project. It couldn't be changed or undone. It could only be weathered.

His mechanical brain wanted to find the solution, though. Or a way to prevent something like this from happening in future.

He channeled all his brooding into his new company, AxSev Engineering.

One of the key differences between himself and Otto was that Otto was a businessman who had taken over his father's engineering firm. Axel was an engineer who had become a businessman. Otto had also been born into wealth. He'd had a cushion to fall back on, so he was more comfortable with risk.

Axel had always taken a more methodical approach to his life, carefully amassing his material wealth to lay a foundation to support his next level. He brought the same attitude to his new company. Each investor and employee and potential project was inspected for quality and durability, like a brick in a structure he wanted to last for a thousand years.

Which wasn't to say things weren't happening quickly. He'd been deliberating on this for years. He knew what he wanted and took profound satisfaction in tapping every brick into place.

He could have been doing this two years ago, of course, but his resentment toward Otto over the delay had lost much of its edge, worn away by something he hadn't expected: Joy.

How could he hate Otto for procrastinating and manipulating him into this marriage when he liked being married to her?

At least he had liked it, before this discord had arisen between them.

He wanted to smooth things over, but Joy wasn't *here*. Even before this, she had been spending a lot of time at the studio and the fitness center, swimming laps to improve her endurance in a way that wouldn't cause her stress injuries.

She was determined to achieve her goals, and he admired her for that, but recognized a small jealousy inside himself over how much of her time was monopolized by it. He didn't want to feel threatened by it, but he did—maybe because he suspected she was using it to avoid him. He'd hurt her by not returning her love, and she had withdrawn.

The weight of being loved was so damned crushing, though. One of his earliest memories was his father saying, *Your Mutti loves you. She's counting on you to look after her when I'm not here.* Then his father had disappeared for a few weeks—serving time, Axel learned much later. What little money had been in his mother's purse had disappeared quickly, leaving Axel to scrounge food from a dumpster behind the grocer.

After his father died, his mother had said similar things countless times. *You're a good boy for taking care of me. I love you.* But those words had never put food on the table. Even when she'd finally embraced sobriety, her love had only felt like something that imposed a certain duty on him. *I know I was not the best mother to you, but I love you. I hope you'll forgive me.*

Axel was doing Joy a favor by not putting that sort of indebtedness on her. He met all her real needs, didn't he? He was giving her a very good life. Wasn't he?

He entered the penthouse to hear her upstairs, talking to someone. Her sister-in-law, it sounded like, judging by the excited babble of a toddler and the gurgle of laughter in Joy's tone.

"Okay, go show Abuela so I can talk with Tía," Carrie was saying as Axel reached the top of the stairs. "He misses you as much as I do, but get back to your text. She wants you as the lead?"

"One of them, yes. I'm very excited."

"That's fantastic! Congratulations! How are you going to celebrate?"

"Oh, I don't know," Joy said in a downplaying tone. "We have a party to go to this evening. I don't know the hosts, but these things are important to Axel, so I'll probably just buy myself a new leotard tomorrow. As if I need more of those!" She chuckled at herself.

"You deserve more than that," her sister-in-law chided. "This is a big deal. We'll do something big when you're here. We'll have a lot to celebrate by then."

"We will—Oh. Axel's home." Joy noticed him. The glow in her eyes dimmed to wariness, and her tone changed to the aloof one he was beginning to despise. "What time is the party?" she asked him. "I can be ready in twenty."

She wore her bathrobe. Her hair was pulled back from her freshly washed face, and she was midway through applying makeup.

"We have lots of time. Finish your call. Hello, Carrie." He stepped into view of the screen.

"Hi, Axel. It's good to see you, but I'll let you go," the very pregnant Carrie said. "I have to get ready for work. I was just excited when I saw Joy's text and wanted to congratulate her. Buy your wife some flowers," she instructed. "I'll talk to you both soon."

The women blew kisses at each other, and Joy ended the call.

"You got in?" Axel asked. "For the performance?"

"I did." A little of the sparkle returned to her eyes, and she couldn't seem to fight the grin that pulled at her lips as she added with shy pride, "As one of the leads."

"Why didn't you call me?" The fact she seemed to have texted her family without telling him was a surprisingly deep cut.

"I was going to tell you when I saw you." She sounded defensive and turned back to her makeup and the mirror.

"Well, I'm proud of you." He drew her back around and into a hug, even picked her up.

She stiffened in surprise as he turned in a circle and set her back on her feet, then she released a soft laugh of surprise, flustered and blushing. "Thank you." Her expression shifted into earnestness. "I couldn't have done it without you so, really. Thank you."

"Don't say that." He knew what dance meant to her. He was glad that he had some tiny part in making this happen for her, but he squeezed her shoulders and rubbed the soft velour of the robe down her arms. "You did the work to earn it."

"I know, but…" She shrugged, then shifted away from his touch.

He simply couldn't stand it any longer. "Carrie is right. We should celebrate. Let's skip the party and spend the weekend in Heiligendamm. The days are warm enough for beachcombing. It won't be overrun with tourists yet."

She lifted her gaze, properly meeting his eyes for the first time in days while her brow quirked with tentative optimism. "Really?"

If it meant she would quit avoiding him? "Yes."

They left within the hour, taking a helicopter to an elegant resort on the Baltic Sea.

Joy had been wallowing in misery for days. She had been okay with being in a loveless marriage before she'd fallen in love herself. Before she'd *said* it.

Maybe, if she hadn't had a bone-deep legacy of being rejected, she could have withstood Axel's rebuff more easily, but she kept wondering whether she was actually lovable. Yes, her family loved her, but they didn't fully understand her. The man who did understand her didn't love her.

The one thing that had saved her this week was dance. It had given her an outlet for her sorrow and loneliness and yearning and unrequited feelings. Inga had hugged her when she offered her the lead, calling her "one of our brightest stars."

In the dance studio, at least, she was truly wanted. Integral, even.

She wasn't sure if Axel was trying to spoil her to make up for their fight—which hadn't even been a fight. She was glad to spend time with him. She loved him. Of course she wanted to be with him, but she also felt as though she walked around without a layer of skin, everything feeling raw and exposed.

She was instantly charmed by the historic buildings, though, all painted white. He had booked them into a tower suite of a luxury hotel, one with two floors and endless views of the water. She couldn't help but relax as they strolled the beach before dinner, then wilted themselves in the sauna. The next day, they had a couple's massage, walked, ate delicious food and made love.

It was good. It always was. She felt as though her soul was wrenched from her body, but when it was over, she couldn't relax in his arms the way she used to do. She made an excuse to use the bathroom, then asked, "Do you mind if I catch up on my sleep?"

He seemed surprised but rose to make a few calls.

This should have been the reconnection they needed, but she couldn't help keeping a certain guard up, even as she called herself a fool for letting his reaction to her confession bother her so much. He cared about her. She knew he did. He gave her a good life. And he was right. They hadn't been together very long.

She tried to let go of her hurt and simply enjoy their time together.

On Sunday, she brought their refilled coffee mugs up to the bedroom and sighed at the glorious view of sunshine and dark blue water. "I could look at that forever."

"Do you want to stay another night?" Axel set aside his phone.

He was on the bench seat that ran under the line of windows facing the sea. He slouched against pillows piled into the corner and rearranged himself, waving to invite her to join him.

She sat in front of him so her back was against his chest,

tailbone in the V of his opened legs. Sunshine poured over them, and a fresh, salty breeze came in through the open windows.

"I would love that, but I can't," she said, trying to relax into his warmth. "I probably won't even have a full weekend free until after the show. We have costume fittings coming up and meetings about set design."

He made a grumbled noise of dismay and draped his forearm across the front of her shoulders.

"I will try not to be impatient while your dancing takes you away from me. I am very proud of you, you know. In fact..." His long arm stretched behind her, to a nearby table, then came back with a velvet box the size of a deck of cards.

"What—? Axel, that's not necessary." A pang hit her heart as she looked at the box. It was a glancing blow, the kind that was an elbow in the face, unintentional, but it still hurt like hell.

"To commemorate your achievement." He opened it to reveal a gold chain of intricate links and a pretty pendant. A freeform pearl was trapped inside a cage of gold where the swirling bars were encrusted with tiny diamonds.

It was beautiful, but... She swallowed.

"You don't like it?" he asked into the silence.

"I—I'll wear it if you want me to." Her voice cracked as she heard how ungrateful she sounded. "I don't want *things* from you, Axel." She sat up and moved down the bench, instantly chilled.

"I don't know what else to give you, Joy. Things are all I have," he said darkly. He turned on the bench so his own feet hit the floor. He snapped the case closed and dropped it in the yawning space between them. "At least you can sell this if—"

"If what?" she asked with alarm.

"I don't know. If you're hungry and don't have anything else."

She saw then how deeply his early years of poverty still affected him. This was why he didn't trust, why he couldn't offer all of himself. "I would never sell a gift from my husband."

"Apparently, you're not even going to accept it."

She stared into his affronted glare, heart aching, and thought, *You didn't want my love when I offered it.*

His phone rang.

He sent an annoyed glance over his shoulder to where he'd left it on the windowsill. They had turned their phones off yesterday, but apparently their second honeymoon was over. He reached to answer it.

Joy tucked her hands under her thighs, staring at the unmade bed with its pillow-top mattress and abundance of pillows and luxury linens.

Look what you have, she scolded herself for the millionth time. Did it really matter that he hadn't said those words back to her?

Or did it matter doubly because she was settling for less than she deserved again, afraid that if she pushed for what she really wanted, he would reject her and she'd have no one?

"Mira?" he said crisply into his phone.

Joy heard the muffled feminine tones, but couldn't hear what was said. She didn't have enough German to follow it anyway. The way Axel went very still, however, pulled her spine and shoulders tight.

He said a few things in a hollow tone, then ended with, "Bis später," which he said to Joy all the time when he was on his way home.

"What happened?" she asked, stomach pulled into knots of apprehension.

"Otto's housekeeper just called her. The police and coroner are on their way. Mira's going there now."

Not an ambulance. "He's gone?" Joy's mind couldn't even comprehend it.

"They suspect a heart event. It seems to have happened when he was on his way to bed last night." His voice was low and somber. "I said I'd inform Umberto and the board."

He was already bringing his phone to his ear, not giving her a chance to say anything. Not giving her a chance to console him.

Did he need consoling? She couldn't tell.

She rose to dress, thoughts as scattered as the belongings they'd littered about the room. They would have to leave as soon as possible. She began to shake out a shirt to fold it for packing.

"Wirklich?" Axel sounded as though the word was punched out of him.

She snapped her head, watching him as he exchanged a few more words, then ended the call.

She dropped the clothes in her hands and went across to him.

"What happened? Are you okay?" She instinctively set a hand on his shoulder. It was both slumped under a great weight and steely with tension.

"No. Yes. Fine," he lied as he rubbed his stubbled jaw. "I told Umberto we're on our way back." He stood and found the trousers and shirt he'd worn to dinner last night. "Mira said the housekeeper called her because she though Mira was his next-of-kin, but given all of this…" He waved between them. "Mira wasn't sure. That's why she called me."

An arrow seemed to spear into Joy's chest. She clutched at the pain there.

"*I'm* not," she protested. "Am I?"

"Umberto said there will have to be a will search, and the validity of Otto's marriage contract is still to be determined by the courts, but as far as he knows, Otto left Vorstoben to me."

CHAPTER FOURTEEN

AXEL WAS IN SHOCK. How could he not be? Otto had been reaching retirement age, but he had seemed in good health. This was the last thing Axel had expected to happen.

Which prompted the chilling thought that he had killed Otto himself by taking such an aggressive stance and putting so much pressure on him.

He saw the same self-recrimination in Mira's drawn face when they came together in Umberto's office that afternoon. Umberto was freshly shaved, but his hair was rumpled and his tie looked as though he'd already given it a yank from his throat.

It was only the three of them there, all in somber suits behind a closed door while rain buffeted the window.

"This will was in place before Otto learned of Joy's existence. Forgive me for being blunt," Umberto said to Mira, "but Otto took the attitude that if he was leaving the company to someone who was not his biological child, he preferred it go to Axel."

"That's not news," Mira said in a strained voice.

"In terms of his other assets, most were acquired during his marriage to your mother and are considered joint property, so he agreed you were entitled to those. We had been discussing other options since he had learned he had a biological child. He had intentions around leaving something to Joy, but as his marriage contract demonstrated, he wanted her to live here and have a firm connection to his life before he made any changes to these arrangements. That's why he stipulated you should be married to her for a year before he would transfer the shares." He turned to Axel now. "At this point, your wife stands to inherit nothing. There is room to challenge that with the marriage contract, if you wish to pursue it."

Did Axel want to enforce the contract and incite more bad blood with Mira so his wife could have a piece of the pie?

"It would muddy things and take time for the courts to make a decision," Umberto warned. "I expect that would have further negative effect on the company." The lawyer was nudging them toward accepting Otto's wishes as they were currently stated.

"I'll discuss it with Joy." Axel rubbed his jaw, still unable to fully take this in. He walked out with Mira a few minutes later, both of them silent until they were in the elevator.

"Drink?" Axel suggested.

"God, yes," Mira breathed.

They walked across the street to the bar in a hotel lobby. It was quiet, being midweek and the hour between the lunch and dinner rush. They ordered, then sat in silence.

"I should have reached out to you sooner. It's been..." How did he describe these last weeks of a whirlwind marriage and breaking away from a man who, it turned out, had wanted him to have the company he'd been fighting to take? "How have you been? Are you and DeStefano—"

"No," she cut in with a strained look on her face.

Axel dropped it. He had warned Mira off Rocco years ago, aware that Otto had a grudge against the man. He still didn't know what that was about, but Mira seemed to have decided Otto's rival wasn't her best ally after all.

She nodded a thank-you as their drinks were delivered and took a deep sip from hers.

"When I spoke to the head of the board, he asked what terms I'd set to come back as CEO," Axel said. The board didn't know yet that Axel was in line to inherit Otto's majority share, but he knew for a fact they'd been at panic stations from the moment Axel had left on his honeymoon. Things had been falling apart ever since, growing worse as Mira had gutted the financial ledgers.

"I had a call from him, too," she said. "They assumed I would be inheriting Otto's shares and wanted to know if I'd support you as CEO or if I would insist on running the company myself."

"What did you say?"

"I wanted to tell them the truth. All of it," she said with embittered weariness. "But I said something noncommittal because I've already done enough damage to Vorstoben. None of this is your fault. Or theirs. The company didn't do this to me. He did. My mother did." Tears of betrayal came into her eyes, but she blinked them away, chin coming up, gaze pointing out the window.

"You're entitled to an executive position, Mira. You've put in the hours. Otto never gave you enough credit or let you shine to your full potential. Tell me what you want."

"I don't even know anymore," she said with a strain in her voice. "I thought I did, for about a minute." She threw him an ironic smile. "It's so true to form that he didn't even give me the fight I wanted." Her gaze turned agonize, but curious. "What's she like?"

"Takes after her mother, one presumes, since she has a big heart." He was being facetious but also sincere. "She dances. Beautifully. She's very passionate about it. She's funny. Gutsy when she needs to be." He was saying too much and set his teeth together.

"You sound like you like her a lot. Did he?" Mira asked with a scathing edge on her tone.

"No," Axel said flatly. "He was furious that I married her without telling him. He took it out on her. I never should have brought her here. It was cruel."

"You mean he was."

Not just Otto. All Axel had wanted was this company, certain Joy's participation in their marriage could be bought for the right price.

I don't want things from you.

She had wanted more than assets from Otto, too. Acceptance. Welcome. Love.

"I knew how he would behave and I brought her here anyway." Like a lamb to the slaughter. He had hoped that she was confusing lovemaking and love again, but guilt was rising in him like a tide. She loved him, and he was hurting her as badly as Otto had.

All of this for something he was going to get anyway.

I helped her, though. She's dancing again. Surely that counted for something?

"I think his death is my fault," Mira whispered, face crumpling with repentance. "I knew he was taking blood thinners. When I saw you'd married her, I knew he would be angry about it. I sent him flowers congratulating him on his daughter's marriage. Vile, right?"

"Don't do that to yourself." Before learning compassion from his wife, it wouldn't have occurred to Axel to stand and draw Mira into a hug, but he couldn't let her wallow in blame.

"I—" She was startled. They'd never been affectionate

with each other, but she let him hug her and briefly rested her head on his chest. He heard her take a shaken breath.

"I did my share of pulling his supports," Axel acknowledged. "I publicly shamed him. Let's remember that he was reaping what he sowed."

"I suppose." She drew back, mouth pouted with sadness, and patted his lapel. "Thank you. I… Can I just say…" She lifted a crooked smile to him. "Our marriage never would have worked. This feels like I'm hugging my brother."

"Agreed," he said wryly and cupped her shoulder so he could set a very brotherly kiss on her brow. "We'll see a lot of each other over the next few days, but call me anytime."

"I will. And don't feel guilty about getting the company, Axel. You put in the time, too. I've always known you were the best person to run it."

Axel didn't come home until well after the dinner hour. He had a five o'clock shadow and his tie was over his arm with his jacket. His shirt sleeves were rolled up, his shirt open at the throat. He looked exhausted. He went straight to the sideboard to pour a drink.

"I've been in meetings with Gerard and some people with Vorstoben, getting out a press release." He sighed wearily. "Otto has some distant cousins, but the funeral arrangements seem to have fallen onto Mira and me. We agree that it's best to hold a service as soon as possible."

"Is there anything I can do?" Joy felt sick every time she thought about the fact she'd only met Otto once. Now her birth father was gone, and she would never have another chance at a relationship with him. Not that she was sure she would have wanted one, but it felt so final to know she never could.

"Heskel is taking lead with one of Otto's assistants."

Axel threw back his drink in one go, then hissed out a breath. "Umberto said Otto's most recent will leaves the company to me. Everything else was joint property with Mira's mother, so it's going to her. If we accept this will, I can start pulling Vorstoben out of its nosedive immediately. Every day counts at this point. But you have the option of suing for what Otto promised to you in the marriage contract." He turned to face her.

She blinked. Then released a husky chuckle that held no humor. "Wouldn't that mean using your money to sue you for half of a company that you would run anyway? And wouldn't I have to wait until we completed our year of marriage?"

"Yes. But you said this was never about the money," he reminded her in a challenging tone.

"It's not." She tried not to be insulted by his assertive tone, remembering he was still processing all of this himself, but she still felt superfluous. Pushed away. "I've never felt I had a right to things that Mira believed were hers," she added in a murmur.

"Good. I need to make some calls." He walked into his office and closed the door.

That was it? Decision made?

She stood there for a few minutes, wondering if she had made a huge mistake in letting go of her option to sue. Her reasons for marrying Axel had never been about getting anything from Otto, but Axel had made certain promises to convince her to marry him.

Her own words echoed in her ears.

Wouldn't I have to wait until we completed our year of marriage?

Biting her thumbnail, she sent a message to her lawyer, then fell into bed. It had been a long day, and her mornings started early now, so she could get her stretches in before heading to the studio.

She didn't speak to Axel until breakfast the next day.

"I need my driver," he told her. "Heskel is arranging one to get you back and forth to the studio. Discuss it with him if you have any issues."

She almost demurred, but she could see he had a lot on his mind. At least, that was what she hoped was behind his terse, distracted tone.

She couldn't escape the thought that Axel didn't need to be married to her anymore. He had only proposed to get Vorstoben, and now he had it. Did he even want to be married to her anymore?

The next few days passed in a blur. LaShonda said she would review the prenup contract and get back to her. Joy then missed an afternoon dance rehearsal to attend Otto's service.

She wasn't sure if it was the somber nature of the afternoon or all that was going on, but she felt very removed from Axel even when she stood beside him. They had barely seen each other since being away. They shared the bed for a few hours every night, but they hadn't made love.

At the service, most of the people were from Vorstoben. Joy didn't know any of them, but she smiled when she caught up with Heskel's husband, Klaus. They'd only met a few times, and she was a little surprised he was here, considering he'd been treated so badly by Otto when he had his accident.

Klaus grinned wryly, saying, "Technically, I've been re-hired by Vorstoben. Axel is keeping AxSev as an ancillary division. I'll be the head engineer there. You didn't know?"

It was another example of how estranged they'd become in a few short days.

"He's been so busy, we've barely spoken," she murmured, then saw Axel was looking for her. "Excuse me." She hurried over to him.

"You two haven't met. Mira, Joy." Axel introduced her to the tall brunette.

Mira wore a black dress that flattered her slender frame. She spoke through the dotted veil on her tiny black hat. "It's nice to meet you."

"And you," Joy said sincerely, holding out her hand. "I'm very sorry…" Her voice trailed off. Was she sorry for Mira's loss? Sorry her birth mother had had an affair with a man who was married to Mira's mother? "I'm sorry this is such a complicated mess," she said with a pained smile.

"Me, too." Mira's lips twisted with pained humor. "I'll also preemptively apologize for stealing so much of your husband's time in the next while. There's a lot to be dealt with, and I don't really have anyone else to lean on." Mira flinched as she said that.

Joy had the impression the anguish in her expression had nothing to do with losing Otto. She almost suggested they have a glass of wine sometime, but the service started.

It was yet another long, draining day. When they got home, Axel said, "Hot tub?"

"I have an early morning. I need to sleep." She could have stayed up with him. The hot tub often led to lovemaking, and she could have used that stress release and a feeling of closeness with him.

Except she wasn't sure how close they were anymore. She kept thinking, *He doesn't need me.* It left an ache in her chest that she avoided by diving into sleep.

They didn't have a proper discussion until two days later, on Saturday. She was dozing when Axel reached across the mattress for her.

"You're here," he said with sleepy discovery, grazing his palm over her hip, then pulling her closer.

Her blood zinged the way it always did when she came into contact with him, but she stiffened, panicking that she would turn emotional—desperate, even—if she made love with him.

"I thought you had the day off," he said as she rolled away and sat up on the far edge of the bed.

"I do, but I have a costume fitting later."

"Joy." He sighed as he rolled onto his back. "We need to talk."

"I know." She didn't want to, though. She would hear things that hurt. Maybe he might even say that he didn't want to be married to her any longer.

She stood and began to dress in yoga pants and a loose shirt.

"Are you angry about the contract? That I said you shouldn't pursue it?" He stayed in the bed propped on an elbow, looking dangerously sexy with his shadowed jaw and heavy eyelids.

"I'm the one who said I didn't want to pursue it." She ran a brush through her hair, then twisted it into a clip.

"What then? You're still upset that…"

She turned to stare at him.

His jaw was clenched, his mouth tight, his gaze flinty.

"You're not going to say it?" she asked on a bitter laugh. "Yes, I am still upset that you don't love me."

"Joy." He flinched.

"I know that's not something you can control. I don't blame you for it." Her voice broke. "I just can't help thinking there's a reason you can't love me. That I lack something—"

"Don't." He threw off the covers and stood, then yanked on his underwear. "The flaw is in me. I don't know how to give you what you need."

"Then why keep me here?" The words blurted out of her.

He paused closing the fly on his jeans to stare at her. "Is there somewhere you'd rather be?" His tone was very deep and ominous.

"I'm asking what you gain if I stay." Her heart was in her throat, thinning her voice to a strident pitch while her lips stuttered out the questions that had been plaguing her. "What do you need me for now that you've got Vorstoben? You don't need to shove me down Otto's throat. You don't need to prove to anyone that this is a real marriage. I don't know how much longer I can keep pretending it is."

His head snapped back. "It's as real as it's likely to get."

"Yes, I know that." That was why she had completely lost faith in it.

His zip was overly loud as he yanked it closed. "So you want to leave?"

"I can't, can I?" Silently, she ordered herself to shut up. She was ruining everything, but her mouth kept going. "I can't leave you unless you release me. That's what LaShonda said. If I walk away, I lose all the support for my father. That's what I get from this marriage, but what do you get? Orgasms? Was I supposed to give you one of those this morning?"

"Those are voluntary, and I was under the impression you liked them as much as I do. But if you want my permission to leave, then you have it," he snapped. "Go. I release you."

She sucked in a breath, astonished by how easily he said it. By how much it hurt. He wasn't even going to try to fight for her? He really didn't want her.

Her phone alarm began to burble. She snatched it up to silence it, remembering why she'd set it. She scooped up her handbag from the table by the closet and started down the stairs.

"That's it? You're leaving?" His voice seemed to echo off the rafters. "That tells me exactly how much you love me, doesn't it?"

She stopped on the stairs and looked backward at him, unable to believe he'd said that.

He stood in the open doorway to their bedroom. His bedroom. His house. She'd never felt more like a houseguest in this marriage.

"I'm due for my costume fitting," she said with the last threads of her fraying poise.

It was a white lie. The alarm was to remind her to wake up in time. She didn't have to leave right now. She only wanted the excuse to leave, before she fully broke down in front of him.

"And you never even wanted my love," she reminded him. "So fine. I take it back. I release you."

"Frau Severin." The doorman looked up with a smile as she came out of the elevator. "This came for you this morning. I didn't want to call up too early—are you all right?"

"Fine," she lied and took the envelope he offered her, shoving it into her bag and walking outside. That was when she remembered her driver wasn't coming for another hour.

She started walking. She knew the route well enough by now that she covered the distance to the studio in steps of blind fury and acute heartache, arriving early for her fitting.

Thankfully, the appointments were staggered, so there were only a few people in the room when Joy walked in with swollen eyes and a face splotchy from crying.

"What happened?" Inga asked with startled concern.

"A spat with Axel." It was so much worse than a spat. *Go. I release you.*

Joy was devastated. Her instinct was to catch the first

plane home, but as she stood for her fitting, she knew she couldn't let a man knock her off her stride again. Even if her marriage was over, her dance career wasn't. She would stay in Berlin at least until after the performance.

How, though? Where?

She was trying to figure things out as she picked up her bag. Her phone was pinging with texts, so she glanced at the screen. There were two from her driver and another from Axel.

Your driver is here. Where are you?

Where did he think? Gawd. She silenced her notifications and dropped her phone into her bag, noticing the envelope the doorman had given her.

She opened it, mostly to put off having to go home to face Axel again. Then she had to lean on the wall, finding herself on the floor by the time she had finished reading.

She started again, trying to take it in.

My dear,
I believe you are my niece. My sister was Lorena Fontaine. I'm in Berlin on business this week. My number is below. I would very much like to meet you if you have time. I'm staying with my wife at—

"Joy?" One of her fellow dancers crouched down before her, asking with concern, "Are you okay?"

"What?" She touched the tickle on her cheek and realized she was crying again, this time for a whole new reason. "Yes." She was better than she'd been in a very long while. "Do you have a car? I need to go to a hotel."

CHAPTER FIFTEEN

AXEL WOULD NEVER have described himself as someone who snapped, but this morning that was exactly what had happened. He'd been trying to hold on to Joy since she had confessed her love, but she'd been slipping away from him, bit by bit.

I don't want things from you. Why keep me here? I don't know how much longer I can keep pretending.

There'd been such rejection and stark unhappiness in her words he'd arrived at his breaking point. There had always been an expiry date on their relationship. She was right. He didn't need her. Not the way he had two months ago when he proposed to her.

Even so, he'd been blindsided by the fact she felt trapped and wanted to leave him. When she had mapped out why she couldn't, a host of emotions had accosted him: guilt at holding onto her. Inadequacy that he wasn't offering enough. Anger that she was reducing their marriage to money and orgasms. Hurt.

Yes, he'd been hurt by the way she'd been shutting him out, so he'd snapped and told her to go. Then he'd been so stung as she walked away, he'd taken a shot that was fathoms beneath him.

She'd responded exactly as he deserved, by throwing his own words back in his face.

You never even wanted my love. So fine. I take it back. I release you.

She might as well have plunged a knife into his chest. Every breath hurt.

The buzz from the doorman yanked him from his brooding.

"Yes," he said curtly.

"Frau Severin's driver is here. I explained that she left an hour ago. She hasn't answered his texts. Did you have any instructions for him?"

"She *walked* to the studio?"

"I presume so?"

Axel tried texting her but didn't get a reply, so he sent the driver to the studio, expecting she would need a lift home.

A few minutes later, the driver informed him she wasn't there.

"Ask Inga to call me," he instructed the driver.

"She was here," the choreographer said when he answered her call. "But she left at least thirty minutes ago."

"Walking? Did she say she was coming home?" Axel asked.

"I didn't ask. Although…" She cleared her throat and lowered her voice. "She seemed upset when she arrived."

Yeah. He knew.

"Let me know if you hear from her," he said gruffly, thinking, *Please. Please let her be all right.*

Of course she was all right, he thought impatiently. It sounded like she had walked to the studio because she was angry with him. She was probably walking home, still clearing her head and cooling her temper. She had started to get her bearings in the city and knew which streets to avoid. She was picking up enough German to ask for help if she needed it. She was resourceful. She'd grown up in

Chicago, for God's sake. She was tough enough to deal with anyone who got fresh with her.

None of that reassured him. A sick churn of gravel sat in the pit of his gut, urging him to hit the Undo button and take back those biting words he'd hurled at her. *Go. I release you.*

What the hell had possessed him?

Restless, he took a quick inventory to see if she'd taken anything more than her handbag. Her dance bag was here. Her passport was in the safe. Her jacket was in the closet.

She hadn't left him. Even though he'd told her to.

The ache in his chest sharpened. Where the hell had she gone?

When his phone rang, he snatched it up, but it was only Mira.

"Yes?" he said tersely.

"I have to get Otto's mansion ready for sale. It occurred to me, there's so much art there. I took what belonged to Mom ages ago, so everything there is something Otto bought. Joy should have a look and take what she wants. It's not family portraits or anything, but she should have something of his, even as an investment."

"I'll mention it when I see her. She's out."

"You sound mad. What's wrong?" she asked with concern.

"We had a fight. She went to the studio and should be home by now, but she's not. And she's not answering my texts." *And it's all my fault.*

"Do you want to talk about it?"

"No."

"Is that the reason you're fighting?" she asked dryly.

"I told her to leave," he admitted. Saying it aloud closed an icy fist around his heart, squeezing it into the base of his throat. How could he be so stupid? So cruel?

"*Why?* You seemed to really care about her."

"I do," he said through his teeth. "But—" *I was afraid to care that much.* Love was sold as a profound source of strength, but in his experience, it was nothing but a sense of helplessness.

So he'd fought against succumbing to it. Yet here he was. Helpless.

"Axel." Her voice turned admonishing. "You said Otto was awful to her. I don't know what it's like to be adopted, but I do know what it's like to wonder why someone who is supposed to care about you doesn't. If you acted like you cared, then told her to leave—"

"I know," he said through his teeth, barely able to withstand the clench in his chest.

I just can't help thinking there's a reason you can't love me.

He had promised to protect her from Otto, then hurt her worse than anyone else ever had.

"I have to go. I need to find her."

Joy had texted Lowell Fontaine that she was coming to his hotel. He met her in the lobby along with his wife, Pascale.

Then he took Joy by the shoulders, and his eyes—eyes that were the same shape as her own—grew damp. "It's like she's here, still with me. You look just like her. I didn't know. I'm so sorry that I didn't know about you." He hugged her.

"Oh, chère," Pascale said. "Perhaps she doesn't want—"

"Je suis désolé." Lowell started to release her.

"No, it's okay," Joy chuckled weepily and hugged him back. Hard. She closed her eyes and drank up what she'd hoped Otto would offer her: instant, unconditional acceptance.

Somehow Pascale herded them into an elevator, and Joy soon found herself in the well-appointed lounge of a suite. Refreshments arrived, but she barely noticed.

"I didn't know if any of her family knew about me," she said. "It seemed like she didn't want anyone to know."

"This is true," Lowell said with regret. "It didn't even occur to me Lorena might have had a child, not until Pascale saw the notice about Otto's death. Frankly, my only thought on Otto's passing was 'good.' I'm sorry if you feel differently about him, but he treated Lorena abominably. She was young, thought herself in love. He dazzled her with gifts, but she was his mistress, so he was ashamed of her. I thought that was the worst of it, but when I learned he had made her give up her child?"

"He didn't know about me." Joy explained how Otto had come to find out. "How did you realize I was her daughter?"

"There was a photo of you and your husband with the article on Otto. Pascale pointed you out to me. She noticed how much you looked like Lorena."

"He brushed me off," Pascale said, taking over. "But reading that Otto was your birth father, I just knew. The timing fit. Lorena missed our wedding because she went to New York. She and I had a terrible falling out over it. She had introduced me to Lowell. She was supposed to be my maid of honor, but she was adamant about leaving. Now I realize she knew she would have been showing on our wedding day."

"Our parents cut her off when they learned of their affair," Lowell broke in sadly. "They wouldn't have helped her if she'd told them she was pregnant. I could have been kinder. She asked me for money to help her get to New York. I was glad she was leaving Otto, but I said she should wait until after the wedding. I don't know where she got the money. Sold some of the jewelry he'd given her, I suppose. It breaks my heart. If I'd been more willing to help her, she might have kept you."

"When she came back, things were still strained between us," Pascale said with equal regret. "I didn't want to forgive her. It seems so childish now, to hold a grudge over something so inconsequential. She must have been so frightened. Heartbroken. She was different when she came home. Older. Quieter."

"But she went back to him?" Joy recalled.

"She did. I never fully understood what she saw in him. He was very rich, obviously. And very handsome," Pascale admitted reluctantly. "Their second affair didn't last long. She told me she thought he was ready to leave his wife, but he wasn't. She said they'd both changed. That's when she moved to Heidelberg and opened the bookstore."

"Did she marry? Have more children?"

"No." There were bright tears in Pascale's eyes. "I always assumed Otto broke her heart. Now I'm sure that giving up her daughter did that."

"Oh." Joy covered her trembling mouth.

Pascale moved to sit next to her and rubbed her shoulders.

"We hope you'll meet our children, though?" Lowell said hesitantly.

"I have cousins?" Joy picked up her head.

"Two boys and a girl," he said with pride. "We haven't told them any of this. We wanted to meet you first and see if you were open to it?"

Fresh tears brimmed her eyes. "I would love that."

Axel went to the dance studio himself, catching Inga as she was leaving for the day.

"I still haven't heard from her," he told her, not mentioning that he could see Joy had her notifications silenced.

The choreographer hesitated, then sighed. "She told me you'd had an argument. I'm sure she's just taking some time for herself. Let me see if she's with any of my dancers." She texted a group chat. "Michael dropped her at a hotel a few hours ago."

She told him which one, and Axel went there, but when he asked the front desk to put him through to her room, she wasn't registered.

Had she met someone here? Who?

Axel ordered a drink in the bar, wondering what the hell he was going to do if she refused to come back to him. He had ignored a dozen calls today along with countless texts and emails, all to do with Vorstoben and projects that meant nothing to him. How could anything hold any meaning for him when the one person he cared about above all others was hurting and avoiding him?

The best case was that Joy was giving him the silent treatment because he'd hurt her. The worst case was that she was looking for somewhere to live because he'd broken her heart.

He had never wanted to feel this powerless, and the worst part was, he'd done it to himself. She wasn't doing this to him. She didn't think he cared about her, but he did. He cared so much it sat as a lump in his throat and was a hard stone lodged in his chest.

He loved her. That was what this agony was. He loved her, and he didn't know how he could push through the life he'd made for himself if he didn't have a reason to be in it.

His phone pinged.

He flipped it over, and his heart lurched when he saw it was finally a text from Joy.

On my way home. Will explain when I get there.

He threw a few bills onto the bar and walked out to the lobby in time to see her hurrying from the elevators toward the revolving doors. "Joy."

She jolted and turned, staring at him in shock as he crossed toward her. "What are you doing here?" she asked with astonishment.

"Looking for you." He looked to the elevator as though he might catch a glimpse of whose room she was leaving. He had never felt so nauseous, so jealous, so terrified in his life. "Who were you with?"

"My uncle," she said with a bemused blink.

There was a taxi outside the hotel. They stepped into it, and Joy nervously relayed the story to Axel on their short drive home. He barely spoke, but he listened intently.

"They live in Lyon," she finished up as they entered the penthouse. "They have children. I have cousins."

"How did you get to the studio this morning? Did you walk? You didn't even take your jacket. Are you cold? Do you want to shower? Rest?"

"No, I'm fine."

"Hungry?"

"No, I had coffee and sandwiches with Lowell and Pascale." She dropped her bag onto the sofa, then lowered to the cushion beside it, blowing out a long breath. "I'm a little talked out, though."

"Good. Because I have a few things to say." Axel paced across her line of vision, then halted to glare at her. "Don't you *ever* worry me like that again."

He didn't raise his voice, but Joy jumped at his vehemence and pushed herself deeper into the sofa. "I didn't—"

"I'm not finished." His hand made a crocodile bite with fingers and thumb, telling her to shut her mouth.

Rude.

"I don't care how angry you are with me or how big of an ass I've been, you will text me proof of life when I ask for it."

"It was two hours—"

"Four and a half. You went to a hotel to meet strangers without telling me—"

"Are you being serious right now? This is an example of you being an ass, by the way. Should I text that to you?" She pretended to reach for her purse.

"I have been an ass since the day we met," he said angrily. "You had no business marrying me. And you claim to have had the bad judgment to fall in love with me. How can I possibly trust you to have any judgment where strangers in hotel rooms are concerned?"

"You're going to throw that in my face again?" She picked up the cushion from the corner of the sofa and hugged it, growing teary and stressed all over again. "I won't have that fight right now. I've had a really emotional day, Axel."

"I know what you're going to say."

"No, you don't!" She didn't let him cut in. "Because I don't. All I know is that I want to dance, and I promised Inga she could count on me. I know that 'show must go on' attitude sounds ridiculous or… I don't know how it sounds." She squeezed the cushion. "I only know that I can't let whatever happens between us cost me my chance to dance. Not again. So I'm staying in Berlin. I don't know what to tell you about whether I'm continuing this marriage or staying in this apartment because I'm really hurt."

"*You* are hurt," he scoffed, glaring at her with outrage, then shoving his hand through his hair. "Do you have any idea what has been going through my mind since the doorman told me your driver was here and you were long gone? You didn't even take a jacket."

That was the second time he'd mentioned that crime. She wasn't sure why he was so incensed about it. The April day had been quite pleasant.

"When I saw you'd turned off your notifications, I thought you were dancing. Maybe punishing me a little. Which I deserved, but I thought you would come home after you were done at the studio. You didn't take a jacket. You hadn't actually left me if all you had was your phone and a credit card."

Oh. She was starting to see why the lack of a coat was such a big deal.

"What other reason could there be then, when time wore on and you didn't come home? I was actually relieved to hear you had gone to a damned hotel with a male dancer because at least if you were having an affair, I knew you were alive."

"I wasn't having an affair."

"No, but if your aim was to show me how empty my life would be if you left me, mission accomplished."

"I've told you where I was. Are you really going to say I shouldn't have gone to meet my birth mother's brother?"

"No. But you didn't have to go alone. I would have gone with you if you'd asked. What does it say about where we're at that you didn't even think to call me and ask me to meet you there? You didn't trust me to be your support in that. Did you?" He ran his hand over his face, but not before she saw the anguish that flashed across his expression.

"I was just reacting," she murmured. "It felt urgent. Like they would disappear if I didn't see them right away. I know that doesn't sound rational."

"I understand why you went, Joy. I do." He dropped his

hand. "And I'm glad it went well, but what if it hadn't? What if it had turned out like it had with Otto, and you were rejected all over again, and I wasn't there to absorb some of that blow? You didn't even know that I wanted you *here*." He pointed at the floor. "For as long as we both manage to live."

Well, why did he have to say that? For someone who was being mostly an ass, he was also being sweet enough to make her blink back tears.

"I never should have told you to leave." His voice thickened with remorse. "It was stupid. Mean. I'm sorry I said it, and I hope you'll forgive me. But, Joy, I want you to be with me because you want to be with me. When you said you wanted to leave, I had to give you that. I don't know how to show how I feel except by giving you what you seem to need." He held out his open palms, helpless. "I feel a lot. I love you."

"Don't…" A knot formed behind her breastbone, but a tiny, tiny hope began to unfurl inside her. "Don't say that word if you don't mean it."

He came to sit on the coffee table and clasped her hands. He looked into her eyes, and there was such a fierce light there, her heart lurched toward hope, but she held it back, fearful.

"Refusing to say it doesn't make it not true," he said with disgruntlement.

"But you think love is something that makes you weak. That hurts to carry. You don't want it." Her voice wavered.

"I said that," he acknowledged. "And it does hurt. It's a terrifying emotion, Schatz. It means that this…" He scanned his gaze all over her. "Any little harm to you might as well be a knife to my own heart. I can't stand when you're hurt. That's why I was so eaten up today when

I didn't know where you were. I had hurt you, and I felt it so deeply. It was a self-inflicted wound, and I couldn't fix it because I couldn't find you. I love you," he repeated, hands tightening on hers.

She searched his face, very frightened she was dreaming and would wake up heartbroken all over again.

"I can see you're having trouble believing me. Look. The kind of love I grew up with was obligation and responsibility, but that's not what this is. I thought love was something that was imposed on you. Some entity I could choose to bring into our relationship or not. But it *is* our relationship. I realized that when you said you would take back your love. I knew you couldn't do that because I couldn't keep from loving you. I want to marry you again."

"What?"

He ran his thumbs across her knuckles and caught the pad of his thumb against her wedding rings. "I want to marry you for no reason except that we love each other. I want you in my life forever, Joy. We belong together. Do you think you would be willing to marry me again? For real this time?"

It wasn't just the words that made her vision blur with tears. It was the pledge. The emotion. The truth. The profound belief that settled over her that she really did have a place in his life, with him. Forever.

She had to bite her quivering lips as sweet love tumbled through her. She placed her hand against the side of his face, barely able to speak past the elation swelling her heart.

"I do."

EPILOGUE

Two years later...

JOY WAS TOO nervous to peek into the crowd before curtain, but Axel had sent her the requisite break-a-leg text, so she knew he was here. When the first notes of the score resounded through the small theater, she became completely focused on her cues and marks and delivering the best performance she could.

The techno-pop musical was loosely based on *The Threepenny Opera*. Mounting this production with fellow students had been part of her final grade, earning her a degree in performing arts. It had been so well received, they'd been able to persuade a local theater to give them a short run.

Singing was not Joy's natural talent, but she could match pitch in chorus numbers, and this production relied heavily on interpretive dance. In fact, she had choreographed some of the numbers, so she knew them through and through.

It was still nerve-racking, especially when she thought about doing this every night for—*No. Don't think about that now. Leap. Twirl. Exit stage left.*

She was sweating and panting at curtain call but exhilarated. The audience was on their feet, likely coaxed there by her family. Axel had bought out an entire row for Joy's family, flying them in for it. Even David was here, probably still trying to calm Carrie's nerves as she checked *one more time* with the professional nanny service minding their children at the hotel.

A short time later, still grinning with triumph, Joy joined everyone at a nearby hotel where her husband had arranged a champagne reception for the entire cast and their various guests. It was a late night for Paul, but he had been napping this afternoon when she left for the theater, and his newest medication seemed to be helping a lot with his symptoms. He and his new girlfriend, Nora, were chatting brightly with Lowell and Pascale.

Everyone was hugging her and gushing enough to make Joy blush.

"I was afraid it would be like one of those little kid plays with bad costumes and scenery falling over, but that was excellent," her cousin teased, winking at her.

Joy still couldn't get over having cousins. They had had a wildly different upbringing from hers, yet they felt so familiar to her, it was as though she'd known them all her life.

Quinn and Micah gave her a ridiculously enormous bouquet, and she received hugs and accolades from Inga, who was round with pregnancy, along with many more of her friends from the festival performance.

Heskel and Klaus were here and had even brought their friend Zander, the dancer who'd evaluated her two years ago. Zander kissed both her cheeks, complimented her performance *and* the choreography and said he would recommend the show to everyone he knew. Her knees almost unhinged.

It was so touching and overwhelming, Joy had a little cry later, once she and Axel were home and getting ready for bed.

"Honigbiene," Axel chided as he drew her into his arms. "What's this?"

"I'm just so happy." She slid her arms around his waist, hugging tight. "I never would have had this without you. Thank you."

"That is far more credit than I deserve. You were always going to find your way back to dancing, shining so brightly you steal every scene."

"I didn't."

"You did. I couldn't take my eyes off you."

"You're biased."

"Yes, but I'm also capable of seeing what's obvious." He brushed a tendril of hair behind her ear. "I won't be the least bit surprised if opportunities come to you after this."

"I hope so, but…" She quirked her mouth. "I want to dance, but I don't want to be away from you."

"Joy. You know I'll spend a year in New York if you want to audition for Broadway. We'll find a way to make it work. Do not let me hold you back."

"Thank you. But I do like our life here, and I wouldn't mind pursuing a master's degree. Also…" Was this the right time to bring it up?

His brows lifted.

"Well, you saw that Inga's expecting? She asked me if I would consider working with her on the festival production this year, since she'll be delivering in the middle of rehearsals. It got me thinking that maybe I could do that, too. Have a baby," she said tentatively. "We don't have to talk about it right now. I know you've always been ambivalent about children—"

He set the pad of his thumb over her lips. His expression was so tender, her heart hiccuped. "I used to think love was something I had to carry. That it wouldn't add to my life, but God, Joy, look at what your love has brought into my life. Everything is brighter. Better. Richer in ways I never would have understood if I wasn't married to you."

"Oh." Her eyes began to sting and well up.

"You think those little monsters of your brother's have no effect on me? Your nephew took my hand when we were crossing the road to come see your rehearsal, and I thought my heart would stop. The level of responsibility was terrifying, but so gratifying when I got him across safely."

She bit back her grin.

"You weren't here to see it, but your niece fell asleep on me the other day. I was annoyed that Carrie insisted on taking her to her cot. I thought, if we had our own, I could hold our sleeping baby as long as I wanted to."

Oh, this ridiculous man. "You really mean it? You want to start a family?"

"I want you to chase your career as long and hard as you need to, so I haven't said anything, but yes. I think about having children with you all the time. When you're ready, I will be ready. And, just to put it on the record, I'm open to adopting, if that's something you ever thought about."

Not a ridiculous man at all. One who was gifting her the world, making her wonder how she had come to deserve it.

"Sometimes I wonder what my life would look like if you and I hadn't been forced together by Otto," she admitted somberly. "That scares me because I love you so much, I don't know where I would have put all of these feelings otherwise."

"Dance," he said simply. "And I would have seen you onstage somewhere and moved mountains to get to you."

Farfetched as it sounded, she believed him.

"Now, we don't have to try making a baby tonight, but maybe we should rehearse how it's done," he suggested.

Laughing, she leaped, and he caught her, then tumbled her onto the bed.

* * * * *

Did you fall head over heels for Business-Deal Bride*?*
Then be sure to check out the next installment in the
Business Proposals duet, coming soon!
And why not try these other stories from Dani Collins?

His Highness's Hidden Heir
Maid to Marry
Hidden Heir, Italian Wife
The Greek's Wife Returns
Boss's Christmas Baby Acquisition

Available now!

WED FOR THE HEADLINES

EMMY GRAYSON

MILLS & BOON

To Dad, thanks for picking Iceland.
Trip of a lifetime.

To Little Man, thanks for encouraging me
to jump into the lake. Worth it.

To Mom, John, Kels, and Jim,
thanks for making it possible.

CHAPTER ONE

Aislinn

My husband's funeral is crowded. Not with people who loved him or genuinely miss him, but with Washington, DC's elite, politicians and bankers and investors who have shown up to supposedly pay their respects as they all play the same game of pretending they care.

Just like Dexter would have wanted.

I shake someone's hand, listen to their lies about what a great man Dexter was. I bite back the bitter words that clog my throat and simply nod. Hopefully most will chalk it up as grief or at least have the decency to pretend like this is a normal funeral.

Pretend like most of us in this room aren't glad Dexter is dead.

I can feel them watching me. Once upon a time I would have felt the weight of every curious gaze, every suspicious glance and pitying smile. Would have been thinking of the newspapers' lurid headlines speculating if Dexter Simpson's wife, a woman nearly half his age who married him in a whirlwind romance just months before his unexpected death, had a hand in his demise.

Now, I feel nothing. Just emptiness. An emptiness that has helped me survive the past ten months since Dexter slithered into my life. Ten months since I had to cut the two people I loved most in this world out of my life.

Tears finally prick my eyes. Diana has texted me faithfully once a week. I hope one day I can tell her how much those texts have meant to me, gotten me through some of the worst days of my life.

And Liam…

My heart twists, tightens. I can't think of Liam. I owe Dexter nothing. But thinking about my friend I've been secretly in love with since I was seventeen while greeting people at my husband's funeral is a low I have no desire to sink to.

A couple moves forward in the endless line, older and dressed in black couture. They tell me how sorry they are. Out of the corner of my eye, I see my parents hovering.

Adoptive parents, I remind myself. Dexter threatened to destroy Liam and Diana's careers if I didn't sever our friendship. But he wanted my parents as close as possible. He couldn't exploit his familial connection to a US senator if I didn't maintain a relationship with my family.

I did think of them as family once. Thought I was the luckiest girl in the world to be adopted just before I aged out of foster care, and by a renowned politician and his wife no less. A fairy tale come true. I thought the man I called "father" was different. A politician of integrity, working toward a better world for the people he served.

God, I was so naive.

Senator Eric Knightley is no saint. He has secrets, dark ones Dexter collected and held over my head all the way to the altar. Given how involved his wife, Stephanie, has been in his campaign, including managing donations, I can't imagine a scenario where she's not at least partially aware of what Eric did to secure his office.

I'm consciously trying not to wipe the palms of my hands on my pants when I hear it. That deep, melodious rumble I've imagined so many times whispering words of love to me. Not the sisterly affection he's shown me for the past eleven years, but passionate words, a declaration that he feels the same way I do.

Out of the corner of my eye I see him. Tall, handsome as sin in a tailored black suit, his face comprised of sharp angles and lines that border on beautiful. When he turns on the charm, which is often, his smile is big and bright. But on the rare occasion I've seen him angry, the cut of his cheekbones and the slash of his jaw can go from sculpted to menacing in an instant.

If I would have told Liam that Dexter blackmailed me into marriage, he would have moved heaven and earth to help me. But I couldn't risk Dexter making good on his threats. He wouldn't have just revealed my adoptive father's secrets. He would have destroyed Liam and Diana, too, simply because he could.

The line shifts, and I see Diana is next to him. A different kind of ache takes hold. I may have developed other friendships over the years, but Diana will always be my first and truest friend. She's trusted me with her deepest secrets over the years, as I have mine with her.

Well, all but one. I don't want my feelings for Liam to ever come between Diana and me. And I know, with how deeply she cares for both of us, she would be caught between knowing Liam never wants to settle down and my love for him. Even if he saw me as more than a sister, he's made it clear he has no interest in ever settling down. I would love to have a life with him, but I want my future to include marriage. Kids. Even now, after everything that's happened, a part of me still clings to the slim hope that those dreams are still possible.

I push that aside. I accepted long ago that Liam and I would never be. I still have his friendship, and Diana's, even after ignoring them for months on end. I'm not out of the woods yet. Dexter may be dead, but I don't know who else may have the information he was holding over my head.

I couldn't care less if the information sinks my adoptive father's political career or not. But I do care about the bill we've worked so hard on for the past two years, one that could improve the lives of foster children around the country. Just a few more months, and once it passes, I'll truly be free to move on with my life. Maybe that step will include renewing my friendship with Liam and Diana.

I bite down on the insides of my cheeks to keep myself from smiling. I can't smile at my husband's funeral. But God, it's going to be so good to talk to them, even if it's just for a few hurried seconds. For the first time in nearly a year, it doesn't feel like the world is ending.

"...congratulations on your engagement."

It takes a moment for the words to penetrate the rise and fall of conversation around me. I swallow hard, try to fight the sudden fluttering panic inside my chest.

It can't be. It's not possible.

I turn to look, just in time to see Liam slipping an arm around Diana's waist and pulling her against him.

My heart shatters. For one moment, I feel it all. Heartbreak, grief, fury, jealousy.

Why her? Why not me?

Knowing he would never settle down had made watching the parade of women streaming in and out of his life tolerable. But this...this is more painful than anything I've ever experienced. All these years I told myself Liam would never settle down, would never see me as more than a friend. It made it easier when his picture appeared in the paper or online with yet another woman on his arm at some gala or fundraiser. Made forcing myself to date and picture a life with someone else bearable.

And now he's engaged to one of my best friends. How

can I renew our friendship now? How can I pretend like I'm happy for them, stand up at their wedding, hold their children…

My stomach pitches up. I can't. I can never be friends with them again.

I've lost everything.

Then, as if my will has asserted itself over my heart, everything vanishes. The shock, the anger, the heartache. All that's left is a yawning emptiness. I slip into that blank space, embrace the nothingness.

"Aislinn?"

I blink. Stephanie is in front of me. The couple I was talking to have moved off to the side but are looking at me with concern, as are several people in line. Including Diana and Li—

No.

Stephanie reaches out and grabs my hand. I start to pull away but force myself to stop. Hurt flares in her eyes, but I ignore it. "Are you all right?"

I nod and gently pat the back of her hand. "Yes. Just tired." I force a tiny smile for the benefit of anyone watching before I withdraw my fingers from her grasp. "As well as I can be."

"You can take a break."

"No." I swallow, tamp down my anger. "I just want to get through this."

I angle myself away before she can push me anymore. Angle toward Liam and Diana as I steel myself against the storm of emotions seething inside my chest.

Diana's tentative smile nearly breaks me as she clutches her hands in front of her. The ring glitters, taunts. "Hi, Aislinn."

Strong. I have to stay strong. I've been stronger than I ever realized I could be these past few months.

Just a little longer, I promise myself. *Then you can rest.* "Hello, Diana."

Her face falls. She glances at Liam, but he doesn't look at her. Instead, he's staring at me, suspicion evident in his ice-blue eyes. It makes it easier to steady myself. To put him in the role of villain instead of the just-out-of-reach hero he's played for so long in my dreams.

"We're sorry for your loss," he murmurs, his voice cool and formal.

"Thank you." I force out my next words. "Congratulations on your engagement."

Diana blinks, a tiny furrow appearing between her dark brows. "You... Did you not know?"

I thread my fingers together. Focus on the pain of squeezing my hands together so hard my knuckles turn white. "No."

Diana glances up at Liam, but he continues to stare at me, his gaze probing. Assessing.

I stand my ground and stare right back. Yes, I've lied, covered for a man who sold his vote for a ticket to a senator's office. But Liam lied, too. He lied to me since the first week I met him when he told me he would never get married.

Pain and anger push at the edges of my control. I push back. I need the emptiness. Need to not only get through this but erase any feelings I ever carried for Liam Whitlock.

Diana clears her throat. "Maybe we could all get together in a few weeks."

Her invitation, coupled with her shy smile and the glimmer of hope in her eyes, makes me tremble. Waver. She's innocent in all of this.

Then her hand comes up to brush a stray lock of hair out of her face. The ring glimmers in the light. Maybe once I would have been capable of putting Diana and whatever happiness she's found with Liam above my own heartbreak.

But the woman I've had to become isn't.

"Perhaps." I nod to the line behind them. "I wish I could talk longer now, but—"

"Of course." I swallow back a bitter taste in my throat as Diana grabs Liam's hand and tugs him forward. "Just…we're here, Aislinn. Always."

I nod, not trusting myself to speak. I meet Liam's gaze one final time. Emotions surge. Loathing tangles with love. I stare at his face, the familiar dark lashes framing ice-blue eyes, the faintest hint of the dimple in one cheek, the strong point of his chin. Remember the countless movie nights, dinners and festivals we attended, the midnight conversations as we shared our dreams for our futures.

And then I turn my back. They're no longer a part of my future.

CHAPTER TWO

Liam

Four months later

A TUXEDOED WAITER passes by with a tray of glass flutes filled with sparkling champagne. A jazz band, set up at the far end of the ballroom, is playing an energetic song. A surprising number of people are on the dance floor. The mood is happy, excited, joyful.

Normally, I would try to match their energy, plaster a smile on my face and pretend. But I don't want to. Not tonight. Not after a year of digging and investigating and coming up against wall after wall. Not after investing my fortune in building up my own company, only to have one of my most important prospective clients inform me that my supposed broken engagement a few months prior had damaged my reputation to the point where he was considering no longer working with me. And he wasn't the only one.

I breathe in deeply in an effort to combat the tension tightening my shoulders. I have done so much for Aislinn, even if she doesn't know it. And now I'm prepared to do even more.

I glance around the ballroom, frowning when I don't see her face. I've attended so many events like this over the years, many of them planned by Aislinn for her adoptive father's various campaign events, fundraisers and galas. She's usually front and center, greeting people like long-lost friends and ensuring glasses and plates are full.

My lips twitch. It's been twelve years since I sat in our high school theater, sullen and irritated that my counselor, Mrs. Scout, had dragged me out of study hall to meet two other foster kids she thought I'd "connect" with. Diana hadn't had the same chip on her shoulder, but she'd carried the same reserve.

And then Aislinn had bounced down the aisle, golden hair tied up in a ponytail and a huge smile on her face. I'd watched Diana visibly thaw in front of me as the sophomore with the shining green eyes and eager voice had told her how beautiful her hair was, how she wished she had Diana's height, how she was so excited to get to know her.

Then she'd looked at me. Her eyes had widened slightly. And then she'd smiled shyly and told me she was excited to get to know me, too.

The friendship that was established that day in the dim theater with the threadbare seats and a cast singing "Without Love" off-key on the stage was the first time in eight years I'd let anyone get close. Diana and I bonded over our shared trauma of being thrust from our former lives into foster care. And Aislinn…

I smile slightly. Aislinn may be the youngest of our trio, but she's always been the mother of the group. She never wanted anyone to feel left out. She saw the best in everyone, even when I didn't.

My hands curl into a fist at my side. Is that what happened with her husband? Did she meet him at an event like this, or did he reach out, make her feel special, and prey on her naive nature before he pulled her into his world?

"Liam?"

My head snaps around. Eric is standing a few feet away, his brow furrowed.

"Are you all right?"

I force my lips into some semblance of a smile and nod. "Congratulations, Senator."

Eric's smile is equally tight, strained. "Thank you."

"Where's Aislinn?"

I don't bother with niceties. I've wasted over a year trying to be methodical, thorough. Trying to do things the right way and not stir the pot. I'm done playing nice.

Eric's eyes flicker up to the series of balconies ringing the upper gallery of the ballroom. "Somewhere up there."

"An odd place for her to be."

Eric's smile disappears. "Everything's been off. Ever since..." He catches himself, clears his throat. "Maybe you can get through to her."

"Doubt it," I grumble under my breath as Eric walks away to greet someone.

It's been radio silence ever since the funeral. Diana, I know, has continued to text her weekly. She recently added an invitation to her upcoming engagement party to my brother.

I wince as I stride across the ballroom toward a marble staircase that circles up to the second floor. It's still odd to think of Diana and my half brother, Ari, being engaged. Getting married. Being in love. Considering I didn't even know I had a half brother until this past spring, finding out that he and Diana had had a one-night stand had been jarring. Not as jarring, though, as realizing they genuinely loved each other. A situation made all the more awkward by Diana's and my fake engagement.

I take the steps two at a time. I had met Dexter a total of three times before he did us all a favor and died. The first had been after Aislinn had stopped hanging out with Diana and me. It wasn't just being busy at work; she'd stopped responding to our group texts and had sent several of my calls to voicemail. So, I'd gone over to her apartment to check on her.

It was seven in the morning. Dexter had opened the door. I'd hated him on sight. Silver hair mussed. Rumpled dress shirt. Belt undone. Even though he was over twenty years older than me, plenty of women would have found him attractive. But when he shot me that slow, smug smile, I barely resisted punching him in the face. He informed me Aislinn was in the shower and would contact me later.

She never did. But I started seeing plenty of photos of them plastered on social media and the occasional feature in the *New York Times* about their attendance at some fancy dinner or political event.

I reach the top of the stairs and glance over the railing. Eric is still chatting with someone. My eyes roam over the ballroom until I see Stephanie, Aislinn's adoptive mother, standing off to the side.

Eric and Aislinn had always had a warm friendship, but as Aislinn had told us, there had always been a distance between them, a recognition that she was not Eric's biological daughter. She'd sworn up and down that everything Eric had provided her with was enough. I knew she was lying, but pressing her on it would have only made her sad. And she had Stephanie, the woman she called Mom and who returned Aislinn's love tenfold.

But from what little Stephanie had said when I'd finally gone to her after months of no contact, Aislinn had cooled things between them, too. Yes, she and Dexter had accompanied Eric and Stephanie to plenty of events around town during their whirlwind courtship and brief marriage. But it was like Aislinn's soul had disappeared, replaced by someone cold, empty.

I start to walk the gallery. How Aislinn had survived her entire life in foster care and still managed to come out with stars in her eyes was a miracle I had no desire to taint. I worried about her sometimes, especially when she started dating in college. Worried no man would ever be able to be enough for someone so…good.

Never in a million years would I have pictured her marrying a government contractor nearly twice her age with a reputation for cruelty in his business dealings.

A man who only escaped being charged with fraud and financial crimes by dying of an unexpected heart attack.

I walk along the gallery, passing behind thick pillars and the occasional alcove shrouded in darkness. All but one. The last alcove before the gallery gives way to three stories of glass overlooking the Hudson River. The doorway is framed by deep red velvet curtains held back with gold ties.

I stop in the doorway, hands in my pockets, shoulders thrown back. Ready to do battle. Instead, I freeze.

I know the woman in front of me. I know the delicate shape of her face, the full lips I'm used to seeing curved in a smile, the big green eyes that could see good in the absolute worst moments. Eyes that calmed me when I was at my worst, held the simmering anger I've never fully been able to escape from since I was placed in foster care.

But now, the green eyes staring at me are anything but warm and soothing. They're ice-cold, void of emotion. Her lips are painted red, a shade that complements her sleekly styled golden hair. It's shorter now, styled to accentuate her sculpted cheekbones and the stubborn point of her chin. She's dressed in black, lounging on a white divan with one slender arm draped across the back and her other hand cradling a glass of amber liquid. She doesn't break eye contact as she raises the glass to her lips.

Heat jolts through me as her lips close around the rim.

What the hell?

I mentally take a step back. This is Aislinn. A woman I've known since she was sixteen years old. A little sister, someone to be protected and cared for, not lusted after.

"You're wearing black."

She tilts the glass back, takes a long sip. The heat starts to rise again, but I squelch it. It's been nearly a year since I've dated. My reaction is strictly biology. And, I think grimly, if Aislinn accepts my proposal, it's going to be even longer before I indulge in sex again. But the return on that investment will far outweigh the costs. Returns that will benefit both Aislinn and me, given our current predicaments.

"Haven't you heard? I'm in mourning."

Her voice is deeper. There's no light, no whisper of joy beneath everyday words. I'm staring at a wraith, a shadow of who Aislinn used to be.

Cold fingers wrap around my heart. Squeeze. All these months I told myself something else was going on. Told Diana over and over whenever she started to doubt. Yet as I watch Aislinn's calm, blank stare, I can't help but wonder if I'm wrong.

"I heard about the Department of Justice."

She blinks. Diana and I always used to tease her about her inability to play poker or any other sort of game where she had to conceal her emotions. She's always been an open book. But now, I can't get a read on her. Can't reach her even though she's just a few feet away.

She stands in one smooth movement, the soft silk folds of her dress following the curve of her hips, the length of her. My eyes flick back up.

"You and the rest of New York." One corner of her mouth tilts up. "Really, the world at this point."

She swishes past me. A dark scent teases me, rose with a hint of spice. The exact opposite of the light, floral scent she always used to wear. Some daisy perfume that came in a bottle shaped like the flower.

I turn, my entire body tensing at the sight of her bare back. Aside from the ties at her shoulders, there's nothing. Nothing but smooth, pale skin all the way down to the base of her spine. Thankfully, silk covers her backside. But with the way it clings, it doesn't leave anything to the imagination. If I didn't think it would piss her off, I'd offer her my coat.

She moves on to the gallery, stopping with one hand on the banister as she gazes down at the ballroom. I follow, stopping just a few feet behind her.

"What are you going to do?"

She turns her head just enough so that her face is in profile. The gentle slope and slight upturn of her nose, the elegant definition of her jaw, the long line of her neck backlit by the golden glow from the ballroom. "Not much I can do."

Anger surges through me. How can she be so blasé about this? "Do you even comprehend the enormity of their decision? The impact it will have on your finances?"

She turns away, giving me the back of her head. Another dismissal. One that has me gritting my teeth.

Has she forgotten everything we've been through? How our friendship was forged in literally saving a life? The years of supporting each other as we fought our way out of high school, through college and to careers and adulthood? She doesn't know the lengths Diana and I went to protect her, doesn't know the engagement was fake. But damn it, we gave up everything to keep her safe. And for what? For her to act like this is all a game?

"It's not just the Department of Justice." I should stop talking, but her silence grates on my last nerve. "The FBI and IRS are both involved, too. All of Dexter's properties were bought with money tied to his criminal activities. You don't have a place to live, and last I heard, most of your finances were tied to his, so you have no money."

"I'm aware."

The anger twists, morphs into fury. I close the distance between us, place my hand on one bare shoulder and turn her to face me. Her skin heats the palm of my hand, feeds my anger. And, deep beneath that, fear. She's right in front of me for the first time in months, and she's never been further away.

"So you're going to do nothing? Just treat this like you have the last year of your life?"

She raises her chin. Then, with defiance flashing in her eyes, she tilts her glass up and throws back the rest. Whiskey, I realize as I smell caramel and vanilla tangled with oak.

"I didn't say that." She sets her empty glass away from her on the banister, then faces the ballroom again. "I submitted my notice to Eric this afternoon."

Eric. Not Dad. Even though they had never been as close as she and Stephanie, she had always called him Dad.

"Why? You love your job."

"And my personal link to a corrupt man could harm his reelection campaign next year."

My head snaps around, my eyes cutting to Eric. He's standing next to Stephanie now, their heads bowed together. They suddenly don't look like the elegant older couple I've always known, but tired, haggard.

"He said that?"

"In less explicit terms, yes."

I think I hear the slightest hitch in Aislinn's voice. But when I glance through the corner of my eye, her face is still set in that blank mask.

"I solved the problem by turning in my resignation, effective after tonight."

I grasp the banister with both hands, curl my fingers around it. "Damn it, Aislinn, you're good at what you do. Everyone knows you were the soul behind the Foster Care Protection Act. You can't let a few rumors drive you out." I want to grab her by the shoulders and shake her. "You can't just give up."

I feel more than see the intention that grips her. I sense the emotion that flashes through her instead of seeing it. But I know it's there. Thank God.

"I call it surviving."

"Semantics," I snap back.

She swallows hard. Her chin dips as she inhales. "Call it what you want, Liam." She spits out my name like its poison. "It's always easier to judge from the outside looking in."

I mentally take a step back. Yes, I'm furious. Hurt. Diana and I have been worried sick about her for months, yet she's rejected us at every turn, making bad choice after bad choice as she spiraled down so fast we couldn't reach out and grab her. Save her.

But I can save her now. I can save us both.

"You don't want to leave." I keep my tone gentle, my voice quiet and as close to friendly as I can manage. I'll never get her to confide in me, to consider my plan, if I'm constantly putting her on the defensive.

I wait. Below us, the music transitions from lively and joyful to something slower, a deep, sultry tune that makes the air feel thicker.

Then, at last, a sigh, so quiet it's almost inaudible below the music. "I don't know what I want."

When I look at her this time, the grief in her eyes is one I feel all the way to my bones. It's always been like this, ever since I first laid eyes on her in our high school theater. She wore her emotions so openly, shared them willingly with no strings attached. I hate seeing her like this, feeling the sadness I'm convinced she's kept from me, kept from Diana, for nearly a year. But a sick, selfish part of me is just so fucking glad she's finally letting me in.

I follow her gaze down to Eric and Stephanie. This time, my anger is directed at the man I'm now convinced has a role in whatever mess she's been caught up in. "He never should have accepted your resignation."

"It was the right choice for his campaign." Her sigh is sad, heavy. "The financial investigation may have cleared me of wrongdoing, but that doesn't mean the public believes it. There are several high-ranking donors who have voiced their displeasure. Eric had to make a choice."

"You're his daughter."

Her shoulders fall a fraction. "But I'm not."

This time, when I lay my hand on her shoulder, I do so gently. My fingers press down on her bare skin. I remove my hand before I let my fingertips trail down her arm. A gesture I've done a thousand times since knowing her. Except right now, it doesn't feel right. Too intimate. "You don't have to face this alone."

She's still quiet, but I can see the cracks in the mask. Can see glimmers of the woman I knew beneath. My friend.

"I have a plan."

A shutter drops down over her face. She takes a step back. "Of course you have a plan." Her voice is cold once more. "You always have a plan."

Insulted, I glare down at her. "You used to like my plans."

She looks back out over the ballroom. "I'm listening."

"As long as your finances are tied up, you don't have much in the way of resources. Especially if you're not working. You need money. Support."

"I need money." Her head swings back around, her blue eyes cool. "I don't need support. I can take care of myself."

The words throw me. I miss Aislinn, miss who she used to be. But I also remember the times she would get caught up in separating emotion from fact, when she would fail to stand up for herself because she didn't want to hurt someone else's feelings. I hate the reason for it, but I can't help but admire the backbone she's displaying in the midst of her life literally falling apart.

"Okay. No support. But you need money. Something to keep you afloat while this investigation drags out. And given that Eric accepted your resignation, I'm guessing you're not going to be getting much from him."

A low blow, but it lands. Her lips thin as her eyes narrow. "I'm not asking him for a damn thing."

"Well, then you need money. And I need a wife."

CHAPTER THREE

Aislinn

MY TRAITOROUS HEART LEAPS. I indulge it for one moment, allowing myself to pretend that Liam actually wants me to be his wife because he's finally realized, after all these years, that he's in love with me just as deeply and irrevocably as I have been with him since I first laid eyes on him.

And then, with the mental snap of my fingers, I suffer the hope and force myself back into reality.

Liam stands in front of me, looking ridiculously handsome in a black suit and tie. There's a smugness about his lips, a confidence in the arrogant tilt of his chin. I hate how handsome he is. I hate how much he still affects me, how I knew he was approaching even before he appeared in the doorway of the alcove.

I once thought my love for him was romantic, an unrequited love story that would match the great romances of literature. I'm a damn fool. There was nothing romantic about how I felt about him. Pathetic, naive, ridiculous—those are far more accurate. Even now, I know he's not proposing marriage because he's had an epiphany. Like he said, he has a plan. He always has a plan. One that takes him one step closer to his ultimate goal of achieving success. A success that does not include goals like mine: a family. Children. Liam's goals include financial success, vacation homes in the Caribbean, maybe even one day a private jet.

I focus on those facts, on how wrong we are for each other, as I gather my next words. "I don't see the correlation between my needing money and you needing a wife."

It's petty, but I enjoy the flash of irritation on his handsome face.

"I'm proposing we marry, Aislinn," he says.

I hold his gaze as long as I can before I look back down at the ballroom. It takes every ounce of effort to conceal my heartbreak. There have been so many times over the past year that I thought I'd been at my breaking point, thought I couldn't possibly sink any lower than I already have. And yet, every single time, I've been wrong. And, I remind myself every single time, I've risen above it. Survived.

"What about Diana?" I ask.

"As I'm sure you're aware, she's engaged to my brother."

Ah. Second best. I hate that I'm envious of Diana. Jealous of her and whatever she and Liam shared. In that moment, I hate Liam for placing me between the two of them.

"Why do you need a wife?" I demand. "You said you'd never get married."

"I'm starting my own firm."

"I remember."

"The clients I've been working with lately are traditionalists. They see marriage as a sign of stability."

I think back to the rotating cast of faces Liam has dated over the years. "Not the word I would use to describe your love life."

He arches one brow. "I didn't realize you paid attention."

Oh, more than you know.

"There were concerns raised about my age, experience and reputation. And when Diana's engagement ended, it caused even more problems."

I frown. "Is that why you got engaged in the first place?"

The singer's voice fills the silence between us, deep and sultry. I force myself to look at him even as I see the answer in Liam's eyes before he says it out loud.

"No. We—"

"Stop." I step back, look back down at the couples swaying in each other's arms to the seductive music. "That's between you and Diana."

"Aislinn—"

"No, Liam." My voice whips out, rough and furious. "I don't want to hear it."

I can't hear that he cared for Diana the way I always wanted him to care for me. Can't hear that Diana will always be the one that got away.

His shoulders shift back as his eyes narrow. I know he's getting ready to argue with me, so I rush on.

"So now you're proposing to me."

He pauses. Watches me. Then he replies with a simple, "Yes." Factual. To the point. No flowery words, no attempts to pretend like this is anything but what it is: a business arrangement.

"I hardly think the widow of a government contractor whose entire estate has been seized by the government and who, until just recently, was under investigation for any links to her husband's crimes is the kind of candidate your clients would accept."

A slow, smug smile crosses his face. "Except you've been officially cleared. And two of my clients hated your husband. When it was announced that you were under investigation, both of them thought you were innocent."

I tap my fingers on the banister. "You've been talking about me with your clients?"

"They brought it up. It's a huge case, Aislinn. Of course people are talking about it."

"So, what? Because they hated Dexter, they'll just accept you marrying me less than a year after my husband died? That doesn't sound like the kind of 'traditional' union they expect out of you."

"They will accept the aggrieved widow of a man many suspect pressured you into marriage. There's also the romance of the situation."

Oh God. This whole situation is so fantastically horrible I don't know whether to laugh or cry. "Romance?"

"Childhood friends. Years of loving friendship. You got married, so I got engaged to Diana. Wrong choice and one made out of heartbreak instead of love. A fact Diana and I both realized and ended the engagement."

Wow. Perfectly spun lies about why people would actually believe we were together, spoken so genuinely I could see people falling for it.

Disgust slithers through me. Did I ever really know him? Or did I blind myself to who he truly was? *Just like Eric.* My stomach rolls. I once thought I was a good judge of character. Another lie I told myself. "Sounds like I'm the perfect candidate for what you have in mind."

"You are."

Not because he loves me. Not because he's had an epiphany and realized he can't live without me. I'm the perfect candidate because I can elicit sympathy, tug on heartstrings with my pathetic fall from grace while making Liam look like someone he's not.

"No."

Liam blinks. "No?"

"No." I incline my head. "You have a lengthy list of past girlfriends and lovers. One of them can fill the role."

"I don't want anyone else."

Heat pricks my eyes. I have to leave. I start to move past him, but he shifts.

"Aislinn."

His voice whispers across my skin, sinks down into my veins. The sound of my name on his lips, spoken with such concern and affection, is pure temptation. One I desperately want to surrender to.

"I can help you, too."

I stare down at the floor. "How?"

"Marry me. You'll have a home, clothes—"

My head snaps up. Fury barrels through me. "So I'm going to be what? A pet?"

I spent months under Dexter's thumb. Now I'm living by the whims of federal government. I may have lost everything—my career, financial security, my friends—but I'll be damned if I give up my freedom again.

"No." He sounds genuinely shocked, frustrated. "It would just be to help you—"

"I don't want your help. Goodbye, Liam."

I brush past him and walk down the gallery. The music transitions from the slow, burning love song to another upbeat tune. I hurry down the stairs, not bothering to see if Liam is behind me or not. I have to put as much distance between us. Have to get out of this hell and back to…

My steps slow as I near the bottom. I pause, lean against the cool marble wall for a moment. I have nowhere to go. I gave up my apartment when I married Dexter. The FBI seized his house in Greenwich and the Park Avenue penthouse. Stephanie offered up the guesthouse at her and Eric's estate in Bedford. But I can't be around them. Not after Eric accepted my resignation without so much as a word of resistance.

A tiny part of me wants to accept what Liam is offering. I wouldn't have his love, but I'd have him in my life again. A touch of normalcy, a chance to rest.

Tempting. But I'm done being a convenience for the men

in my life, being of use until they decide they no longer need me.

No more.

I square my shoulders and walk down the remaining stairs. I'll get a hotel room for a couple nights, find a short-term rental. I'll find a job by the end of the week. I worked for a cleaning service in college and even bartended one summer to pay for a trip with Liam and Diana to Paris. Not where I saw my career in my late twenties. But I have skills. I can take care of myself. I don't want to leave New York, but if that's what it will take for me to survive, so be it.

I skirt around the edges of the ballroom and slip into the hotel lobby. Guests mill around, but thankfully no one looks twice at me. Most days I can handle the curious glances, the accusing stares when I walk through the building Eric's New York office is housed in.

Right now, though, I just want to go to a hotel—one I can afford—and fall asleep.

"Mrs. Simpson."

My shoulders climb up before I can stop them. I hate the sound of my married name. I haven't heard it in months, didn't think I would hear it again. So when I turn to face the man who uttered it with such casual familiarity, I'm angry.

Angry and instantly on guard as soon as I lay eyes on him. Tall, nearly as tall as Liam, but broader with thick shoulders, beefy arms and a slight smile that leaves a chill in its wake.

"I go by Miss Knightley now."

He doesn't shift. Doesn't blink. Just continues to stare with that tiny, creepy smile. "I'm sorry about your husband."

Few people at the funeral seemed genuinely remorseful about Dexter's passing. But beneath the blankness, there's a glimmer of glee. As if he's enjoying this.

The chill digs into my skin. "Thank you."

"Perhaps he mentioned me. Augustus Marston."

"No. He didn't. If you'll excuse me—"

Marston's hand shoots out and clamps down on my wrist. His palm is dry, cold, his grasp too tight.

Panic flutters in my chest. I force myself to stay still. He strikes me as the kind of man who wants me to be afraid, to run so he can chase. I raise my chin. Liam accused me of running away. He doesn't know how capable I am of fighting. No one does. "Are you planning on engaging in kidnapping tonight, Mr. Marston?"

His slow, reptilian blink is a victory. "No. Of course not, Mrs. Simpson." His leer deepens. "Excuse me. Miss Knightley. This is a business meeting."

I glance down at his hand. "Feels more like the beginning of unlawful restraint."

Augustus slowly releases me. "Dexter said you were timid."

"Dexter was a bastard."

Marston's chuckle sounds like the beginnings of a cartoon villain laugh. "Agreed. Which is why I'm here. Dexter owed me fifty thousand dollars. I'm here to collect."

Now it's my turn to blink. "Excuse me?"

"Fifty thousand. A high-stakes poker game he lost two days before he died." The smile vanishes. "I want my money."

"As I'm sure you're aware, I have no money." My voice stays level even as the fear deepens. I can handle dealing with the FBI and any other federal agency. But a poker boss I'm guessing has very strong ties to the criminal underworld in New York is something else entirely.

"You're too modest." He leans down. "Your adoptive father is worth an estimated four million dollars. You've rubbed plenty of…shoulders in your line of work. Politicians, investors, bankers, movie stars. You have multiple resources."

"And that's where you and I differ," I snap back. "I don't ask other people for money."

His eyes harden. "Then we have a problem."

Dreams of a quiet night disappear. The flickering hope that maybe, just maybe, the worst is now truly behind me evaporates. I'm in the lobby of one of the most glamorous hotels in New York surrounded by people. And I've never been more alone.

"I'm not involving anyone else in this." I maintain his gaze even though I want to sink into the floor. Want to throw back my head and scream. "What about a payment plan—"

"As you just pointed out, you have no money. As of tonight, according to my sources, no steady source of income." The smile returns, sharp and predatory. "Payment in full in one week or we'll have to work out another…arrangement."

The suggestion in his voice makes me want to gag. I managed to keep Dexter off me throughout the duration of our relationship. I'm not going to give my body to another man against my will.

But Marston won't play fair. There won't be any investigation, no due process or day in court. There will just be yet another man pressuring me, hunting me.

Bone-deep exhaustion seeps in. I'm suddenly so tired I can barely stand. I suck in a quick breath as the fear starts to take over. When will this end? I just need this to end.

No. I'm not going to let this be the moment that breaks me. I've come too far, survived too much, to let this man I've never met take control of my story now.

I lean in, close the distance between us. Marston moves back, just a fraction but enough to give me a desperately needed sense of power.

"I would rather jump in the Hudson in the middle of winter than spend another second in your company, let alone your bed," I spit out. "Unlike Dexter, I keep my promises. So you can either get your money in time, or I will use every single one of my connections to drag you into the spotlight and ruin you."

Marston reaches up, runs a finger down my hair. "I like your spirit, Miss Knightley."

I barely hold in my shudder. I'm about to retort when awareness pricks the back of my neck. My spine straightens a second before Marston's gaze shifts to a point over my shoulder. My satisfaction at seeing the blood leach out of his face is short-lived as Liam speaks from behind me.

"Hello, Marston."

CHAPTER FOUR

Aislinn

I WHIRL AROUND. Liam is standing just a couple feet behind me. The rage etched onto his handsome face catapults me back to another cold winter's day, one where I barely stopped Liam from killing Diana's foster father. His neck is corded, his pulse throbbing in his temple. Marston's eyes were blank, like staring into a void. But Liam's pale blue eyes are sharpened into icy daggers.

My gaze drops down. Liam's hands are curled into fists.

"Liam." I keep my voice gentle, my tone soft as I approach him slowly. "Liam, I'm all right."

Slowly, he drags his attention away from Marston and looks down at me. He grabs my wrist and starts to tug me to his side, his fingers gentle on the skin Marston gripped so hard just a couple ago. I wince.

Liam's gaze shifts down. I follow his eyes, see the lingering red marks from Marston's grip. "You're not all right." The guttural growl of his voice shocks me. Before I can reply, he steps forward and inserts himself between Marston and me. "I didn't think you were this stupid, Marston."

I tilt my head so I can see around Liam. If I thought Marston pale before, it's nothing compared to the whites of his eyes blending into the chalkiness of his skin. His lips stretch into another smile. But this one is forced and full of fear as he inclines his head to Liam.

"Mr. Whitlock." He clears his throat. "I didn't realize you and Miss Knightley were acquainted."

"Engaged."

My mouth drops open. "Liam—"

"Do you have a problem with my fiancée?"

Marston withers before my eyes. His shoulders curl in as he glances at me, then quickly looks down. "I didn't realize…when?"

"A recent development." Liam's voice is razor-sharp and furious. "Answer my question. Is there a problem?"

Marston slowly inclines his head in a deferential gesture I'd enjoy if Liam wasn't inserting himself into my problems. "A misunderstanding. That's all."

"Good. I'd hate to have to reach out to my lawyers or the FBI."

"No need." Marston clears his throat again. "Consider the debt paid in full." He nods to me. "My apologies for any inconvenience, Miss Knightley."

He's gone before I can say anything. I stand there, questions whirling through my mind. Why is a poker boss scared of Liam? How does Liam know him? Did Marston truly forgive the debt, or was this just to satisfy Liam and he'll come after me later?

And why did Liam call me his…

"Fiancée?" I choke out the word as Liam turns around to face me.

"It worked. He made an assumption. I played along."

My fingers curl around my clutch. Better than slapping him across the face in a lobby crowded with people. "If you have that kind of power over him, you could have just told him to leave me alone."

"Claiming you as mine will ensure your safety."

Mine. The word pulses between us. His eyes flare for a split second, ice to fire in the span of a heartbeat. But it's gone so quickly I wonder if I've imagined it.

Wished it, I think grimly. Even now, after everything, there's still a stupid part of me clinging to broken dreams. "And ensure you get what you wanted."

I nearly flinch as his gaze turns glacial. "Your opinion of me has certainly dropped."

I start to speak, but the all-too familiar sound of a camera clicking has me turning my head. There's a photographer ten feet away, a young woman dressed in black pants and a glittering black top. She snaps another photo before turning and darting toward the door.

"Security!" Liam bellows. "Stop her!"

The guard near the door lunges but just barely misses grabbing the photographer as she rushes out onto the street. Faces swivel from the door back to Liam and me as the room quiets for one second. Then the noise rises once more. Voices chattering, swirling around me as I stand in the midst of a vortex of public speculation.

"Was that a pickpocket?"

"Did you see what happened?"

"Wait, isn't that the senator's adopted kid? The one who married that man who…"

My heartbeat surges as invisible fingers dig into my chest and squeeze. My breathing quickens. A hot flush smothers my skin like a heavy blanket I can't escape from. The fear pushes to the surface, orders me to find an exit. Escape.

"Liam." I manage to gasp out his name even as my throat tightens. Before I can look up to see if he's heard me, a strong arm wraps around my waist. I lean into the comforting heat of his body.

"Aislinn?"

"I…" Heat pricks my eyes. "Help me. Please."

I've barely finished speaking when Liam dips and scoops me into his arms. I cling to him, not caring how I look, what people think. I just need him to get me out of here.

Liam's arms tighten around me. "Almost there."

The cold winter air is harsh against my bare back as he walks outside. More flashes go off, light after light, voices shouting. My heartbeat accelerates, pounds against my ribs so hard I'm sure it's going to burst out of my chest. I try to fight it, to remember the grounding techniques the counselor taught me. But there's so much noise, and I just need it to stop, or I won't be able to breathe—

"I've got you, Aislinn."

His voice penetrates. I mentally latch onto the sound of his voice, sink into it. I bury my face into his neck and breathe in the warm spiciness of his cologne. A scent he's been wearing for years. I release a shuddering breath as the familiarity of it washes over me, takes the edge off my panic.

"Hold on."

A moment later he eases me into the back of a vehicle. The door closes, shutting out the lights and the noise. It comes back for a split second when another door opens. I hear more shouts, but try to shut them out as I focus on the sounds around me. The quiet murmur of the radio. The loud click of the other door closing, followed by the softer click of a seat belt. I wiggle my fingertips, then clench and unclench my hands. Each sound, each movement, gradually lessens the tightness in my chest. My heart is still racing, my breathing still fast. But the panic is receding.

I force my eyes open. Buttery leather seats on the opposite side of what I now realize is a limo. The lights of New York outside my window.

And Liam sitting next to me.

Slowly, bit by bit, I regain control. My breathing slows, as does my pulse. The pain in my chest eases. But it leaves room for the subsequent exhaustion to rush in, drag my eyelids down as I sink into the seat. I'm too tired to be embarrassed by letting Liam see what I've been struggling with for months.

"How long?"

My head lolls back against the headrest. "What?"

"The panic attacks."

I want to reply with something smart. But it would take too much effort, so I opt for the simple truth. "Eight months."

Dexter and I had argued. I'd started for the door. He'd grabbed my arm, swung me around and flung me onto the couch. When I'd tried to get up, he'd pushed me back down into the cushions, held me there as my pulse had skyrocketed and my breathing had started coming out in sharp, frantic gasps. When it was finally over, and I'd become aware of my surroundings again, Dexter had been sitting in the chair across from me, a brandy in one hand and a sneer of disgust on his face.

So fucking weak.

The words had been a switch. One minute I'd felt disoriented, violated, frail. The next I'd been…empty. Felt nothing. A merciful nothing that had kept me sane through the tangled mess of my new life.

But I can't tell Liam any of that. Don't want him to hear how feeble I'd been. I breathe in a deep, cleansing breath. "I'm seeing a therapist."

"That's a start."

"Don't." I slightly shake my head. "This isn't your fight, Liam." God, I can't even open my eyes. I've always experienced exhaustion after the attacks, but never this acute.

"It is now."

"We are *not* engaged." I force myself to open my eyes, to meet his gaze. "Marston is the only one who heard you. Given that he's a poker boss at best and probably has ties to organized crime, I doubt the press are going to pay attention to him."

Liam stares at me for a long moment. Then he shrugs. *Shrugs.* Like the fake engagement or marriage or whatever scheme Liam concocted isn't that big of a deal. Except to him, it's probably not. The marriage isn't important. The boost to his image is.

"Where should I take you?" he asks quietly.

I hesitate. "Chelsea."

"You moved?"

"Temporary lodgings."

"Address."

I wince. "Could you make that sound less like a bark and more like a request?"

"No."

I mentally roll my eyes. "It's a hotel, Liam."

"A hotel."

Fatigue pulls at me, whispers in my ear and encourages me to just tune Liam out for a moment. "Yes. Until I can make other arrangements."

"Why didn't you reach out to Diana and me?"

Pain tightens my chest. *Because I couldn't. Because I was trying to keep you safe.* "Things change, Liam." I can't fight it anymore. I relax back into the leather. "I appreciate your help tonight. Would you wake me up when we get there?"

I hear a muted reply but can't discern the words. I try to process, then quickly give up as I spiral down into a blissful state of nothing.

Liam

The limo stops outside the brownstone home in the quieter Upper East Side. It's been twenty minutes, and already security at Fifty-seventh Street notified me there are paparazzi on the sidewalk outside my penthouse in Billionaires' Row. It's only a couple miles away, but we might as well be in an entirely different world inside this peaceful, elm-lined corridor.

Aislinn wanted to believe no one heard our run-in with Marston, so I dropped it, let her have a few minutes to rest. But my instinct was right. There's no way out but forward.

My eyes flick to Aislinn, still asleep on the opposite side of the car. She'd been so focused on Marston and then me, she'd failed to notice how many people have been paying attention to our little drama unfolding.

I rub at my jaw. I'd been so focused on her that I had failed to notice the photographers by the door until they'd raised their cameras.

My phone dings again. I glance down and stifle a groan when I see Diana's name on the screen. It's the third time she's called in seven minutes. I send this one to voicemail, too.

I'm not worried about her being angry or jealous. Our engagement was fake. There wasn't a single moment during our whole charade when I experienced anything but the same feelings of friendship we'd had for years. On the few occasions I've seen Diana and my brother together, the way she looks at him and he at her, almost made me envious for a relationship like theirs.

Almost. I wish them well. I want nothing but happiness for them. But I also know how cruel life can be, how swiftly it changes from light to dark. I have no desire to invite the potential for loss back into my life. It's one of the reasons I've struggled to bond with Ari.

I glance over at Aislinn again. Strands of gold have fallen across her face. Her lips are parted, her breathing even and peaceful. Her face is relaxed, serene, yet I can still see the darkness etched into her skin beneath her eyes. The responses I've had tonight—the awareness, the small flares of attraction—are concerning. Not once did I experience this with Diana, and that was after touching her, dancing with her, pretending to be in love.

My phone chimes, signaling a text message. I open it and grimace when I see Diana's screenshot of me carrying Aislinn out of the hotel, her head tucked into the crook of my neck. A social media post with the caption *Crook's widow already engaged to legendary investor!*

I'll get my feelings under control. There is no other choice. The news is out, and we have to move forward. Starting with finding a safe place for Aislinn to stay.

Anger stirs. The address of the hotel she gave me was in a seedy neighborhood, the kind where drug deals take place in broad daylight. Every choice she makes is a clear indicator that the worst-case scenario is preferable to accepting my help.

Yes, it's a ding to my ego. But it cuts, too, damn it. I thought we were closer than this. Thought she trusted me. How many times had I told Diana that Aislinn was doing whatever it was she was doing for reasons we didn't know about yet?

"Sir?"

I nod to Paul, my driver. "Could you get the front door, Paul? I'll carry Miss Knightley."

I get out and circle around the limo, keeping an eagle eye out for photographers lurking behind parked cars or hidden in the shadows. But there's no one. A quiet, private neighborhood with gated trees and neighbors that include ambassadors, TV actors and investment bankers. When I decided to open my own firm, I bought the townhouse primarily for use by my clients—a secure getaway when they come to the city that offered quiet luxury and privacy. I thought of every detail, planned for every eventuality.

Not once did I think my personal life and some misguided,

overly conservative opinions about dating would drag everything I've been working for to the brink.

I open the limo door slowly. Aislinn doesn't stir. I stare, relieved when her chest moves up and down. I lean down, unbuckle her, and gather her into my arms. She murmurs something and curls into my chest, her face resting once more against my neck, one hand wrapping around the hem of my jacket. My arms tighten around her.

I went after her because I was worried about her, yes, but also because she didn't give me a chance to dive deeper into how our marriage of convenience could benefit her, give her a start at a new life. Her facing down Marston had catapulted me back to that freezing winter afternoon when Aislinn and I had heard the snap of leather, followed by Diana's pained scream and a puppy's frightened yelp. The same rage, the same determination to stop whatever was happening by any means necessary.

But as I'd stalked across the hotel lobby, seen Aislinn lean in, shoulders thrown back and her spine straight, other emotions had reared their head. Fear. Admiration. And, most concerning of all, possessiveness. I'd seen the look in Marston's eye as he'd stared down at Aislinn. He wanted her. Just for that look alone, I could have punched him right in the face.

I walk up the stairs and shift Aislinn in my arms so that I can punch in the security code. Once inside, I tap the button to lock the door and go upstairs. The house boasts three bedrooms for clients who may have guests or family with them. But so far, I'm the only one who's used it, crashing in the master bedroom on late nights when I didn't feel like making the trek back to my penthouse. The first two bedrooms are unmade, but the last one, the one I've slept in, has fresh sheets, a clean blanket and a few amenities to make it feel more like a home.

I carry her in and lay her gently down on the bed. She

stirs but doesn't open her eyes. I pull the blanket up over her and tuck the edges around her shoulders. I start to turn away, then freeze when her lips curve into a small smile. She inhales deeply, then releases a breath, as if she finally knows she's safe.

My hands clench into fists. Extreme emotional reactions after nearly a year of being separated from a woman who's like family to me. Of seeing her eviscerated in the media, abandoned by her adoptive parents and on the verge of losing everything.

Yes. That has to be it.

I'm at the door, my hand on the knob, when she breathes out a single word that stops me in my tracks.

"Liam."

My fingers clench down on the knob. I imagined it. Misheard it. Or even if I didn't, she's asleep. Whispering the name of the last person who helped her when she was losing control in a crowded room in front of prying eyes and flashing cameras. It means nothing.

I close the door behind me. Nothing.

I go back downstairs and turn on the light in my study before powering on my laptop. A couple minutes of research confirms that news of our engagement is everywhere.

Not how I pictured things playing out. But as I scroll through the pictures, the hastily written articles, the speculation in the comments, I can't help but smile. Most of the attention is positive, romantic, with writers and commenters fixated on my getting in-between Marston and Aislinn, carrying her out of the hotel. There's a few mentions of Dexter and his criminal activities, but it seems most outlets are following the lead of the initial article and highlighting how the FBI and DOJ's recent investigation cleared Aislinn of any wrongdoing.

Satisfied, I lean back in my chair. I imagined something

more formal when it came to announcing our engagement. But this media coverage is good for both of us. In less than an hour, public opinion is already shifting in her favor.

My phone rings again. I frown when I see Eric's name pop up. Stephanie reached out several times over the last few months to see if Diana and I had talked to Aislinn. But Eric hadn't reached out. Not once.

The phone barely stops ringing when Eric texts me.

Where is she?

My jaw tightens. Eric saw what was happening to Aislinn, had to have known something was wrong when she started dating Dexter. When she fucking married him. How could he have missed how miserable she was?

Eric didn't protect her last time. Hell, I failed to protect her. But I'm not going to now. For better or worse, she and I are tied together for the foreseeable future. She's going to be pissed when she wakes up. But once she sees the media coverage, sees people are finally on her side, she'll see that this might be the best possible thing that could have happened.

I type back two words: With me.

Bubbles pop up showing he's typing a reply.

I switch my phone to silent and turn it over. I don't care what he has to say. As far as I'm concerned, he and anyone else who has hurt Aislinn can go to hell.

CHAPTER FIVE

Aislinn

SUNLIGHT WARMS MY SKIN. I snuggle deeper under a soft blanket and breathe in the delicious, sexy scent of cedar and spice.
Liam.

My eyes fly open as I sit up. I look around frantically. My heart jumps into my throat as I take in the unfamiliar surroundings. The huge bed with its mahogany frame. The thick navy blanket. The plush leather chair and ottoman tucked into an alcove and a stone fireplace where flames are crackling over several thick logs.

I blink and bite back my panic. It's been three months since my last panic attack. Three. I'm angry at myself that I lost control in a public setting, and in front of Liam, for God's sake. I'm not going to do that again. Especially when I don't know where I am.

I glance down and breathe a sigh of relief. I'm still in the same dress. There's no sign that anyone else has slept in the bed with me. This looks far too nice and homey to be a hotel. I distinctly remember telling Liam where I wanted to go last night, but after falling asleep, I remember nothing. Nothing but a sensation of being held. Of being safe.

I shake my head. This isn't Liam's penthouse on Billionaires' Row. As nice as his home in the sky is, it always felt more like Liam showing off his wealth than a place he could call home. This room, however, seems more like the kind of place he would enjoy. The paintings on the wall, mostly watercolors of the sea. I know he and his parents have spent a lot of time at a beach in Rhode Island. Water has always been calming for him. The colors seem like him, too: brown leather and dark wood trim with dark blue walls. Some might find it too dark, but it feels restful. Peaceful.

I can't remember the last time I would ever describe Liam as being peaceful.

Okay, stop. I need to stop psychoanalyzing the man I should not be in love with, especially after the ridiculous idea he proposed last night. Instead I need to focus on figuring out where I am, how I got here and what I'm going to do next.

I notice my phone lying on an end table. I reach over and grab it, frowning when it vibrates in my hand. I open the screen, and my mouth drops open. Dozens of text messages and numerous missed calls from Eric, Stephanie, coworkers I once considered friends…and Diana.

I press my lips together. I miss her. I miss her so much it hurts. But every time I think of her, I think of her hand tucked into the crook of Liam's arm. Think of the ring glittering on her finger. Feel the snapping of a connection I never thought could be broken. The severing of a friendship I once believed would withstand anything.

It's a pain I have to carry alone. Diana did nothing wrong. And while I can't stand the man Liam has become, with his twisted proposal and scheming to further his career, he had no idea his first engagement would crush me.

I scroll past Diana's texts and open one from Jamie, one of Eric's press assistants.

How did I not know you were dating Liam Whitlock? And now you're engaged?!

I freeze. Beneath the text is a screenshot from social media of Liam carrying me through the hotel lobby. There's a link. Slowly, I force myself to tap it. More pictures come up of Liam with his arm around my waist at the beginning of my panic attack, carrying me outside the hotel and trying to shield me from the cameras with his body. Liam setting me inside the limo.

I scroll through the text, the links. Shock turns into anger. I didn't like what Liam proposed yesterday. But going behind my back while I slept off a panic attack is something I never would have expected of him.

I sling back the blanket and scramble out of bed. My bare feet hit the floor. I stalk across the room and throw open the door. A quick search reveals no one on the second floor. In fact, there's no furniture in any room except the bedroom I was in.

Still angry and a little bit creeped out, I hurry down the stairs to the first floor. The scent of food hits me. My stomach growls. I don't even remember glancing at the time, but obviously it's the next day. The last time I ate was lunch. I couldn't stomach anything more than a couple of forced bites of appetizers at the gala last night.

I follow the scent toward the back of the house and step into the kitchen.

Liam is leaning casually against a granite top counter, one long leg crossed over the other. He's dressed casually in a hunter green shirt, a trio of buttons undone at the throat and the sleeves rolled up to his elbows, and a pair of black jeans. Silver platters crowd the table next to him. He has his phone pressed to his ear, but as soon as he sees me, he ends the call.

"Good morning."

"You bastard."

One eyebrow arches up. "Not the greeting I was expecting."

"What did you expect?" I cross my arms over my chest. "For me to just sit back and let you tell everyone we're engaged while I'm sleeping off a panic attack?"

The air in the room drops ten degrees. Liam pushes off the counter and starts walking toward me with slow, measured steps.

I stand my ground. I'm not going to be intimidated by him.

"Did you ever like me?"

The question takes me back. "What?"

"You think I'm capable of the most heinous acts." He spits the words out, his voice sharp and lethal. "It's a wonder we were ever friends if this is what you thought I was truly capable of."

Guilt tries to seep in, but I push it away. "The man I used to know is not the man standing in front of me today. The man standing in front of me," I say, "used what happened last night—"

"I did nothing. As you were sleeping across from me, my phone started blowing up. They snapped compromising photos of us. Someone overheard our conversation with Marston and told the press we were engaged."

There's no hint of lying in his gaze, no tell. The guilt pushes back, hard. Am I being so hard on him because he deserves it? Or because I'm still angry? Hurt? "Okay," I say. "Have you tried to tell everyone it's not true?"

Liam grabs his phone, taps it a couple of times and hands it to me. It takes me a moment to focus on the words, to look past the photo of his body arched protectively over mine as he carries me out of the hotel. A dramatic photo. Both of us in black, with snowflakes swirling around us. No wonder it's getting so much press.

I continue scrolling, then stop. The title screams in all capital letters: Fairy Tale at Last for Innocent Victim, Government Criminal.

I scroll down farther. The story paints me as an innocent young woman seduced into marriage by an older man. It's the kindest portrayal I've seen of myself in the media since Dexter died. "Why do people care?"

I hate that my voice cracks. Hate that the words of a writer I've never met can make me feel something when I've spent so many months burying my emotions.

"Everyone loves a fairy tale," Liam said quietly. "You used to."

I scoff and shove his phone back at him. "I grew up. Just like you always said I should."

Silence falls. Slowly, I look up.

Liam is gazing at me with a tenderness that I have to consciously steel myself against. It's not romantic. It's not sweet. It's pitying. "I never meant like this, Aislinn."

"No. You were right. It was time to grow up." I look up at him. "Happily-ever-after is an illusion."

Liam's eyes sharpen. "What do you mean?"

Part of me wants to confide in him right then and there. To tell him how Eric looked the other way on just who was funding his first campaign, how he rubbed shoulders with men just like Dexter. Manipulated our country for their own financial gain and reputation.

Yet something holds me back. I don't owe Eric any loyalty, but I'm not quite ready to throw him to the wolves.

"I'm asking a lot of you," Liam says quietly. "But this arrangement will help us both."

"Why do you want to work for clients that dictate how you live your personal life?"

"Arthur Tarsney. William Luther. Anne Singleton. Know the names?"

A face appears in my mind. Sharp nose, dark gray hair combed back from a prominent brow. "I know Tarsney." He's been a generous donor to Eric's campaign over the years. Luxury real estate developer.

He's been a donor for over two decades. Is he one of the ones who bought votes with his support? Did he influence legislation so he could make more profit?

"And Luther," Liam continues, "is a former NASA engineer turned inventor with a patent on some of the latest technology being utilized by cell phone companies as they develop enhanced satellite systems. And Singleton took control of her husband's shipping company when he passed away in a car accident and turned it into an empire. They're the best."

"And you want to work with the best."

Liam has always wanted the best. I never begrudged him for it. How could I given the way he, Diana, and I grew up? But right now, it makes me sad. First it was getting into the best school for finance and accounting, then securing the best internship, and then a job with the most prestigious wealth management firm in the city. Now it's putting together his own management firm and having the wealthiest clients while owning a slate of New York's most impressive real estate.

Will any of it ever be enough?

"I'm the youngest investor in our firm's history to make partner. I took my own salary and turned it into a fortune nearing one billion dollars. I can do the same for my clients."

He speaks factually, earnestly.

"Then why does your dating life matter?"

"Luther's the one who brought up his concerns about what he referred to as my cavalier love life." His face darkens. "My accomplishments have been in a short amount of time. There's no longevity to back me up, and Luther, along with the others, have concerns that the way I've lived my personal life will be how I live my professional life. They want to see endurance, commitment."

"I'm sure Luther wasn't a saint back in the day."

"Back in the day, it doesn't matter because Luther was an engineer who wasn't under scrutiny by multimillion-and billion-dollar clients looking for an investor to manage their wealth. An investor they need to know won't back out of his obligations."

I open my mouth to argue, then decide what's the point? Liam's obviously ready to sell his commitment to bachelorhood for a chance to rub shoulders with snooty clients.

"Did you like everyone Eric did business with?"

The question is an arrow straight to my pride. "No."

"Did you still work with them?"

"Yes," I ground out.

"Being able to open up my own firm and have clients like Tarsney, Luther, and Singleton cement my firm's future. I owe it to…"

He stops himself, glances away. I frown, but before I can press, he turns back to me.

"This is what I want. This marriage can help us both. You read those comments. You won't have to sign off and start a new life somewhere. You can get your old life back or start a new legacy without always wondering if someone's going to recognize your name."

Oh, he's good. All the things I told myself I'd gotten over, that I no longer wanted, he's now offering to me on a silver platter. I still have no desire to go back and work for Eric. But to have my reputation back, to be able to figure out what I want to do with the rest of my life without constantly looking over my shoulder…

"Think about it while we eat." He nods to the table over my shoulder. "Before the food gets cold."

The very mention of food has my stomach growling again. Wincing, I glance back over my shoulder. My eyes widen as I take in the number of serving dishes. "What is all this?"

Liam moves around me and starts removing lids. Steam rises off a plate of thick omelets, with small bowls of chives and caviar sitting next to it. Oysters chill on ice. One platter hosts bagels sliced in half and piled high with smoked salmon, strips of red onion, capers and dill. Another offers sugar-coated donut bites with plump raspberries perched on the rim. There's a pitcher of mimosa with freshly sliced oranges resting on the surface and a coffeepot next to a plate of scones.

"Food."

I roll my eyes. "I can see that. Are you expecting company?"

"Just you." Liam grabs a plate and starts serving himself. "I ordered your favorites."

I blink rapidly as emotion wraps around my heart and squeezes. "The donut bites are from the bakery on the Upper West Side."

"Yes."

"But the omelets…that's from the restaurant on Roosevelt Island."

"Like I said, your favorites." As I stare at the food, Liam sets the plate down at the far end of the table and pulls out a chair. "Come sit."

His voice is gentle again, friendly. I respond to it before I can stop myself, placing one foot in front of the other as I cross the kitchen and sit down. I pick up my fork and cut off a small piece of omelet and force myself to eat slowly. It's hard when the omelet is cooked to perfection, savory with a hint of butter, when each bite is made all the more indulgent with the caviar and dill.

I keep my eyes on my food as Liam moves around the kitchen and fills his own plate. It's all so…ordinary. Domestic. Peaceful.

Liam will never love me. I know this. Will have to prepare myself for those moments when weakness will try to creep in. But the thought of having something like this, a calm friendship I can enjoy as I stitch myself back together, is no longer a simple temptation. It's something I desperately want.

CHAPTER SIX

Liam

"How long?"

I try, and fail, to suppress the triumph in my voice. "Five years."

She glares at me. "Two," she counters.

I lean back in my chair, pick up my glass of mimosa and smirk at her. I've been dealing in mergers and acquisitions for eight years. I know how to make a deal. "Five."

"This isn't one of your conference rooms."

Her retort, the fire in her voice, has me sitting up straight. This isn't the Aislinn I'm used to, the friend with the soft voice and kind smile who tries to make sure everyone is happy. No, this is a fiercer Aislinn, someone who won't back down.

"You need me." She points her fork at me, making me grateful we're sitting on opposite side of the table. "You're offering a good deal. But don't think for one second that I will not turn around and walk out the door if I don't like the terms."

The air between us shifts. Crackles. The attraction from last night rears its head, slams into me with a force I can't ignore. My eyes drop down to her mouth, then back up to her mesmerizing eyes. For a moment, I imagine I see a similar desire in the familiar emerald—

Stop. I've always enjoyed verbally sparring with the women I've dated. Aislinn's newfound confidence is just intriguing.

"Four."

Before she can reply, her phone rings. Aislinn looks down at it and grimaces.

"Who is it?"

"Stephanie."

Her voice is resigned. But beneath I can hear the sadness, the bone-deep ache that comes from missing someone who's still here.

An ache I've fought off every day since Aislinn disappeared.

She starts to lay the phone on the table, then stops. "I should probably take this."

I think back to the way Stephanie's face looked the last time we talked, the fear and hopelessness as she tried to figure out why her daughter had distanced herself. "She'd like that."

Aislinn nodded and stood. I heard her faint "Hi, Stephanie" as she moved down the hall.

I prop my elbows on the table and scrub my hands over my face. From single to engaged—again—in less than twenty-four hours. The path had been choppier than expected, but I'd done it. Goal achieved.

But there was no satisfaction. No thrill of conquering the next step. No, right now all I felt was worry for my friend who had changed so drastically.

I stood and moved to the window. The snow was still falling, thick, heavy flakes that quickly piled on top of the branches outside. This corner of New York was quieter than most. With the snow smothering most of the sound, and obscuring my neighbors' homes from view, I could almost pretend I was back in the country.

Grief hit me hard and fast. Inevitable whenever I think about my parents. When I remember the early years spent in upstate New York, hot summers running through the fields along the river and winters spent cozied up by the fire watching Christmas movies and sipping on Mom's hot chocolate, I feel the twinges of a peace I haven't experienced in years. The comfort of Mom's hugs, the reassurance of Dad's deep, rumbling voice.

I still remember sneaking down one winter's night to look at all the presents piled under the tree and catching them stealing a kiss under the mistletoe, Mom's hand on Dad's cheek and his arms wrapped around her like he never wanted to let go. I'd had the usual *ick* response of any eight-year-old boy. But it had also made me feel…safe. I was lucky to have two parents who had wanted me, who told me whenever I asked that my birth mom had loved me so much, she'd given me a chance at a better life.

A life altered just six months after we moved to the city. A car racing too fast down a side street through a red light. Police at the door of our apartment in the middle of the night.

My fingers curl into fists at my side. The man who killed them is serving a long sentence for the crimes he committed that night. But it didn't bring them back. It didn't stop the deep, heart-wrenching ache as Child Services searched for any record of my birth mother or any family members and came up with nothing. It didn't change the fact that at age ten I was thrust from a loving, happy family into a system struggling to serve the hundreds of thousands of children in its care.

I glance back at the door. I can still hear the quiet murmur of Aislinn's voice. I would give anything right now to have Mom and Dad here with me, to tell me what to do to help her. I can't remember the last time I let myself remember, let myself feel.

But in this moment, I miss them so fucking much it takes everything inside me not to let out a yell of rage that life could be so cruel. Not just to me, but to two of the best people I've ever known.

My eyes flick over to my jacket hanging off the chair. I think back to the photo inside a small plastic bag. One Ari gave to me the last time he was in New York. A photo of the woman who had done even more than I could ever imagine; given up her life so I could have one. I haven't looked at in nearly two weeks, but I carry it around just the same. Some days it feels like a subtle way of honoring her. Other days it feels like penance. Logically I know her death isn't my fault. But that doesn't chase away the guilt.

The floor creaks behind me. I swallow the pain, the anger, and smooth out my face before I turn to face Aislinn.

My fiancée.

She's still in the damn dress, the one that makes a man think of sliding the straps down her arms and revealing more of her naked skin. Of watching it pool in a black silken heap at her feet before—

God, stop.

I mentally grasp onto other thoughts—finance reports, investment summaries, numbers and data—to stop the lust. Lust I have absolutely zero business feeling. If Aislinn agrees to this relationship, it will be strictly platonic. I may be battling back a need I've never experienced before, but I'll be damned if I'm going to let it get in the way of rebuilding my friendship with Aislinn.

"Everything all right?"

She listlessly places her phone on the table. "As well as it can be, I suppose. She's worried about me, which is nice, I suppose." She sinks into her chair, and I follow suit, pouring her a tall glass of mimosa. She takes it and downs a good third of it.

"Careful now." I grin. "You'll be on the floor of the living room groaning about how the room is spinning before too long."

Her lips quirk at my reference to her first time drinking, when Diana and I made the mistake of taking our lightweight friend bar-hopping in SoHo for her twenty-first birthday.

I miss those years. Miss the casual ease of our friendship, the brightness of our futures. Miss when Aislinn was happy.

Aislinn sets her glass down on the table, folds her arms, and leans forward. "Now, as I recall, we were in the middle of a negotiation."

Blood hums in my veins at the challenge in her tone. I lean back in my chair and smile at her again. "Your move, Knightley."

Aislinn

"Three," I shoot back.

"Three and a half."

I bite down on my lower lip to prevent the reflexive smile at his ridiculousness. I mentally calculate. In three and a half years, I'll be just over thirty. Three and a half years to get my life back in order, get myself financially stable. Then, maybe, I'll be in a good place to still pursue the one personal goal I have left.

"Three and a half. And while we're on terms," I continue, ignoring his smug smirk, "I'd ask that you keep any affairs as private as possible."

Liam's smile evaporates. His eyes narrow to slits. "Excuse me?"

"Not only would it hurt your persona, but I just don't feel comfortable—"

"I'm not going to be sleeping with other women while I have a ring on my finger." The disgust dripping from his voice has me looking down at my plate. "I have always been upfront with the women I've dated. My affairs have been brief, but I have never once been unfaithful."

I look down at the floor and suck in a deep breath. "I wasn't trying to insult you. I just didn't think that you would put your romantic life on hold for three and a half years."

"Well, think again." He pushes away from the table and stalks over to the window.

Once upon a time, I would have gotten up, too, laid a comforting hand on his shoulder, would have invited him to tell me what was wrong. But those times are long gone. Liam and I are both very different people now than we were almost a year ago.

"I expect the same of you," he snaps over his shoulder.

I take the shot. Yes, I don't like the way he's doing things, but I have no room to judge. And now, I'm a willing participant in his scheme.

God, I don't even recognize myself anymore. When did I become this person? A schemer, a liar? The bright-eyed girl who met Liam and Diana all those years ago in the high school theater would be disgusted with the woman I've become.

"I'll be faithful," I say quietly.

His fingers knot into a fist at his side. "I'll have a bank account started for you. Deposits of—"

"No."

Liam glances back at me. "No?"

Now it's my turn to stand. "I'm not accepting payment to be your wife."

He opens his mouth as if to protest, then stops. "It won't be like it was with him."

I swallow hard. Liam and Diana could always read me. Not too hard when I always wore my heart on my sleeve. But it's just concerning to know, lately, he can still see me, still know me—even when there are so many days when I no longer know myself. "I just can't."

"An alternative suggestion then." He pauses, waits for my reluctant nod. "I know you have limited funds, but you have some. You won't have to worry about rent or utilities for the foreseeable future. Give me half and let me invest it for you."

I want to say no purely on principle. But Liam's talented. Otherwise, he wouldn't have caught the interest of someone like Arthur Tarsney. "All right."

Liam picks his phone back up and taps the screen. "Next Saturday?"

"For what?"

"Our wedding."

My throat constricts. "That soon?"

"Take advantage of the good press, start the countdown on our contract."

"And make sure I don't change my mind?"

"A consideration, yes."

I look away. It's all moving so fast. Just like last time. One day, I woke up happy, content. In the span of a couple of hours, I lost everything. My friends, the relationship I had with my adoptive father, my beliefs about the world. Everything, gone in an instant.

But I remind myself, Liam isn't Dexter. This arrangement is different. I'd be a fool not to take advantage of it. Maybe, just maybe, it'll change not only the public's perception of me but the people at the foundation. Maybe, after all this is through, I'll at least have some of what I've dreamed.

"Should we shake on it?"

Liam eyes my hand. "Given that we're going to have to kiss in front of people next week, maybe we should start practicing now."

My lip curls in disgust at Liam for suggesting it—and the desire that surges from my stomach straight down into my core at the thought of his mouth on mine. Can I do this? Separate myself enough to survive three and a half years married to Liam? I have to be. No time like the present to test myself.

"All right."

Surprise flares in Liam's eyes. He steps forward.

My pulse jumps. My breasts grow heavy. God, can he see how badly I've wanted this? How many nights I've dreamed of kissing him, the feeling of his hands on my skin—

My phone rings.

I look down. Eric. The sight of his name has the same effectiveness as someone dumping a bucket of ice water over me. My conversation with Stephanie had been...hard. I miss her. Miss the relationship we had. The genuine concern in her voice had nearly undone me. I'd almost asked her.

But what if I was right, and she confirmed she'd been involved all along? Or, worse, what if she knew nothing about it, and I upended her life the same way Dexter had ruined mine?

Eric, though... I had no interest in talking to Eric. But I needed to get away from Liam. Needed space to breathe and think.

"I... I should get this."

I don't look at Liam as I hurry out over the kitchen. Wait until I get to the foot of the stairs before I hit Ignore. Eric will be furious, spouting off about image and damage control. What will the voters think of his adopted daughter getting engaged within a year of her husband passing? A husband who was a crook?

Takes one to know one, Eric.

But one good thing Eric's call did was interrupt that ridiculous moment in the kitchen. I hurry up the stairs and don't stop moving until I'm back in the bedroom with the door firmly shut behind me.

CHAPTER SEVEN

Aislinn

For the second time in a year, I'm staring at my reflection in a mirror and contemplating how different my wedding dress looks from what I'd always imagined for myself. When I married Dexter, I wore a tan sheath dress. I hadn't been bold enough to wear the black I'd wanted to, but tan had felt like a small middle finger to the man who had taken control of my life. The small satisfaction had carried me through the ceremony.

Today, though, I took a different tactic. I wanted a dress that would make me feel like a princess. More like my old self.

It's lovely, probably too opulent for a courthouse wedding. But when I saw it in the window of a gallery earlier this week, I couldn't resist sneaking back a few hours later to try it on. Taking a private car to the back alley entrance after hours had felt ridiculous, but it was a better alternative than giving the creeping vultures who seemed to photograph my every move these days a chance at seeing my wedding dress.

Worth it.

A full princess ball gown, with a bell-shaped skirt made of fluffy tulle and a sweetheart neckline decked with tiny jewels. The corset-like bodice adds a touch of sexiness, while the gauzy swaths of tulle that gently wrap over my upper arms feel like wings. The stylist I booked kept my makeup simple, my hair done in loose curls.

I smile slightly at my reflection in the mirror. For a moment, I see her—the old me. The one full of hopes and dreams and fairy-tale endings.

Then I raise my chin and see the woman I've become. Hard, cold, pragmatic. I have one dream I've held on to with an iron grip. But I've let everything else go, surrendered it to reality. There's strength, yes, but there's also a deep loneliness I've never experienced before. Not just from lack of friends or family, but a lack of...well, myself. I don't know who I am anymore. Don't know who I want to be. Right now, in this moment, that makes me feel the loneliest out of everything happening in my chaotic life.

I cut the cord on the pity party and rearrange one of the gauzy sleeves. At least today's ceremony will be cut and dry—a quick elopement in a courthouse just outside the city with two witnesses. Miles away from the prying eyes of the press, granting Liam and me the privacy we so desperately crave after our mutual turns in the spotlight.

Although, I think with a slight smile, hopefully I can ask someone to snap a photo of me with their phone. Even though marrying Liam is still not in my list of top choices, I like the way I look today. Years from now, this will be the moment I focus on. That for the first time in a very long time, I feel beautiful and hopeful. The future looks nothing like what I dreamed of so long ago. But it's far better than where I was just one week ago.

I shake my head. One week, yet it feels like a lifetime. I spent most of my time at the brownstone out of sight of the cameras. Given that Liam will be officially opening the doors to Whitlock Investments a week after we return from our honeymoon, he's been gone most days and quite a few nights, too, finalizing licenses for his advisors and brokers, ensuring his agreements with banks and investment platforms and confirming his client list.

A list I overheard him saying on the phone now included his top three clients.

My humor disappears. Liam could have been a lot of things. But even from the first time I met him, he was always driven to succeed, to do better and be better. He told Diana and me a little about his adoptive parents. He also hinted that the foster homes he grew up in had been less than kind. Given his near-constant state of alertness, I had always assumed he'd experienced similar levels of abuse as Diana had. Yet he rarely talked about it. He always offered a listening ear, a teasing smile and a protective streak—whether Diana and I wanted it or not. But he always held himself back.

I do seem to have a knack for getting involved with emotionally unavailable people. Liam. Eric. My birth family.

I glance down at my dress. I have something new, obviously. I chose pale blue lacy underwear at the encouragement of the salesperson at the bridal boutique. Not that Liam will be seeing it. But I bought it for myself, not for him.

Still, I think with a touch of tightness in my throat, I'm missing the something borrowed. The something old. A parent beside me to walk me down the aisle.

The tightness shifts down, wraps around my heart as I fight back a sudden wave of tears. I wanted to ask Stephanie so badly to be here. But I can't. Not only would she ask if Eric could come, but I don't want to establish that connection again only to have it broken down the road. Broken when I learn she was involved or broken when she turns away from me for ruining the image she has of her husband.

I raise my chin. I was always told by my foster care parents how sweet I was, how if they were in a place to adopt me, they would. I clung to those words, to that hope, throughout my childhood. I knew life wasn't perfect, but I was fortunate to have kind families who genuinely supported me, who helped keep that hope alive. A hope Stephanie and Eric had validated when they'd adopted me.

But I know better now. Pinning my hopes and dreams on others does nothing but leave room for disappointment and heartache. When I depend on myself, I can make my own way.

I refocus on the mirror. I have three and a half years to plan and prepare for that dream. Today, though, I need to focus on getting through this ceremony. I turn one way, then the other. Doubt creeps in. Is it too much? Did I really need to purchase an actual wedding dress?

Yes.

Even if I'm nervous, even if there's that nasty weak streak in me that wants Liam to like it, I wanted to wear this for myself. I won't marry again. Two loveless marriages are enough in one lifetime. But if this is going to be my last wedding, I'm going to look good walking down that aisle.

A knock sounds on my door. I frown. Liam said he was traveling ahead to the courthouse to make sure everything was ready and the security detail was in place. Did he forget something?

"Yes?"

"It's me. Diana."

I never thought it possible to have one's heart jump and sink at the same time. I swallow past the sudden thickness in my throat and smooth my hands over the tulle skirt as I walk to the door. I grab the knob, whisper a quick prayer and open it.

"Aislinn!" Diana's smile is so bright it nearly blinds me. I blink, unsure of what to say, but she beats me to it by letting out a very Diana-like squeal. "You look so beautiful." She starts to reach for me, then pauses. Uncertainty flickers across her face.

I debate for less than a second before I step forward and hug her.

Her arms come around me, and she crushes me to her. "I missed you, Aislinn."

I have to fight to keep the tears at bay. "I missed you, too."

She squeezes me one more time before leaning back and sweeping me from head to toe with her shining eyes. "This is such an amazing dress."

She doesn't seem jealous or upset. But I'm still not sure what to say, what to do. How to feel as I stand in front of one of my best friends in the dress I'll wear to marry her ex-fiancé. "Thank you."

Her eyes come back up to mine. She frowns. "Are you all right?" She lays a hand on my arm. "Are you sure you should be doing this?"

I pull away and walk over toward a window. Even though she's engaged to Liam's brother, does she still have feelings for Liam? Or, like so many in my life, does she have a mean streak I never saw and just doesn't want her ex to be with someone else? "I can only imagine how hard this is on you."

"What?"

"My being engaged to your ex-fiancé."

Silence reigns behind me. Each passing second feels like a sharp needle pricking my skin. Then, finally, "Did Liam not tell you?"

"No. I...no."

Diana lays a gentle hand on my arm and turns me around. I should have let Liam tell me whatever happened between the two of them. Shouldn't have put it off so that I'd be finding out all the heartbreaking details the morning of my wedding—

"The engagement was fake."

My brows draw together. "What?"

Diana rolls her eyes. "Looks like I'm not the only one who doesn't share."

Confused, I frown and repeat, "What?"

Diana waves her hand in the air. "Nothing. Long story, and one best told over a glass of wine. Preferably a big, big glass."

"Yeah, but... I don't understand." Anger creeps in. Liam told me his and Diana's engagement had nothing to do with the controversy with his clients. Did he lie to me?

Diana runs a hand through her thick, dark hair. "I'll tell you anything you want to know. I don't know how much you want to hear about Dexter on your wedding day."

"You know why Liam and I are getting married, right?"

"I do. It doesn't change the fact that today is still your wedding day, and unlike before, you and Liam care about each other."

My whole body goes on alert. "Care?" I repeat.

"I know the three of us haven't been close lately. But a friendship like ours isn't one that just fades away after a few months."

I breathe out. "No, I suppose not. Still, I'd like to know. I've been worrying that my getting engaged to him so soon after your broken engagement might hurt you. So hearing what actually happened would be helpful."

Diana winces. "Sorry. I didn't think about that. Although..." She hesitates again. "It has to do with Dexter."

The mention of his name doesn't hit as hard as it used to. There's still an unpleasant twinge, sometimes a flash of his face in my mind. But compared to my skin breaking out in a sweat and glancing over my shoulder for a solid hour afterward, I've made huge strides. "I need to know."

Diana nods and moves toward the window. "Shortly after you and Dexter were married, Liam ran into him. I forget where, but Dexter accused Liam of being in love with you."

The ground drops out from under me. I stand, immobilized by a torrent of emotions I can't even begin to unpack. "He what?" I finally croak out.

"And Dexter was convinced that the two of you were secretly in love and that Liam might one day try to make a move, initiate an affair or even convince you to leave Dexter."

I start laughing. I laugh until my sides hurt, and I wonder if I'm going to split the stitches of my dress. It's either laugh or cry.

"Aislinn?"

I wipe away a couple of tears. "Dexter is even more of an idiot than I thought he was if he thought that Liam was interested in me romantically."

Diana cocks her head to one side.

I turn and look out the window, not wanting to risk the possibility of her seeing my feelings for Liam reflected in my eyes.

"The way you say that makes me feel like you don't think you're good enough for him."

I shake my head. "One, Liam is like a brother to me, and I'm like a sister to him. Always have been, always will be. Two, once upon a time, I wanted marriage and kids and fidelity. A commitment. You and I both know Liam loves and accepts who he is. The things I want out of life, or wanted, are not the things he does."

"Okay." Diana doesn't sound completely convinced, but she lets it go. "For whatever reason, Dexter thought there was something there. He threatened Liam and you and me."

My head snaps around. "What?"

"So Liam decided to cover his tracks by saying that he was already engaged. He used me as the fake fiancée, partially to protect me because we were friends and he thought we could pull it off, and because a part of him was hoping that the shock of your two best friends suddenly getting engaged would encourage you to reach out."

God, Dexter had all of us dancing to his tune. So many threats, so many threads in his web that we could all barely move without getting caught.

A heavy knot of guilt settles in the pit of my stomach. I was so abrupt to them at the funeral, ignored all of Diana's texts over the last few months. All because I was angry. I never once thought myself capable of this. But when I look at the actions I've taken over the last year, when I think back to the secrets I've concealed all in the name of the greater good, the people I've shut out of my life, I don't even recognize the woman I've become. And now, learning that Liam and Diana were just trying to protect me gouges a far deeper wound in my heart than Dexter could have ever inflicted.

A red cardinal flies into view and lands on a snow-covered branch just outside the window, a flash of red against stark white. I stare at it, keeping my gaze focused outward as I speak. "I was so angry and hurt when I saw the two of you at Dexter's funeral. I had no right to be, but I was."

"Why?"

Because I thought you were engaged to the man I've loved for twelve years. I don't think I'll ever be able to tell her the whole truth, so I settle for bits and pieces of it.

"I had thought after the funeral the three of us might be able to reconnect. I had no right to feel betrayed, but there had been so much change, and that was the final straw. At the end, I didn't know how, even if I did reach out, our friendship would survive." I grimace. "That probably seems unfair with Liam and I now being engaged, but this is different. It's just two friends helping each other out." I finally suck up enough courage to turn and face her. "I understand if this affects—"

Diana holds up a hand. "Don't. One day, I will need to know what happened. With you leaving, your marriage, all of it. But today is not that day." She holds my gaze. "Are you sure you want to do this? Liam can be very persuasive, and

I know a part of me felt like I had to say yes when he asked me to be his fake fiancée after everything he's done for me over the years. I don't want that for you."

"I didn't at first," I admit. "But I know this will help Liam. It feels deceptive, but I also don't agree with his clients pressuring him and monitoring his personal life. And," I add quietly, "people are enjoying the story. It feels like one giant lie, but no one has supported me since Dexter died. I want the chance to have a new life."

"Then I'm here for you. I'm here for you," Diana repeats as she lays a hand on my shoulder.

I blink rapidly. "Thank you."

"You're welcome. Now," she adds with a big smile, "Time to get you to your wedding."

Nerves flutter in my stomach as Diana walks across the room. She stops and glances back, frowning when she sees me still standing by the window.

"Aislinn, you don't have to—"

"I'm fine." I force out a tight-lipped smile. "Truly. This is what I want."

We both know I'm lying. I want the benefits from this arrangement, not the marriage itself. The initial relief I felt at knowing Liam and Diana's engagement was fake is gone. It was so much easier to keep myself emotionally distant, to be angry, when I thought they'd gotten engaged out of love. Knowing they did it for me opens up the door to all the feelings I spent the past four months burying.

I was strong enough to survive Dexter. But am I strong enough to survive three and a half years married to the man my heart won't let go of?

I glance down at the solitaire diamond on my finger. The sunlight catches it, casting sparkles onto the wall.

I made a promise. I'll keep it. The rest is mine to deal with.

I nod to Diana, more confident than I feel. "Let's go."

A sleek black car is waiting outside. A chauffeur opens the door and helps bundle the billowing skirts of my gown inside.

"How long until we get there?" Diana asks as the car pulls away from the curb.

"Twelve minutes, ma'am."

"Twelve minutes?" I frown. The courthouse is at least twenty minutes away, and that's in good traffic.

"We're not going to the courthouse," Diana tells me.

"Oh?"

Diana reaches over and squeezes my hand. "It's a surprise."

I once loved surprises. They didn't have to be big or extravagant. Something as simple as Stephanie showing up with my favorite latte could brighten any bad day. But the last time someone told me I was getting a surprise, Dexter had his hand wrapped around my neck like a vice and was dragging me out of the back of the car onto a California beach.

Diana gives me another reassuring squeeze. "It's a good surprise. I promise."

CHAPTER EIGHT

Aislinn

THE CAR WINDS its way through New York. The city is always busy, but a little less frantic on Saturday morning as the snow deafens the noise; it makes everything seem cleaner, brighter. Lights glimmer in the windows of cafés and storefronts. Towers and skyscrapers reach up and disappear into the low-lying clouds. People walk along the sidewalks, dressed in bright pops of color. Red, blue, even a pink-and-white-striped winter coat with a matching pink hat. So many details I used to enjoy. So many things I haven't paid attention to in the last few months. It was easier to shut out the world, draw into myself.

Yet as I watch the world pass by, I realize how much I've missed it.

That cautious ray of hope, the same one I felt the morning of Dexter's funeral when I saw Liam and Diana in line, flickers to life. Part of me wants to squelch it.

But as I glance over at Diana, then back out at the people on the streets, I find myself wanting just a little bit more. I can never go back to the way I lived my life before. I've seen too much to believe the world is a rosy, happy place. But maybe I can find a middle ground, a place in between where I can enjoy bits of happiness and small victories. Or I can find some good in this arrangement with Liam while still keeping my heart safe.

I glance down at the engagement ring on my left hand. Delicate bands of silver twine over one another like the branches of a tree to the center of the ring, where an oval-shaped diamond glitters between two drops of emeralds. Sweet and delicate. Liam surprised me at breakfast three days after we agreed to an official engagement. I was going stir-crazy from being cooped up. He'd dropped to one knee in front of my chair and popped open the lid on a deep blue velvet case to reveal the stunning ring. And damn my heart, it had shot into my throat faster than a shooting star.

Got to do at least one thing traditionally. He'd said it with a small smile as he slid the ring onto my finger. And then he stood, kissed me on the forehead like a brother would a little sister and left.

I curl my hand into a fist and turn it to the side so I can't see the ring.

The car turns onto Billionaires' Row, then makes another turn into the private parking garage.

"Are we going to Liam's penthouse?"

Diana shakes her head. "Nope."

A few minutes later, we're in a secure elevator racing up toward the sky. I watch the numbers, my confusion growing as Diana presses the button for the one hundred and thirty-first floor, several floors above where Liam's penthouse is.

"Friends in high places?" I joke.

Diana chuckles. "Something like that."

As the elevator ascends, I glance once more at my friend. She's always been beautiful. But now she's glowing. There's a contentment about her, a peace I never saw. A far cry from the woman who befriended me in a high school theater, who held on to my hand like it was a lifeline as she lay in a hospital bed after suffering through an attack no child should ever experience. She was so brave, but she shouldn't have had to be. She should have been cared for, loved.

My eyes slide down to the ring on her finger. "You're happy?"

Diana glances at me, startled. Then a smile comes over her face, so bright and happy it brings tears to my eyes.

"You love him?"

Diana nods. "I do. More than I ever thought possible."

I hesitate. Then, quietly, "Maybe at the end of our honeymoon, we could have that big glass of wine."

Diana's eyes are shining as she reaches over and hugs me again. "I'd really like that. You're going to love Iceland, too."

I'd been surprised when Liam had suggested Iceland for our honeymoon. But I'd never been, and knowing his birth mother and brother were born and raised there, it seemed like a good location for both of us. He's arranged for a couple days in Reykjavik, including a few dinners at some high-end restaurants and even a visit to the opera house for a ballet performance, before we head north for a quieter stay at a remote villa.

I frown. Every time I've tried to get Liam to talk about his brother or his birth mother, he changes the subject. Just like he used to whenever Diana or I would ask about his childhood before foster care or his adoptive parents. We learned quickly that those were topics not even we were privy to. Something Diana had accepted, but something that, despite my best intentions, had hurt.

Apparently, I think with a quiet sigh, some things haven't changed. Liam wants to know all about my time with Dexter, my ugly, painful secrets, while he gets to keep his hidden away.

Another reason, I remind myself, to not let myself think this arrangement can be anything permanent.

At last, the elevator stops. Floor one hundred and-thirty-one. The top of the tallest building in New York. I mentally rack my brain. I can't remember who owns this.

The doors open to reveal a two-story living room. Diana and I walk out, the elevator doors closing quietly behind us. I walk across the floor to the window. On a clear day, I'd be able to see not only New York but the ocean and the surrounding states. Right now, though, clouds blanket the city. Only the tallest skyscrapers are visible.

"Welcome."

I turn, then do a double take. I know intrinsically the man walking into the room isn't Liam. Just a touch taller and slimmer, with white-blond hair instead of Liam's dark brown. But the face, the sharp blade of his nose, the chiseled cheekbones and angular jaw... He could be Liam's twin.

He doesn't notice me. He only has eyes for Diana. He crosses the room to her, his arms going around her waist and pulling her against him before he covers her lips with his in a passionate kiss.

I stare for a moment before embarrassment floods me, and I turn back to the window. Beneath the embarrassment, envy pumps through me. Sick, ugly poison. I bite down on my lower lip. After everything Diana has been through, how can I possibly be jealous that she has found someone to love and respect her? To cherish her?

"Aislinn?"

I swallow hard, get myself under control, then turn and face Liam's brother.

"Ari, this is Aislinn." The pure joy in Diana's voice makes me want to sink into the floor.

"Hello."

Ari smiles at me. "So you're Aislinn?"

"I am. Yes." Flustered, I thread my fingers together in front of me. "I know this is probably awkward—"

"Not at all." He crosses to me and holds out a hand. I shake it. "Diana and I are used to the unconventional. I'm glad that you and Liam are able to help each other out." His eyes narrow slightly. "As long as you're sure this is what you want."

I can't help but let out a small chuckle. "I take it you also have a protective streak?"

"I may have only known Liam for a few months, but in that time, I've come to discover how persuasive he can be." His indulgent smile dims as his voice softens. "And you've been through a lot."

The simple acknowledgment touches me. "Thank you. And I appreciate you asking, but I do want this."

"All right. Well, if you're ready, Liam is waiting for you."

Warmth flows through me. *It's an illusion*, I remind myself. *None of it's real.* "All right."

"You look beautiful."

I smile at Ari. "Thank you."

Diana and I follow Ari. He leads us out a glass door onto a stone terrace. Snow swirls around us. We walk around a corner, and my eyes widen. A huge greenhouse takes up this portion of the terrace. Behind the glass is another world, bright blooms and exotic trees.

We walk into a small vestibule. Ari closes the door behind us, waits a moment and then, at the sound of a soft bell, opens another door into the greenhouse. Warm, fragrant air rushes over me. I shrug out of my coat as I stare around in wonder. Huge, fuchsia-colored blooms drip from a bougainvillea tree. Other flowers, ones I've never seen before, show off a stunning array of colors. Violet, burgundy, deep jewel tones throw us into a world of summer.

"Where are we?"

"A secret garden."

My head snaps up. Liam is standing just a few feet ahead on a stone path, legs spread and hands tucked into his pockets. He looks so incredibly handsome. Black tuxedo tailored perfectly to his broad shoulders and thick arms. I've never been a fan of bow ties, but Liam wears his with masculine confidence. He's smiling at me, cocky and proud.

"A secret garden," I repeat.

"Your favorite book."

My lips part. "You remember that?"

"Every time I'd find you in the library or the food court or out on the green, you always had that book with you."

No. No, no, no. He can't do this. I don't want him to make me feel special. I don't want him to make me feel anything. I wrench my gaze away from him. My heart's pounding so fast it's making me lightheaded. "So we're getting married here?"

"Is that all right?"

The thread of concern underlying his words makes me look back. He's watching me, the smile still in place. But there's something else in his eyes. Worry.

For a friend. Just a friend.

Like the time he brought Diana and me coffee at two in the morning when we were both cramming for exams. Like the numerous times he walked Lucy, Diana's dog, when she got caught late at her internship. Like the time I brought a birthday cake to the wealth management firm where he was interning because he couldn't get off. He's doing what friends do. Remembering the little things and caring for each other.

"Yes. Thank you."

"You're welcome." He gestures down the path. "Shall we?"

"Coats first." Diana fans her face. "It's hot in here."

Ari moves behind her and helps her out of her coat. She kept it simple with a long, black evening gown, but she still looks like a dark-haired goddess. Judging by the way Ari's eyes flare, he's imagining what she looks like out of it as he sets the coat down on a bench near the door. He holds out his arm and smiles at Diana as he escorts her down the path.

My lips quirk as I slide mine off. The sound of a sharp inhale has me looking up.

Liam is staring at me. His blue eyes are hot, flames burning bright as his gaze travels up and down my dress. I stand, immobilized by my own desire and wonder. I can feel his stare as if it were his fingers instead of his smoldering eyes on me. I press my thighs together, but it doesn't stop the heat. Thank God the bodice is thick. Otherwise everyone would be able to see my nipples hardening, pressing against the fabric.

Liam's gaze snaps back up to mine. Beneath the currents of lust pulsing between us is something new: awareness. I've always admired Liam from afar. Ached for him in a romantic sense, the way I imagine Jane Austen heroines pining for their loves. But this sensual need is different. Incredible.

Terrifying.

Apparently, Liam has the same thought because the desire vanishes as quickly as it appeared. "Ready?"

His voice is still friendly, his face relaxed and open. But as I set my coat down on the bench and move toward him, I see the tightness in his jaw, the blankness in his eyes. I'd be lying if I said I didn't feel just a bit more beautiful. Powerful. Even sexy.

But his ability to turn off his emotions, to shut me out as quickly as he just did, is just another sign. No matter how much I may care for him, no matter how attractive I find him, we'll never be compatible. I want a family, children. He doesn't.

Once I'm free of this marriage, I'll create my own family. Follow through on all the vague promises of my former foster parents and adopt children who deserve a loving home. A decision I know Liam and Diana will both support, especially given the far harsher experiences they both had in foster care.

But not something Liam wants for himself. And even if he did, even if we were compatible, I don't think I can ever trust myself to be in a committed relationship again.

I almost laugh. For once, Liam and I have the same goal; to never get married to anyone else. Never let ourselves fall in love. That, coupled with my feminine satisfaction at knowing Liam at least finds me attractive, too, gives me a much-needed boost of confidence.

"Yes."

Liam holds out his arm. I slide my hand into the crook of his elbow, focusing on the incredible foliage around me instead of the feel of his arm beneath my fingers.

A stream winds its way through the flowers. The soft babbling of the water feels like sinking into a hot tub after a long day. When a bird flies overhead, I can't help but laugh. This bit of summer in the midst of a New York winter is incredible.

Liam's arm tenses beneath my fingers. I glance up to see him looking down at me with a small smile.

"What?"

"I haven't heard you laugh in a long time."

"It's been a while." I give his arm a gentle squeeze. "Thank you."

The path curves past a tree with rambling roots and moss hanging from its rugged branches. Just beyond the tree is a stone patio. Huge pink blooms have been threaded through a wooden arch. Diana is standing on the bride's side with two matching bouquets in her hands. Ari is on the groom's side, chatting quietly with a young woman in a black dress and an older man in a white shirt and tan slacks.

"Our officiant and a photographer," Liam murmurs. "They're unaware of our agreement."

I push back the spurt of guilt. We're not marrying for love. But we are marrying. We're committed to the arrangement. I'm sure it's not what Liam's archaic-minded, high-and-mighty clients had in mind, but it shouldn't matter anyway.

That above all else helps me slip into my public relations mode as the older man glances over his shoulder. He has a craggy, well-worn face, with a square jaw and lines carved deep into his forehead.

"Liam." He walks over and holds out his hand to me, a big smile on his face. "And you must be Aislinn."

"Yes." I return his smile. "Thank you for officiating our ceremony... I'm sorry, I didn't catch your name."

"Bill. And it's my honor." His smile deepens. "Never thought when I got certified to officiate my daughter's wedding a few years ago I'd have the chance to use it again."

"Well, thank you."

"Of course." His eyes are kind as he gestures toward the arch. "I hope this is to your liking."

This time there's no pretending. "It's beautiful." I steal a quick glance at Liam, give him a small smile. "Just like a secret garden." I look away before I let myself feel too much. "I can't thank you enough for making this possible."

Bill looks back and forth between Liam and me. He almost looks satisfied.

Odd.

"Normally it's just my wife and myself who make use of it. My daughter lives in Portugal and my son is away at college in London. It's nice to have people here again." He looks back at Ari, Diana and the photographer. "We're ready if you are."

As ready as I'll ever be. I keep my eyes on Bill as I nod. "I'm ready."

I walk up to the arch with Bill and Liam. Diana hands me my bouquet, gives me a hug and then my second wedding begins.

The photographer is good. Aside from the quiet clicking of her camera, I barely notice her as Bill talks. I stare at Liam, my fingers clenching and unclenching around the stems of my bouquet. Thankfully the large petals hide my knuckles. Otherwise I'm sure everyone would see how white they are.

"And now the vows."

Diana gently nudges me. I turn and hand her my bouquet, trying to look calm before I turn back to Liam. I brace myself as he takes my hands in his.

"Liam, do you take Aislinn to be your lawfully wedded wife, to have and to hold from this day forward, for better or worse, for richer or poorer, in sickness and in health, to love and to cherish until death do you part?"

Or three point five years from today.

"I do."

His voice is a gentle, familiar rumble. I remember the first time I heard it in the high school theater. The kind of play we're acting out now, though, has far higher stakes for both of us.

I squeeze his hands and give him a small smile. He blinks, a tiny furrow appearing between his brows. I hold his gaze as I repeat my vows.

"The rings?"

Ari hands Liam the rings. Liam hands me a thick silver band, which I carefully slide onto his finger. He slides a matching slimmer one onto my finger, the same woven bands of silver holding tiny diamonds in their grasp. A perfect match for the engagement ring.

At least this time I'm not stuck with an ostentatious jewel that could be seen from space. I like the simplicity, the casual elegance.

"I now pronounce you husband and wife. You may kiss the bride."

You can do this, you can do this, you can do this.

I freeze. Do I put my arms around his neck? Do I lay my hands on his shoulders? How does one kiss one's best friend and make it look like I care while hiding the fact that I actually do care?

My mind's spinning. I know it is. I'm so focused on making it stop that when Liam slides an arm around my waist and pulls me close, I simply relax into him. My hand automatically comes up to rest on his shoulder. The other settles on his chest. His very muscular chest.

Heat floods my body. Startled, I look up just as his hand settles on my cheek in a gentle cradle that makes my lip part.

And then he's kissing me. Liam, one of my best friends and the only man I've ever loved, is kissing me. I stay still, not wanting to do anything wrong, not wanting to give any hint of how much this simple touching of mouths is making my body so hot I can barely stand it.

Until Liam's lips part. My mouth responds. The sudden intimacy of it, of sharing breath as his fingers firm on my cheek and his arm tightens about my waist, as he *groans* into my mouth, turns the heat into a raging wildfire.

It's a good thing I've already committed to never getting married again. Because no kiss will ever top this.

Then just like that, it's over. Liam pulls away. He smiles down at me, his eyes still that same blue blankness from just before we walked down the path. The camera clicks, the sound now like a gunshot as I remember.

That wasn't a real kiss. It was theater.

Bill, Diana and Ari approach us, offering congratulations and thankfully giving me a reprieve from looking at Liam.

My husband.

I ignore Diana's concerned frown and Ari's speculating gaze as we all make small talk about the wedding, the honeymoon, our plans for when we return to New York. If they think there's the possibility of something romantic between Liam and me, then we're off to a good start with this farce of a marriage.

A chill creeps over my skin. I glance down at the engagement ring, now joined by the wedding band. It's strange how such slender pieces of jewelry can suddenly feel so heavy.

CHAPTER NINE

Liam

I GLANCE OUT my window as the plane soars over the Labrador Sea. There's nothing but a star-speckled sky above and a dark blue carpet thousands of feet below.

As I reach for my old-fashioned, my ring clinks on the glass. It feels strange, cold. Even knowing there's an expiration date for wearing it, it doesn't negate the tightness around my finger, the heaviness pressing on my skin.

My gaze slides over to where Aislinn is seated on the opposite side of the plane. We've barely said ten words to each other since we boarded. She changed out of her wedding dress into a long-sleeved navy shirt and wide-legged burgundy pants. Her golden hair is tucked behind her ears, her eyes focused on her laptop screen in front of her.

Aislinn. One of the few people in this world I trust. My friend.

My wife.

My chest tightens. When she took off her coat, I nearly swallowed my tongue. The billowing skirt reminded me of a princess. Sweet, romantic, just like Aislinn used to be. But the top of her dress…just thinking about the way the fabric clung to her slender waist, the dip in the front that teased me with a view of the swells of her breasts, the see-through scraps of fabric draped over her arms, made me hard in an instant. I've never really noticed a woman's shoulders before. But I noticed Aislinn's, noticed her bare skin, imagined what it would be look to kiss her there as I slid the bodice down and lowered my head to her—

Fuck, stop.

I look back out the window, my hand clenched around my glass. What the hell is wrong with me? I've always thought Aislinn was beautiful. But ever since that first night at the gala when I saw her in the black dress, I've been cursed by an awareness of her as a woman. A stunning, sensual woman who is far stronger and confident than I ever realized.

Yet she's holding back. This entire last week, every time we talked, she was distant. Muted. When she laughed in the greenhouse, when I saw her smile, it was like finally being able to take a deep breath for the first time in over a year.

There you are.

The old Aislinn, the one who loves fairy tales and greeted everyone by name and played hide-and-seek with kids in Central Park simply because they asked her to, is still in there. She's just buried herself so deep no one can get to her.

I bite back a smile. I have three and a half years to find out what happened. To help Aislinn get out of this hole she's hiding in. To do what I should have done last year and fight for her.

Fight for her, not kiss her.

The blend of bourbon, bitters and a dash of sugar is smooth, sweet. I focus on the scent of orange, the glimmer of light through the caramel-colored drink. Anything but the way Aislinn felt in my arms. The way she tasted.

God, she tasted good.

I can't think this way. Can't let Aislinn in this way. I'm much more of a coldhearted bastard than I realized, enjoying my friendship with her even as I kept parts of myself concealed. Worse, when I think about how Aislinn opened herself up and let me in from the very beginning. It was one of the things that drew me to her, that dauntless kindness and trust. How even after years of not having her dreams fulfilled, she still thought the world was good.

And I took everything she offered without hesitation.

Disgusted with myself, I stare at the curled orange rind artfully arranged in my glass. It's not just my heart I want to protect. It's hers, too. She deserves far more than my selfish self can give her.

I set the glass down harder than I intend. It clinks on the hardwood of the table and sloshes up over the rim. I curse as Aislinn glances up with a frown.

"Everything all right?"

I give her a tight smile. "Yes. Just clumsy."

She nods and turns back to her computer, which just pisses me off even more. I saw the way she looked at me when she first took off her coat in the greenhouse. She felt something, too. I know desire when I see it; Aislinn found me just as attractive as I found her. But she had no problem switching it off.

Which is a good thing.

Maybe if I repeat it enough times, I'll stop gritting my teeth at the memory of her lips parting beneath mine. Of wishing I had had just a moment longer to feel her body pressed against mine.

I suck in a deep breath. Which is a mistake because somehow I inhale the scent of spiced rose.

I stand and stalk toward the galley at the front of the plane. When I reserved the private jet, it seemed like a good idea to both keep prying eyes at bay and continue to sell the secret romance that's been so popular. I just hadn't anticipated it turning into a private hell of my own making.

I reach the galley. Light gray cabinets, green quartz countertops and soft lighting give the kitchen a cozy feel. The size of it rivals the kitchen I had in my first apartment. Two attendants are moving about, pulling pans out of the oven and arranging food on plates.

"Mr. Whitlock."

One of the attendants smiles at me. Kacey, I remember. Long red curls pulled back with a clip, a big smile and huge green eyes. A year ago, I would have flirted. If she'd flirted back, I would have invited her to dinner, drinks, a night in whatever hotel I was staying in.

Now it's like looking at a painting. I can acknowledge she's beautiful. Yet I feel nothing. Not even a flicker of attraction. It's odd, but I'm grateful for it. Three and a half years of celibacy will be interesting. But I meant what I said to Aislinn. I have never been unfaithful, and I never will be, even if our marriage is a business arrangement.

"Just stretching my legs."

"Understandable, sir. Dinner will be served in five minutes."

I walk back to the main cabin. Aislinn is still on her computer, oblivious to the world around her.

"Shopping?" I ask as I sit back down.

"Job hunting."

I frown. "Already?"

"Yes." She shakes her head. "More like reapplying."

"For?"

Her eyes flick to me. She hesitates, then lets out a long sigh. "Working for the Foster Foundation."

I snort. "They should be begging you to come work for them."

She gives me a sad smile. "Thanks."

Warning bells clang. I keep my voice cautious, my tone even as I pick up my glass again. "What happened?"

Her walls are thankfully down, allowing me to see the debate playing out across her face. Once she would have told me everything. Now it's like prying a favorite toy away from a child to get her to share just a small piece of her life.

"I knew last month that continuing to work for Eric wouldn't be a good idea. He hadn't said anything yet," she adds as my hand tightens around my armrest, "but I knew. So I started applying for other jobs. One of them was for a director of public relations with the Foster Foundation."

"They rejected your application because of Dexter."

At her nod, I grab my phone.

"What are you doing?"

"Contacting one of their board members." I pull up my contacts. Anger seethes inside me. After everything Aislinn has done for kids in foster care, all of the attention she's brought to the Foster Foundation and other organizations, and they reject her because of her ass of a husband?

"Don't." Her voice whips out.

Slowly, I turn my head. She's gripping her armrests, as if physically restraining herself from jumping out of her seat to stop me.

"I'm just trying to help."

"And I didn't ask you to."

"No," I reply coldly. "Because you don't need help anymore, do you?"

A lock of hair falls from behind her ear. She tucks it back with a violence that seems to surprise her as she slowly leans back in her seat. "I'm not trying to be ungrateful, Liam." Now her voice is calm, almost eerily so. "I just want to do some things for myself for once. I don't need my husband taking charge again."

Ice sinks into my skin. Slowly, I tuck my phone into my pocket and pick up my glass.

"Liam." Her heavy sigh fills the cabin. "That wasn't—"

"Comparing me to Dexter?" I swirl the contents of the glass before taking a long drink. "Good."

Except we both know that's exactly what she was implying.

Silence falls between us. For the second time that day, I question whether this marriage was a good idea or not. The reason this time, however, is not my inconvenient physical attraction to a friend. It's my wife's continuous reminders that she has a low opinion of me.

I let down my guard with Aislinn and Diana. Not completely. But more than I have with anyone else since Mom and Dad died. I spent months digging for information on Dexter, first to find out why Aislinn had chosen him and then to help her as she faced down public opinion on her involvement in Dexter's crimes. Every time Diana wondered if Aislinn had simply changed, I defended her. Every time a newspaper article or news report questioned whether or not Aislinn had been involved, I dug deeper.

No more. She wants to compare me to her manipulative dick of a husband, fine. But I'm not going to waste any more time trying to help her. Hell, at this point, I'm not sure our friendship is even worth saving.

"Liam."

She says my name so softly I barely hear it over the roar of the engine. I don't look at her.

"I'm sorry."

Her words pierce me. This is why I don't get romantically involved, why I hold a part of myself back from everyone, including Aislinn and Diana and even Ari. Ten-year-old me would have been ecstatic to learn I had an older brother, a mother who had loved me before I was born, who no doubt would have loved me if she hadn't passed away in the hospital shortly after I was born.

But the man I am now, the man forged by years of anger and grief and rejection in foster care, keeps his walls up. When you feel too deeply, you give people power.

I finally look at Aislinn. Remember that moment I found my parents kissing under the mistletoe, the moment I felt like everything was good and right in the world. A high that made the fall ten times more painful when I was left alone. I don't regret loving them for one second. But I'm smart enough to not open myself up to that kind of pain again.

CHAPTER TEN

Liam

KACEY AND THE other attendant thankfully arrive with dinner. They set down two plates and two water glasses on the long, sleek table close to the back of the cabin, followed a moment later by a third attendant with a bottle of wine and wineglasses.

Aislinn joins me at the table, her eyes downcast and her face wan. She barely touches the burrata salad with tomatoes, the filet mignon with roasted carrots and béarnaise sauce, or the pistachio mousse. The glass of wine remains full.

My anger slowly ebbs as she moves a slice of carrot around her plate with her fork. "I'm sure the attendants could find something else."

"No. Thank you. It looks delicious. I'm just not hungry."

Each word sounds like it's been being dragged out of her. I want to tell her to eat. I want to shout at her for ever thinking I could be anything like Dexter. I want her to trust me again.

I pause with my fork halfway to my mouth. Is that part of why this is eating at me so much? Am I hurt more by her comment or by her distance?

You failed to keep her safe before. You could fail again.

Irritated with my subconscious, I set my fork down. But before I can say something, Aislinn's phone rings. She gets up and goes back to her seat, grimacing as she glances at the screen.

"Stephanie. She probably heard about us getting married."

Surprised, I lean back in my chair. "You didn't tell her about the ceremony?"

"No." Aislinn waits until it stops ringing before she speaks again. "We haven't been close for some time."

Part of what has made me good at my career is my ability to pick up on subtle tells, intonations, to read people. Beneath Aislinn's casual dismissal of her adoptive mother, there's a deep vein of pain.

"I'm sorry."

Aislinn nods slowly. "Thank you." She finally picks up her spoon and dips it into the mousse. My eyes follow the spoon, my body growing hard as her lips close around it, and she lets out a small sigh of contentment.

Thank God I'm sitting down. Walking would be a challenge.

I have to get a grip. Have to stop thinking about Aislinn this way. It's never going to happen.

Can't happen, I firmly remind myself.

"It was nice to meet Ari."

I breathe out. A neutral topic. "I'm glad."

"You two could be twins."

One corner of my mouth tilts into a half grin. "I've told him more than once I'm the more handsome of us two."

Aislinn smiles slightly. "I'm glad you're getting to know him."

My grin fades. I've been trying the past few months. After my fake engagement to Diana ended and she took a job for my brother, I was worried about her. I knew she was hiding something from me. So when an opportunity to meet with a client in Iceland popped up, I'd seized it, using the trip for both business and to check up on my friend. Finding out she'd slept with my half brother before learning of his relationship had been a shock. Discovering that she and Ari truly loved each other had been another twist I hadn't seen coming.

I'd told Ari on that trip I wanted to get to know him more. And I meant it. But it quickly proved to be much harder than I had anticipated. Listening to his stories about my birth mother—our mother—and imagining a life that could have been if she'd survived giving birth to me... That was a guilt I hadn't expected, knowing she gave her life and left behind a son to be raised by a coldhearted tyrant.

And if she had survived, I never would have met my adoptive parents, a fate I couldn't even begin to fathom.

The pain and the guilt had been too much. So I'd pulled back. Ari hadn't pushed, which deepened the guilt even more. Inviting him to the wedding had been a massive step, one I'd forced myself to make for Ari and Diana.

I pick up my wineglass. "I'm trying."

Aislinn tilts her head to one side, her eyes thoughtful.

Worried she's going to try and delve into my feelings, I ask, "Did you ever hear back from the DNA test?"

She freezes, her fingers tightening around her spoon. Slowly, deliberately, she lays it down on the table and leans back in her chair.

Aislinn used to say she could feel Diana's and my emotions like they were her own, a concept I struggled to understand. But I understand it now. I can feel the pain in the way her fingers grip the arms of the chair, the grief shining in her eyes, the anger in the tightness of her lips.

"Aislinn," I say quietly. "You don't have to tell me—"

"For so many years I dreamed about her." Her voice is so quiet I can barely hear it over the hum of the plane engines. "I thought she might have chosen foster care over a violent household, over not having enough money or an unsupportive family of their own. Maybe someone who had had that choice made for them while they pieced their life back together."

I wait as she pauses, picks up her wineglass and stares down into it with a blank gaze. Rallying herself for whatever.

"I got the DNA results back shortly after Dexter...after we started dating."

I note the pause, barely force myself to not pursue it.

"I found my birth mother on social media, had seen the pictures of her with a husband and two teenagers. Pictures of them in front of a little house in some suburban neighborhood, playing on a beach, going to one of the kids' baseball games." Her voice catches. "It hurt. It hurt so much. But I'd comforted myself with the hope that maybe she'd been searching for me all these years."

I stand and circle around the table, crouch next to her and grab her free hand with mine. She grips my fingers tightly with a strength that surprises me.

"I messaged her. She messaged me back, said she was glad I'd done well for myself and had found loving adoptive parents. She had moved on with her life and didn't want to dig into the past. Not when it could potentially hurt her husband and her children."

Rage swells inside me. Of all the people in this world who deserved a happily-ever-after, it was Aislinn. For her to experience the cruelest possible outcome, especially after all she'd been through, was unfathomable.

"Her children," Aislinn repeated softly. "A term that didn't include me."

I pluck the wineglass out of her hand, set it down on the table and pull her to her feet. I wrap my arms around her and hold her tight, one hand cupping the back of her head as I rock her.

She stays stiff in my arms for a long moment. Then she shudders, as if holding in the grief is too much, and slowly wraps her arms around my waist.

I don't know how long we stand there. But I don't let go

until she gently pats me on the back and steps away. "Thank you."

She sinks down into her chair as I circle back to mine. Her eyes are red, but there are no tears. "Unfortunate, but she made her choice."

"A cruel, selfish woman."

Aislinn shrugs. "I don't know enough about why she made the choice to judge her. I'm just...sad."

"You give people too much credit."

"I used to." The lack of emotion in her voice sets off warning bells. "But I don't anymore. Logically, there are any number of reasons for her to have made her choices back then and her choices now. A touch of sadness is understandable. But to give in to anger or grief would be stupid."

I grit my teeth as I try to tamp down my own anger and find the right words. "Trying to suppress your emotions isn't healthy, either."

Aislinn arches one dark golden brow. "Are you the pot or the kettle?"

Impressed and completely aware of the double standard I live by, I incline my head.

Before I can say anything else, her phone beeps again. She glances at it, then rolls her eyes. "Our wedding is already hitting the news." She sends me a small smirk. "More good PR."

I nod, even though acknowledging it makes me feel like dirt.

"What other campaigns do you have lined up? For your investment firm?" she asks as she reads the article on her screen.

I rattle off the list that my head of publicity came up with, including high-quality videos, client testimonials and press releases with some of the top publications in New York.

"Hmm."

I arch a brow at Aislinn's noncommittal sound. "Hmm?"

"It sounds good."

"But not great."

She shrugs one shoulder. "I think you should start a blog."

I stare at her. "A blog?"

"Yes. Topics that would appeal to your top-tier clients, of course, but articles that could be helpful to anyone. Building generational wealth, estate planning, investment diversification."

I blink. I've never been big on social media and having an online presence. But it's not a bad idea.

Aislinn looks up from her phone. It's a good idea. But it's the tiniest flare of interest in her eyes that has me nodding.

"I like it."

"I could write something up for you."

I smile at her. "I'd like that."

The smile she gives me, bright and hopeful, is worth writing a hundred blog posts. She glances back down at her phone. A moment later her body goes rigid. "Bill."

"Bill?"

Slowly, her head comes up. Her face is stricken, her eyes full of pain. "William Luther."

"Yes?"

She lets out a soft moan. "God, I'm an idiot."

I lean forward. "Perhaps I'm missing something."

"It was never about giving me a 'secret garden.' It was about putting on a show for your client and making sure he had a front-row seat." She holds up her phone.

The photos from our wedding are splashed all over a tabloid article, with a title touting the "elopement of the century" in a private greenhouse owned by billionaire William Luther.

Trepidation whispers across the back of my neck. Of course she would have to find this out right after reliving one of the worst moments of her life.

"Having Luther there was a benefit, yes." I reach for her

hand, but she snatches it back. The small rejection is a kick to the gut. "I wanted to surprise you, too, Aislinn. To thank you."

She shakes her head. "Just stop. Stop, okay? I would have been fine with a courthouse wedding, Liam. I don't need all this pretense."

"No, but the public does." Damn it, I regret the words as soon as they're out of my mouth.

She closes her eyes and pinches the bridge of her nose. "Yes. The public." She lets out another long, harsh breath. "I apologize. You were just following our agreement—"

I stand. "Forget the agreement, Aislinn." I stalk around the table and stop in front of her, wait until she finally looks up at me. "Yes, I had the photographer leak the photos to someone in the press I knew would spread them quickly. And yes, Luther being there was a bonus. But he's the one who offered to marry us. My initial plan included an officiant, Diana, Ari, you and me."

"And the photographer," she adds quietly.

"Yes, and the photographer." I run a hand through my hair. "Damn it, Aislinn, that's part of why we're doing this."

"I know. I just…" She closes her eyes. I stare down at her, at the dark sweep of lashes against her cheeks, the full lips pressed so tightly together as she fights her demons alone. Again. When she finally opens her eyes, her walls are back in place. She's as cold and remote as she was the night I found her in the alcove at the gala. "I'll be all right."

"Don't do this."

"A few minutes ago, you had nothing to say to me."

"Yeah, while now I do have something to say." I reach out and grab her hand, tug her closer. "Don't push me away."

She braces her other hand on my chest.

The heat of her palm sears my skin through my shirt. The sudden, instant arousal nearly has me backing down. But I'm not giving up. Not now. I have to fight through it, focus on what's important.

Aislinn narrows her eyes at me. "I'm not pushing you away."

"Liar."

Temper flares in the emerald depths. I'm probably going to hell for finding it satisfying and oddly arousing. "I am not."

"Yes you are." I lean down. "You forget, I can read you like a book. Just how many secrets are you hiding, Aislinn?"

She stands her ground, her chin tilted up and her eyes fierce. As we stare each other down, awareness slams into me with the force of a freight train. My chest rises and falls as our breaths mingle. She shifts. Her breasts brush against my chest. The sound of her sharp inhale makes time stand still.

My eyes drop down to her mouth. How did I never notice how perfectly shaped it was before? Full, ripe lips. Soft and yielding when I kissed her just a few hours ago.

I need to kiss her again.

Just one more taste.

The first time I kissed her, I told myself it would be quick, passionless.

This time, I know better.

She meets me halfway as I crush my mouth to hers. The first time she was hesitant, testing. Now, she's on fire. She sinks into me, her arms circling around my neck as she kisses me back with a passion that rocks me to my foundation. I band one arm around her waist as my other hand sinks into her hair. Cool silk against the fire raging out of control under my skin.

I told myself one taste. But I can't walk away from this. Not yet.

I tease the seam of her lips with my tongue. Her mouth parts on a gasp, and I take the kiss deeper, drink in every scent, every touch. Her hands move up my neck, her fingers diving into my hair. The slight tug makes me growl as my entire body goes hard. I press my hips against hers, shudder as she presses back against my cock.

There's a bedroom at the back of the plane. We have hours until we land. Hours for me to strip her naked and explore every inch of her body. Drive myself inside her and claim—

Stop. NOW.

I wrench myself away.

Aislinn stumbles back a few steps, swollen lips parted and her breath coming in short, rapid gasps. Just like mine as I fight to get myself back under control. Her eyes are wide, still bright with desire.

As I stare at her, try to grasp onto the threads of my sanity, a chill creeps into my chest. I'm not seeing Aislinn as my friend. I'm seeing her as a woman. A woman I want more than I've wanted anyone else in my life.

What the hell did I just do?

"Aislinn, I'm sor—"

"Stop." She raises a hand to her lips. Guilt punches through me as she touches her mouth with trembling fingertips, then looks away. "Just… I need to be alone."

I want to reach out, stop her. Apologize and figure out a way we can put this behind us. Go back to the way things were.

But as I watch her disappear into the bedroom at the back of the plane and close the door, feel the loss of her yet again, I know things will never be the same.

CHAPTER ELEVEN

Aislinn

THE BALLERINA SNAPS her fan shut and taps it on the shoulder of the male dancer in front of her. Basilio, I remember, the handsome barber. And the ballerina, Kitri, who has fallen for him instead of the wealthy man her father has picked out for him.

I've never been to a ballet before. I took dance classes when my favorite foster mother signed me up to attend with her daughter. I loved it; the leotards with the filmy skirts, learning the different positions, the routines set to relaxing classical music.

But this is different. As Basilio sweeps Kitri into his arms and draws within a breath of kissing her, my breath hitches. I recognize some of the movements. But everything else is so much more than I ever imagined a ballet to be. I've smiled a few times as Don Quixote and his bumbling but well-meaning lackey Sancho Panza stumble about. I've watched with wide eyes as the entire cast danced in unison.

And now, as Kitri caresses Basilio's face and he lifts her up in front of a red sky with a lone windmill in the background, I'm mesmerized by their love story.

Liam shifts in the seat next to me. I probably look like a child leaning forward to see everything from our private box on the left side of the theater. But it's not just so I can see everything happening on stage. It's also so I can keep as much distance between Liam and myself as possible.

We arrived in Reykjavik yesterday. A private limo took us to a hotel overlooking the Old Harbor, not far from his brother Ari's geothermal energy company headquarters. We barely said two words to each other on the drive. Thankfully Liam had reserved a two-bedroom suite for us. I'd taken the coward's way out and slipped into my room seconds after the concierge closed the door behind us.

I'd managed to make it to the bed before I let my tears fall. I buried my face in the pillow so Liam couldn't hear me cry. Those moments after the kiss on the plane had been like taking a knife to the chest, one he twisted when he'd started to apologize. I jumped between loving him and loathing him as tears ran down my face. Loving him for giving me a wedding he thought I would enjoy. Loathing him for turning it into a PR ploy. Loving him for coming after me, for not letting me hide. Loathing him for changing his mind and pushing me away.

I didn't just cry for him. I cried for the last year of my life, for my lost innocence and the fool I'd been. I'd cried for the months of lost friendship with Diana, especially the last four. Four months I can never get back because of my own pride and poor choices.

It was easier to focus on Diana, on my lost relationship with Eric and Stephanie, on how much my life had changed, than to think about Liam. To remember how being held by him, kissed by him, *wanted* by him, surpassed any dream I'd ever had.

Just a few seconds. But I know no man will ever make me feel as alive as Liam did.

Liam had left me alone until dinner. It had given me time to write up some more on my blog proposal, as well as a couple more ideas with sponsoring charity events and collaborating with financial journalists. It had given us something to talk about during dinner at a restaurant on the water. The venue had been stunning, with candlelit tables and chairs draped in faux fur blankets. Each dish had been a work of art, from a snow crab salad dressed with fennel greens to grilled sole surrounded by a ring of clams and dressed with a side of pickled plums.

I'd tried to focus on that instead of my husband. A challenge when I knew we had to at least look like we were enjoying ourselves. I saw more than one cell phone raised to capture a "discreet" photo. The only thing that had made conversing with Liam on a blog publication strategy bearable was the tension etched into the lines about his mouth. Knowing he was just as miserable as I was made it easier.

We had barely made it back inside our suite when alerts started popping up on my phone.

Lovebirds in Reykjavik!

Cinderella love story continues in Iceland.

Trouble in paradise? Exclusive insider says honeymooners barely speaking.

The last headline had been accompanied by a picture of me looking decidedly glum as I stared off to the side. Liam looked equally miserable, his mouth set into a grim line, his hands folded on the table.

I wanted it to just be over. But I showed Liam the headline before I went to bed.

"Tomorrow," he said quietly, "we'll have to do better."

And then he turned and went inside his room, closing the door behind him. The click had been loud in the quiet stillness of the suite.

Down on the stage, the lovers dance off as Don Quixote lumbers onto the stage in his clunky armor. I smile slightly as children dance onto a miniature stage and reenact the events of the first act.

"I'm impressed."

Liam's quiet murmur in my ear, coupled with his warm breath on my skin, makes me start.

"Oh?" I whisper back.

"The children dance better than Don What's-His-Name."

I bite my bottom lap to keep from laughing. "They're supposed to."

"Hmm."

I smile over my shoulder at him. He gives me a small grin back. For a moment our bond clicks into place, years of friendship arcing between us.

Liam's eyes drift down to my mouth. I breathe in sharply. His eyes dart back up to mine, and then he looks away. The bond snaps like it never existed.

I slowly turn back to the stage and sit up. I watch the rest of the second act like I'm seeing everything through a hazy mirror. I try to focus on the music, the dancers, the scenery. But it's hard.

It's so hard when the man I've loved for so long, the man who kissed me like he'd die if he didn't, has treated me with cold indifference ever since. I walked away, yes. But I needed time to collect myself, to sort through what had happened. I also couldn't bear to hear him apologize, not when it had just replaced our wedding kiss as the best kiss of my life. Not when I felt, just for a moment, that maybe something could be possible between us.

Yet I should really be thanking Liam. I had just promised myself hours before our plane ride that I wouldn't allow myself to entertain any thoughts of our marriage turning into something more. That kiss had lured me toward that very thought. His almost-apology and subsequent silent treatment had plunged me back into cold reality.

The curtain falls down, marking the end of the second act. The lights come on, illuminating the vivid red birch walls of the concert hall.

Liam stands and turns to me with a smile. "Shall we?"

I force a small smile and take the offered hand.

Liam guides me through the throng of people outside our door to an elevator that whisks us up. My breath catches for an entirely different reason as we walk out onto the eighth floor.

The wall, a collection of geometric glass shapes that remind me of a beehive, looks out onto the Old Harbor. The sun set hours ago, but I can still make out the distant outline of a mountain on the other side of the water. Reykjavik hugs the shore, a collection of tall, slim buildings that slope down as the city spreads farther north.

"Beautiful, isn't it?"

I turn as Liam hands me a flute of champagne. He puts a hand at my back and guides me toward a tall table. I try to ignore the heat of his fingers through the fabric of my dress. And fail miserably.

"Yes, it is," I say before I take a generous gulp of my champagne.

"A little more refined than our high school theater."

I chuckle. Our school theater was a disaster; threadbare seats, a stage that groaned at inopportune times and curtains that always smelled of mothballs. But it also played host to one of my happiest memories; meeting Liam and Diana. "Hard to believe it's been twelve years."

"Twelve years this month."

Surprised, I glance at Liam. "You remember?"

He frowns. "Of course I remember."

A thought pokes me, a memory I can't quite grasp. And then it appears suddenly and with complete clarity.

"I stay in touch with Mrs. Scout, our old counselor," I mention casually.

Liam tenses beside me. "Oh? How is she?"

"She retired last year."

"Imagine that," he murmurs.

"And she received a check from a foundation for five hundred thousand dollars for 'exceptional service.'" I watch him like a hawk, note the slight tap of his fingers on the tabletop. "Know anything about that?"

"Good for her."

Warmth fills my chest as I gaze at Liam. I don't know why he holds everything so tightly, why he keeps us at a distance. But I know, no matter the challenges we're struggling with right now, that he's a good man.

Which makes my current predicament ten times harder. Each layer I peel back, each new detail I learn about him, the more I struggle to stay away from the edge of loving him.

Loving a man who will never share the same goals and dreams I do.

I swirl my champagne in my glass, watch the bubbles dance. "Why did you decide here for our honeymoon?"

I barely catch the hesitation in Liam's answer. "Unique. Beautiful. A chance to see Ari and Diana at the end."

I bite back a sigh. More secrets. Always more secrets.

The glass is nearly to my lips when Liam quietly says, "I wanted to see the country I may have grown up in."

I lower my glass and face him. "That makes sense."

He huffs a small, frustrated laugh. "Does it? Seems maudlin and unnecessary."

"But you're here," I say gently. "I'd give anything to know more about my heritage."

He looks at me then, his blue eyes surprisingly kind and warm. "A good point. Just..." He smiles slightly. "I'm not one to share."

"I know."

I don't mean to say the words out loud. But nonetheless they hit with accuracy as Liam's eyes darken. I look back out over the harbor.

An awkward thirty seconds of silence passes before Liam speaks. "Do you like the ballet so far?"

I nod as I watch a small boat, maybe a fishing boat, navigate across the harbor, its faint lights tiny against the dark expanse of water and sky. "It's a little sad, though."

Liam frowns. "What is?"

"Don Quixote is living in a fantasy world. No one's telling him the truth."

More silence. I mentally kick myself. After what I shared with Liam on the plane, I need to do a better job keeping my mouth shut. I can't confide in him the way I used to.

"He's happy, though," Liam says quietly. "Isn't that enough?"

I sigh. "I used to think so."

Liam moves closer until we're arm to arm. I keep my eyes focused on the boat, on its trek through the darkness, and off of my husband.

Unfortunately, I don't have to be looking at Liam to know he's there. To feel the warmth of his body through the sleeve of his suit, to hear the softness of his breathing and smell the rich cedar of his cologne.

"What would make you happy, Aislinn?"

I almost don't answer. But then I realize this is an opportunity. To once again remind myself of the boundaries I must keep. Liam is attracted to me, yes, something that once would have made me ecstatic. Now it's just painful. I'm under no illusions that that attraction will turn into love. And even if it did, there's no future for us.

I look up at him, meet his pale blue gaze head-on. "A family of my own."

His eyes widen slightly. Understanding, empathy and a hint of fear that tells me, perhaps even more than Liam could ever say himself, that we will never be. "Aislinn..."

"Not us, Liam." I smile slightly. "You've always been vocal about how you feel about being a parent. And I have no desire to marry again after we..." My voice fades, and I glance around to make sure no one is eavesdropping. "After we part ways."

"Adoption?"

This time my smile is real. "Yes. I want children. I want a home with kids running around, happy and well-fed, kids who know they're safe and loved and will never have to worry about not having a roof over their head again."

Something dark flits across Liam's face. "It sounds nice."

"What is it?"

He shakes his head. "It's nothing. I—"

"You asked me on the plane to not shut you out." I give in to the urge to reach out and gently squeeze his hand. "You still want me to share."

He stares at me, his eyes uncharacteristically bleak. "Aislinn…" His gaze shifts and locks onto something over my shoulder. The bleakness vanishes in an instant, replaced by a cold cunning that induces an involuntary shudder. "Phones. People trying to snap pictures of us."

Tension grips my shoulders. I start to turn, but Liam reaches out and cups my face in his hand. Heat washes over me as I meet his eyes.

"Focus on me." His thumb strokes along my cheekbone, igniting little sparks that turn into fires racing across my skin. "There's just us. No cameras, no nosy bastards."

The uncharacteristic profanity startles a laugh out of me. "Liar."

He smiles down at me. "But it made you laugh. I wish you'd laugh more like that. Like you used to."

He leans down, and I sway forward to meet him, my eyes drifting shut…only to fly open when he brushes his lips across my forehead.

Before I can sort through my racing thoughts, the lights flicker and a bell dings.

"Since we have a private box, we're allowed to take our champagne back in," Liam murmurs.

I nod, not trusting myself to speak.

He once again lays a hand at the base of my spine and steers me back to the elevator. Out of the corner of my eye I see a woman raise her phone in our direction. I suck in a deep breath, then slip an arm around Liam's waist and lay my head on his shoulder. His body tenses beneath my touch.

He may not feel any of the emotions I do. But at least I have the satisfaction of knowing he's just as physically unsettled as me.

Cold, hollow satisfaction.

Liam

The elevator doors whoosh shut. I spend the next seven seconds focusing on the descending numbers and keeping my eyes off my wife.

My wife, who is the definition of a siren tonight, dressed in a scarlet sheath dress that clings to every curve I never paid attention to. She chose another off-the-shoulder design that reminds me of her wedding dress. Never in my life have I thought a woman's shoulders to be sexy. But now, as the doors snick open, and she walks out ahead of me, I entertain graphic images of kissing along her ridges, the curve of her arm, scraping my teeth along her skin.

It's not just the physical I find sexy. It's the whole woman: strong, powerful, determined to rise above the parade of heartbreaks she's suffered.

As we move into our private box, I'm aware of more than one man eyeing her appreciatively. With my ring sparkling on her finger and her hair falling in a smooth, golden waterfall to her shoulders, she's beautiful.

I wait for her to sit before taking my own seat. Then, with a nasty thought for the men lusting after my wife, I slide my arm around her shoulders. She stiffens but doesn't pull away.

The lights dim. The curtain rises on the third act. Slowly,

Aislinn relaxes. Despite her best intentions to remain aloof, the ballet pulls her back in. The tightness about her mouth eases as her lips curve up.

It's not hard to picture her as a mother. Reading her favorite books to them at bedtime, cheering them on at a game or wiping away their tears.

My heart twists in my chest. But this time, instead of the bone-deep certainty that kids are not a part of my future, there's a flicker of something else. Something I've never experienced before.

Longing.

I squelch it before it can take root. Having children is something I crossed off my list after a few years in foster care. I can barely summon enough emotion for my friends, let alone my long-lost brother. There's no way I'd be emotionally capable as a father. And given how many kids I lived with who had been abandoned by cold, detached parents, I'm not risking passing that trauma onto another child.

Even if I've occasionally wondered what it would be like to be a dad, all I have to remember is the words of the last foster father I ever had before I was moved into the group home.

I hope you never have kids.

I'd already decided I didn't want a family. Much as I loathed my final foster family, the words cemented my choice. I wasn't cut out to be a dad. Never will be. But things I can control—my career, the wealth of my clients—those are goals I can pursue. Milestones I can achieve without worrying who I'm hurting or who I might lose.

It also gives me vicious satisfaction every time I think of the words uttered during my time in foster care. I heard more than one foster parent murmur to their spouse or a social worker that they'd be surprised if I amounted to anything after graduation. Now, I'm wealthier than any of them will ever be. I have the stability they never offered me.

I glance at Aislinn out of the corner of my eye. Even if I sometimes wonder what life would be like with someone in it, I've made the right choices.

The third act continues. I try to pay attention to the dancers, the elaborate sets, the orchestra. But it's hard to focus when the realization that Aislinn and I will never be compatible pulses through me, a certainty that shouldn't matter.

But it does.

At last the curtain falls. The cast comes out for several curtain calls. Aislinn stands and applauds, a slight smile on her face.

I hold out my arm as she turns to me. "Ready?"

She nods and takes my arm without looking at me. I catch more than one curious glance directed our way as we make our way to the coat check.

I lean down to whisper in her ear. "Who would I be best as? Don Quixote or Sancho Panza?"

The question works. Her full lips, colored the same red as her dress, slide up into a smile. "You could look good in armor. But somehow I think Gamache is more your style."

I arch a brow. "The rich, spoiled nobleman?"

She reaches up and flicks her finger against my hair. "You'd look good in a tri-corner with a feather."

A flash interrupts our teasing.

Aislinn's face falls a moment before she smooths out her expression into a bland mask. "Well done."

"Ash—"

She shakes her head slightly even as she keeps the fake smile pasted on her face. "It's fine, Liam. I'm tired and on edge. It'll be okay."

Just a couple hours ago I was apprehensive about spending time together in the villa Ari recommended in northern Iceland. There will be no fancy restaurants, no operas or other opportunities for photographers to keep us under their microscope. Just Aislinn, me and miles of endless snow and ice.

Right now, as I feel her pull away even while she presses her body closer to mine, I want that time with her. Want a chance for us to hit Reset after the months of being apart, after my stupid decision to kiss her on the plane.

Want us to get back to where we were before Dexter entered her life and changed everything.

We step out into the winter air. I glance toward the dark outline of the mountain and the snow-drenched slopes. The first time I was in Iceland, my primary focus had been Diana and finding out why she had been so distant. I'd been aware of the fact that this was my homeland.

But now, with the picture of my mother tucked snugly in the pocket of my suit, I'm all too conscious of my heritage. The guilt is ever-present: guilt for what happened to my birth mother; guilt for wanting to know more about her after everything my adoptive parents gave me. It's a constant companion, one I haven't been able to shake ever since I laid eyes on her picture.

I surprised myself when I suggested Iceland to Aislinn. It had been the morning after I gave her the ring. I'd walked in to see her at the kitchen table, reading a book and stirring a spoon in a cup of hot tea. The urge to share Iceland with her, not just a whirlwind trip but a true visit to both the glittering city my brother called home and the northern shores where my birth mother was raised, came out of nowhere. But it was an urge I couldn't shake.

I don't know if I would have taken this step if I wouldn't have known she'd be by my side. I doubt I'll ever be able to express to Aislinn how much her being here with me means.

As I open the door of the limo for Aislinn, a cruel voice echoes in my head.

Not able? Or too afraid?

CHAPTER TWELVE

Aislinn

CHRISTMAS IN NEW YORK used to be my favorite part of winter. The bright lights, the huge Christmas tree and skating rink at Rockefeller Center, the snow-covered trees in Central Park.

It's nothing compared to Iceland.

The landscape passes by as Liam navigates the Jeep down the road. Snow-drenched land stretches out on either side of the road before sweeping up into soaring hills. Farmhouses and trees dance in and out view through the swirling snow.

I burrow deeper into my coat. The Jeep is warm, my seat heater on full blast. But the temperature between Liam and me rivals the frigid weather outside.

"I posted my first blog post."

Surprised, I glance over at Liam. "Oh?"

"Just on LinkedIn. It's a start."

I pull out my phone. There's just enough of a signal for me to pull up his profile and the link. "'Securing Your Family's Future,'" I read out loud. "'Build and Protect Generational Wealth.'"

"Lengthy and a touch austere," he replies.

"I like it, though." I scroll through the article. It's well-written, with a touch of humor that makes me smile even as it makes me think about things I could be doing to prepare for the family I hope to have one day. "I like it a lot."

"Thank you."

The sincerity in his voice has me glancing over. But Liam is staring straight ahead, his eyes fixed on the horizon.

I stifle a sigh and lean my head against the glass of the window.

The three days in Reykjavik flew by. I spent most of the days following the ballet wandering the streets and ducking into various shops. We went out a couple of times to sell the story of a couple in love on their honeymoon and managed to make stilted conversation. But aside from those brief moments in public, we barely saw each other. Even on the flight from Reykjavik's airport to the regional airport in Akureyri in northern Iceland, we barely spoke.

I saw a few pictures of the villa. Four bedrooms, glass walls and stunning views of the mountains and the deep blue waters of a fjord. Plenty of places for me to spend the next week taking what joy I can out of this honeymoon and staying as far away from my husband as possible.

At least in Reykjavik, I could wander. But that came with the price of paparazzi following everywhere I went. Sometimes they were brazen. Sometimes they were sneaky. Pictures appeared online within an hour of us returning to our hotel room every time, and sometimes even a few photos of just me. Each one made me feel like a liar, even as it reminded me of the reason why I'm here.

But here in the northern part of the country, I'm going to be stranded with Liam out in the middle of a frozen wilderness. I'd almost rather deal with the paparazzi. I'm surprised Liam picked a spot so far away when the goal of this honeymoon was to sell our romance.

I hear the clicking of the blinker and glance over. "Are we stopping?"

"Yes." Liam's face has turned unusually tense, his fingers tight on the wheel.

Confused, I look forward and see a sign. "Goðafoss Waterfall," I murmur.

"Waterfall of the Gods," Liam replies as he steers into a parking lot and puts the Jeep in Park. "It's nearly a fifty-minute walk to the waterfall."

My eyebrows shoot up. "Okay."

He stares straightforward out the windshield. "You can stay here."

I bristle but bite back my initial retort. Something else is going on. "Do you want me to stay here?" I ask.

He taps his finger against the steering wheel. Once. Twice. Then, finally, "It would be nice to have you there."

The admission costs him. Whatever is going on, it's enough for us to put aside our differences.

"All right."

We take a few minutes to get bundled in our winter gear and then set out along the path. The wind is fierce, but the winter pants, coat and face covering are relatively cozy as we walk along the snow-dusted path. A rope lines most of the way, tracing a trail through craggy rocks, up and down hills.

"A lava field," Liam finally says when he catches me crouching down to look at one of the formations. "Thousands of years old."

Amazed, I barely stop myself from touching it. "And here I thought that some of the oldest places in New York were incredible for being hundreds of years old."

The rest of the walk is silent. Yet, unlike the silence since our unfortunate kiss, this one is companionable. By unspoken agreement, we've decided to put aside our differences for the moment. I want to ask questions, but I don't have the right. Whatever demons Liam is facing are his to battle.

And, as I've learned from past experience, he'll most likely keep them to himself.

The onset of sound is so gradual it doesn't register at first—a shushing that grows into a dull roar. We crest a hill, and my jaw drops.

"Wow."

Torrents of water tumble over the lip of a cliff, forming several falls that descend to a large pool. Curtains of ice drape over the edge and have formed clumps in the pool—winter trying to make its mark despite the river's persistence. It's like something out of a dream.

I look at Liam. He's pulled his balaclava down so that I can see most of his face—the tightness of his jaw, lips pressed together.

Slowly, I reach out and lay a hand on his shoulder. "Liam?"

Wordlessly, he reaches up, unzips a pocket over his chest and pulls out a clear bag with a photograph in it.

I take it. My heart drops.

It's an older photo, slightly faded at the edges and creased in a few places. But the image is still clear: Goðafoss in summer, the lava rocks dotted with green, and the water sparkling clear as it tumbles over the basin.

And there, just on the edge of the photograph, is a young woman with dark hair, pale blue eyes and a round belly.

I turn the photo over.

Mamma og ungbarn.

Liam translates softly. "Mama and baby."

"Your mother." I flip the photo back over and stare at the smiling woman who, just months later, would lose her life.

"The photo was taken a few months before I was born. Ari and our mother used to take long drives, weekend trips, whenever Ari's father was home. This was the last place they came before she had me."

I trace a finger over her face—the sweet smile, the eyes so like Liam's.

"She loved you," I say.

The words slip out. I mentally curse, but before I can say anything else, Liam looks down at the photo.

"She did."

We stand there together, staring down at the photo, listening to the roar of the falls.

A million thoughts run through my head, a thousand possibilities of what I could say. But none of it seems right. Liam has lost not only one mother, but two. What does one say to that? Especially to a man who keeps himself bottled up so tightly?

I breathe out as my eyes roam over the stark, wintry landscape. Liam has hurt me, yes. But he's also been there for me more times than I can count over the years. Him sharing something so deeply personal is a gift I can recognize through my own pain.

So I stand and wait.

Liam

My mother smiles up at me from the picture in Aislinn's hand. I never met her, yet she feels so familiar that I can almost imagine her voice, hear her laugh as the photograph was taken.

Aislinn glances up at me. There are no empty platitudes, no mumbled words of apology or false statements of hope. That's something I've always appreciated about her. Even though she always maintained such a sunny outlook on life, I never once heard her say something just for the sake of saying it. She always knew when to listen, when to give space and when to give support. That, at least, hasn't changed. And God, I'm grateful for it.

The last few days have been torture. One minute I'm furious with myself for kissing her, for wanting her as badly as I do. The next I'm angry with her for once again being able to withdraw so easily, to go out to the ballet and dinner and act like everything's fine even as I'm burning on the inside.

"I don't know what to feel."

I feel like I'm wrenching the words from some deep pit buried in my chest. I don't share. But right now, it feels like the right thing to do. The last year may have been different, but the eleven years prior to that, Aislinn has always been there. Small gestures I once took for granted until suddenly they were no longer there.

"Understandable."

I hold my hand out. She lays the photo in my palm. I hold it up, positioning the picture so I can see exactly where my mother stood thirty-one years ago.

"Losing Mom and Dad..."

Grief tightens my chest. Most days I don't think about them. Don't think about the counselor pulling me out of class, the principal sitting next to me and awkwardly patting me on the shoulder as they told me my parents were dead. I stared at them. Screamed at them. Begged.

None of it changed the fact that my parents were gone.

"They never concealed my adoption from me. I wondered sometimes, but I was happy." I look at the picture once more before slipping the picture back into my pocket and zipping it up. "When they died, Child Services did a search for any living relatives. They didn't find anyone."

Aislinn shifts beside me. "A different kind of pain. The not knowing, wondering why."

"It made me angry. So angry I scared the first foster family I was placed with. I didn't last four weeks."

Aislinn's head whips around, and she stares at me, eyes wide. "I didn't know that."

"Not something most people respond well to." My jaw tightens. "They automatically think of you as the stereotypical foster kid. Don't get me wrong, I was an ass. I talked back to my foster dad and snapped at my foster mom. And then their son told me I needed to show them a little gratitude for taking in a runt."

"What?"

The outrage in Aislinn's voice makes my mouth quirk up. "I punched him."

"Good."

"Good except I got kicked out." I remember every moment of the walk from their porch to the car waiting to take me to my next home. Hot summer day, sun beating down on the back of my neck, mirroring the anger inside me. The anger covering a grief so large I didn't know to process it. So I concealed it. "It's been hard for me to connect with people since then."

"Again, understandable." Aislinn shakes her head. "The system is overworked. But it still failed you. You were ten years old, and you'd just lost both your adopted parents. Of course you were angry and grieving."

"Angry is one thing. Rage…" I breathe in deeply. "Rage is another beast."

My mind flashes back to another winter's day. The snow wasn't white and sparkling but gray and sludgy. Aislinn walking beside me talking a mile a minute as we headed to Diana's to walk the little puppy she'd sneaked into her backyard.

The cry had barely sounded before I was running. I knew the sounds—the whip of the belt, the frightened howls of the dog—knew what they meant. And when I barreled through the broken backyard gate of Diana's foster home, I wanted to kill the foster father who had beaten her.

I can still remember the fury, feel the murderous pulse in

my veins as I'd punched the old drunk over and over again. His eyes had rolled back into his head as he fell to the ground. And still I hit him.

It had only been Aislinn screaming my name that broke through my focus, only her small hands clutching my arm and tugging me away that kept me from killing a man that day.

I curl my hands into fists at my sides. "I almost killed someone, Aislinn."

"Don't." She lays a hand on my arm, almost the exact same place she laid her hands twelve years ago. "You stopped, Liam. You made a choice that day. You saved two lives and possibly others."

"I wanted to hurt him."

"As did I." She rubs soothing circles on my bicep.

I can barely feel it through the thickness of my parka, but I'm so damned grateful for it. Grateful for the comfort she's offering, the understanding.

"If you need someone to forgive you, Liam, I do."

My throat constricts even as my chest lightens, released from a burden I hadn't realized I'd been carrying all these years. I glance down at Aislinn, at this woman who even after all she's been through can still see straight to the heart of everything. A woman who has been a constant friend through all my ups and downs. One of the few people to stay.

And I nearly screwed it all up by kissing her. I don't know why, after years of friendship, I'm suddenly struggling with these feelings. But it has to stop. I almost lost Aislinn once. I'm not going to lose her again just because I can't keep myself under control. Aislinn may be telling herself now that she never wants to get married again, but she deserves more than casual sex. And that's all I have to give.

I've been down the road of losing people I care about one too many times. I don't think I'm capable of opening my heart up to anyone again, and even if I were, I don't want to. Standing here, feeling the grief clawing at me, the memories from my past like a persistent knock at the base of my skull, are reminders enough.

"Going through all of that changed me."

"Yeah, it would change anyone."

I breathe in deeply as I force out the next words. "What I'm saying is it's one of the reasons why I don't do relationships."

She stares at me for a long second, then nods. "So this isn't you finally sharing something from your past and opening up to me?" she asks. "This is a warning?"

Irritated, I turn and face her. "I just shared one of the most painful moments of my life with you. Explain to me how that's not sharing."

"You shared, yes, and I appreciate that, Liam. You've hardly shared any bit of yourself with Diana or me over the years."

The pain in her voice surprises me. "I told you, I'm not used to sharing."

"No, but you sure were content to let Diana and me share. Hell, you even encouraged it. And the one time when I think that you're finally opening up to me, you just turn it into a way to drive us apart even further." She shakes her head. "If you were wondering if our kiss was suddenly making me picture this marriage reaching its fourth anniversary or that I might be imagining a nursery for our kid, I know better. I know you, Liam. I know those things aren't in your future, and if you think that I would pressure you into something I know you don't want, then you don't know me, either."

She's walking back down the path before I can even respond.

I stand, staring at the spot where she stood just a few moments ago.

What the hell just happened?

Aislinn and I had always had the easiest friendship. I could be myself with her, relax, let my guard down. No, I wasn't into sharing bits and pieces of my past. But damn it, not sharing doesn't make me a bad friend.

Her accusation that I encouraged her and Diana to share lingers, though. Yes, there's some merit to it. I wanted to keep them safe. I wanted to be the friend, the brother they never had.

And you liked being their protector. Having something else to focus on.

I silence the ugly voice in my head and start back down the path, the waterfall continuing its incessant roar behind me.

CHAPTER THIRTEEN

Liam

ARI'S RECOMMENDATION DOESN'T DISAPPOINT. The villa, constructed of stone and glass, sits on top of a hill overlooking the narrow strip of sea below and the snowcapped mountains in the distance.

"Wow."

Aislinn walks from wall to wall, her eyes drinking in the sights. I smile slightly. She always sees things I don't. Diana notices details, too, but like me, she tends to focus on people, on reading their tells and signs so she can anticipate, prepare. Aislinn, by whatever miracle, simply saw the good. It used to worry me, made me think of her as a little sister to be protected from the truth of the world.

Definitely not a little sister anymore.

Blood rushes south. My cock starts to swell. I mentally swear, then leave Aislinn in the living room as I explore the rest of the villa.

All the rooms boast soaring ceilings and massive windows. The master bedroom is at the back of the house with its own private door onto one of several patios. This one, I remember as I note the steam rising from the far end of the patio, has stairs that lead down into a hot spring mineral pool.

I wander back out into the living room. "Do you have a preference on bedrooms?"

"No. Thank you," Aislinn adds, almost as an afterthought.

"The one toward the back has a private patio that opens onto a hot spring."

She quirks her head to the side. She's always done that when she's interested, a minute gesture most people probably miss. "That sounds nice."

"Then you take it."

She turns, her breath coming out in a heavy sigh as she crosses her arms. "We're stuck here for three days. I don't want to fight anymore."

"I don't, either."

"Okay. So we kissed. It happened. Now it's over."

I slide my hands into my pockets—clear, concise, emotionless. A dream response. So why the hell does it settle like an incessant itch between my shoulder blades? "Sounds good to me."

Aislinn nods. "We both had rough years. We've barely seen each other. Ours is a business arrangement, but the nature of it is rooted in ideas of romance and love."

She spits out the last few words with a derision that makes me ache for her, or rather the woman she used to be. I want nothing to do with love, but I wanted it for her. It's only understandable that we would get caught up.

I nod. "Yes. Understandable."

Aislinn lets out a deep breath. "So we're on the same page. No more kissing."

"There might still be occasions in the future when the situation warrants the kiss."

She rears back so drastically that I don't know whether to be amused or offended. "There are plenty of couples out there who don't kiss in public."

"Couples in love?"

"Yes."

"Like who?"

She blinks rapidly. "British royalty. Isn't it like against royal protocol or something?"

"As flattered as I am that I'm being compared to a prince, I think their situation is a little different than ours."

I step closer, intrigued when Aislinn takes a step back.

"We just agreed that we weren't going to talk about the kiss anymore." Color creeps up her neck—a soft, delicate rose that makes her skin glow.

"I'm not suggesting we kiss now, or anytime soon." Another step forward on my part. Another step back on hers. "I'm merely pointing out the possibility of it in the future."

She runs a hand through her hair, dislodging several strands that frame her face. I hope she grows it back long. I remember a night three years ago when she wore it loose—a political fundraiser. I asked her to dance, and as I spun her in a circle, she threw back her head and laughed, her hair falling down her back in a golden cascade.

I stop. Did I really think that? Back then?

"Can we talk about that later?" Aislinn's question yanks me back to the present.

"Of course." I glance around the massive living room. "Obviously no need for it here."

"Yes."

The doorbell rings.

"I'll get it." Aislinn darts forward like a frightened bunny. As she passes by me, that dark scent of rose lingers.

I walk over to the window and lean my head on the cold glass. It's bothering me—the realization that four years ago, I was noticing the way Aislinn's hair looked as we danced. Have I been wanting her all this time?

I should be disgusted. Instead, I'm thinking about how I want to sink my hands into her hair, feel the silk against my fingers.

"Catering delivery."

I turn around. Aislinn is standing on the far side of the living room, her arms crossed over her chest, her eyes wary.

"Sounds good. Are you hungry?"

She shakes her head.

"Then maybe I'll see you at dinner."

"Yeah. Okay." She starts to turn away, then stops. "The caterer said there's a snowstorm they're keeping an eye on, but they think it'll pass south of here."

I shrug. "Iceland is used to snow. I'm sure we'll be fine even if the storm does hit."

I watch her walk away. Force myself to let her. She's in the same house. She's not going to disappear anytime soon. And I need this time to figure out what the hell is going on with me.

For so many years, I've shut out most of my feelings. Loving Aislinn and Diana, accepting them as sisters, was the closest I got—a huge leap for me, but one that still provided some distance. I threw myself into the role of protector, partially because I wanted them to finally be safe, to have the lives they deserved.

But I can also admit that part of it was selfish. Protecting them, being their friend, gave me a purpose—something a little more personal than my goal of achieving my own wealth and independence, of never having to depend on anyone ever again.

Mercenary. Self-centered. Does it matter whether I've subconsciously noticed Aislinn before all of this? Even if I could let down my walls, I'm not the kind of man she deserves.

Which means no matter how much I want to kiss her, I can't. She's been through hell. I'm not going to drag her into mine.

My phone rings. "Whitlock."

"Mr. Whitlock? This is Bjarki, the manager of the villa." He sounds relieved. "Did you and your wife make it to the villa all right?"

"Yes, thank you."

"Good." Bjarki clears his throat. "I'm glad because I was just informed that the bridge leading off the highway to the villa collapsed."

"Excuse me?"

"Five minutes ago. A glacial outburst flood overwhelmed the bridge. The catering staff just made it across before the water came." His tone takes on an edge. "Foolish engineer used a timber pile foundation, and I warned him—"

"Is there another way out?" I interrupt.

"By helicopter, yes. Except…"

"Except what?" I ground out.

"High winds are forecast for the next several days. If it holds, the soonest I could get a helicopter to you would be early next week."

I stand there with the phone pressed to my ear, blood roaring in my ears. What are the odds that a split second after I decide to keep my distance from my wife, I'd be trapped with her in the middle of nowhere?

Aislinn

I throw back the covers and stand, grateful for the thick rug spread out across the floor. I grab a robe I tossed over a nearby chair and shrug into it before walking over to the window. There's nothing outside but snow, the white muted by the night as the storm howls around us.

This can't be good.

I drag a hand over my face. Three days. It was supposed to be three days in Iceland. If the wind keeps up like this, the helicopter won't be visiting anytime soon.

Another gust slams against the villa. I glance at the clock. Only one in the morning, but I'm not going back to sleep anytime soon. Not with the storm raging and my thoughts swirling in my head.

I quietly ease open my door and glance down the hall. Low lights along the baseboards create a warm, comforting glow. I pad softly down the hall.

Liam picked a bedroom on the opposite side of the house. Which is a good thing, I remind myself as I head toward the kitchen. The more distance between us, the better. Especially after he started talking about the potential of us having to kiss in the future.

My pulse went wild with the possibility of it. I don't need that right now. Can't deal with it. Especially when he made me feel like he was hunting me in the living room that first day, teasing the possibility of another kiss.

The man is so confusing. One minute, I think he's opening up to me emotionally and trying to reestablish our friendship. Then he reveals that he's reminding me that we can never be more than friends, right before he starts teasing me about us having to kiss again to sell our fake marriage. And now, since we learned about the bridge, he's been nothing but respectful, polite last night during dinner and cordial when he bid me goodnight before going to his room.

It's driving me crazy.

I walk into the kitchen and head for the fridge. I'm reaching for the handle when a voice speaks from the shadows.

"Good morning."

I shriek and spin around.

Liam is leaning casually against the counter with a steaming mug in his hands. And, damn it, he's only wearing pajama pants. Black silky pajama pants, the waistline clinging to his muscular hips, the silky material following the long line of his legs. One barefoot is crossed over the other at his ankle, and I have no idea why I find that sexy. But I know why I find his upper body sexy. Carved muscles dusted with a dark smattering of hair. Bulging biceps as he braces one hand on the counter behind him.

"Are you flexing?"

His smile is quick and white in the darkness of the kitchen. "Is that a pickup line?"

I roll my eyes, but I'm grateful for his humor. "What are you doing in here?"

"I could ask the same of you."

I glance toward the wall of glass at the far end of the kitchen. Still more white. Endless white. The storm.

"Guess the caterer was wrong."

I nod, my eyes focused on the swirling snow. "Do you think we'll be stuck here?"

I hear the tremor in my voice before I feel it in my chest—the tightening, the feeling of the world starting to press in on me. I try to keep my breathing even, try to fight it, but it's so hard.

"Aislinn." Liam's voice washes over me. I mentally respond to the sound of it, hold on to it like a lifeline. "Why are you in the kitchen?"

I breathe in deeply. "The storm. What else?"

I can't tear my eyes away from the snow, but I can sense him, can feel the heat of his body as he moves closer. The refrigerator hums. The furnace. Good. Two more. My heart beating. His footsteps on the floor.

"Close your eyes."

I follow his gentle command. My eyes drift shut.

"What do you smell?"

I inhale deeply, then release a cleansing breath. "Some kind of cleaner. Chocolate. Some kind of alcohol, like whiskey." I smile slightly. "My shampoo. And..." *You.* "Cedar."

"What else?"

My eyes fly open.

Liam is standing just a few inches away, his eyes burning into mine.

"Your cologne."

Liam's eyes drop down to my mouth. God, I want him to kiss me so badly. When he kissed me on our wedding day, it was unexpected and sensual. When he kissed me on the plane, he showed me a world I had never experienced. And now...now I can only imagine what our next kiss would be like.

I raise my face to his, start to lean forward, and then Liam steps back.

I jerk back like I've been slapped.

"Are you okay?" His words sound like rock scraping against rock—harsh, rough.

"Yes. I'm better." I glance back at the window. "It's just situations when I feel trapped, like there's no escape. Thank you."

He nods, then holds up his mug. "Drink?"

I swallow hard. Normal conversation. That's what I need. "Sure."

He walks over to the stove and pours what I realize is hot chocolate out of a kettle into another mug. I watch the ripple of muscles across his back as he moves about the kitchen. My fingers ache to reach out, follow the lines of his body. He turns back to me and sets the steaming mug on the counter, along with a bottle.

"I'll let you pick your poison."

I grab the bottle of brandy, uncap it and pour a very generous amount into my mug.

Liam's eyebrows shoot up. "Do I need to check on you later?"

"No." I hold up my mug in a toast to him. "Thanks for the drink. And the help. Good night."

I'm halfway across the kitchen when I hear him murmur my name. But I keep moving, walking out and back down the hall to my room.

CHAPTER FOURTEEN

Aislinn

I CLOSE THE door behind me and walk over to the bed, flicking on the switch that turns on the fireplace as I go. Flames crackle to life around the synthetic logs as I shrug off my robe and ease back under the covers.

Things will be different once we're back in New York. Once we both have things to distract us—Liam opening his firm, me figuring out what I want to do… I glance at my phone. Figuring out things like whether or not I want to accept the job offer I received this afternoon from the Foster Foundation. A month ago, they wanted nothing to do with me. And now they want to hire me without even conducting an interview.

My fingers tighten around the mug. I'm alone in my bedroom in northern Iceland in the middle of a snowstorm. I'm going to grant myself a couple of minutes to have a pity party. It seems like a cruel joke that I could be wanted by so many people, yet never for myself—only for what I can do for them. By Eric to elevate his campaign. By Dexter to use my political connections to both protect him and advance his agenda. By the Foster Foundation, for my newfound notoriety as the heroine in a love story so outlandish people want to believe. And Liam. Once upon a time, Liam wanted to be friends with me simply because he liked me. But now...now that's all changed, too.

I take a sip of my drink. My eyes widen. Wow, I had a heavy hand with the brandy on that one. At least it's good brandy. Great, actually. Some of the best I've ever had. And beneath the strong vanilla and spice of the alcohol, I can taste the richness of some of the best hot chocolate I've ever had. The same scents I smelled as Liam helped me stabilize.

A pressure grows between my thighs. I shift my legs, sit up in bed, take another sip of my drink.

None of it helps. And now there's the tingling to deal with. Subtle threads of sensation traveling up through my belly, winding their way through my body until every nerve ending is pulsing.

This is ridiculous. I should not be having this kind of reaction simply because a man stood a few feet away from me. But I am, and aside from getting drunk, which will just leave me with a horrible headache in the morning, there's only way reasonable way to deal with this.

I set my mug on the nightstand and ease down into the pillows. I close my eyes and breathe in, then out. Slowly, my muscles relax despite the need now beating a demanding rhythm in my veins. I reach up, cup my breasts in my hands and moan as I remember how it felt to be pressed against Liam's chest. I pull my top down, lightly graze my bare nipples with my fingertips as I imagine his mouth closing over one, then the other.

I arch my hips up off the bed and ease my sleep shorts and panties off. I keep one hand on my breasts while I skim the other over my stomach, past my hips, and down to my core.

When my fingers brush my skin, I hesitate. My thighs are damp, my skin hot. Slowly, I explore my body, imagine that it's Liam's fingers, hands, mouth on me. I've never indulged in a daydream like this before.

And it's so damn good.

The pressure builds. Presses against me. I'm climbing up, moaning, saying his name as I imagine him grabbing my hips and—

My door opens. Mortification roots me in place as Liam and I make eye contact.

This can't be happening. This is a dream. A nightmare. I'm going to wake up anytime…

Except one hand is still pressed between my thighs. The other is still cupped around my breast. I'm naked except for the tank top shoved down below my breasts.

I start to sit up, to reach for the blanket at the bottom of the bed as I fight against the sheer humiliation of being caught in such a vulnerable position. Did he hear me say his name? Will he even want to continue the marriage after this?

"Don't stop."

I freeze. Then, slowly, I turn my head to stare at him. Liam is still standing in the doorway, hands fisted by his sides, his bare chest rising and falling as he devours me with his gaze.

Bad idea. Very, very, very bad idea.

Slowly, I lean back into the pillows. The humiliation lingers, adding an edge of discomfort. But the fire in Liam's eyes, seeing the tension in every taut line of muscle, the way his fingers are curling, then uncurling, gives me a sense of power. Pure feminine satisfaction.

Liam wants me. I want him. If this is as close as we're going to get, so be it.

I slide my hand back between my legs. This time I tease, taunt myself and him as I glide my fingers up and down my thighs. The slight scratch of my fingernails, the softer touch of my fingertips, has my breath catching and my back arching.

I glance over at Liam. Then moan when I see him ease the waistband of his pants down and grip his cock with one hand.

His very large cock.

We stare at each other as he strokes himself. My hand moves to my core. I slide a finger inside myself, my hips bowing off the bed as I imagine Liam between my legs. He strokes faster, his breathing intensifying as his eyes roam over every inch of me.

The pressure is back, pressing harder, growing with every touch until I feel like I'm going to burst. I keep my eyes locked on Liam, try to memorize every single detail so I can remember him forever. Raw, masculine, barely controlled as he grips the doorframe with his other hand, muscles straining as he strokes faster.

"God, Aislinn."

I shatter. Waves of sensation swamp my body as I press my hand against my core and cry out his name.

He growls, yanking his pants up a moment before he grunts my name and his body shudders with his release.

My body collapses back into onto the bed, and my eyes drift shut. Delicious warmth flows through me, leaves me feeling sated and blissfully weak. That was more satisfying than anything I've experienced in my entire life.

The door clicks shut. I smile, anticipation making my skin pebble.

But all I hear is the howling of the wind.

I open my eyes and look over. My door is shut. I sit up and look around, my heart starting to pound against my ribs.

Liam is gone.

I don't know how long I sit there in the dark. Emotions try to worm their way in: mortification, grief, anger, regret. I choose numbness, wrap it around my almost naked body like a blanket.

I keep telling myself I can handle this. But it's become painfully obvious that I can't.

Starting tomorrow, I'm going to keep my distance from

Liam. It'll hurt, but it's the best thing for both of us. And once we get back to New York, I'm going to find somewhere else to stay while I live out the terms of our agreement. We can't be alone together.

That more than anything nearly breaks down my walls. Once I could go over to Liam's penthouse and relax on his couch with a movie and popcorn. I could even sleep over if I had an event the next morning that was closer to his place than my apartment.

Now we can't even be in the same room without setting each other on fire.

I pull my top back up and wiggle back into my shorts and underwear. I crawl under the covers, burrowing deep beneath the fleece.

For one moment, I let myself think *what if.* What if Liam could let himself feel again, fall in love with me? What if he did want to get married? Have a family?

And then I push the thoughts away. I've already made plenty of mistakes in this marriage. I'm not about to make the worst mistake of all and let myself hope for a future with Liam.

CHAPTER FIFTEEN

Aislinn

The world is still white. Endless white, as far as I can see. But unlike last night, or rather early this morning with the snow swirling in the wind and the howling storm, the day is calm. The storm is gone. Gray clouds lay like a thick blanket above, but I can still separate land from sky, can still see the fjord below our cliff and the mountains surrounding us.

Whoever manages the villa left a pair of binoculars in the living room, as well as a book about the different kinds of wildlife in the area. A quick look confirms that the road leading from the villa to the main highway is covered in snow.

I set my mug of tea down on the counter. I've never enjoyed giving myself pleasure as much as I did last night. But every time I woke up, it was like I hadn't found any release. Instead, there was an ache, one that deepened every time I thought about his eyes burning into mine, his hand stroking up and down his cock, him growling my name…

I pick up the tea and chug it, wincing as it burns my tongue. At least it gives me something else to focus on besides the pulsing between my thighs.

My phone buzzes. I roll my eyes at the notification of yet another news article, then stop as I catch one of the words in the title.

...philanthropist...

Confused, I click the link. There are the usual photos of Liam and me, some from the opera house and some from our time out and about in Reykjavik. The vultures are speculating about where we've gone for the next part of our honeymoon.

But farther down is a paragraph about Liam. It mentions his donations to a foster support program, a mentorship network for teenagers in care, and something called the Carpenter School. My finger trembles as I click on the link for the school. My eyes grow hot as I read aloud.

"Established five years ago by Liam Whitlock in honor of his parents, Robert and Norrine. To give the next generation a chance at a future."

He's never once mentioned any of this. From the little I can dig up, his support has been almost exclusively financial. No public appearances, no fancy galas. Just Liam giving money to causes he believes in.

I shove my phone back in my pocket and stand. Every time I turn around, there's a new layer to uncover, another aspect to the man I thought I knew so well. His time in foster care, the impact his adoptive parents' death had on him, his feelings about his birth mother... And now this, a generosity he won't let anyone else see. Another layer that deepens the emotional love I haven't been able to shake myself free of.

Coupled with our experience last night, I'm in deep trouble.

Restless, frantic energy propels me into the living room. The desire Liam has ignited in me is strong—too strong. It was so much easier loving him from afar, entertaining the occasional daydream about what life could be like. I never allowed myself the fantasy of imagining what it would be like to kiss him, to go to bed with him. Entertaining dreams like that only made it hurt worse when I saw him with a date on his arm.

But now, with each passing day, our friendship is receding as this new dynamic takes root. Which means that even after all I've done to protect Liam and Diana, I'll still lose him in the end. After what we shared last night, there's no going back to being just friends. Or moving forward, either.

I stare out over the swells of snow. Do I wish Liam would change his mind about a family? Fall in love with me and ask me to marry him? Yes. But I will never ask that of him. I won't be like William Luther and tell him to change himself so I can accept him.

God, I need to get out—away from the house, away from sharing a roof with Liam.

I grab a sleek binder off the coffee table that has all the information about the villa. I open it to the amenities page and run my finger down the list of activities the villa has to offer: on-site hot spring-fed mineral bath, gym on the lower level, snowshoes, skis, snowmobiles, sledding, archery.

The mineral bath would be relaxing. But it would still be in the house, where I might glimpse Liam at any time. Same for the gym. I've never tried snowshoeing before. Archery would be impossible with the wind. It's not as bad as yesterday, but Liam received a text message that the winds are gusting hard enough at the airport to prevent the helicopter from taking off. Skiing is an experience I'd rather forget. Nothing like falling flat on your face and knocking a tooth loose in front of a group of US senators.

But snowmobiling… It's been a while since I've driven one. Over two years, I admit with a grimace, when Eric and Stephanie took me on a weeklong getaway to Colorado. That had been around the time Liam had been dating an ice-skating champion and pictures of them kissing after one of her competitions had been splashed all over the news, with one article speculating the skater just might be the one to tame Liam into marriage.

I'd spent hours on the snowmobile, navigating the trails around the log cabin as I tried to keep my mind on nature and off the image of Liam with his arms around another woman. It had taken awhile, but eventually I'd found my rhythm with the snowmobile, alternating between speeding around curves and gliding down long stretches of trail. Exhilarating at times, peaceful at others.

I need the peace more than anything right now.

Decision made, I snap a photo of the recommended routes. The trails themselves will be covered, but the landmarks noted on the map will still be visible. The wind will make things interesting, but I want to get out.

Have to get out.

I hurry back to my bedroom, grateful when I make it without seeing Liam.

A couple minutes later I'm in the garage, bundled up in thick, fleece-lined winter gear. The snowmobile is brand-new, with a sleek frame and wide skis that will make navigating the recent snowfall a breeze. Excited, I grab the oversize dolly at the back of the garage and maneuver it into place before pushing the snowmobile outside.

The air is ice-cold. I breathe it in, savoring the clean taste of it as I straddle the snowmobile and turn the key. The engine hums to life.

"What the hell are you doing?"

I was so close. So close to freedom.

I glance at the throttle. Maybe I should just hop on and gun it. There's only one snowmobile. It's not like he could catch me anytime soon.

Except I didn't grab the helmet yet. Damn it.

Slowly, I turn and look up.

Liam is glaring down at me from the deck above.

"Going for a ride."

"By yourself?"

I grit my teeth. "Yes."

"Without telling me?"

Okay, that part was stupid. "Hey. I'm going snowmobiling."

"Not without me, you're not."

Oh yes, let's add the hot hunk of a man I can barely keep my hands off to the back of my snowmobile and have him intimately pressed against me on an hour-long ride. That'll cool me off.

"No."

"It wasn't a question, Aislinn."

"I've been snowmobiling before."

"I don't care."

I explode. "Damn it, Liam, I'm a grown woman. I don't need a babysitter."

"I'm fully aware you're a grown woman—"

"So leave me alone." Tears prick the backs of my eyes. Horrified, I look down. He's already seen me in one vulnerable position. I can't handle crying in front of him, too.

I look away and stalk into the garage. I grab a helmet off the shelf and am nearly back at the snowmobile when Liam runs out the door in the same black silky pants from last night and a T-shirt.

My mouth drops open. "Where's your coat?"

"I'm a grown man," he fires back. "Aislinn, we need to talk—"

"I don't want to talk! I just want…" I gesture out toward the snow-covered fields. "I just want to go. I want to be away from this house and away from you and us and what happened last night, and I—"

Liam reaches out and grabs my arm. "Then let me go with you. Make sure you stay safe."

I force out a laugh. "God, even after all this time, that's all you can see me as, isn't it? Poor little Aislinn with her head in the clouds. I can't tell a lamb from a wolf. Too foolish to see the bad in the world." I wrench my arm out of his grasp. "Like I said, Liam, I grew up. I'm not the stupid girl you once knew."

Liam stares at me. "Stupid?"

"Yes," I snap. "And guess what, you were right. The world is dark, and the people you love and trust can betray you without ever blinking an eye." A tear slips out, and God, it's cold. "I'm not perfect, but I'm not weak like I was."

"Would you stop?" He grips both my arms and hauls me close to him. "I have never once thought you were stupid or weak, Aislinn. Not once."

I blink. "But…you always said…"

"I always said I worried that people would take advantage of your kind heart. I never thought you were weak because of it, Aislinn." He leans down, his breath feathering across my face. "You were stronger for it. Stronger than I could ever be."

The world tilts. I open my mouth, but no words come out.

"I want to come with you because you've never been snowmobiling in Iceland before. We're snowed in. The helicopter can't take off, so an air evacuation is out if you get hurt. I'd rather not risk you getting injured and me spending hours looking for you."

All rational arguments. Ones I didn't consider when I came up with my brilliant plan, which unfortunately reinforces his point.

"Give me five minutes to get dressed?"

I nod, not trusting myself to speak.

"We need to talk about last night. But," he adds softly as I tense, "later. Let's just enjoy the moment."

He's back in less than three. I climb on the snowmobile, forcing myself not to react when he gets on behind me. As soon as I press down on the throttle and start forward, my rear slides back. His legs are on either side of me, his body cradling me as I navigate us through the snow.

I don't know exactly when it happens, but at some point, I start to relax. My body is still acutely aware of Liam sitting behind me. But with patches of blue sky peeking through the clouds and pale beams of sun making the snow glitter, it's hard to hold on to the turmoil that drove me out of the villa and into the snow.

I've seen snow before, mountains and lakes. But Iceland is raw, untamed in a way I've never seen before.

The snowmobile skims over the snow. Off to my right, steam rises from one of the things on the map. We pass by and continue on to where a lone pine tree stands tall and proud. I pull the snowmobile under its thick branches and turn it off.

"We shouldn't go too far toward the mountain." I nod my head in the direction of a soaring peak. "About a hundred feet that way, the cliff drops off into the fjord." I stand and shake out my hair.

"When did you learn how to drive a snowmobile?"

I glance over my shoulder. Liam is standing just a few feet away, his helmet in one hand and his balaclava in the other. His hair is messy, like someone has just run their fingers through it.

God knows I'd like to.

I mentally curse as I turn and face the mountain again. "A couple of years ago. Eric and Stephanie took me to Colorado. I spent most of the week exploring the trails."

Snow crunches softly behind me. I tense, all too aware of how close Liam is when he stops just behind me.

"He should have stood by you."

Hurt gnashes through me, but I shrug. "He had bigger things to worry about."

I always hated the term *greater good*. Except I, too, chose the greater good over doing what was inherently right. How can I possibly judge when I also made decisions I never thought myself capable of? When I've let Eric's misdeeds go unpunished all these months?

An ugly, wicked thought winds itself around my lungs and squeezes. If Liam knew that I'd kept Eric's secret to ensure the passing of the bill, that I continued to keep it because of my own inner conflicts, would he still see me as someone good and kind? Or would he turn away from me?

I hear Liam's soft inhale, as if he's about to say something else. Something moves to my left, a quick flash of white on white. I turn and gasp.

There, standing in the snow, is a fox—brilliant white fur speckled with gray, large, inquisitive eyes fixed on Liam and me.

I grab Liam's arm and squeeze. "Look."

I don't know how long we stand there, but finally, the fox turns its head and slowly pads through the snow. It pauses every now and then, sniffing the ground, even hopping up into the air a couple of times. Just as it's about ready to disappear beyond the hill, something else moves to my right. Another fox bounds across the snow, its stride long and its movements almost happy. It runs up to the first fox, gives it a gentle nuzzle with its snout, and then the two turn and disappear over the hill.

My breath comes out in a rush. "Did you see that?"

"I did." He sounds amused, but I don't care.

"That was amazing!" Even when I was in Colorado, the only animals I saw were deer. But an arctic fox?

I move out from beneath the tree and crane my neck up toward the sky. The clouds are rapidly disappearing, leaving a blanket of brilliant blue above. "This place is incredible."

Liam

She's stunning. Absolutely beautiful. How did I not see her before?

"Incredible," she repeats again as she turns in a slow circle. Her eyes sparkle. Roses bloom in her cheeks. Her hair falls in messy golden strands around her face. Even in her puffy jacket and snow pants, her hands encased in fur-lined gloves, she's the sexiest woman I've ever laid my eyes on.

"Last night."

Her joy disappears almost instantly. She goes still, almost like the fox we just saw. Wary, trapped. "I thought we were going to enjoy ourselves."

"We are," I say quietly. "I'm enjoying this."

"I was."

My mouth tilts up into a grin. Never in my life did I picture Aislinn being sassy. But God, I enjoy it.

"What is there to talk about?"

My amusement disappears as I stare at her. "You're joking, right?"

"Look, we talked about this. We're friends helping each other out. A relationship wasn't supposed to cross that far into intimacy, but it did. So let's chalk it up as an accident and move on."

"An accident?" I repeat. "That was no accident."

"Oh. So you walked into my room on purpose? Did you know..." Her voice trails off. She clears her throat. "Did you know what I was doing in there?"

It's twenty degrees outside, but it might as well be in the hundreds on a tropical island with how quickly heat swamps me.

"I came to check on you. I heard you moaning. I assumed you were sick or hurt. So yes, I opened the door."

I nearly swallowed my tongue. When I saw her stretched

out on her bed, nearly naked, one hand capped around her full breast, the other buried between her legs, my body went so hard I wouldn't have been able to move from her doorway even if I'd tried.

"No, I didn't know. I would never violate your privacy like that."

She looks down. "I'm sorry. That was unfair." She shakes her head. "I've been unfair to you a lot."

It would be easy to go down that path, to ask her why she's been pushing me away ever since that night of the gala. But I'm not about to be distracted now.

"I didn't know," I repeat, "but I'm damn glad I opened that door."

Her head snaps up. She stares at me, her eyes wide. "What?"

I walk toward her, much like I did the first day we arrived here—slow, measured steps. She's tense, frozen. But she stands her ground. I keep walking until nothing separates us but a sliver of winter air.

"I have never seen anything sexier or more beautiful than the sight of you touching yourself."

Her lips part. "You don't mean that."

"I do."

Her eyes drift down towards my mouth. She leans in. I tilt my head down, my body hard, ready to feel her lips—

She puts a hand to my chest. Firm, flat. "I need a moment."

Every fiber of my being is on fire. Demanding I kiss her again, take things further, deeper. Claim her. But I have no idea how she feels about all this. Yes, it was my name on her lips last night when she came. And God willing, before this honeymoon is over, I'll know what her body feels like wrapped around my cock.

But I'm not going to push her. When she comes to my

bed, it's because she won't be able to fight this attraction between us any longer.

I should be fighting it. But that ship has sailed. I can't fight it anymore. Not after seeing her laid bare and just out of reach.

"We should get back." She blinks, shakes her head slightly. "Liam—we've been out for a while. It's cold. Let's not push it."

She's been pushed and bullied enough. I still don't know why she married Dexter, although I've got a pretty damn good idea, and it wasn't willingly. Still so many pieces to sort through. But we have a couple of days here, at least, not to mention the rest of our marriage.

I glance at her out of the corner of my eye as we walk back toward the snowmobile. When we first agreed to the terms of our marriage, three and a half years seemed like a long time to play being in love, committed.

But now, as Aislinn pulls on her helmet and throws one leg over the snowmobile, it suddenly doesn't seem that long at all.

CHAPTER SIXTEEN

Aislinn

I WALK DOWN the hall to the bedroom Liam claimed as his own. Nerves flutter in my stomach, but I keep going.

After we got back from our ride, Liam helped me get the snowmobile in the garage and then disappeared inside. I went to my room and took a long, hot shower. At first, I just focused on the blazing water on my back, the steam clouding the room.

But as I scrubbed soap up and down my legs, my hands drifting over my breasts, I made a choice. One that absolutely terrified me. But after what Liam had told me by the tree, the way he looked at me, I know I will always regret it if I don't take this step.

I stop at Liam's door, sucking in a deep breath, and knock.

Footsteps sound on the other side, then Liam opens the door. "Aislinn…" His voice trails off as his eyes drop down, going from passive to burning in an instant when he realizes all I'm wearing is a towel.

"I want you, too."

The words are barely out of my mouth before he's hauling me against him.

His mouth fuses to mine. I moan against his lips as his fingers dig into my hips. He bands one arm around my waist and drags me inside, kicking the door shut behind us. We move to the bed, hands frantic, breath mingling.

I step back long enough to drop the towel. The towel falls to the floor, leaving me completely naked.

Liam stares at me, his eyes moving over my body with an intimate thoroughness that thrills me to my toes. "How did I not see you?"

Before I can respond, Liam picks me up in his arms, kissing me senseless as he turns and lays me down gently, then covers my body with his. His hands are on my back, then gliding up my sides, cupping my breasts with an exquisite tenderness that brings tears to my eyes.

"Liam," I murmur against his mouth.

Liam lifts his head.

I freeze. Is he going to pull away again?

"You're so beautiful, Aislinn." He leans down and brushes his lips against the swell of my breast.

My eyes flutter shut as I moan. It feels so good, the wet heat of his mouth on my skin, the teasing touch of his fingers as his hands shift down to my waist. When he scrapes his teeth over my nipple, I tense. When he sucks my nipple into his mouth, I cry out. Each caress of his lips, his tongue, heightens the sensation from through my body. I thread my fingers through his hair, hold on as he shifts to the other breast.

His mouth is fire on my skin. Did I think my own hands could even begin to compare to what Liam is capable of? He trails kisses down the sides of my breasts, beneath, kissing sensitive skin no one else has. I stare down at him, momentarily jolted by the site of my friend, the man I've loved for so long, kissing me in ways I never thought possible.

And then his mouth moves lower, over my stomach and farther down. My breath starts coming in short, frantic gasps as he captures my hips in his hands. His breath fans over my core, cool and soothing as I restlessly shift my legs.

"Please, Liam. Please."

His chuckle reverberates across my skin. And then he lowers his head, tracing his tongue up and down the seam of my most intimate skin.

Then he feasts. Kisses, licks, teases with the faintest scrape of his teeth that drives me wild.

I reach down, finally tangle my fingers in his hair and press his mouth deeper. "Liam!"

His name comes out on a sob. I can feel myself spiraling up, shooting toward something I've never experienced before. He's relentless, driving me higher, finding every vulnerability I have and exploiting it with his mouth. I come apart, arching into his touch and screaming as pleasure fills me, pours out of me.

Gradually, I come back down to earth. I give a half-hearted laugh mixed with a groan as he presses one last kiss to my skin before sliding up my body.

I peel open my eyes to see him propped up on his elbows above me. "You," I say as I trail a hand down his chest, "are overdressed."

He smirks and pushes himself up onto his knees. I watch as he grabs the hem of his shirt and whips it over his head.

"Better?"

"Getting there."

He rolls off the bed and rids himself of his pants and boxers. I swallow hard at the size of his cock. Thick, hard. He wants me. He really, truly wants me.

He joins me on the bed again. He starts to lower himself on to me, but I stop him with a hand on his chest.

"My turn."

He huffs out a laugh even as I push him onto his back. "Not what I expected."

I pause. None of this is what I expected. I never imagined

when I saw Liam just two weeks ago that we would end up in bed together after all these years.

"Hey."

I blink, focus on his face.

He reaches out, traces a finger down my cheek. "You don't—"

I lean down and flick my tongue against the tip of his hardness.

He groans, his hips arching up. "Tease."

I smile at him before sliding my mouth down his length. I love the way his body moves beneath my hands, love the taste of him, the feel of him as I both give pleasure and take it with every moan, every muffled curse.

"Enough." He sits up, grabs me by my arms and has me on my back within seconds. "I need you, Aislinn."

My throat tightens. For years, I just wanted to be wanted for myself. And now, in this moment, I finally am. "I want you, too, Liam."

He suddenly freezes. "Damn it. Condom."

"I'm on the pill. And I'm clean. I haven't…" Embarrassed, I shift beneath him. "It's been a couple years."

He stares down at me. "Years?"

Slowly, I nod.

"It's been over a year for me, too," he says softly. "I've never not used a condom before."

I have no right to feel relieved. But I do. To know that it's been so long makes me feel special. There will be other women after me. But for right now, Liam is mine.

"I want you," I repeat. I reached down between our bodies and grab his cock.

He presses himself against me, his cock hard against my wetness. He slowly slides himself in, stretching me, filling me up. I moan his name, my hands traveling up and down his back as he eases his full length inside me.

"God, Aislinn, you're so tight."

We quickly find a rhythm, our hips moving together as the pleasure builds once more. We whisper each other's names, our fingers stroking, pressing, urging each other onward.

"Liam… God, I can't…"

"Let go, Aislinn. Just let go."

I do, coming on a scream as I clench my legs down around his waist.

His thrusts grow deeper, harder, and then he arches back and groans. "Aislinn."

Warm heat fills me. I wrap my arms around him, arch my neck as he presses his face against my skin and kisses me.

My eyes drift shut. Between our excursion and the incredible lovemaking, I'm exhausted. The bed shifts. A moment later I'm covered by a thick blanket.

"Sweet dreams, Aislinn."

I drift off to sleep, dreaming of Liam and me dancing in the snow, oblivious to the storm gathering on the horizon.

CHAPTER SEVENTEEN

Aislinn

I WAKE UP SLOWLY. Warm sunlight fills the room. My eyes are open long enough to see the curtains pulled and a fire still flickering in the hearth.

A hot, heavy arm slides across my waist.

Liam.

He presses a soft, tender kiss to my cheek. I turn and look at him. Is this even possible?

"Good morning." His voice rumbles through me. So familiar, yet so different as we lie there, naked in bed.

"Good morning."

His smile is slow and languid. Satisfied. And given that he woke me up around midnight and made love to me again, I'm not surprised.

"How do you feel?"

"Tender. Sleepy." I smile shyly. "Happy."

His smirk disappears as he leans in and kisses me.

My body responds instantly. I roll over and straddle his hips, brazenly rubbing myself against his rapidly hardening cock.

"Aislinn," he groans.

I grab him with bold confidence, angle myself and then sink deep down, moaning as he fills me.

His hands clamp down on my thighs like a vice. "Ride me."

I move up and down, need coursing through me as he fills me. I cup my breasts, gently tug on my nipples.

"Fuck, yes," he groans. "I love watching you touch yourself."

I move faster, sinking down even deeper, watching the play of emotions across his face. He's so handsome. So sexy. A man who knows me far better than anyone else.

A man I love and will always love, even if he can never love me back.

Liam thrusts his hips upward. My orgasm hits, sends me spiraling over the edge. Liam follow the moment later, filling me with his heat.

I slump forward on his chest.

He chuckles into my hair. "Good morning."

"You already said that."

"Well, now I'm saying it again." He presses a kiss to my hair.

I scrunch my eyes tight. This is far more than I ever thought I would have with him. Yes, in a few days we'll go back to reality. But I need to take this gift I've been given and make the most of it.

"Are you all right?" He's watching me, alert and curious. Perhaps even suspicious.

"Yes. Just overthinking things."

His face softens. "Let's get breakfast."

We bundle into our robes and walk down the hallway. He grabs my hand halfway down the hall, wrapping his fingers tightly around mine. He makes quick work of pulling out various dishes left by the catering company: bagels piled high with thick slices of lox and topped off with dill and capers. Skyr, Icelandic yogurt that could classify as a dessert with its thick creaminess, topped with honey and frozen raspberries. Rich, thick coffee that makes me moan as he sets a cup in front of me.

"How am I ever going to go back to breakfast burritos?"

Liam chuckles as he scoops up a spoonful of yogurt. "We could always eat like this back home."

I nearly drop my fork. "Yeah. That sounds nice."

"Okay," Liam says. "What's going on?"

I set my fork down, put my elbows on the table and scrub my hands over my face. "I feel…uncomfortable."

His face sharpens. "With me?"

"No. With me. Myself." My heart starts to pound. "You keep telling me I'm this amazing person. That I'm strong and good."

"You are strong and good."

I lay my palms flat on the countertop, steel myself. "But what if I'm not?"

Liam sets his spoon down and leans back in his chair.

I resist the urge to squirm under his gaze. Why did I bring this up? Because of the guilt I felt yesterday while we were snowmobiling? We were having a pleasant morning. And what if after he hears the truth my worst fear comes true? What if after I've finally gotten to be with Liam he pulls away? "Maybe we shouldn't talking about this."

"No." He shakes his head. "You can't run from this, Aislinn."

Hurt spears through me. "Is that what you think I did? Ran away?"

"I don't know. I don't know, because you never once reached out for help. You never told Diana or me anything. You just disappeared."

"I wasn't…" I sigh. "I wasn't thinking. I was stupid."

"Stop saying that," Liam snaps. "You're one of the smartest people I know. Look at Eric's campaign before and after you came on board. You took his career and turned it into a powerhouse. Yes, he's done good work, but you're the one who told his story, told the story of the people whose lives he changed. You're not just smart, but you know people. You open yourself up to them, and they, in turn, open up to you." He leans forward, eyes blazing. "How could you ever think that was a weakness?"

"And what if Eric wasn't who we thought he was? What if he did something bad?" My throat grows thick. "What if he did all of these good things, but he's still a selfish person?"

Liam's face softens. "You married Dexter to protect Eric."

Slowly, I nod.

"Aislinn. Why didn't you come to me? To Diana?"

"Because he threatened you, too."

Liam's face hardens, his eyes going ice-cold.

A shiver creeps down my spine as I remember the way he pummeled Diana's adoptive father. I have no doubt that if Dexter were still alive, Liam would be planning a way to hunt him down and hold him accountable.

"He threatened to tank your firm, to ruin Diana's career. He knew so many people, had so many people's secrets in the palm of his hand…" I suck in a shuddering breath. "But at least I learned a valuable lesson."

"What?" Liam snaps. "That people screw up? That sometimes the world's not perfect?"

Angry, I turn and face the mountain again. "You don't understand."

"What don't I understand? We've led different lives, but I know what it's like to lose, to be disappointed, to be hurt."

"And what about used?" I face him again, my hands curled into fists at my sides. "What if every single person in your life wanted you, not because of who you were, but because of what you could do for them? And what if you spent your whole life thinking that one day, one day, it would get better? And you pretended like your adoptive father didn't adopt you because it looked good for his reelection campaign? And your adoptive mother went along with it because she was the dutiful wife and wanted to make her husband happy? What if the first time I was proposed to was because a madman wanted to use me and my connection to my father to further his own ambitions? And what if—"

My voice trails off. I'm angry. So angry. But I don't want to hurt Liam.

"What if one of your best friends proposed to you for a business arrangement?" Liam finishes quietly.

We stand there, the only sounds the occasional whisper of the wind or snow falling from the trees onto the ground.

"Is Stephanie involved, too?"

The pain cuts deeper. Eric's distance stung, but he still gave me so much. Stephanie, on the other hand, had been what I'd always dreamed of—a mother. Until I saw her signature on several of the documents Dexter had kept. I can't see a scenario where she's not involved in some way, no matter how badly I want things to be different.

Maybe I'm making excuses for myself, but when I made those choices, it was with the thought of protecting a bill that would, in turn, protect thousands of children. What Stephanie and Eric did only benefited themselves.

"I don't know. We haven't talked much since everything happened."

"Why did you decide to keep Eric a secret?"

"We had been working on that bill for years. Years," I repeat. "It's something that should have been discussed and passed within hours. That's not the way the system works, but it should."

Frustrated, I stand and start to pace. "I know that's my idealistic self talking. But it just doesn't make sense. This should be a no-brainer. Dexter must have done his homework on me because he knew how important the bill was to me. He knew how involved I was and threatened to make sure it would never get passed." I snort. "God only knows how many other senators and legislators he had in his pocket."

"So you concealed your adoptive father's breach of ethics to ensure that foster kids would grow up in better environments?"

It sounds so cut and dry. "I did it for the children, so it must be okay, right?"

"So what's holding you back from accepting that?"

"Because I still did it. I still made a choice. A choice to lie, to conceal, and not about something small. And as soon as I kept that lie, then another took its place. I pretended like I was falling for Dexter. I shut you and Diana out. I told Eric and Stephanie everything was okay. And Stephanie asked a lot." My lips curve up into a sad smile. "I always told myself, even when I was little, that even though I didn't have a family, I had myself. Rules, beliefs to live by. That even if no one wanted me at the end of the day, I could still be true to myself." I finally look at him. "And now I don't even know who I am anymore."

Liam stands and circles the table. "In all the years I've known you, I never realized how high of a standard you hold yourself to. But it's okay that you're not perfect, Aislinn. No one is."

"I know that. I make mistakes, but this…" I grab the folds of my robe and pull them tightly together at the base of my neck. Hiding. Shielding. "I hated him, Liam. I hated him, and when I found him, I was glad he was dead." Tears pour down my cheeks. "Who thinks like that? What kind of person is happy that someone else's life is over?"

"He abused you, Aislinn." Liam slowly reaches out.

When I don't pull away, he tugs me closer until I'm standing in the circle of his arms.

"He manipulated and used you. He was willing to sacrifice all the children that would have benefited from that bill for his own personal gain." He leans back, looks down at me. "And you still gave him respect. He'd earned none of it, but you gave him a funeral, a wake. You never once disparaged him to anyone." He presses a gentle kiss to my forehead. "You're human, Aislinn. And in this case, I wouldn't even say that you made a mistake. You went through something horrific. You had difficult choices to make. If I had been in your shoes, I would have probably made the same ones."

My lips tremble as I barely manage to hold in my sobs. Finally telling someone everything, having him hear my darkest secrets and still be standing in front of me, takes the weight off my heart. "Thank you."

He tucks a strand of hair behind my ear. "Don't let Dexter take away who you are." He lays a hand over my chest. "You are kind, Aislinn. And yes, now you've seen that you can be harsh. But you know it can be good, too. And the second that you stop believing in that and fighting for it, that's when Dexter will win."

He's right. It's going to be hard, opening back up. There was something so easy about not feeling much of anything.

Liam's smile chases away the last lingering clouds. "Something I have noticed is your confidence."

"Oh?"

"Before, you would always tiptoe around, making sure everyone felt heard, seen." His teeth flash white as his grin widens. "The Aislinn I've seen the last few weeks stands up for herself."

"Still diplomatic—unless it's you," I joke, half teasing, half apologetic.

"True. But it's good, Aislinn. You're important, too."

I breathe in. For the first time in over a year, there's no pressure on my chest, no tightness in my lungs. I'm finally breathing again.

CHAPTER EIGHTEEN

Liam

The moon has turned the landscape into silver. Stars dot the night sky with tiny drops of light. I'm sitting in the mineral bath just outside Aislinn's bedroom. The water is hot, a sharp contrast to the cold on my shoulders. Champagne bubbles in flutes perched on the stone wall that circles the bath. Overhead, a shooting star streaks across the sky. The perfect honeymoon.

Except our honeymoon was never supposed to be like this. Two friends selling a story to the public, her to recoup a public image, me to establish a private one. But now that I've had her, seen her, I can't get enough of her.

After her confession this morning, we finished breakfast before I sweet-talked her into taking a shower. By the end of it, I had her facing the wall, hands braced on the tile, my hands on her hips again as I drove myself inside her.

I forced myself to stay away after breakfast while I answered emails and reviewed expenses for the office. Prepping for the opening has consumed my attention for well over a year. But just receiving an email from her halfway through the morning with a detailed public relations campaign made me crave her. The sight of her name made me hard.

Reading the details on what she proposed, a campaign that seamlessly blended high-end luxury with subtle outreaches to communities in need, made me want to see her, talk to her.

The woman is brilliant. How had I not ever talked with her about my plans for my business?

And then I came face-to-face with the ugly realization that I hadn't shared because my business was an extension of myself, of my own dreams and desires rooted in years of pain. Yet another piece I hadn't been willing to share.

I forwarded her recommendations to my head of public relations and requested a check made out to my wife for consultation services. A check, I thought with a smile, she'd probably argue with me over. And damned if I wasn't looking forward to that argument, to silencing her with a kiss and…

I stopped that thought process, shaken at how easy it was to suddenly see Aislinn in my future. Was I actually contemplating this? Contemplating something more with a woman I used to refer to as my little sister?

How can I offer her a future when the thing she wants the most—a family—is something I'm not capable of?

Except as I sat at my desk and thought about Aislinn, thought about her with a child in her lap or a baby in her arms, the longing that flared in Reykjavik dug deep into my skin. It was unsettling to consider that the things I told myself I wasn't capable of having or didn't want are all things I might have just pushed away out of fear.

I turned back to my work and made it one more hour after her email.

She was in the living room, wrapped up in a pile of blankets, watching a movie. I joined her, and we spent the rest of the afternoon lounging on the couch and indulging in the high-end snacks left by the caterers: handcrafted chocolate truffles, gourmet popcorn with real flecks of gold.

I took advantage of her lying in my arms to let my hands wander beneath her shirt, tease the waistband of her pants. But there were also long stretches of time where I was content to simply hold her, listen to her laugh at the movie or murmur an observation.

I can't recall the last time I felt so satisfied with a romantic partner. All of my previous relationships have been rooted in sex and mutual interest in physical pleasure that, once gone, meant the end of the relationship.

But I don't think I would ever lose that with Aislinn.

The thought of not having her in my life, being with someone else at some point in the distant future, makes me sick. And the thought of her with someone else, another man holding her hand, kissing her cheek, daring to touch a single hair on her body, has me wanting to punch something.

Careful.

Part of the reason I shy away from emotions is simply because I don't want to get hurt again. But part of it is because I've also seen what I'm capable of. Punching my first foster brother in the face was just the tip of the iceberg. What I did to Diana's foster father, even though it was ruled in defense of someone else, was confirmation that emotions can be violent, unpredictable.

Dangerous.

We only have one more day, maybe two at the most. The winds have finally died down enough for the helicopter to take off, only for one of the machine's parts to break. A new part is on its way, and there are no more storms in the forecast.

Twenty-four hours until we leave our unexpected paradise and confront the real world again.

Movement catches my eye.

Aislinn opens the sliding glass door of her suite and steps out onto the patio, bundled up in her thick white robe. She walks over to the bath, her shoulders hunched against the cold. "Please tell me that water is boiling hot."

I arch my brow at her. "Come in and find out."

She stops at the edge of the water. She closes her eyes, takes a deep breath and yanks on the belt of her robe. The robe parts.

My mouth dries at the sight of her in a red one-piece swimsuit with a deep V-neck that gives me a very generous view of the sides of her breasts.

"Cold. Cold." She darts toward the stairs and enters the water, letting out a hiss as she descends. She sinks down until just her head is above the surface. "That's better."

I smile as she drifts over to me. Since we talked this morning, she's been happier. More like herself, but still with that edge of confidence I see. I hand her a glass of champagne.

She sits next to me, her thigh brushing mine, and tilts the glass up. "That's delicious." She tilts her head back and looks up at the stars. "Do you think we'll see the Northern Lights? Ari says there's a good possibility. And Diana saw them on the southern coast. She said it was the most amazing thing she's ever seen." Aislinn glances at me. "Thank you, by the way. For what you and Diana did. I just wish it would have worked the way I had intended." She shakes her head. "My best guess is that Dexter didn't tell me about your supposed engagement because he knew the chances were high of me reaching out, even though he told me not to."

I think back to that morning when Dexter opened Aislinn's door, when I assumed he'd just left her bed. The rage I felt that morning takes on a new meaning as I sit next to her, my fingers stroking over her bare back. Even then, I felt something for her.

I'm just not sure what to do about it.

The thought of not having Aislinn in my life like this, from the mind-blowing sex to these casual, intimate moments I've never had with another lover, seems impossible. Yet marriage, a real marriage, doesn't feel right. Not when I can't open up and fully be the man she deserves. Not when she wants a family.

"Can I ask you something?" Aislinn murmurs softly.

"Yes."

"If you had all the money and all the prestige in the world, what would you do?"

I smile. "Anything's on the table?"

"Yes."

I sit there for a moment. "When I was seven, I wanted to be a firefighter. The dream of many little boys. And when I was nine, I wanted to be a carpenter."

"A carpenter?" she repeats.

"Yeah. Like my dad. Every time I smell sawdust, I think of him. I remember the row of wooden carvings I kept in my room—toys Dad crafted for me over the years. Toys that were lost when I was put into foster care."

"What were they like?"

"Some of the kindest people I've ever met. They would have loved you."

Aislinn's smile flashes white in the darkness. "From what little you've said, they sound like amazing people."

"They were." I pause. "The boy I was before they died and the man their deaths forced me to become are two very different people."

Aislinn lays her head on my shoulder. The simple contact releases some of the tension from my body. "I'm so sorry."

"I learned quickly that if I cared about what others thought of me, I wouldn't survive foster care. Not emotionally. Once I had the reputation for being angry and sullen, I couldn't shake it. Foster families anticipated it. I didn't help with how I responded to situations, but still, they were automatically reserved and ready to mete out punishment. More than one said I'd amount to nothing."

Aislinn twists so she's looking up at me. I look down to see understanding in her eyes. "And look at you now." She leans up and kisses my jaw.

The simple contact surges through me straight to my heart. "I switched myself off. Apathy kept me stable. I worked toward my goals of becoming independent, of achieving the kind of success that meant I would never have to depend on anyone again."

For a moment, Aislinn is silent. Then, she speaks. "You never really answered my question. Firefighter? Carpenter? Karaoke singer?"

"I actually really enjoy what I do. Helping people build their own wealth is immensely satisfying."

She frowns at me. "But you're already working with people who have a lot of money."

"I saw a lot of families struggling during my time in foster care. There were some decent ones, but there were a lot of them that did it for the money. I promised myself I would never find myself in that position. Once I realized what I could achieve, it just seemed like a no-brainer to reach as high as possible."

Aislinn's frowning at me. "But does it make you happy?"

"Happy?" I repeat.

"All the money. The penthouse."

I start to respond, then stop. *Does it make me happy?*

It's unsettling to realize I don't have a good answer. It should be an unequivocal yes. I made clients millions, and in some case billions, when I worked for the firm. I'm opening my own financial advising practice. My investments have paid off to the point I own a penthouse on Billionaires' Row, a brownstone in one of New York's elite neighborhoods, and I've vacationed all over the world.

But when I think back to what's truly made me happy over the years, the first thing to come to mind is my parents. The second is Aislinn and Diana. People who loved fiercely, who stood up for others gave them a voice. While I hoarded money and climbed corporate ladders, all for the sake of reaching independence. Keeping people as far away as possible.

What would make me happy?

I think back over the past week—even with the tension—I've had some of the happiest moments of my life with Aislinn. Apprehension knots my chest. I don't know when it happened, but at some point, Aislinn became far more than I had ever anticipated. I care about her. Deeply. More than I ever have any other woman.

I've lived most of my life with the conviction that being alone is better.

But I can't remember a happier time in my life than these last few days with her. When I think of my future post-divorce, there's no satisfaction at accomplishing my goal, no relief at returning to my old lifestyle. Instead, there's an ache, a knowledge that one of the best things to ever happen me will no longer be there.

"I don't know." A bald-faced lie, but I don't know how to share yet the conflict inside me.

Thankfully, Aislinn doesn't push. Instead, she grabs my hand under the water and squeezes. "You're a good guy, Liam."

I huff out a laugh. "I'm a selfish bastard."

"Foster Connect. The Big Kids Network. The Carpenter School." She says the name softly.

My muscles tighten with each mention. "What about them?"

"You've been donating to the first two for years. You created the third on your own." Her voice hitches. "A carpentry program for kids aging out of foster care. I didn't realize the connection to your dad until now."

"I give money, Aislinn," I say firmly. "It's not anything close to what you do. The campaign you shared—which my head of publicity thought was phenomenal—wasn't just smart. It had heart, Aislinn. You naturally care, and it shows in your work, just like it shows in what my brother does with his company." I pause. "That's not me."

"So change it." She gently nudges me. "You could use one of those for your charity fundraisers—"

"No," I cut her off. "I don't want to use any of them to help my business."

Her slow smile is sexy, knowing. "Any other man would have jumped at the chance to use those organizations for public relations. But you care."

I shake my head. "You're giving me too much credit."

"That campaign was created based on the work you've already done, Liam. Yes, you cater to top-tier clients, but you've made impacts with your money. Thoughtful ones. For crying out loud, I know you were the one who gave Mrs. Scout that money when she retired."

I try to look away, but she reaches out and lays a hand on my cheek.

"You don't give yourself enough credit. Maybe it's time to re-evaluate."

"And what about you?"

She blinks like an owl. "Me?"

"You're good at what you do. Great, actually." I lean over and give in to the urge to kiss her cheek. "When are you going to grab your life with both hands and start living again?"

"Well... I did get a job offer from the Foster Foundation."

My whole body tightens. "The ones who rejected you until you suddenly became famous?"

Her shoulders sag. "I know. I just... What if it's my only chance?"

"What would make you happy? Professionally," I clarify.

Aislinn's brows draw together in a frown. "Working in PR. But..." Her smile is slight, shy. "Starting up my own foundation. I wouldn't want to run it, but mold it the way I want it to be run, then make sure it gets the attention it deserves."

I smile. Of course Aislinn's professional goals are tied into something that helps others. "So why not do it?"

She stares at me for a long second, the steam adding a sheen to her skin. Then, slowly, she looks down. "Because I'm afraid." She draws in a deep, shuddering breath. "I've failed so much this past year—"

I reach over, snake my arms around her waist and draw her into my lap. She lets out a soft squeal that drives me crazy. I kiss her hard until she's melting in my arms.

I pull back, smooth a strand of wet hair out of her face. "You also were the driving force behind a bipartisan bill that is going to help hundreds of thousands of children. You did everything you could..." My voice breaks for a second, and I look down. "You protected me. And Diana." I look back up at her, my chest tight and my throat thick. "I wish you could see yourself the way I see you."

Her eyes are shining, full of emotion that both ensnares and terrifies me. But before I can begin to decipher her emotions and my response, she looks up. Her arms tighten around my neck.

"Liam, look."

The breathless wonder in her voice makes me look up.

Light arcs across the sky, shades of green and violet rippling through the inkiness of night. It almost looks like the tendrils of light are dancing.

My eyes flick to Aislinn. She's staring up, a huge smile on her face and wonder in her eyes.

What if I break her?

Aislinn has been through so much, survived so much. I always thought there would never be a man good enough for her. Over the last twelve years, I did exactly as Aislinn accused me of and took everything she and Diana had to offer, encouraged them to share, to depend on me while I held myself back.

Even now, after everything she's shared, I'm still holding back. Still selfish. Still not wanting to let go of my control and let her in.

I want to be the man for her. But just sharing the bits and pieces I have over the last few days has been like pulling blood from stone. It's hard, unnatural. Yeah, I've donated money. But I haven't done anything of purpose. Nothing that hasn't benefited myself.

Aislinn deserves someone who will match her, who can make her feel just as loved as she'll make them feel. Someone who can see the world the way she does.

Not someone who's world exists solely around himself.

The thought has my hands curling into my fists beneath the water. I want it to be me. But what if the best thing for Aislinn is letting her go?

She turns to me with shining eyes. "I'm so glad I got to share this with you."

I pluck the champagne glass from her fingers and set it on the rocks. I pull her on to my lap, positioning her until she's straddling my legs. I slide my hand up her neck and bury my fingers in her hair. I kiss her deeply, drink her moans.

Her head drops back, exposing her neck to my lips. I slide the straps of her bathing suit down, fill my hands with her breasts as my name comes out on a breathless whisper.

I shift enough to slide my swimsuit down and release my cock. I slide the material of her suit aside and in one long thrust, I fill her. She arches back, calls out my name. I slide my fingers back into her hair, anchor her head and kiss her as I take her.

I make love to her under the stars and the glimmer of the Northern Lights, knowing it will most likely be one of the last times.

CHAPTER NINETEEN

Aislinn

THE PHONE RINGING wakes me. I stretch in bed and roll over. My hand falls on a cool sheet.

I frown and glance around. My room is empty. Liam's phone is on the nightstand. I reach over and grab it. A quick glance at the screen shows it's a local number. Feeling a little guilty, I answer. "Hello?"

"Mrs. Whitlock?"

The small smile that crosses my face is reflexive. It's the first time someone's addressed me by my married name since our wedding day. "Yes."

"This is Bjarki, the villa manager. How have you been holding up?"

I glance at the rumpled sheets and bite down on my lower lip. After making love under the stars, we wandered back inside for a late dessert and more wine.

And more sex.

In the shower just before bed.

In the middle of night when Liam woke me to see the aurora borealis shifting into a spectacular sea of red and violet before sliding into me from behind, one arm pinned around my waist, my back against his chest.

"Really well."

"I'm glad to hear it. And also glad to share that the helicopter is ready."

My heart sinks. "Oh."

"Is that all right?"

"Yes!" I force a smile onto my face, try to infuse some pleasantness into my tone. "Yes, it's just a surprise."

"The winds have died down, and we finally got the part we needed. Would two hours from now give you enough time?"

I look around the room. Two hours. Two more hours of just Liam and me.

It's not nearly enough.

"That sounds great."

"The pilot will meet you behind the villa. I'll call when he's over Akureyri."

I place Liam's phone on the nightstand after we hang up. I realize then it's quiet. No wind, no storms racing down the mountains and barreling across the lava fields. I glance out the window, the same window where just hours before Liam was reflected in the glass, his face just over my shoulder, his lips on my neck as he made love to me in front of the Northern Lights.

Now there's not even a cloud in the sky, just endless blue. The perfect winter day in Iceland.

And I'm miserable.

I don't know what happened last night between the mineral baths and going inside. But I could sense something was off. Even though Liam worshipped me, took his time loving every inch of my body, there was an edge to him. A slight distance.

The door to my room opens. Liam walks in wearing the silky black pants and carrying two steaming cups of coffee. "Good morning."

The upswing in my mood quickly takes a downward turn at his barely there smile, the shuttered expression in his eyes. He hands me the coffee and then turns away.

I cup my hands around the mug. "Bjarki called. I hope you don't mind, but I answered."

He sits down in a chair near the fireplace. "What did he have to say?"

"The helicopter's on its way. Two hours."

Liam's gaze shifts to some point outside the huge glass windows.

I turn and look. My body clenches at the sight of the mineral bath at the end of the patio. Our robes lie in crumpled white heaps next to the stairs, our slippers in a jumbled pile next to them. Snow-covered fields stretch out behind the pool. In the far distance, the lone pine tree stands tall and proud.

"Can you be ready by then?"

I blink furiously. When we first got here, I couldn't wait to leave. Now, I don't want to go. I know what's coming. Have known ever since I made the decision to walk into his room. But God it hurts. "Yes."

He stands, sets his cup down and moves to the bed, sitting on the far end. He might as well be on the other side of the fjord for all the distance it puts between us. "After today…" His voice trails, and he lets out a deep breath. "I've really enjoyed our time together."

How many times, I wonder, has he given this speech? How many other women? "Me, too."

"When we go back to New York, we should abide by the original terms of the agreement."

"No sex."

He blinks at my bluntness. "Yes."

"I agree."

His brows draw together in a slight frown. "You do?"

"You've been clear about your expectations from the beginning, Liam. I'm not going to ask for more."

His lips part. He starts to lean forward, his hand coming up. Hope surges…then splinters into fragments as his fingers curl into a fist and he stands. "All right." He grabs his phone off the nightstand.

I wait until the door closes behind him before I roll onto my stomach, bury my face in my pillow and sob. I cry for myself. I cry for the friendship that will never be the same. I cry for the man I love, the man I wish could see himself as I do.

Thirty minutes later, I walk out into the living room with my suitcase trailing behind me. Liam is standing by the door, dressed in a crisp white shirt and black pants as he talks quietly into his phone.

"All right. Yes, Tuesday. Thank you, Bill."

Bill. William Luther. We haven't even left Iceland yet, and already his focus has shifted back to his work. Back to the reason he married me in the first place.

It's not just the pain of rejection or the sting of finding yet another person who can't let me in. No, it's the hurt of seeing a man like Liam, a man who is smart and intelligent and giving, live his life for the next achievement, the next goal in his never-ending quest to be better, instead of letting himself be happy.

I stop a few feet away. "I'm ready."

He glances up, nods, then looks back down at his phone. "Bjarki called. The helicopter should be here in fifteen minutes."

"All right." I clear my throat. "When we get back to New York, I'd like to move into the brownstone."

Liam's head snaps up. His eyes are narrow, his jaw tight. "What?"

My grip tightens on the handle of my suitcase. "I don't think we should continue to live together in the same house."

"That's not going to work."

"Plenty of couples live separately."

"And what will we do when the tabloids pick up on us living apart?" he snaps.

"Appear in public together." I keep my voice calm. "As long as we play out our roles in front of the camera and whatever functions you need me at, we don't need to live together."

"Why?"

Because I love you. Because sleeping apart from you will feel like a part of me is missing. "It'll be more comfortable for me."

His face darkens. "I make you uncomfortable."

"Not you specifically, but our situation, yes. Have you ever lived with an ex-lover after you broke up?"

The glower on his face gives me my answer. "This is different. We're..." His voice trails off.

"I don't think either of us know what we are anymore."

I will always cherish what Liam and I shared in this villa. What we discovered about each other here in Iceland. But that doesn't mean there won't be moments when I pine for who we used to be, what we were to each other.

I sigh. "I've had a hell of a year, Liam. If something comes up in the future, let's deal with it. But I don't want to live under the same roof just because someone might write an article about it. I don't want the awkwardness of living with my best friend-turned-lover-turned ex." My voice grows heavy. "I just want to rest."

Away from him, from temptation. From pain.

He stares at me for what feels like forever. Then, in the distance, we both hear it. The low thwap-thwap-thwap of a helicopter's blades.

"Fine."

As Liam grabs his suitcase and coat, I look out the window, watch as the helicopter lands. Snow jumps into the air.

The honeymoon is over.

I had a few days with Liam, wonderful days. That will be enough. It has to be.

CHAPTER TWENTY

Liam

Two weeks later

THE OLD HARBOR is dark. Midnight blue against the even darker backdrop of night. I can dimly make out the shape of whatever mountain is on the side of the harbor. Lights from a couple of boats glide across the water. The towers and buildings of Reykjavik cradle the harbor in a crescent. Nowhere near as tall as the buildings in New York.

I glance toward the west. Thousands of miles away, my wife may be having lunch or going for a walk in Central Park. Or regretting she ever married me.

I raise my glass to my lips and take a long, satisfying drink of my gin and tonic. The last two weeks have been hell. The helicopter ride to Akureyri had been short. Aislinn had stared out the window the whole time. I'd been too angry to try to talk with her. Her wanting to live separately had been a physical blow to my pride.

It had also just plain hurt. Putting the brakes on our physical relationship had been the right thing to do. But I never thought living in the same penthouse, a sprawling monstrosity with plenty of room, would be too painful for her.

I pause with my glass halfway to my lips. I wonder for what feels like the umpteenth time why it was so painful.

There were times when Aislinn looked at me, the way she would touch me, that almost made me think she felt something more. I know she cared about me. Desired me.

Doesn't matter.

I need to stop thinking about Aislinn and focus on business. As soon as I got back to New York, my three coveted clients booked meetings to officially open up their accounts with Whitlock Investments. The office space is leased with furniture arriving next week. My secretary is more efficient than I am and already has a map for each room with the furniture placement marked. And Aislinn's PR campaign, including my blog post that went viral on LinkedIn, has already netted me a guest spot on a morning talk show and a growing list of clients.

Including one living in Reykjavik, which is why I'm back in Iceland just two weeks after I left.

I should be on top of the world right now. But all I can think about is how the seat next to me shouldn't be empty. I built my firm, worked for it with long hours and long nights. But her recommendations have humanized my firm, made it stand out from the rest. A detail I wouldn't have bothered with a few months ago. Not when I had my investment record to talk for me.

It matters now.

Someone plunks a glass down in front of me. I frown, ready to ask the waiter to be a little more gentle. Then I groan. "What are you doing here?"

Diana is staring at me, hands on her hips, dark eyes narrow. "Why are you here and not home with your wife?"

"I'm here on business with my brother." I glance over her shoulder. "Where is he?"

"Parking the car. I asked for a few minutes." She sits in the chair across from me and holds up a hand to the bartender.

"Please, join me," I say sarcastically.

I don't know why she's angry. I can't believe Aislinn would have told her about what happened between us at the villa. But I can't think of another reason why Diana would be so angry.

"What happened between you and Aislinn?"

Okay, so she doesn't know. Relieved, I drain the last of my first drink and pick up the second. The bartender comes over to take Diana's order, giving me a moment to compose myself. "What are you talking about?"

"Something's happened." Her eyes widen. "The FBI? The investigation?"

I shake my head. "No. The investigation into her has been formally closed. There's not much we can do about the joint assets. But she's in the clear."

"What about Eric and Stephanie?"

I stay silent. "It's not my story to tell."

Diana's shoulders sag. "We're supposed to get together sometime soon, but..." She sighs. "I hate how distant she is."

Me, too.

I had anticipated tears when I told her we needed to stop the sexual aspect of our relationship. Tears or at the very least some sadness. God knows I didn't want to stop. Seeing her in the bed where I'd made love to her just hours ago and not touching her had been physically painful.

But she just accepted it. Accepted it and then took things a step further by asking if we could lead separate lives.

I was surprised by how much that part of it hurt. I had enjoyed my time with Aislinn. Yes, it had been punctuated by periods of intense emotion and hard confessions. But walking out in the mornings and seeing her there, sharing meals, talking with her with the added intimacy of knowing her body just as well as I knew her mind, had made me... happy. Content.

Does it make you happy?

In the last two weeks I've gotten close to one of the biggest goals I've spent over half my life working toward. I have the money, the prestige and now the recognition.

I haven't felt happy. Not once.

No, I concede. There was one moment. Aislinn texted me to inform me she had turned down the job offer from the Foster Foundation. I was happy for her. Proud of her. And then I spent the next two days with my pulse jumping every time my phone dinged.

She hasn't texted again.

"She looked really sad."

My head snaps around. "Aislinn?" At Diana's nod, I lean in. "When did you see her?"

"Video call. Earlier today." Diana's watching me with an intensity that puts me on guard. "She told me about turning down the Foster Foundation job."

I smile slightly. "I'm proud of her."

"I am, too." Diana quirks her head to one side. "But she still looked miserable."

I look away. I've talked to Diana before about past lovers. I never did with Aislinn, though, I realize with a frown. I never confided in her the way I did Diana, never sought out her advice. "Did she say why?"

"She's recovering from 'everything.'" Diana holds her fingers up in air quotes. "But she's hiding something."

The bartender comes back and sets a glass of wine on the table.

Diana waits until he's gone before she speaks again. "You're hiding something, too."

"I'm not hiding anything," I snap.

"Are you harassing my brother, dear?" Ari walks in, dressed to kill in a black suit.

Diana's intensity evaporates as she smiles at Ari and leans in for a kiss. I look away. It's better than it was, but it's still odd to see one of my best friends kissing my big brother. "Just a little friendly questioning."

"More like an interrogation," I shoot over my shoulder.

Ari sits down across from me. It's so odd to see my eyes staring back at me. Our mother's eyes.

A fist clenches around my chest, squeezes. I never knew her. Never heard the sound of her voice, never felt her arms around me. But I miss her. I miss the woman who loved me, who gave up her life for mine.

I wish I could have known her.

This time, instead of shying away from grief, I pause. Let it in, bit by bit. But it's not just grief. There's admiration, longing, gratitude.

"I went to Goðafoss."

Ari gives me a small, sad smile. "Beautiful, isn't it?"

"Stunning."

Diana reaches over and grabs Ari's hand, squeezes it. "I wish I could have known her."

"She would have loved you." Ari leans over and kisses Diana on the forehead with casual intimacy.

It's strange seeing my brother so relaxed. The first time he was uptight, cold. Now he's relaxed. Content.

Happy.

Ari turns to me. "You said you had some business questions?"

"Yes." I gaze down at my gin and tonic. "Your company, the way you run it. How do you decide what community initiatives to invest in?"

My question surprises Ari and Diana both.

"A lot of the focuses were already established by my grandfather. But we also host community meetings and town halls at least once a year to make sure we're investing in the right things and addressing any concerns."

"I hadn't thought of that."

That approach will be a challenge in New York. There are over one million people in Manhattan alone. But it's not impossible.

"What brought this on?" Diana asks as she picks up her wineglass.

"A conversation I had with Aislinn." I swirl my drink, watch the slice of lime spin inside the glass. "I've been focused on myself for a long time. I want my company to be more than just an investment firm that helps wealthy people stay wealthy."

The thought of expanding what token gestures I'm currently doing into something that will make an impact is more exciting than any of the clients I've signed.

Aislinn was right. She had always been able to see to the heart of me.

I pause with my glass to my lips. The same is true for me. I saw all of the things she never gave herself credit for: her compassion, her wit, her passion. Yet I never allowed myself to see her as a woman. Ignored the feelings that have been there for years because I didn't think I'd ever be able to be who she needs.

But I never asked her. I never talked to her, never told her about the feelings rising to the surface. I did exactly what she accused me of; making decisions for her and taking away her choice.

"I love Aislinn." A smile spreads across my face. "I'm in love with her."

"I knew it!" Diana turns to Ari and holds out her hand. "You owe me later."

I glare at her. "You bet on me being in love with our best friend?"

"Oh please." Diana rolls her eyes. "The way the two of you were looking at each other before your wedding ceremony was hot enough to burn the greenhouse down."

"And you?" I ask, turning to Ari.

Ari holds up his hands. "I thought you might have feelings for Aislinn. But I wasn't sure how she felt about you."

The possibility that Aislinn might not feel the same way makes my chest tight.

"She does," Diana says softly. "I knew on your wedding day. I saw the way she looked at you."

My fingers tighten on the glass. "I pushed her away. I didn't think... God, I didn't think."

Diana reaches out and grabs my hand. "I did the same thing, Liam. You know Aislinn." Her eyes glint with unshed tears. "You've always known her. You never gave up on her. Don't give up on her, or yourself, now."

"I won't. But," I say with a smile, "I could use some help."

CHAPTER TWENTY-ONE

Aislinn

One week later

I STIFLE A yawn as Diana's chauffeur navigates the car down the road.

"You'll have a better view of Hvannadalshnjúkur in just a minute," Viktor, the chauffeur, says from the front row.

I glance out the window. It is impressive, a huge sprawling mountain covered in snow. Dawn is still a few minutes away, but the peak of the mountain is bathed in an orangey rose. Stunning.

And I can barely summon any emotion for it.

It's been nearly three weeks since I returned to New York and moved into the brownstone. I've seen Liam a couple of times, once for dinner with William Luther and his wife and another for a going-away party at his old firm. Each event drained me, left me feeling like a husk of myself. Holding on to Liam's arm, smiling and pretending like we're in love, is ten times harder after what we shared.

After Liam rejected it all.

Except, I remind myself as the car speeds down the road, he doesn't even know the extent of my feelings. And that is the worst part of it all. Never once in a million years did I think Liam would be attracted to me, let alone make love to me. But even after we shared our bodies and our beds, I still didn't tell him how I felt.

I gaze out over the sea, still dark just before the dawn. What if I had told him how I felt? Maybe he would have still rejected my feelings.

But maybe, after what we shared, it would have changed things for him.

Diana offered me a reprieve when she called me a couple days ago and asked me to fly out and help her look for a wedding dress. She mentioned she and Ari had grabbed drinks with Liam, but when I pressed her, she'd told me that as far as she knew Liam had concluded his business with his client.

I stare out the window. We found the dress yesterday. Diana will make a stunning bride. And, I think with a small smile, I'll get to be her maid of honor, just as she was mine. At least one dream survived.

To celebrate, Diana suggested an overnight stay in southern Iceland. I'd wanted nothing more than to just go home and curl up in bed, but I didn't have the heart to tell her no. So we drove down to Black Sand Beach, then farther on to a bed-and-breakfast near the infamous Diamond Beach. Somehow I let her talk me in to getting up before dawn to see the beach at its most glorious.

The car slows down. Viktor steers into a parking lot next to a bright blue lagoon.

Diana sits up and yawns. "Oh good!" She checks her watch. "Just a few more minutes to sunrise. Ready?"

I stifle another yawn and nod. "Sure."

We get out. It's still cold, but the wind is thankfully mild.

"Okay, Diamond Beach is—" Diana's phone rings. She glances down at the screen and frowns. "Damn. It's one of my clients from Japan." She shoots me an apologetic glance. "I'm sorry, Aislinn, I have to take this. You should go on ahead."

"I'm not going without you."

Diana shoos me. "I don't want us both missing it. I'll be right behind you."

"I'm going to stay with the car," Viktor adds. "But if you just walk across the road and then follow it down, you'll see the beach."

Disappointed and a little frustrated, I turn and start walking. The wind picks up, and I burrow my face deeper into my scarf. I'm so focused on how cold and tired I am that it takes a moment for me to realize I've reached the beach.

My jaw drops. Chunks of glittering ice cover the black pebbled beach. The pebbles give way to smooth, fine sand before it descends into the ocean. The hunks of ice come in all different shapes and sizes, from small wedges to large slabs of shimmering glacier. The sun starts to creep up above the horizon. Light shoots through the ice, turning the broken bits of glacier from white to violet, pink and orange.

I turn in a circle, trying to take everything in. I feel the same contentment, the same peace, as I felt standing on edge of the fjord watching the foxes prance across the snow.

I wish Liam was here.

The thought strikes my heart like an arrow. My eyes well up with tears. It's so beautiful, and I'm so fortunate to be here, to be with my friend.

But I miss him. I miss him so much it hurts. Even at my lowest points, he never stopped believing in me. Even when I couldn't see what I was capable of, he always did. Because of him and his encouragement, I'm applying for jobs I never would have before. Because of him, I see the strength and courage I've developed during the dark periods in my life.

I smile through my tears. Liam helped me see the good in the bad. Helped me see I'm still there in the mess. I'm not the girl I used to be, and that's okay.

The sun rises higher. The colors fade, replaced by sunbeams that pierce the ice and turn them into sparkling diamonds. The waves fall on the beach, a gentle roar that soothes some of my pain.

I need to see Liam. I need to tell him how I feel. Then, even if our lives don't align, I'll know I gave it my all.

Someone stops next to me. Irritated at the mood being broken, I glance over my shoulder, then do a double take. My heart starts to pound.

"Liam?"

Liam

God, I missed her.

Aislinn is standing in a puffy winter jacket with a scarf wrapped around her neck, hands shoved in her pockets, a hat pulled down over her hair and her nose bright red from the wind.

She's never looked more beautiful.

"Hi."

"Um…hi." She looks around. "What are you doing here? I thought you were back in New York."

I take a step closer. Not pulling her into my arms is almost killing me. "I wanted to see you."

She cocks her head to one side. "Okay. Not that this isn't beautiful, but why not just stop by Diana and Ari's place? Or come see me back in New York?"

I've gone over this probably a hundred times over the last week. Asking myself if I was sure. Not for me, but for her. I need to be one hundred percent sure that I can stand behind everything I have to offer.

And then I smile. There's fear, yes. There will probably always be fear. But I want Aislinn, want a future with her, more than anything.

"This seemed like a more memorable place to tell you I'm in love with you."

For a moment there's nothing but the gentle roar of the ocean and the murmur of the wind.

"You're what?" Aislinn finally says.

I yank my gloves off and cup her cheeks with my hands. Her skin is cold, but I don't care. I just want to touch her. "I love you, Aislinn Knightley. I have for a long time. I was just too stupid to accept it."

She shakes her head. "This...this is crazy."

"Is it?" I lean down and kiss her forehead. "You know me better than anyone, Aislinn. And I know you. You've always been there for me. You're smart, kind, compassionate. You make me want to be a better person."

"Liam..." She tries to step back.

My heart clenches as I release her. God, am I too late? Have I hurt her too much?

"I... I feel very...strongly for you, too."

Is this what a heart attack feels like? Sharp pain stabbing over and over again as I brace myself for whatever she's going to say next?

"But I want kids." She shakes her head as tears course down her face. "I can't give that up. Not even for you."

"And I would never ask that of you." I take a step toward her, grateful when she doesn't step back. "I'm going to be honest, I'm terrified to be a father. I'm afraid I won't live up to the example my father set. I'm afraid something will happen that will rip my family apart. But," I add softly as I stop in front of her, "I realized I've been living my life in fear. I never fully let anyone in, including you and Diana."

She's watching me again with that emotion shining in her eyes. This time there's no fear, just hope as I reach out and touch her face once more.

"I'm sorry, Aislinn. I'm so sorry for always keeping you at arm's length. I can't promise I'll be perfect from now on, but damn it, I want to try. For both of us."

She swallows hard. "And kids?"

"I want a life with you, Aislinn." I lay a hand at her waist, close the distance between us as my heart pounds in my chest. "I want kids with you, whether it's kids of our own or adopting or however we create a family. I never pictured myself having kids, but when I finally stopped looking at it through a lens of fear, I realized I've wanted so many things I told myself I didn't." I press my forehead to hers. "I want a family with you, Aislinn."

She sobs my name and throws her arms around me.

I crush her to me. "God, Aislinn, I'm never going to let you go again." I slant my mouth over hers, kiss her until we're both panting and breathless.

"Did Diana help you set this up?" Aislinn asks with a laugh.

"She did. Aislinn..." I lay my forehead against hers. "I told Luther the truth about the arrangement of our marriage."

She leans back, eyes wide and luminous. "You did?"

"Yes. I told him if that meant he didn't want me as a client, so be it, but I wasn't going to live my personal life for anyone but myself." I smile. "He wasn't happy about it, but telling him I loved you and was going to do everything in my power to get you to stay mollified him."

Her eyes glint with unshed tears. "Liam... I love you."

I suck in a breath. "You do?"

"Yes." She starts to laugh. "I have for years."

I pull her against me. "Then I'd say we have a lot of time to make up for."

Her smile is brilliant. "I agree." Her expression dims. "I never thanked you."

"For what?"

"For always believing in me. For giving me grace even when I didn't think I deserved it." She smiles as she glances around the beach. "Just like Sleeping Beauty."

"Oh?"

She leans up and kisses me with a passion that rocks me to my core. "It was your kiss that brought me back to life."

I grin. "Does that make me Prince Charming? I like that a lot better than a spoiled nobleman."

She laughs. The sound fills me with a contented happiness I never let myself before. I pick her up and twirl her in a circle in the middle of Diamond Beach, laughing with her as the sun climbs higher in the sky.

I finally set her down. "I propose a change to the terms of our agreement then. Removal of the expiration date and the no intimacy clause."

"I accept."

And we seal our new deal with a kiss.

EPILOGUE

Aislinn

One year later

"You look so beautiful." Stephanie comes up behind me and lays her hands on my shoulders. Her smile is proud, motherly.

I reach up and pat her hand. "Thank you, Mom."

Stephanie's eyes glisten for a moment as she leans up and kisses my cheek. "You're welcome."

She drifts away, and I turn back to the mirror. It's not often a bride gets to wear her wedding dress twice. But Liam surprised me four months ago by dropping to one knee at the lookout point of Goðafoss and proposing a vow renewal ceremony.

Our first wedding was a little rushed, he said as he slid the stunning ruby onto my finger. *I want you to have everything you missed out on.*

At first, I'd told him it wasn't necessary. We were together. We were in love. That was enough.

But I have to admit the last few months have been fun. Finding the perfect venue, picking out invitations, perusing flower arrangements... I smile over at Stephanie as she fluffs my veil for the half dozenth time. Having people there I love.

After Liam and I reconciled, he accompanied me to Eric and Stephanie's house when we got back to New York. I sat in the living room I'd spent so much time in, my hand clenched around Liam's, and told them everything.

When I finished, there was a moment of silence.

Stephanie was shocked and heartbroken to hear about everything I'd been through. Eric sat there looking resigned, defeated.

And then he surprised us by admitting to all of it. Favoring certain government contractors who contributed to his campaign, sharing legislative information with companies to help them invest during those early years of his campaign. He also said that while Stephanie had signed off on some of the checks, they'd looked like straightforward donations. She'd had nothing to do with any of it.

I'd seen the emails, the financial records. I knew it was true. But hearing Eric admit it, while incredibly painful, had also been freeing.

Tears prick my eyes. It had also given us a new foundation, one Eric had created when he'd asked if he could hug me.

I don't deserve you as a daughter. But God, I'm going to try to be better.

He took things a step further by holding a press conference the following week. He admitted everything and told the people of New York that it would be their choice to decide whether or not to trust him again. When he won by a very slim margin, he asked me to come back and work for him.

I appreciated the gesture. But it was time to move on.

"Are you all right?"

I give Stephanie a watery smile in the mirror. "Yes. It's just...it's been a crazy year."

"It has." She reaches up and slides the clip of the veil into my hair. "But it's been a good one."

I nod. Liam's firm is growing. Luther surprised him by staying on and recommending other clients. He and his wife have become close friends. They'll be in the conservatory today watching as we renew our vows.

Liam also moved fast on the foundation. Six months after our wedding, we opened the doors of the Boundless Foundation. Liam wrote a check and stepped back, letting the board of directors and my leadership team take control of the foundation's focuses on adoption, independent living for older foster kids about to age out and foster family support.

The one thing Liam has thrown himself into has been the Carpentry School. He spends several nights a month at the school, visiting with students and even taking a few classes alongside the kids.

And our nights are spent in our new home, a condominium in Central Park South that we've made into a home.

Stephanie's phone chimes. She glances at the screen and smiles. "The pastor is ready. I'm going to do one more check, and then we should be good to go." Stephanie slips out, leaving me in the dressing room just off the conservatory.

Just over four dozen guests are seated inside the luscious New York Botanical Garden. In a few minutes, Liam and I will say our own vows.

A knock sounds on my door.

"Yes?"

I can't discern the mumbled reply from the other side, so I get up and open the door.

"Liam!" I laugh as he slips inside. "You can't see the bride in her wedding dress."

"I already have." His eyes flare as he looks me up and down. "I forgot how gorgeous you are in it."

I have zero willpower as he pulls me into his arms and kisses me.

"You do realize Diana will kill you if she finds you in here."

"She's making out with Ari down the hall, so I doubt she'll care too much."

I chuckle. "This seems…impossible."

"What?" Liam asks quietly as he traces a finger down my cheek.

"This. All this happiness."

"You deserve it," he murmurs. "You deserve everything, Aislinn."

I hesitate. Do I tell him now? Or do I wait until after the ceremony? Going with instinct, I grab his hand and guide it to my stomach, lay it flat against the slight swell beneath the waistline of my dress.

He stares at my belly for a moment before his head snaps up. "Really?"

I nod, my throat tight. "I know we just filed the papers to adopt, so maybe—"

"So maybe we'll just have two." He says it with such certainty it brings tears to my eyes.

I watch him as he stares at my stomach with a smile that tugs on my heartstrings.

"I…oh my God." His fingers tighten for a moment before he draws me into a gentle hug. "You're going to be an incredible mother."

"And you a wonderful father." I kiss him. "I love you, Liam. Always."

"Always."

*****

Did Wed for the Headlines *sweep you off your feet?*
Then you're sure to love the previous instalment
in the Red-Hot Icelandic Nights duet,
Enemy in His Boardroom*!*

In the meantime, check out these other stories
from Emmy Grayson!

Prince's Forgotten Diamond
Stranded and Seduced
Deception at the Altar
Still the Greek's Wife
Pregnant Behind the Veil

Available now!

MILLS & BOON®

Coming next month

BODYGUARD'S ROYAL TEMPTATION
Abby Green

She felt incredibly delicate and yet he sensed a latent strength.

He had a feeling he shouldn't underestimate her. After all she'd managed to ditch her bodyguards and avoid her brother.

He looked down at her and she lifted her face. She smiled. It made something inside Ares ache. Why was she so smiley? So perky? She was a princess way out of her depth. She could have been unconscious somewhere now if it hadn't been for him. But again, he had that sense that perhaps she would have surprised him by managing to get out of that predicament. She was using a false name to avoid detection.

Then his gaze went to her mouth. It opened slightly and he had a glimpse of pink tongue. White teeth. A fire started raging in his blood. He'd never been more tempted by a woman. By a woman who was so far out of his bounds that –

Before Ares could formulate another word, she'd reached up and pressed her mouth to his, a chaste and surprisingly sweet gesture. But any thought of *sweet* fast dissolved as *sweet* morphed into burning hot *heat* and intense need. Ares couldn't resist.

Continue reading

BODYGUARD'S ROYAL TEMPTATION
Abby Green

Available next month
millsandboon.co.uk

Copyright ©2026 Abby Green

COMING SOON!

We really hope you enjoyed reading this book.
If you're looking for more romance
be sure to head to the shops when
new books are available on

Thursday 26th March

To see which titles are coming soon, please visit
millsandboon.co.uk/nextmonth

MILLS & BOON

FOUR BRAND NEW BOOKS FROM
MILLS & BOON MODERN

Indulge in desire, drama, and breathtaking romance – where passion knows no bounds!

OUT NOW

Eight Modern stories published every month, find them all at:

millsandboon.co.uk

TWO BRAND NEW BOOKS FROM
Love Always

Be prepared to be swept away to incredible worldwide destinations along with our strong, relatable heroines and intensely desirable heroes.

OUT NOW

Four Love Always stories published every month, find them all at:

millsandboon.co.uk

OUT NOW!

Available at
millsandboon.co.uk

MILLS & BOON

LET'S TALK
Romance

For exclusive extracts, competitions and special offers, find us online:

- MillsandBoon
- @MillsandBoon
- @MillsandBoonUK
- @MillsandBoonUK

Get in touch on 01413 063 232

For all the latest titles coming soon, visit millsandboon.co.uk/nextmonth